120 DAYS

120 DAYS

RONALD L. RUIZ

MY THANKS to Jay Amberg, Sarah Koz, Amanda Wilson, Robert Brown, Annie Smith and Allen Cetto for their help and encouragement in writing and publishing this book.

First Edition   ISBN 13: 978-1-937484-67-5
AMIKA PRESS   466 Central AVE #23 Northfield IL 60093   847 920 8084
info@amikapress.com   Available for purchase on amikapress.com
Edited by Jay Amberg and Ann Wambach. Cover art by Phe Ruiz. Cover photography by Amanda Wilson and Elvis Santana. Author photography by Amanda Wilson. Designed and typeset by Sarah Koz. Body in Espinosa Nova, designed by Cristóbal Henestrosa in 2010. Titles in Lapis, designed by Jim Rimmer in 2006. Thanks to Nathan Matteson.

"You have a stupid, meaningless, worthless, wicked, sick old crone, no good to anyone, who doesn't know herself why she's alive, and who will die on her own tomorrow,... Kill her and take her money, so that afterwards with its help you can devote yourself to the service of all mankind and the common cause."

—Fyodor Dostoyevsky, *Crime and Punishment*

I

"OBJECTION, YOUR HONOR! Argumentative! Asked and answered! Irrelevant! Counsel is intimidating the witness!"

"Intimidating the witness? How can a woman my size intimidate a police officer his size?" Blake was a petite, dark-haired woman in her late thirties.

There were snickers from the jury. Judge Williams's gavel came down hard on his desk even before Bill Thompson shouted, "Objection!" again.

Defense Attorney Barbara Blake knew she had gone too far. She stopped her slow, deliberate pacing. Judge Williams liked her, but she had crossed the line. She liked him as well, and she knew he would invariably give her as much as he could, but he had his limits. She looked up at him. His face had reddened and his mouth had thinned. "Counsel, if you want to address the district attorney's objections, address them to the court. Otherwise your gratuitous remarks will not be tolerated in this courtroom. Is that clear?" It was a high-ceiled, wood-paneled courtroom in an old courthouse building.

"I'm sorry, Your Honor, I meant no disrespect to the court. I was just taken aback by the district attorney's outrageous remark." She was not the least bit sorry, and she had just taken another jab at the DA. And she saw that her apologetic tone and her look of innocence were working. The judge's mouth had softened and the red on his face had receded. After a few moments he added some conciliatory words. "Counsel, the court understands that in the heat of battle, tempers will rise and inappropriate remarks will be made. Nevertheless, you are a very experienced, able lawyer and I ask that you refrain from further gratuitous remarks. The district attorney's objection is sustained. Please proceed with your cross-examination."

"Thank you, Your Honor. Now Sergeant Brennan, do you recall telling us this morning that you interviewed the alleged victim, Jane Doe, on January 30, 2004, two days after the alleged sexual molestation by my client?"

"Yes, ma'am." Tall and rangy even as he sat in the witness chair.

"For the record, Jane Doe is six years old?"

"Yes, ma'am."

"And isn't it true that during that interview Jane Doe told you that she had been molested only once by my client, her father?"

"Yes, ma'am." Tolerant, permissive. He knew this was defense counsel's role.

"Well now, Sergeant, that's quite a bit different than the ten times you testified to on direct examination earlier today, isn't it?"

"Yes, ma'am."

"And as a qualified expert in child molestation cases, you told us earlier that it is not uncommon for a child to change the number of times she has been molested by an individual especially when the perpetrator is someone near and dear to her?"

"Yes, ma'am."

"You prepared a report concerning your January 30 interview with Jane Doe, didn't you, Sergeant?"

"Yes, ma'am."

"And in that report you describe Jane Doe as being calm, collected, and forthright, correct?"

"Yes, ma'am."

"How long have you been working child molest cases, Sergeant?"

"For over ten years now."

"And over the course of that time, you've interviewed hundreds of victims, haven't you, Sergeant?"

"Yes, ma'am."

"And by now you can pretty much tell when a child is lying to you and when she's not, can't you, Sergeant?"

"Not always." Irritated now.

"Does that mean never...or some of the time...or most of the time...or always?"

"Probably most of the time."

"What does the word 'forthright' mean to you, Sergeant?"

He hesitated and she could feel that familiar excitation stirring in her.

"Did you hear my question, Sergeant?"

"Yes."

"And your answer is?"

"Aboveboard."

"Does aboveboard also mean truthful, Sergeant?"

"You could say that, yes."

"It's not what I say that's important, it's what you say that counts, Sergeant. Does forthright mean truthful?"

"Objection! Argumentative, and I'd ask the court to admonish Ms. Blake to stop her editorializing."

"The objection is overruled. Proceed with cross-examination, Counsel. Please answer the question, Sergeant Brennan."

As the district attorney voiced his objection, Barbara Blake watched Sergeant Brennan. There was uneasiness in his eyes. Her stirring increased, and she could feel her blood pulsating. She knew that her mind was clear and quick then—ready to focus and stay focused, ready to pounce. He was hers, and it was only a matter of time until she made that clear to all.

Jane Doe's parents were locked in a bitter divorce battle. One of the court's temporary orders gave the father visitation rights that allowed the child to spend every other weekend with him. After each visitation, Jane Doe's mother questioned her in detail about her visit. Some three months into the visitation Jane Doe revealed that on some nights she had slept with her father. The mother was outraged and threatened to have the father's visitations terminated if the practice continued. The father's response was that the child had always slept with them. Soon Jane Doe began resisting the court-ordered visitations, telling her father that she had no one to play with at his house...that all her friends lived far away near her mother's house. The mother began questioning the child even more closely, specifically asking after every visit if her father had touched her "privates." After several weeks of that questioning, Jane Doe answered yes. Her mother called the police, and her father was arrested.

As part of police protocol Jane Doe was introduced to Mary Atkins, a social worker from the Child Protection Agency who met with her and began regularly taking her to a "child-friendly room" at the agency. There she was given snacks and treats and encouraged to play with stuffed animals and other toys while Mary Atkins attempted to question her about the illicit touching. Sergeant Brennan and the child's mother watched unseen behind a two-way mirror in an adjoining room into which every word of the child and Mary Atkins was transmitted. Ostensibly all of the sessions between Jane Doe and Mary Atkins were videotaped, but as it was later shown, the switch for the recording device was not always turned on. There were ten sessions recorded and at least five other sessions that were not recorded. All the recorded sessions had the child saying that her father had touched her private parts. The number of instances varied from one to ten and to an unspecified number beyond ten. The ten recorded sessions were turned over to the defense as part of the standard discovery packet. It was only during the cross-examination of the mother that Barbara Blake was able to establish that on some of the unrecorded sessions the child had maintained that her father had not inappropriately touched her.

On the afternoon that Barbara Blake was cross-examining Sergeant Brennan, she had already been practicing as a criminal defense attorney for almost fifteen years. Over that period she had developed a unique style of cross-examination that had drawn the attention, if not the admiration, of judges and fellow attorneys alike. So much so, that young public defenders and even deputy district attorneys and seasoned criminal defense attorneys would often come into the courtroom to watch her cross-examination of principal prosecution witnesses. There were times during those cross-examinations that Barbara Blake underwent a transformation in the courtroom. She was a small, soft-spoken woman who was courteous and polite to all until she felt that her client was in danger. Then she became loud and assertive, pouncing and attacking, even accusatory when she found it useful or necessary. She was acutely aware of the transformation and other attorneys made endless references to it. But she never discussed her cases with anyone—once a case was over, it was over. Nor would she talk about the transformation itself. But she thought of it often, prided herself in it, and explained it to herself as, "This is where I live."

She would rise from her chair at counsel table whenever the witness to be cross-examined was an important one, because she knew she would not be able to sit still when and if that surge, that excitation, came. Better to be standing, pacing, and moving—easier to spread the tension— than to be confined to a chair. During those times her mind seemed white hot. She did not need her notes, did not need the counsel table; her mind could do it all, calling up anything and everything of any importance to challenge and demolish the witness. It was far from her everyday state of mind, which would flit and flitter from image to image, from thought to thought in instants. This was truly where she lived.

When she stood, she paced with slow, deliberate steps about the courtroom, sometimes beyond the counsel table a few feet closer to the witness than the table would permit, but usually farther from him than the table allowed, along the railing, into the courtroom corners, next to the jury box and the captivated jurors, as she questioned. When the witness would begin to reel, her voice grew louder and her questions came in rapid-fire succession, and her movement about the courtroom became more pronounced, not faster, rather more definite, more certain, as if every inch of that courtroom floor was hers. She would turn her back on the staggering witness, walk away slowly, and, as she did, fire another question at him in a voice so loud as to be nearing a shout. Then she would watch the mesmerized faces of the audience and that spurred her on all the more. And when the witness's answers came back weak, thin, quiet, and confused, she would spin and come back at him again and fire still another question, another blow, and watch as he reeled even more, about to fall.

As ready as she was to dismantle Sergeant Brennan, she reminded herself not to lose control.

"From January 30, 2004, the date of your first interview with Jane Doe, until the beginning of this trial on April 16, 2004, some seventy-five days, how many times was Jane Doe interviewed by law enforcement, and that includes Mary Atkins?"

"At least ten."

"Meaning the ten tapes that were turned over to the defense?"

"Yes."

"What about the five unrecorded interviews testified to by Jane Doe's mother? You know the ones that included denials of any inappropriate touching. You're aware of those aren't you, Sergeant?"

"Yes."

"And you interviewed Jane Doe alone a second time, which was not recorded?"

"Yes."

"So that would make it sixteen, wouldn't it, Sergeant?"

"Yes."

"And during the two weeks immediately preceding the start of this trial Jane Doe was interviewed by the district attorney, wasn't she?"

"Yes."

"How many times?"

"Three."

"And you were present during those interviews, weren't you, Sergeant?"

"Yes." He was flustered. His eyes were shifting constantly. His head jerked from place to place. Twice he looked over at the district attorney, but Bill Thompson was hunched over a legal pad, apparently taking notes.

"So if there were nineteen interviews, why did you tell the jury that there were 'at least ten'?"

Now Sergeant Brennan's eyes latched onto Bill Thompson, but Thompson wouldn't look up. Barbara Blake's eyes were on the sergeant, but he wouldn't look at her. Her mind was clear, controlled now, ready.

"...I don't know. I guess I thought you were asking how many tape-recorded interviews there were."

"Sergeant, my question was very specific. I asked for the number of interviews with Jane Doe over a seventy-five-day period. The court reporter can read back my question if you like. Would you like that? Would that refresh your recollection?"

"No. No. I was just confused."

"So how many interviews were there with Jane Doe over that seventy-five-day period?"

"Nineteen."

"Why were nineteen interviews with Jane Doe necessary?"

"It's difficult interviewing six-year-olds. Their attention spans are very limited. They can't sit still for very long. A complete stranger has to gain the child's trust and confidence so that the child can be comfortable in that setting. They're not used to talking to adults about serious matters like these over long periods of time." Looking at the jury, he nodded through his explanation.

7

"How long were these interviews?"

"They varied. Some were thirty or forty minutes long. Others were two or three hours long."

"Could we say that some twenty hours were spent interviewing Jane Doe?"

"You could say that."

"What did you hope to gain? Why was it necessary to interview this child, some twenty hours about the facts of this case?"

"We were trying to get at the truth."

"What is the truth in this case, Sergeant? Is it 'Daddy never touched me' or is it 'Daddy touched me one, three, five, seven, or ten times or beyond'? Take your pick, Sergeant."

There was something resembling a weak smile, a sneer, a scoff on Sergeant Brennan's face as he looked directly at Barbara Blake for the first time in a while. It was a look of contempt, one you saved for a scum who was unashamedly trying to deceive you, take advantage of you. He held that look for several moments before he answered, meeting his persecutor's challenge for the first time. Then he said evenly, firmly, "Your client touched his daughter's vagina ten times."

"How did you make that determination, Sergeant?"

"His daughter said so."

"Didn't she also say that he touched her but once?"

"Yes."

"Three times?"

"Yes."

"Five times?"

"Yes."

"Seven times?"

"Yes."

"More than ten times?"

"Yes."

"And didn't she say in at least three of those interviews that he had not touched her at all?"

"Yes."

"What was so captivating about the number ten, Sergeant?"

The sneer was gone, and his eyes were shifting. He was the hunted again. "It made the most sense."

"How so?"

"The visitation period was a little more than five months. He slept with the child on numerous occasions during that time, even after the child's mother threatened to take him to court. If he molested her once he certainly molested her several times over those months, and ten makes the most sense."

"So was she lying to you when she said he had molested her only once?"

"I wouldn't say she was lying."

"What would you say, Sergeant?"

"That she was confused."

"Was she confused when she said three times?"

"Yes."

"Confused when she said five, seven, and beyond ten times?"

Something of the sneer reappeared, but weakly. He was no longer challenging, standing his ground; he was no longer sure. He held the look for a few moments before he answered, "Yes."

"Was she confused when she said that her father had never touched her?"

"Yes, and there, as I said earlier, she was probably trying to protect her father."

"Was she confused, Sergeant, when she said that he had molested her ten times?"

There was shifting in the jury box, and Sergeant Brennan turned and saw the look of concern on some of their faces. "No." But it was a barely audible no.

"What was that again, Sergeant? I'm sorry, but I just couldn't hear your answer." She wasn't sorry and she had heard his answer.

"No." Louder.

"Sergeant, you just told us that Jane Doe was confused when she said that there had been no touching and when she gave numbers other than ten, is that correct?"

"That's correct."

"Could you tell us what that confusion looked like? I mean, when a person is confused, he'll usually have a confused look on his face. Could you tell us what the girl's look was like when she recited any number, or non-number, other than ten?"

"No, I don't remember what she looked like then."

"Well, in your report of the January 30 interview when she told you that her father had molested her once, you describe her as calm, collected, and forthright, correct?"

"Yes."

"So, you did not see any confusion then, did you, Sergeant?"

"No, apparently I didn't."

"How about when she said it was ten times. You told us there was no confusion then. Did her look differ in any way from the look you described seeing on January 30?"

Sergeant Brennan paused. He looked down and around at the courtroom floor. He sighed audibly and then looked in the direction of Bill Thompson, but Thompson was still focused on his notepad. Most of the jurors were not looking at the witness. Some were busy looking through their notebooks in the absence of any testimony; others had their eyes downcast, perhaps embarrassed for the Sergeant; and two were looking stoically across the courtroom at the opposite wall. Those who did look at him did so only intermittently with puzzled, frustrated looks—puzzled by the pathetic testimony of a sworn law-enforcement expert in child molestation cases and frustrated because they took their seats as jurors fully expecting to convict the defendant of those dastardly crimes charged. But now they found themselves stymied instead of aided by this awkward garbled evidence.

"Did you hear my question, Sergeant?"

"Yes."

"And your answer is?"

"I don't remember."

Barbara Blake's mind was at its keenest now. One question suggested two or three more; one answer raised even more. The questions came from everywhere: from her voluminous case file, from her life experience, from common sense. They arrived instantly and queued-up like a deluge of water about to spill over a dam, lapping for a chance to be spoken. Sergeant Brennan had testified at a preliminary examination some eight weeks before that in his opinion Jane Doe had been molested five times. Barbara Blake reminded him that he had been under oath then as he was now, and then she led him step by painful step down the path that brought about his change of position and again proved to be based on the changing numbers given by Jane Doe over the course of nineteen interviews.

Barbara Blake then explored the importance of the parents' bitter, ongoing divorce. Sergeant Brennan saw little consequence in the parents' dispute and said that divorce was often in the background of molestation cases. But it wasn't long before Barbara Blake had him backpedaling again. Yes, he admitted, the mother's questioning after every visit was excessive and suggestive, especially in the latter stages. Yes, he was aware that Jane Doe had slept with her parents for years and there had never been any indication of molestation on the father's part. Yes, it was perfectly normal for a child to resist visiting a parent every other weekend when that parent lived far from the child's friends and normal social activities. Yes, he reluctantly admitted, now looking sheepish and worn, a child of six in Jane Doe's situation might conclude that she should answer yes when her mother asked over and over whether her father had sexually molested her.

By this stage in the cross-examination, Sergeant Brennan seemed battered and dazed, but Barbara Blake wouldn't let up. Everyone in the courtroom now looked at each question, no matter how innocuous on the surface, as a building block for the next blow. Deputy District Attorney Bill Thompson was also being humiliated by Barbara Blake's lethal cross-examination. Sergeant Brennan was not just a witness, he was Thompson's expert witness. He had strutted Brennan's credentials before the jury during his opening statement. He had assured them Brennan would explain the ugly phenomena of child molestation in such a way that they would have absolutely no trouble in finding the defendant guilty on all ten counts. Each new thrust by Barbara Blake seemed as painful to him as it was to Sergeant Brennan. In an attempt to cut short the cross-examination, Thompson began objecting again and again. They were desperate, specious objections with no legal bases. Perhaps the saddest series of objections were the half a dozen he made about the tone of Barbara Blake's questions. With each objection he shot up from his chair with looks of outrage and exasperation, once pounding on the table and another time throwing his pen down and saying in a loud, angry voice in a variety of ways, "Objection! Counsel is badgering the witness! She is yelling at the witness, Your Honor! This is totally unacceptable and impermissible and is bordering on misconduct!"

Barbara Blake knew that her voice had become loud, but she had no idea how loud it had become. Others had told her that at times she came close to screaming at a witness, but once her fervor took hold, she had no way of gauging it. Judge Williams's reaction to Thompson's first objections was to meet his glare and say nothing until Thompson looked down or away. And then he said quietly and firmly, "The objection is overruled." It was only when Thompson added, "And I ask that the court admonish counsel to lower her voice," that Judge Williams said, "Mr. Thompson, when you lower your own voice when addressing this court and show a modicum of respect, then the court might take a more tolerant view of your otherwise spurious objections. Let the record show that while Ms. Blake's voice is certainly animated, it is not unduly loud. The objection is overruled."

Next Barbara Blake turned to the subject of the three interviews in the child-friendly interview room. As she laid foundational questions for those interviews, she turned her back to Sergeant Brennan and moved slowly and deliberately toward the audience as she waited for his answers and then asked another question. As she did so she noted for the first time that the courtroom, empty for most of the proceedings that day, was now almost full. Most of the spectators were young attorneys from the public defender's and the district attorney's offices. There were also a few private practitioners—among them, Greg Olsen. She focused on the looks of awe and respect on those young faces, and though it had been a long cross-examination those looks reinvigorated her.

"Isn't it true, Sergeant that on three of the ten tapes that were turned over to the defense that Jane Doe said she didn't want to talk anymore, that she didn't want to answer any more questions, that she just wanted to go home?"

"She may have said that. I really don't remember."

"Would you like me to play those tapes for you here in court to refresh your recollection?"

"No, no, I'll take your word for it."

"My word doesn't matter, Sergeant, it's yours that counts."

"Yes, she did say that."

"Isn't it true that the questions she did not want to answer had to do with whether her father had molested her?"

"Yes."

"And was she allowed to go home when she asked to go home?"

"No."

"And on two of those tapes she then cried for her mommy to come and take her home, didn't she?"

"She may have."

"Any doubt in your mind about that?"

"No...she did."

"On each of those occasions when she cried, she had already been in that child-friendly room for questioning for at least an hour, am I correct?" Stopping, standing, pointing with self-righteousness at the sergeant.

"Yes."

"And after she cried for a while, a break was taken and the child was taken out of the room, wasn't she, Sergeant?"

"Yes."

"And after the break she was brought back into the child-friendly room for additional questioning, correct?"

"Yes."

"Were any of those breaks tape-recorded?

"No."

"Where did those breaks take place?"

"Mostly in an employees' lunchroom."

"And who was present at those breaks?"

He paused, hesitating, "Jane Doe, her mother, Mary Atkins, and myself."

"How long were those breaks?"

"Fifteen, twenty minutes, half an hour."

"And during those breaks, did any one of the three of you tell Jane Doe that once she answered the questions about her father molesting her, she could go home?"

"No."

"You're certain of that?"

"Yes."

"Was Jane Doe's mother comforting her during those breaks?"

"Yes."

"And during those breaks did you ever hear Jane Doe's mother tell the child to answer those questions so that they could go home."

"No."

"And of course neither you nor Mary Atkins ever suggested that to Jane Doe during those breaks?"

"We did not."

"Yet each time when she returned to that child-friendly room after those breaks, she answered those questions, did she not, saying that her father had molested her on various occasions?"

"Yes, she did."

Then Barbara Blake played a portion of a videotape dated March 18, 2004. Staring down at Sergeant Brennan she asked, "Isn't it true, Sergeant, that on that tape Mary Atkins tells a sobbing Jane Doe three times that the questioning will stop and she can go home as soon as she answers the questions about whether her father molested her?"

"Yes." A quiet yes.

"And isn't it true that she says these things to the child just a minute or two before the break is taken?"

"Yes." Eyes downcast and another quiet yes.

Barbara Blake then played a portion of a videotape dated March 28, 2004, and elicited from Sergeant Brennan that here too, just minutes before a break was taken, Mary Atkins twice told a sobbing Jane Doe she could go home as soon as she answered the questions about whether her father had molested her.

She had him. She had the son of a bitch. She had hunted him, stalked him, cornered him, and now he was hers. *Don't let him slip out now, Barbara. Don't gild the lily. Keep it simple, direct. One more question, two at the most. He has nowhere to run, nowhere to hide. He's in the open. Take him now. He's yours.* She had reached her peak. She knew that. Her body knew that as well. It was taut, at the breaking point, reminding her, *Calm yourself, calm yourself. Now get him.*

"But it's your sworn testimony here today that not once during those breaks was Jane Doe advised by you or her mother or Mary Atkins to answer the questions regarding whether her father had molested her, isn't it, Sergeant Brennan?"

"Yes."

She glared at him with scorn and contempt. She made no attempt to hide her disgust. He was a sworn liar. Everyone in the courtroom had to know that. Except for the shifting in the jury box, where the discomfort was obvious, there was complete silence. If the spectacle of a lying cop was so disturbing to the jurors, then let them squirm. Not one of them was looking at him now. They dared not look—look at his confirming, sickening, beaten expression. His eyes shifted from place to place but found no refuge. Judge Williams cleared his throat, signaling that he was not going to permit the stare down to go on any longer.

"I have no further questions of this witness, Your Honor."

THE COURT recessed for the day, and as Barbara Blake was gathering her notes, folders, and exhibits, Greg Olsen came up to the counsel table and gently put his hand on her shoulder and said,

"That was a helluva cross, Barb." The hand and the voice told her it was Greg. "Thanks," she said, looking up at him briefly, self-consciously, as if she had exposed too much of herself to him and everyone in the courtroom and now needed to conceal the uncontrollable twitching and quivering her body was experiencing on its descent to the accustomed Barbara Blake.

"How about a cup of coffee? The cafeteria will be open for another forty-five minutes. The coffee will taste like mud, but the place will be quiet and empty."

OK, she nodded several times as she stuffed her last folder into a valise-like briefcase.

BARBARA BLAKE and Greg Olsen had entered the public defender's office a year apart. Because of the lack of office space, they shared an office for about a year. They became friends. Barbara's first marriage had already ended. Greg was married, but Barbara had sometimes thought that if it hadn't been for Greg's two kids, more might have come of their relationship. As it was, Greg's wife, Molly, was openly relieved when they were assigned separate offices. Barbara learned later that unbeknownst to Greg or herself, Molly had approached the chief and demanded that her husband and Barbara either be given individual offices or be reassigned to other attorneys.

After seven years in the public defender's office, Barbara and Greg left to open an office together. By then Barbara had married Brian Stone, so Molly voiced no opposition. Their practice flourished. They worked long hours and weekends. It was not uncommon for them to sit around the office, often with drinks in their hands, long after their day in court, long after the secretaries and the clients had left, discussing their cases or office matters or finances. Nor was it uncommon for Molly to call, irritated, asking what time Greg would be leaving the office or reminding him that he was late for dinner or telling him the kids wondered where their daddy was. When Molly learned that Barbara and Brian had been separated for some time she went wild. The following day she stormed into Barbara's office, and a loud, angry, and demeaning confrontation took place for everyone in the office, including clients, to hear. By the week's end the partnership was terminated.

The breakup was especially hard on Barbara. Greg Olsen was a dear friend; sometimes she thought he was her best friend. In some ways she had been closer to him than to any man in her life. Now not only was she losing him, but she was going to open a new law office alone. What she would never know was that for weeks after she left, Greg sat in his office at the end of the day, after the others were gone, staring off into space and wondering if he had made the mistake of his life in letting Barbara go...in not going with her. But always, at the end of that void, in the distance stood Timmy and Jenny, his son and daughter. Barbara and Greg saw each other occasionally after the breakup—at first for lunch, then for breakfast, then for coffee—and then not at all. Now, five years later, their practices were flourishing, Barbara as a sole practitioner and Greg as a partner in a seven-attorney law office. But for the past several months, Greg had been finding more and more reasons to call her, talk to her, meet with her.

"HEY CARL, how long's this coffee been sitting here?" Greg Olsen could be big and loud. He was big and loud then.

Carl was at the far end of the otherwise empty courthouse cafeteria washing dishes. "Not gonna lie to you, Greg, I made it a couple of hours ago. But no one's saying you have to drink it."

Barbara Blake was trailing behind Greg pulling her enormous briefcase on wheels. Greg stopped at the darkened coffee pots. "Wanna cup?"

Barbara shrugged, "I don't care." She was drained. She had left every fragment of care and emotion and energy in the courtroom. Her shoulders ached and her legs were stiff, tight. Everything within her from her neck to her hips seemed to have been siphoned off.

Greg took two paper cups and half shouted to Carl. "You sure I can pour this stuff, or am I gonna need a spoon to scoop it out?"

"All outta spoons," Carl answered.

Greg poured two cups of coffee and then led Barbara to the nearest table where they sat. "You were great, Barbara. Magnificent!"

Barbara Blake felt neither great nor magnificent. She felt spent and exhausted. But Greg's words soothed her. *You never get tired of being appreciated and admired,* she thought.

"You think they'll walk him?"

The question stirred her, irritated her, and then angered her a bit. "Come on, Greg. Nobody walks these days, least of all a man accused of molesting a child. You know that. We can run circles around a DA. Half the time they're unprepared. We can chew them up and spit them out. We can work all day and all night and weekends, too, and blitz right over them. But the jury will still convict. You know that." Her words surprised her. She hadn't thought she had any emotion left. She went on. "It's fear, Greg. It's fear. This whole damn country is motivated by fear. We're afraid of everything. We're spooked by anything. Mark my words, lazy Bill Thompson's going to stand up there in closing argument and tell that jury that this community can't afford to have men like my client walking the streets. That they have an obligation to protect our children, keep them safe from child molesters, from men like my client. It doesn't matter he hasn't proved a damn thing. It doesn't matter that my client might even be innocent. 'You can't risk it,' he'll tell them. 'You can't chance it. Do the right thing,' he'll say. 'Find him guilty.'"

She stopped. What had flowed so smoothly and nonstop in the courtroom was now rasping and scraping her insides. She had had enough for one day, but the hypocrisy of it all still riled her. She went on, not with the fire and vigor of an hour ago, but rather with softly spoken words uttered through gritted teeth. "This process is so much bullshit. Have a kid accuse a man of child molestation and the man has no chance, not in this society. So much for all that nonsense of the accused being innocent until proven guilty beyond a reasonable doubt. Have you ever had a defendant in a child molest case walk into a courtroom on the opening day of trial and at that point think that his prospective jurors presume him innocent? Not for a second."

Greg Olsen watched as a shadow of her courtroom fervor returned. He knew Barbara felt passionately about the preconceived notions of a defendant's guilt in child molest cases. As he watched, it occurred to him that he cared more about her now than he had years before when he had wondered if he had made the mistake of his life by letting her go. Maybe that was because there was hope now. His kids each had one foot out the door. Soon, they would be out of high school and gone. When that happened, he had promised himself he would not spend another day with fat, drunken Molly. Not that he was any prize. But he knew he could lose weight and cut back on his drinking, if it meant a life with Barbara. Yes, there was hope. Or was there? Life being what it is, after all these years of being single, Barbara would probably take up with another guy just about the time Jenny was graduating from high school. On the other hand, how much did the kids need him even now?

Two DAYS later, after Barbara Blake made an impassioned plea for justice and fairness under the law, the jury convicted her client of three counts of child molestation and acquitted him on seven counts. The verdict made no sense. Jane Doe's testimony had been that ten times and "way more than ten times" her father had put his finger on her "privates." How could he be not guilty on seven occasions but guilty on three others? Conversely, how could he have been guilty on three occasions but not guilty on seven others —or "way more than ten"? But it mattered little. The pain and hurt of a loss never lessened, and the losses were always there. This one had been particularly galling. She had made flagrant liars of Sergeant Brennan and Mary Atkins, and Jane Doe had served up so many different versions of what had happened and not happened, as to be ludicrous. But it was the man sitting next to her, her client, who had suffered the ultimate loss. Forcing herself to be mindful of that, she turned to him, trying to set aside her own hurt, and tried to comfort and console him, but instead she stumbled through the only words she could call up, worn clichés. It didn't matter at all. His face was ashen and frozen in horror and disbelief. He hadn't heard a word she had spoken. Once the jury left, Judge Williams remanded him into custody and the bailiff and a deputy sheriff whisked him away. He was facing a minimum mandatory prison sentence of ten years.

Then the spectators left and only Barbara Blake remained. Slowly she put her folders together and into her briefcase, waiting until she was sure that the jurors had left the hallways and the courthouse—afraid of what she might say if she encountered one of them—and not wanting to let anyone see her cry. Once she had filled her briefcase, she sat for a while longer, crying softly. Ten minutes after the jury left, Judge Williams came back into the courtroom, still wearing his black robe, and went to the counsel table where she was sitting. For a few moments he stood across from her, watching her, searching for the right words. Then he said, "Barbara, don't be hard on yourself. You did all you could for your client. In the thirty years I've been in this business, I've seldom seen a better cross-examination or a better closing argument than what you gave to this case. That may not be much of a consolation, but you were truly remarkable."

II

SHE DROVE HOME INSTEAD OF
going to her office. It wasn't five o'clock yet, but she did not want
Suzie, her secretary, to see her in this condition. The phone calls
and e-mail messages could wait until Monday. She drove to a
beige, stucco, two-bedroom home in San Cristobal's Tower District. She bought the home some fifteen years before with funds
from her parents' estate. She had lived there with her first husband, Bob Johnson, and later, briefly, with her second husband,
Brian Stone. It was a small house with a kitchen, dining room,
living room, bathroom, a bedroom converted into an office, and
her bedroom. She could have afforded a larger, more luxurious
house or a pricey apartment in one of the new high-rises that had
sprung up around San Cristobal, but the little house was home.
She knew everything about it: each room, each window, and each

cupboard and door. She knew where the creaks were in the old wooden plank floors and for much of the year enjoyed walking barefoot over those smooth, worn planks. Time and time again the little house had provided her with refuge from life's ups and downs. True, she could visualize places where she and her ex-husbands had stood or sat during some of the more disappointing moments of their marriages, but that mattered so little because now she understood she had not known either of them, and, worse, neither of them had known her.

As she closed the kitchen door behind her, kicked off her high heels, pulled off her pantyhose, and felt her full weight resting on the familiar planks, a sheet of exhaustion and disappointment washed over her. But here she could slouch and droop, hang her head, and cry if she wanted to. Here there was no need to present her lawyer front: strong, self-assured, knowledgeable, and able to offer the soundest advice in the worst of conditions. Here she was whatever she was. She poured herself a glass of white wine and went to the living room and sat in an overstuffed armchair.

SHE HAD fallen in love with and married Bob Johnson four months into her first year of law school. It seemed like the perfect match. Bob's rugged good looks, his strong baritone voice, and his ability to verbally spar with the professors in the classroom signaled a bright courtroom future. With Barbara's quick grasp of legal principles and her ability to analyze complex legal issues, they seemed destined to be a dynamic legal team. But when they received their first-year grades three weeks into their summer vacation, Bob had flunked his exams and Barbara had finished at the top of the class.

Bob was devastated. He paced or sat around the house during the day and slept very little at night. Barbara was tormented by his failure and her success. She tried to lift his spirits while downplaying her accomplishment. She finally convinced him that there had to have been a mistake, that the law school had somehow attributed someone else's test scores to him. Bob went to the registrar's office. The exam books were retrieved. There had been no mistake and Bob wasted no time in berating Barbara for heaping this second round of humiliation upon him.

Next came the rage. "Stop pitying me! I don't need your pity!" "Stop making excuses for me; I'm a grown man!" "What the hell gives you the right to pity me! Who in the hell do you think you are!" Then came the scenes, often and everywhere. In public at a restaurant: "Don't try to hush me! If I don't like the goddamn salad, I have every right to say I don't like the goddamn salad! I don't give a damn who's watching or listening!" At home over a broken glass: "I know that was your favorite glass! I understand that it came from Poland or Czechoslovakia or Timbuktu or wherever the hell it came from! Believe me, I know that this house and everything in it is yours and yours alone. So tell me, should I get the hell out of here now? Should I? Should I?"

The summer days dragged by. Every day, Barbara thought, this too will pass. It had to pass. Things would get better. They had to. He had to get a job—but she didn't dare suggest it. Quietly she volunteered to work for a law office, telling Bob that they had called and were in a bind for the next six weeks. Then Bob began looking for a job. He wanted nothing more to do with school: the entire educational process in the country was idiotic. Barbara was overjoyed. He had to do something or he would drive them both crazy. But there was not a great demand for a liberal arts major who had just flunked out of law school in his first year. That brought on more depression, but at least there were no more outbursts. Instead, Bob became withdrawn. Still, he continued looking for work. There was an abundance of sales jobs—jobs selling life insurance, pesticides, fertilizers, automobiles, home appliances. But selling products, "hawking things" as Bob put it, was beneath him, and he withdrew a little more. Finally, Bob took a job with a bank in a management training program. It was not just "any old job," he said, but a job that would put him in management, if not today, then in the very near future.

He was more himself again, or so it seemed. He talked loud and long about the bank and about its history and place and importance in society. They started him out as a teller, not permanently, just for a few months, so he could learn the banking business from the ground up. For the next six months, Bob talked endlessly about his everyday experiences as a bank teller: the failures to balance at the end of the day, the customers at his window, the envy of the career tellers who understood he was being groomed for management, and even about the safeguards against armed robberies. Then Bob was transferred to a small branch as an operations officer. Now his talk shifted to managing staff and the everyday operations of that branch. He read bank texts on management skills and didn't hesitate to explain their intricacies to Barbara. Not once in that year was there any discussion of Barbara's law courses. The only mention of her attending law school was if one of her school activities was going to conflict with Bob's work schedule. For all of the hours Barbara spent poring over her law books, she might just as well have been knitting, because whenever Bob poked his head into the room where she was studying, they never talked about her academic work.

When Bob was sent to San Francisco to train as a loan officer, he took a small apartment there. They were both relieved. At first he would come home on Friday night and leave early Monday morning. By the end of that six-month training, he was coming home on Saturday morning and leaving on Sunday night. The weekends were awkward. He always managed to busy himself with some project, and Barbara, of course, had her studies, which meant they spent very little time together. She was in her last months of law school then, but the conversations they had on those weekends dealt with the bank, Bob's training program, and San Francisco. At night, she changed for bed in the bathroom, donning one of two ankle-length, cotton nightgowns. Each was careful to stay on his or her side of the bed, and any accidental touching or bumping would provoke an "I'm sorry" or an "Excuse me."

Then Bob was promoted to junior loan officer at the same small branch of the bank. He had been there a little more than four months when he made his announcement.

"Barbara, I'm leaving."

"Where you going?" she said, looking up from her bar-review outlines. She thought he might be going to the store or for a walk and that he must have told her earlier, but it hadn't registered because there were just two days left until the bar exam.

"I'm leaving," he repeated.

"Yes, but where are you going? What time will you be back? I'd like to have an early dinner."

"I'm leaving, Barbara. I won't be back for dinner. I won't be back for breakfast. I'm leaving, period. I'm leaving your house. I'm leaving you."

"What!" A shaft of pain and disbelief—and relief, too—shot through her. She grinned a mirthless smirk and shook her head in tiny motions, fighting back tears. Not for the breakup... that was bound to come, was too long in coming, but for them, for their failure, for the grand beginning that had come to nothing and melted away in sadness.

"You're kidding, of course, aren't you?" she said, when in fact part of her was hoping he wasn't kidding.

"No, I'm not kidding. I'm leaving."

He *was* leaving. The solemn look on his face said he *was* leaving. Tears fell silently on the open pages of her bar-review course. "Oh, Bob, I know things haven't been good between us. I know I've been studying for the bar exam and you've been working, but it's almost over. On Tuesday I'll take the bar, and on Thursday I'll be finished, I'll be free. Then we can get back to normal—do things together again, enjoy ourselves, and enjoy each other again...have a life again." She said these things wishing them perhaps but needing it to be over, too. Not wanting the corpse to be dead and, yet, not wanting the corpse to come back to life either.

"No, Barbara, it's been over for a long time. These past two years have been hell for me and they haven't been a picnic for you either." He was finally shutting the door on the humiliating pain he had endured since their first year in law school. His only regret was that he hadn't done it sooner.

Through the blur of her tears she said, "Can't we talk this out?" knowing they could never talk it out and not really wanting to talk it out.

"There's nothing more to say, Barbara. It's over. How or why it happened, I'll never know. But we both know it's over."

SHE SAT and thought. It wasn't the hours and weeks of effort and emotion that she had poured into that child molest case that was exhausting her, rather it was the defeat itself. Had she won, she would be out having dinner or drinks with Suzie or even out shopping, repaying herself for all her hard work. But today criminal defense lawyers never win, except of course on television. How she deplored the lawyer shows on television, the reruns, in which the dogged defense attorney won every time. In her mind, those trials didn't even rise to the level of caricature. Most of the speeches, questions, and answers there would never have been permitted or even dared in a real court of law. Underdogs were always falsely accused and yet prevailed at the last moment against overwhelming odds. If the scripts were written with a police or prosecutor slant, the prosecutor never lost despite facing every obstacle known to man. And of course, just as often as not, romance was woven into those episodes.

She dozed off. When she woke, light was slanting through the kitchen windows; the sun was in its last stages. She got up and unbuttoned her skirt, let it drop, and stepped out of it on her way to the kitchen, where she poured herself another glass of wine. She returned to the armchair, rolled her blouse off, and sat and let the defeat seep in, telling herself that in two weeks this would be only a bad, passing memory. But for now, she would have to deal with the bitterness. Her mind flitted from scenes to words to images, to the preparation of the case for trial, the trial itself, and then the actual verdict—three counts of guilty of child molest, the defeat itself. Then it stopped because the final note had arrived: she was thirty-nine and alone with her defeat. Thirty-nine and completely alone in the emptiness of her little house. More and more she was experiencing these bouts of abject loneliness, not just after a loss but sometimes as she prepared a case for trial, too. And then, as she sat with her wine glass in that absolute silence, she could hear the sound of loneliness, clearer and clearer with each loss. She stood and in one quick motion turned on the TV. The hum of the set warming. Not fast enough, but at least a real sound...something. Then the first colors, the first images, and finally words. But what she saw and heard was a rerun of an *LA Law* episode. A dashing, young lawyer was crushing a fat, male witness on cross-examination with questions and statements that had long since been outlawed by the Evidence Code. In a rage, she threw her glass of wine at the television set. After the shattering of the glass, there was silence once again.

III

THREE HUNDRED MILES NORTH, Donnie Sanders flipped up a metal slot, leaned toward the opening, and said, "Roll 'em up, Soto!"

Alejandro Soto was hunched over a small dictionary searching for the word "incandescent" when he heard the command. He knew the voice and despised its owner. He paused before he looked up at the two-by-eight-inch peephole on the upper half of his steel door. Then slowly he turned his head sideways and upward and sneered at that part of Sanders's face visible through the steel mesh. But he said nothing.

"You hear me, Soto! Roll 'em up!"

Alejandro Soto continued staring but said nothing.

"OK asshole, have it your way. I'll be back in ten minutes. If you ain't rolled up by then, I'll get the boys down here to roll you up. They'll roll your ass up good." Then he was gone.

Sanders typified what Alejandro Soto loathed most about some of the guards assigned to the Secured Housing Unit at Arroyo Grande: fat, white, and sadistic. If he could ever grab Sanders... A minute was all he needed. A minute with his hands free. The pleasure he would get from sinking his fingers into that fat white neck until Sanders's eyes popped and his body collapsed would be better than any pleasure Soto had ever had: the best fuck, the best blow job. What more could they do to him? He was already serving two life sentences without the possibility of parole. He was going to die in prison. So what if they gave him the death penalty for Sanders. He was forty-three now; by the time they got around to executing him with all those appeals, he'd be sixty-eight, almost seventy. And who the hell would want to live that long in this hellhole anyway? Besides, with all he had done to his body as a youngster, he was sure he would die long before that. But he knew he'd never get the chance to grab Sanders. They cuffed him even before they entered his cell. "Back up, Soto." He'd step to the cell door, turn around, and stick both hands through the food tray slot. Click. Then two or three of them would come into the cell and put on the leg irons and the waist chain.

What was it that he hated most about Sanders? How many times had he asked himself that question? The answer was always the same: Sanders represented everything that was evil. Now they were moving him, probably to another cell or unit. They never said where or why.

ALEJANDRO SOTO had been in the infamous SHU for more than eight years. They had brought him there from the Adjustment Center in San Quentin eight months after he had been convicted and sentenced for the murder of Carlos Sanchez and his mother. When he was leaving San Quentin, he had had no idea where he was going. Even after they had been in the air for an hour, the answer was still the same: "Shut up, Soto." Once they landed and he saw the signs saying he was in Butte City, he knew he was going to Arroyo Grande, going to the SHU, a prison within a prison, the housing for the Department of Corrections' worst of the worst. They skirted the town and drove several miles down a deserted county road. When he saw the lights of the three-story buildings, he wondered which one was the SHU. First they drove toward the lighted buildings, then away from them. But where they were taking him was none of his business. It was only two years later when his lawyer showed him aerial photos of the prison that he understood that he was living in one of the round, mound-like structures that seemed to come up out of the ground.

They called the units within those structures "pods." His first impression of a pod was that it was the cleanest, quietest, most well-lit cellblock he had ever been in. But the word was that guys went crazy in the pods. And when they did, they went so crazy with all their screaming, it was almost like they wanted to take everyone with them. At first glance he saw nothing to support that. The mounds had been cleverly designed so that the circular, glassed-in controls were at the center of each gigantic mound pie that had been cut up into slices all around it. The entry to each pod was located at its tip, which was close to the control center and broadened gradually until its two sides met at a triangular base some 100 feet away. Each pod was twenty feet high and had no windows; all lighting was artificial. The cells were located on two tiers, ten cells to a tier. Everything was concrete painted a pale green. A large, round white thermometer was mounted in the center of the wall opposite the cells. It read seventy degrees. Always.

Each cell was eight by ten feet. A one-foot-thick, three-by-six-foot slab of concrete was attached to the left wall, three feet off the floor. On top of it was a rolled-up mattress and on top of that a blanket, a sheet, and a towel. A metal toilet bowl was bolted to the floor at the far right end of the cell. Next to it was a metal washbasin mounted to the wall. The cell door was made out of solid steel, except for a food tray slot in the center and an upper peephole. Cell lighting was provided by a florescent, steel-encased tube along the upper-right-hand wall.

Once inside the cell, Alejandro Soto was issued a yellow jumpsuit, a pair of jockey shorts, a pair of white cotton socks, and shower clogs. At the end of each week, his clothing, sheet, and towel were exchanged for clean ones. They said that breakfast was served at 4:00 A.M., lunch at 10:00 A.M., and dinner at 4:00 P.M., although Alejandro had no way of knowing. Meals were served through the tray slots. All trays and unfinished food or drinks were to be returned fifteen minutes after they were served or the inmate risked forfeiture of the next meal. Like the pod temperature, the pod lights and cell lights remained constant, with the same light on twenty-four hours a day, 365 days a year. Each inmate was allowed out of his cell three hours a week for exercise in an exercise yard. Failure to follow the pod's rules and regulations meant the loss of exercise privileges. There was to be absolutely no talking or note passing between inmates.

As ALEJANDRO Soto began readying himself for Sanders's move, he thought back to those first minutes in his new home. He had sat on his cement bunk next to his rolled-up mattress remembering what others had said about the SHU. "They go crazy up there, man. It's the place. It's the way they got it set up that will drive anybody crazy." Thinking, *So this is how they drive you crazy. Total isolation. Nothing ever changes. The light, the temperature, and the silence never change. And you never know whether it's day or night or what day or week or month or year or season it is. Their absolute cleanliness, their even temperature, and good lighting go a long way to protecting themselves against charges of brutality.*

He couldn't remember how many days or nights he had been there when he first heard it. After sleeping several times he lost track of what day or time it was. But it was early on when he heard it. It was the first sound, other than his own, that he had heard since he had been put in his cell. The sound continued, steady, constant, distant. The whine of a small motor maybe? No, now it was high, very high, then low and thin, and then gone for a moment or moments, only to begin again. A distant siren? No. Sharp, muted, punctuated sounds. Then a long shrill sound again, but distant. Then cough-like, guttural sounds. And he knew. There was no denying it. Someone, somewhere in the pod, was cracking up. The sound stopped and he thought, hoped, he'd been wrong. He began counting one, two, three...each second confirming that he had been wrong, thankfully wrong. But the sound began again. Long, shrill, muted cries, stopping only long enough to allow whoever it was, wherever he was, to catch his breath. Then there were softer, muted sounds, muted shouts, muted screams. He listened and knew. It was the other inmates telling whoever it was to stop, to shut the fuck up, yelling at the guards to make him stop. But the guards weren't in the pod. They were in the circular, soundproof, bulletproof, glassed-in control room. Could they hear? Of course they could, if they wanted to. Could they turn off the sound? Of course. The bastards were probably sitting back laughing as another one of the "worst of the worst" went mad and was about to take some of the others with him. The sounds went on and on for an eternity it seemed. Or was it only an hour? Or less than an hour? Was it day or night? The bastards! He had no way of knowing. The light would always be the same. Artificial light. Always there. He didn't know if the sounds stopped first or if he fell asleep first. All he knew was that when he woke, the sounds had stopped. He still didn't know if it was night or day. Had he had slept an hour, ten hours, or for days? But the sounds had stopped. What had happened to the crazy, he didn't know. What had happened to the other inmates, he didn't know. What he did know was that he needed to guard himself now as he had never guarded himself before.

THE PEEPHOLE flipped open again. "You got five minutes, asshole." It was Sanders. "If you're not rolled-up in five minutes, my boys will be in there to roll you up just like they did the last time."

He never forgot the last time. Sanders had told him to roll them up just like he had just done. Soto had been in his cell for a few years by then. And strange as it seemed, he didn't want to leave his cell. He didn't want to lose his cell. It was his home. It was everything he had. So he didn't roll 'em up. And a bunch of goons came in and beat the holy shit out of him and dragged him out of his cell and searched it. That's all they wanted to do, search it. But he had thought they were moving him. They didn't find anything and they dragged him back in unconscious and left. It was no different now. He still didn't want to leave his cell, but he sure as hell didn't want to have the shit beat out of him again.

"You got four minutes asshole." Sanders again. How he hated the pig.

Sanders had actually been in his cell only once during those eight years. He had come in with three guards not long after Soto had been there. What he first saw was a big man with huge jowls in a khaki uniform. Behind him were the guards.

"Well, look who's here. Another badass. This one's from Dos Palos County. We've had a few from Dos Palos. They cracked too, didn't they boys?" He smiled and looked Soto up and down.

"Looks to be in pretty good shape, doesn't he boys? Hell, I'd be in good shape, too, if all I had to do all day was lay around and wait for my next meal." The upper part of Sanders body ended in a large paunch that hung out and over what was probably a belt. "Shit, if it was up to me, I'd burn the worst of these assholes and put the rest of them in a chain gang. Make them earn their keep. It's really tough paying taxes when all you see day in and day out is how your hard-earned tax dollar is being pissed down the drain on scumbags like this asshole."

Sanders. The mass of added flesh on his face narrowed his eyes to slits and left his nose as a tiny, shiny knob between two massive, red-streaked cheeks.

"Listen up, Soto. We play the music here and you do the dance. We run things to suit us, not you. You step out of line and we can make it plenty rough for you. Follow the rules and mind your own business and we'll get along just fine. Not that we'll have much to do with you because we won't. Everything's automatic around here, everything's by the computer. Today's an exception. We're here to make sure that you have only what that ridiculous law says you can keep in here. You're allowed two ten-by-fifteen-inch boxes in your cell—one for your legal work and the other for your books and papers. Lieutenant makes us come down here with every fresh fish and sort through what came with him from his last prison. Fuck, if it was up to me, I'd burn every damn thing that came with you assholes. Some of these assholes come here with fifteen boxes. You seem to be different. There was only a box and a half that came with you from Quentin. There's legal papers enough for half a box, and the rest of the stuff is just books, twelve of them. No letters, no photos, no gifts. What's the matter, don't nobody out there love you? No mother, no sister, no girlfriend, no boyfriend, no nobody to write to you?"

He didn't answer. Instead he looked down at the roll of fat that hid any sign of a belt and tried to imagine the ugliness of the hairy red paunch that might some day reach and cover Sanders's dick.

"OK, believe me, I'd rather not talk to you either. Fact is, I'd rather not even be standing here with you piece of shit. But just so we're clear, just so there's no bullshit, no 'you-never-told-me' bullshit later on, you're only allowed five books and a Bible at any one time.

"You got twelve books that come with you. You got to pick out five besides the Bible. Do that now… Billy, hand me those two boxes. Curtis, bring in those legal papers and the books."

The guard behind and to the right of Sanders stepped forward and laid two empty cardboard boxes on the cement floor and stepped back. Then the second guard stepped up on Sanders's left with two boxes and their contents and placed those on the floor.

"OK, put your legal papers into one of the boxes. Then put five books and the Bible into the other."

"He doesn't have a Bible," Curtis said.

"No Bible! What the hell's the matter with you, boy? Don't you believe in God?"

He kept his eyes lowered and his head still. It was better not to answer.

"Well, fuck you too. We don't need to be talking to you either. Go on, pick five, before I burn the whole goddamn thing."

He knelt and picked *Crime and Punishment* first and placed it in one of the empty boxes. Then he picked *One Hundred Years of Solitude, Pedro Páramo, A History of Mexico,* and finally *Webster's College Dictionary.* Then he stood and fixed his eyes on Sanders's paunch again.

"OK, you picked your five books. You understand that all the books you didn't pick will be burned?"

He didn't answer.

"You understand everything I've told you here today?"

No answer.

"Have you got anything you want to ask us?"

He kept his eyes on Sanders's ugly roll of fat and said nothing.

"Play your silent game, asshole. I could care less. Die slow." Then they were gone.

THE PEEPHOLE slid open again. He didn't turn or look up. He didn't want to give Sanders that much satisfaction. But he did move to the two boxes. It wasn't Sanders.

"Soto, let's not have a repeat of the cell search incident." It was the lieutenant. Soto turned and faced the peephole. "I don't know what the problem is between you and Sanders, but I can sure as hell tell you that there are six guards standing outside the pod just dying to roll you up."

"Where am I going? Where you taking me? There's nothing to search for. Why do I have to move to another cell? This has been my house for more than eight years and all of a sudden that asshole comes down here and says, 'Roll 'em up!' just like that. And he expects me to roll up everything and move out in five minutes, just like that? Where am I going? Where you moving me too?"

"I don't know, and even if I did know, I couldn't tell you."

"Are you moving me to another pod? What for? Except for Sanders, I haven't had any problems here."

"No, we're not moving you to another pod. You're leaving the

SHU. You're leaving Arroyo Grande. That's all I know. That's all I've been told. That's all I can tell you."

"Leaving? Where in the hell am I going to? I'm a double lifer."

"I don't know, Soto. And frankly, I could care less. All I'm concerned with now is how to avoid having your teeth kicked in once again... Look, it won't take you more than five minutes to roll 'em up. Let's deal with that now. Are you going to roll 'em up, or am I gonna have to let those guards come down here and roll you up?"

"I'll roll 'em up."

"Thanks." The peephole slid shut and the lieutenant was gone.

He rolled up his mattress and folded his blanket, sheet, and towel. He put his dictionary, tablet, and pencil in the one still half-empty box; put on his jumpsuit and shower clogs; and was ready, ready to move out. Then he sat on the cement bunk concerned and confused. Leaving the SHU? Where could they be taking him? What had he possibly done to deserve being taken from the worst of the worst? He didn't trust them? What could be worse than the SHU? He waited. Waits could be for minutes or for hours—he would never know. He looked around the cell and thought of the millions of exercises he had done there, the thousands of hours spent, day after day, week after week, month after month.

His feet were resting in the five-by-six-foot, imaginary rectangle where he had sat and lay and stood to do those exercises. One, two, three, four...one thousand one, one thousand two... The counting had been almost as necessary as the exercises themselves. It kept his mind from wandering, kept his mind focused on the task, each number another grain in his wall of resistance against madness. Even though a federal judge had ruled these conditions were inhumane and that once an inmate lost it, he had to be removed from the pod, inmates were still going crazy and staying right where they were. Two thousand nine hundred ninety-seven ...two thousand nine hundred ninety-eight.

He looked at his boxes. One was half filled with his appellate papers. The other was always less than full, varied by the changing sizes of the books his lawyer brought him. Two books always remained. Of those, *Webster's College Dictionary* had been changed once, but only for a larger version when he had upped his quota of definitions to be memorized to twenty-five a day.

Crime and Punishment had never left his possession. Always stacked in the same place in the box, it was a smooth, worn paperback edition that he had read through completely four times in those eight years and read passages to himself hundreds of times. Because he was, he thought, no different than Raskolnikov—Raskolnikov lying on his couch, pondering the uselessness of his despicable old landlady's life. Just as he had pondered the worthlessness of Carlos Sanchez's life. Carlos Sanchez, the cruel, sadistic, barrio dope dealer who enjoyed watching his clients, men and women, writhing with fear and pain as they begged him for just "a little taste," promising him everything and doing whatever he fancied then and there for that little taste. Until one day, Alejandro Soto had heard and seen his gruesome laughter one too many times, and he crept up Carlos's apartment stairs. At a time when Carlos was known to be napping, when Carlos was not to be disturbed, he crept up those filthy back stairs with Johnny Moncado's gun; jiggled the door lock loose; put the gun to Carlos's head, an inch from his skull, even as Carlos slept with a gun in his hand; and pulled the trigger not once but twice and felt pieces of Carlos's flesh splatter onto his face and hands. And then he stood motionless telling himself that he had done the right thing.

What Alejandro had not counted on was that Carlos's mother was in the apartment visiting. When she heard the shots, she came running into the room screaming hysterically, and, before he knew it, Alejandro had shot and killed her as well. There had been talk that the district attorney would seek the death penalty for the double killing. But such a trial would have uncovered some questionable dealings two undercover police officers had had with Carlos Sanchez. Instead, at the trial the district attorney had asked for two life sentences without the possibility of parole, which the jury gave him in less than a day of deliberating.

The other box contained only letters and legal papers sent by his attorney. Alejandro's father had been run over by a train when Alejandro was thirteen. His mother died of a broken heart two weeks after his homicide convictions. His brothers and sisters had disowned him long before the double homicides. His marriage to Julia, his wife of six months at the time of the killings, hadn't lasted six months more once he was jailed. It took him years to wipe out the memory of Julia whispering, "Love of my life. I'll love you forever and ever and ever." Her jail visits had slackened by the fourth month. She visited only twice during the fifth month and then sat sullenly on the other side of the glass partition as he first accused her of infidelity and then abused her and then tried every word, every cue, every ploy he had so successfully used to control her out on the streets. Her response had been to sit silently and morosely, occasionally looking at her watch until it was time to go. Then she was gone for good. She had never come to the SHU. She no longer accepted his collect calls, and his desperate letters came back stamped: Return to Sender.

"Get yourself a fat, ugly woman," was the prison refrain. "The fatter, the better. And ugly too. Because they'll stick with you. They'll wait. They need love too. They'll send you money and things, anything you want, and they be regular on those visits, too. The fine-looking ones, the juicy ones never last." He had heard this refrain so many times before as forlorn inmates returned from waning visits. He heard it again just after Julia's last visit.

Once Julia left, another piece of jail-spun advice stuck with him: "If you're looking at some serious time, cut her loose now, quick like, 'cause you'll do hard time in here trying to control her out there. That's just not happening. Never has. Never will."

In the eight years and three months that Alejandro had been locked up in Arroyo Grande, the only visits he had received were from Fred Solomon, his court-appointed appellate attorney. But then, making inmate visits as difficult as possible had been part of the Department of Correction's elaborate scheme to establish Arroyo Grande as a state-of-the-art maximum security prison. The prison was located ten miles from the Oregon border near the tiny town of Mills. The majority of inmates were brown and black men. Most of these men came from the Los Angeles metropolitan area. Public transportation from Southern California or even the San Francisco Bay area was all but nonexistent. It was a fourteen-hour drive from Southern California and the spare lodgings in Mills became even scarcer and more expensive once the local white innkeepers laid eyes on their new, would-be lodgers. At the same time, the prison was the largest employer in the area and there was a real deference paid by the local citizenry both to the prison's policies and its employees.

AFTER HE rolled up, Alejandro Soto was transported back to San Quentin where he was housed once again in the Adjustment Center. All he was told was that he was facing new charges in San Cristobal County, nothing more. Early in the morning of the fourth day he was moved to the San Cristobal County jail. No sooner had he been processed, when he was rushed in leg irons and waist chains through a tunnel to the courthouse and placed in a holding cell. Sometime later, he was taken into court, alone and still in chains, to a room full of people, more people than he had been with for years. He was advised that he was being charged with the murder of Santos Estrada some ten years earlier. Perplexed, he had to run the name Santos Estrada through his mind several times before he realized who the judge was talking about. He was appointed a lawyer, a Mr. Something Olsen, a big, soft, blond-haired guy, and once the charges had been read to him, that lawyer and the district attorney went up to the judge's desk for a long time and argued about something in whispers.

The charges were completely bogus; still, what could they do to him? Give him another life sentence? Once the shock began to lessen, he became aware once again that for the first time in almost eight years he was in a room full of people. He turned and looked out at those people. Most were staring at him. Angry, defiant, he stared back and all turned away except for a woman sitting on his side of the railing. She had to be a lawyer, he thought, because she was dressed like a lawyer and was sitting where all the lawyers sat. He looked past her and then came back to her. Her eyes hadn't shifted, rather they were staring at him. When he stared back, she seemed to stare harder. *Fucking cunt,* he thought. *Trying to stare me down. Self-righteous bitch knows nothing about my case but has already convicted me. Knows I'm guilty and wants me to know that she knows. Has no use for me. Her husband's probably a cop. Thinks she can put the fear of God in me with her two-bit stare. Make me confess right here on the spot—yell out that I'm guilty. Lady, put that stare away, you'll never outstare me. I'll never cop to something I didn't do.*

Much to Alejandro's surprise, that Olsen guy followed him into the holding cell once the court proceedings ended.

"What do you want?"

"What do you mean what do I want? I'm your lawyer."

"I never made you my lawyer."

"No, but the court did."

"Oh, bullshit!" That soft dummy sat down across from him, angering him. *This big white asshole, make-believe lawyer couldn't defend his dog. Soft as shit, couldn't last a round with me. Watery blue eyes and a slit for a mouth. All that red on the bottom of his cheeks says he's a drunk. Look at that sorry fat bastard. Every time he breathes he's wearing out the inside of his white shirt. And he has lines of skin and fat hanging over his collar's edge.* "You guys all eat out of the same trough. You think I'm stupid or something? You think I don't know that the same county that pays the DA is the same county that pays the judge and is the same county that pays you? You gonna tell me you're gonna bite the hand that feeds you? Come on. You get uppity with the judge in defending me, a guy everybody in that courtroom hates and thinks is guilty of murder, and the judge doesn't appoint you anymore and you've just lost a shitload of money because I'm telling you I'm innocent and this case is gonna go to its bitter end."

He stopped and stared at Olsen, an angry, hateful stare. "I ain't pleading guilty to nothing. You'd better understand that from the get. I don't know a fucking thing about you, other than that you're on the same payroll as that asshole judge out there. I don't know

40

if you even know how to try a case. You're probably just another dump truck like all the other public defenders. First thing out of your mouth is gonna be how I better plead guilty or they're really gonna fuck me over. Well, what can they do to me, give me a third life sentence when I only got one life? No, I know, you'll come out with: 'They're gonna shoot for the death penalty.' Bullshit! And besides, if you were a top-notch defense lawyer that handles murder cases all the time, you wouldn't be taking my case for the nickels and dimes the county pays. Bottom line is I don't want you for my fucking lawyer." Then there was complete silence and Alejandro Soto thought, *The punk didn't think I'd come at him and tell him like it is.*

Greg Olsen sat inches from the chained man looking down at his polished shoes, letting the silence multiply. Finally, he looked up at Soto and stared into his eyes for several moments before he quietly said, "Are you finished?"

Surprised and then enraged, Soto said emphatically in a raised voice, "Yeah, I'm finished with you! I'd rather have Charley McCarthy representing me! At least he'd do what I'd tell him to do straight out!"

Again Greg Olsen looked down at his tasseled loafers and waited before looking up. And Soto waited too, ready to spike whatever wimp comeback the dump truck had. But there was nothing wimp in the dump truck's eyes when he looked up this time and met and held his look.

Rather, there was a calm, self-assuredness in those eyes, with not a trace of anger, hurt, or hostility. Which again surprised Soto, but this time it unnerved him and left him completely open to the dump truck's quiet, confident question, "Can I say something now?"

"Go ahead, man, say all you want. Who the fuck's stopping you?"

"First of all, if you have the funds available you can hire anyone you want. Without those funds, the public defender will represent you. But in this case, the public defender has a conflict because they represented the victim, Santos Estrada, in the past. With that in mind, the court then chooses a qualified lawyer from a panel and he or she is your lawyer, like it or not, unless you show the court that you are not being competently represented. For your information, Mr. Soto, I have a highly successful criminal law practice. I'm not a public defender. I don't need your case. The only reason I'm in it is that Fred Solomon asked me to do what I could to get appointed to your case. Mr. Solomon thinks—"

"How do you know Solomon?"

"Fred Solomon and I were roommates during law school. He's one of my best friends. He doesn't think they've got much in this ten-year-old case, and he believes they are filing it only because they're afraid that the federal court's going to cut you loose on the prior homicide convictions."

Now it was Alejandro Soto who looked down...but at his leg irons. He felt sheepish. Fred Solomon had earned his trust and respect as no other person in his life had. His letters and visits and books and court-ordered phone calls had kept him from madness. His legal briefs had given him hope, something to live for, a future. His encouragement had given him his first and only measure of self-esteem. No one, other than Fred Solomon, had ever said, "You're bright, Alejandro. You owe it to yourself to read and learn, to make the most that you can of yourself, for yourself, and no one else." He would forever be indebted to Fred Solomon.

"So, um...," his voice had softened and his mind was clutching for words and his eyes were looking away. "Um, how do I know you really know Mr. Solomon? How do I know I can talk to you? How do I know you're not really a cop? Except for Mr. Solomon, I ain't talked to anybody face-to-face like this, and then with Solomon it was with a glass partition between us for more than eight years. Besides Mr. Solomon has told me over and over not to talk to anybody about my case until I clear it with him."

"We don't have to talk about this case now. Fred said he's coming down Saturday to talk to you. He wanted to be here this morning but the whole thing came up so fast that he couldn't make it."

Alejandro felt like a fool. Everything this man had told him rang true. He searched for something else to say because he didn't want the man to leave. After eight years to be this physically close to a human being he trusted felt good. But there was nothing more he could find to say, and he was afraid that any moment now the man would get up and say that he was leaving. "Do you have a card?" he blurted out. "You know, I don't even know or remember your name."

As Greg Olsen handed him his business card, Alejandro thought of something else to say. "Who was that lady lawyer giving me the evil eye in court, trying to put me down?"

"What lady lawyer?"

"The one in the green suit with the brown hair. She was sitting with all the other lawyers. She was sitting next to this mousey little blonde thing. She's thirty-five or forty. Kind of good-looking. Lot of legs. Good legs."

Green suit, brown hair, sitting next to a mousey blonde had to be Barbara Blake, Greg Olsen thought. *These guys never miss a beat. Probably the first female legs he's seen in years. And Barbara is leggy. Sorry bastard has to be horny as hell.* "I know who you mean. She wasn't giving you the evil eye. She's a defense attorney and a good one."

"Then why was she staring at me?"

Poor bastard. Barbara might have glanced at him. Eight years is a long time. Now he'll probably fantasize about her all night. Beat his meat. "There've been a few articles about your case in the paper. She's probably just curious."

"What's her name?"

Now Greg Olsen found him offensive. *The sorry son of a bitch is here on what could turn out to be a death penalty case and all he can think about is sex. Sniffing after anything that even glances at him. If he wanted to know any other female's name in the courtroom, that would be one thing, but Barbara's...that's another. Still, there had been enough awkwardness in their first meeting, and he didn't need any more. Besides, Barbara could handle this goon just as she had handled hundreds of goons before him.*

"What's her name, man?"

43

"Barbara Blake. She and I are very good friends. In fact, we had a law practice together. We were partners for several years." *There was something he didn't like about Soto. Or was it about himself? How much longer could he keep fantasizing about Barbara?* "I've got some cases in another department. I'd better get going. I'll get back to you once you've talked to Solomon."

In his cell, Alejandro Soto replayed the woman's look a thousand times or, rather, her look came back to him a thousand times. Time and again he gave, or tried to give, that look meaning. It was more than a look. He had stared, and she had stared back. She had to want something. She wasn't a cop. She wanted him to see her staring. She didn't look away once. He had been around enough women to know that when they returned his look, stared back, they wanted to play. Smile or no smile—and she hadn't smiled—they wanted to get it on. Sometimes when they didn't smile, when they just looked back and stared, it meant that they were dead serious and they wanted to get right to it. She wanted to get right to it with him. But how? And why? She wasn't fat and ugly. She wasn't some sappy thing on welfare with seven kids. She was a lawyer, and a good one, that Greg guy had said. There must be millions of guys out there on the street who would jump at a chance to make it with her. So why would she...?

For the rest of the day no matter where his mind went, whether to listen to a guard writing up another inmate or to yell at some fool on the tier to turn the fucking TV down or to try to devise some way to look at himself in his mirror-less cell, she and her look returned. It calmed him to allow himself to think and believe that she wanted him, wanted to be with him, wanted to be his lawyer, so she could win his case and they could be together. But after a while, that was followed by a feeling of being ridiculous, of knowing there was nothing he could give her—nothing she could want from a double lifer without the possibility of parole. So he would resolve to stop thinking about her, hours after the look. But she would come again. The look would come again, beckoning him. Shake his head as much as he wanted, it never left.

When the trustee brought his dinner, he asked, "Do you know Barbara, the lawyer?"

"Who?"

"Barbara Blake, stupid. Barbara Blake. A good-looking broad with fine legs. She's a defense attorney, a good one, too."

"Naw, I ain't never heard of her."

"How long you been doing time?"

"Too long."

"How long you been doing time out of this county?"

"Too long."

"And you ain't heard of Barbara Blake?"

The trustee paused, postured. He had heard that this guy was out of the SHU at Arroyo Grande, and it didn't hurt any to act as if he were giving the matter some thought. He put his hand to his chin and fingered the edges of his mouth and looked off into recollection land and after a while started slowly shaking his head before he said, "No, I can't say that I've heard of her. What she look like, man?"

"Get the fuck out of here, punk! You're worthless!"

As Alejandro Soto was eating his dinner with the metal tray on his lap, it occurred to him he had almost missed a golden opportunity. He got up, went to the commode, and flushed down more than half the meal. Then with his bar soap he scrubbed the tray repeatedly in his miniature sink until it was as clean and shiny as he could get it. He dried the tray with his towel and then combed his hair. He took the tray to the cell bars and held it up to the walkway's light. He placed his face in front of it and saw a very blurred image of himself. He turned the tray and his head in several different directions, but the results were worse. Angry, he flipped the tray through the bars. The crash brought the guards running. When they asked what had happened, he wouldn't answer.

Everywhere he went she was there. She was in his dreams. He woke several times when he was about to touch her, only to find that he was alone in a new and different, darkened cell. She was in his exercises: one thousand one...Barbara Blake...one thousand four...Barbara Blake... The days that followed brought more of the same. He did everything from possess her to flee from her. His dreams turned sexual. He would waken to his smelly, creamy, sticky wetness. He never knew what had or had not happened in those dreams, just that she was in them. Even if he couldn't see her, he could sense her, smell her. He talked to her all the time, both in his dreams and in his cell.

"What's the matter, man?" a passing trustee might dare to ask. "Don't be losing it."

"Fuck you, punk. I'll be losing you if you don't stay out of my business."

FRED SOLOMON came to see him. He had more pleadings and brought him up-to-date on the progress of the writ. He spoke of Greg Olsen in glowing terms. He said that he had begged Olsen to get involved in the case and implored Alejandro to trust and cooperate fully with Greg. Just before he left, Solomon asked, "Do you have any questions?"

"Yeah, who's this Barbara Blake?"

"Who?"

"Barbara Blake, the lawyer. Olsen says that they used to be partners and that she's a damn good attorney."

"Barbara Blake? Don't know her...Barbara Blake...? Seems to me that Greg was associated with a Barbara Blake. But I never met her. Don't know her."

"Why can't she be my lawyer?"

"What!"

"Yeah, why not?"

"If you've got the money to hire her and she's willing to take your case, then yes, she can be your lawyer. But when you don't have the funds to hire a lawyer, you can't go around picking and choosing who your lawyer's going to be."

"Why not?"

"Because for one thing the court's in a much better position to know who's best qualified to represent a defendant. Much more so than the defendant himself. So who's been talking to you about this Barbara Blake?"

"Nobody in particular. It's just that everybody around here says she's a dynamite lawyer."

"Who's everybody?"

"Everybody here at the jail."

"You mean the other inmates?"

"Yeah."

"That's nothing to write home about."

Two days later, Greg Olsen came to visit. No sooner had Greg sat down on the other side of the glass partition than Alejandro Soto asked, "How do I get me another lawyer?" Greg Olsen bristled. *This son of a bitch needs to know that I won't be played with.* "The day I fuck up you can make all the motions you want to get rid of me. But not a minute sooner. I haven't fucked up yet. Hell, we haven't even started yet. Once we do, I don't intend to fuck up. I have too much respect for myself... Now, do we understand each other? I hope so, because I've seen you twice and we've had this discussion twice. I'm here until the court runs me off, and only the court." The two men glared at each other. But Greg had made his point and now he calmed himself.

"Now let's get down to business. The lab reports indicate the bullets that killed Santos Estrada were fired from the same gun used in the killing of Carlos Sanchez and his mother."

That got Alejandro Soto's attention. *Johnny Moncado must have panicked and then he lied. Fucking asshole laid it on me.*

"You know a Johnny Moncado?" Alejandro nodded. "Apparently, about a year after the Estrada killing, Moncado got picked up with a pound of heroin. Given his rap sheet, he stood to do a lot of time. Well, he cut a deal with the cops and the DA. In exchange for telling them that he had been with you the night *you* killed Estrada, he got two years for the heroin. He's out now. Where, I don't know. But I'm sure the DA does."

Alejandro sat back and looked away. *The truth was that Moncado had shot and killed Estrada when his fucking scheme blew up in his face. I didn't even know Estrada. How was I even gonna get near him.*

THE SECOND court appearance arrived and Alejandro Soto went hoping that Barbara Blake would be there. He went to court also hoping he would recognize her. Because having thought of her so many times, she had changed, it seemed, a little each day, and after eight days and nights he was no longer certain what she looked like. But the moment he stepped into the courtroom he saw her, recognized her. She was talking to Olsen. Once Olsen left her, her eyes went to him, fastened on him for a moment, and everything became a blur, until he felt Greg Olsen tugging on his arm. "Have a seat, Soto. The judge is going to hear another matter first."

The courtroom was empty save for Judge Williams, court personnel, Greg Olsen, Alejandro Soto and the three guards who escorted him everywhere, and Barbara Blake and District Attorney Bill Thompson, who were seated at the counsel tables. Alejandro Soto had no idea why he and Olsen were sitting in the jury box or who they were waiting for or why they were waiting. He was aware only of Barbara Blake and though he had looked over at her several times, she had not returned his look. Suddenly the lock on the holding cell door clanged loudly and the great iron door slowly swung open. A young, white male in brown jail garb stepped out into the courtroom. The brown clothing meant that the inmate was in protective custody in the jail, and more than 90 percent of the browns wore it because they were child molesters. *Wait till the punk hits the joint. He'll get his,* Soto thought. When the brown-clad man took his seat next to Barbara Blake rather than next to the DA, Soto became more agitated, mumbling, "Punk better not end up in Arroyo Grande." Greg Olsen nudged him back into silence.

It was a sentencing hearing for the man in brown who had been convicted of child molest five weeks earlier. The district attorney was asking the court for the maximum twenty-five-year prison sentence based on the psychological trauma the child had sustained. The probation department had recommended a mid-term

48

sentence of seventeen years and Barbara Blake was seeking the mandatory minimum ten-year sentence.

The prosecution called two witnesses in support of its position: Jane Doe's mother and a clinical psychologist who had been seeing Jane Doe on a weekly basis since the inception of the case.

When Barbara Blake rose to begin her cross-examinations, Alejandro Soto watched intently. He watched as she strutted about the courtroom, approaching the court clerk with the school records and requesting that they be marked for identification, then approaching the witnesses with the records and asking them to examine them. She stood just a few feet from the witnesses with her arms crossed, looking casually about the courtroom as she waited calmly and confidently for them to finish their task. He was stunned by her agility, her facility, in the courtroom. He watched as she cross-examined each witness, moving easily, stepping toward and away from the witness, leaning against the jury box railing, turning her back on the witness, and striding away even as she asked another question and then another, apparently ready even before the witness had finished answering the previous question. He didn't understand most of her questions or the answers, but she was by far the better of the two attorneys, and the best he had ever seen at work in a courtroom. When she finished her final argument, the judge gave the inmate in brown a ten-year sentence. Alejandro Soto was overwhelmed and then thoroughly deflated, depressed. How could someone of her caliber want anything to do with someone like him?

In those moments after the judge pronounced sentence, all of his fantasies about Barbara Blake had been crushed, and he was too embarrassed to look over at her as he followed Greg Olsen out of the jury box and slowly made his way to the counsel table. But as he neared the table he looked up and his eyes met hers, and she stared at him only to have Greg Olsen step between them.

THEN HE was in his cell again. It had all happened so quickly and so intensely that at times he wasn't certain that it had happened at all, only to know in the next moment, without the slightest doubt, that she had stared at him, not with hostility or contempt or fear even. She had not looked away; she had returned whatever jumbled look he had given her. She was interested in him, she was attracted to him, and there could be more...there had to be more. Sometime that night he woke and realized once again that he was alone and helpless in a strange, dark cell and that he would not be returning to court for another three weeks and that she could never be his.

In the days that followed he asked the trustees about her. "Hey, I ain't talking about no broad, punk, I'm talking about a class-A attorney. The best. Understand?" The urgency in the voice of the double lifer from Arroyo Grande made it clear to the trustee that his response would have to be very different than what it had just been.

"No disrespect, man. I mean I don't know the lady, the lawyer, I mean, personally, but I be hearin' that she's a hella lawyer. An ol' homey of mine down on the second floor be havin' her for a lawyer and he be doin' a lot of time and knows good lawyers from dump trucks. And he says she's a hella lawyer."

That was how Jacobo Lopez came into possession of two notes from Alejandro Soto for Barbara Blake, notes that Soto knew would bring Barbara Blake to visit him and make her his lawyer.

IV

SHE WOKE STARTLED. THE SUN
was full against the bedroom blinds. "Oh my God, I'm going to
be late!" She looked at the clock: 8:35. *The damn alarm didn't...* She
started to mentally rearrange her day and then stopped. It was Saturday. Yesterday's loss returned. The hurt hadn't stopped. This
one was going to take a couple of weeks to get over. "How long
can I keep doing this?" she asked.

She plopped back down on the bed and looked up at the ceiling. There was a time when the wins were sandwiched in with the
losses. Not anymore. She needed to take some time off. Go down
to Big Sur for a week and take in that magnificent coastline. But
that fantasy lasted less than a minute. A woman alone. There was
nothing sadder to Barbara Blake than a woman her age alone on
a vacation. What could be more depressing than sitting at a table

in some fancy restaurant eating and pretending not to be aware that she's alone? And, longing for a man to come along.

She wondered how long she'd been lying idly on the bed. It didn't matter because she'd already decided not to go to the office that day or tomorrow and maybe not all of next week, even if it meant she just hung out at the house. There was no reason why she couldn't just lie there all day if she wanted. But within minutes, she tired of that.

She decided to take a long, hot shower, unlike the ones she usually took. She languished under the shower until the hot water began to run out. Then she made a breakfast of bacon and eggs with a side of pancakes and some coffee. She ate slowly, thinking how nice it was not to be rushing out the back door with a cup of coffee and toast. But yesterday's loss was still hurting. It hung over everything. No matter how much she thought she was enjoying her leisure, the defeat was still there, biting at her. She read the morning paper, read it all, including her client's conviction, which was featured on the front page of the local section. She noted several inaccuracies in the report, all in favor of the prosecution. She brushed her hair carefully and applied her eye shadow meticulously. Then she slipped into a pair of jeans, a T-shirt, and sandals and decided that this might be all she'd wear for a week. She washed the dishes because this weekend she'd be eating at home and her cleaning woman didn't come until Monday. No, she remembered, a cleaning woman wouldn't be coming on Monday. Another one had quit. She'd better pick up that broken glass herself before she forgot and stepped on it. They all wanted more than one day a week, even though she didn't need cleaning more than one day a week. Once, she had decided to go without a cleaning woman. After a month the house was filthy. But she wasn't about to become a housekeeper. She had seen what it had done to her mother.

She went outside and sat on the cement landing and studied her backyard, the same yard that she seldom looked at as she made her way to her car every day. It was a sixty-by-forty-foot lot with a thick, rich lawn in the center, a variety of flowers growing along the garage on her right and along the neighbors' fence on her left, and dense ivy covering the back fence. She took off her sandals and walked out on the lush grass and felt its thickness and softness. She moved to a rosebush and gently touched its velvety petals and smelled its fragrance. She went to a large camellia bush with its beautiful white, perfectly shaped petals and a scent that purified the air around it. She wondered why it took a loss in court to make her see and appreciate the fragrance and beauty of her backyard? Then there was ground cover of blue-white, needle-like leaves that served as a background for brilliant orange blossoms, and she thought of Manuel, her gardener, and how much he enjoyed his work. She poked her slender arm through the deep, vibrant green ivy and touched the fence. There were sunflowers blooming in the far left corner of the yard and more flowers than she could identify. Finally, she watched the silvery leaves of her young olive tree glistening in the morning sun. When she reached the olive tree, she plucked a new leaf off a thin branch, examined its color for the silver, but found only a powdery white-green. When she pinched the leaf she saw bright green. She told herself again she had to make more of an effort to talk to Manuel, to personally thank him, rather than just sending him another check in the mail.

Calmed by the beauty in her backyard, she sat on the landing again. She sat for a good while at peace with herself and yesterday's loss. But then she began thinking of what to do next, how to fill her day. She usually went to the office on the weekends to catch up on all the paperwork her time in court had left her. Not this weekend. She decided to take the whole week off and forget the law for a bit. Not go to the office. Let Suzie handle everything for a week... Well, maybe not for a whole week. There was so much she had put off during the three weeks she was in trial—correspondence, pleadings, meetings, clients, phone calls. And then, too, there was the Dawson case, a homicide, a trial she was scheduled to begin in four weeks. No, there's no way she could take off the entire week. But this weekend was not negotiable. She wasn't going to the office, not this weekend anyway.

But what to do? She wasn't a shopper. She seldom went shopping and when she did, she went with Suzie. Suzie was the shopper. But Suzie wasn't home that weekend. A movie? Why put herself in a pitch-black cave on a beautiful, sunny day to watch something that at best would prove to be mediocre? No, thanks. She didn't play bridge. Had no interest in it. She'd never volunteered for any community service group: never had time for it. Aside from her law practice she had nothing. That thought had occurred to her before, but it had never mattered, because her law practice had always been enough. But what if in eleven years she was still killing herself with effort and coming home with losses? At fifty. What then? She had seen and heard what happened to trial lawyers who kept trying cases into their sixties. Not a pretty picture. That was a long way off. No need to think of that now. Still, the latest series of losses were taking their toll.

When Barbara Blake graduated at the top of her law school class, two of the big law firms in San Cristobal offered her a position as an associate attorney. The offers were flattering, but she wanted to be a trial attorney, and the chance that she would be one with either firm was years away...if ever. She could never articulate why she wanted to be a trial lawyer. She sometimes thought it was because all the important attorney roles in the movies and on television were those of trial attorneys, and they were always played by men. Maybe it was in part, too, because she had flourished and been brilliant in the law school's moot court trials. Law school had also shown her that she was more astute, more articulate, and quicker than her male counterparts. So she took a job with the public defender for a quarter of the starting pay the two private firms had each offered.

On her third day in the public defender's office, Barbara Blake had her first jury trial. Her client was a sixty-six-year-old man who was charged with a misdemeanor drunk in public. He was in custody and had seventeen prior convictions for the same offense. It was a pathetic trial for a pathetic old man. And Barbara Blake stumbled around the courtroom in her ignorance, offending first the deputy district attorney, then the judge, and then the jury who convicted her client in less than twenty minutes of deliberation. The judge sentenced the defendant to the time he had already served, which prompted the deputy district attorney to say, "That old guy will probably be in custody by tomorrow morning, and maybe Ms. Blake can start representing him again before the end of the week."

Barbara Blake wasn't offended in the least. She was well satisfied. She had already had a jury trial, which, in her mind, was more than 95 percent of the lawyers in America would ever have.

In two months, Barbara had seven jury trials—two- and three-day misdemeanor trials to be sure, but seven nevertheless—which was impressive. She showed no fear. She volunteered for everything in the office. On the days she wasn't in trial, she roamed the courthouse halls looking for cases being tried by more experienced attorneys. Finding one, she would sit, taking notes on methods to be emulated as well as on those to be avoided. At home during dinner and into the evening, she began reading texts on how to try cases before a jury.

From the beginning Barbara Blake loved being in trial. It didn't matter who she was representing or what he was charged with or how offensive he might appear to be. None of that reflected on her. Being in trial, she thought, brought out the best in her. This was where she belonged, where she was supposed to be. And in front of a jury, she was friendly and open and able and always well prepared. The jurors saw that and respected her.

It wasn't long before Barbara Blake found it much more productive to charm a judge with her ignorance rather than annoy him with it. She did it by openly admitting her inexperience while at the same time stressing her desire to learn. She took rulings seriously, as well as any trial tactics the judge suggested. And she was astute enough to include the clerk, the court reporter, and the bailiff in her cultivation. Early on she felt that they were ignored or taken for granted by the attorneys who practiced in their court-room. It didn't take much for her to treat them with a sense of importance and respect. And it didn't take long for the judges and their personnel in the two departments where she was trying cases to single her out and speak highly of her to their colleagues.

By her fifth month in the public defender's office, Barbara Blake was receiving not guilty verdicts in almost half of her cases. That was extraordinary, especially for a new public defender. Jim Tobin, the head of the misdemeanor unit, took note and at first attributed it to her relentless hard work. It was clear to him and everybody in the unit that Barbara Blake was always working—morning, noon, and night...and weekends. And because of her success she was already being assigned the more serious misde-meanor cases.

Her success continued. More curious than impressed, Jim To-bin sat in on one of her trials. When he returned to his office, he called Steve Hastings, the public defender. "She's a natural, Steve. Within a year, she'll be as good as any defense attorney in and out of this office. I hope we can keep her."

The San Cristobal Municipal Court was housed in a three-story, brown-brick building along Rupert Street, the main street to and through the county civic center. It had eight departments, a clerk's office, and an office for the misdemeanor unit of the pub-lic defender. By Barbara Blake's seventh month there, many of the people in the building either knew her or had heard glow-ing reports about her. And Barbara could feel the admiration and respect that was there for her wherever she was in the building. For that matter, she could feel that admiration and respect in the morning when she parked her car and started across the lot and street to the courthouse, all of which made it easy for her to have a warm smile and a ready greeting for everyone. But then that's how it should be, she often thought, because that's where she belonged, more at home there than anywhere else.

Even the deputy district attorneys respected her. Those who

had been in trial with her advised those who hadn't: "If you're going to be in trial with her, you'd better be prepared because she sure as hell will be. She's bright and quick and she doesn't play games. And she's not afraid to try a case, any case, no matter how bad it might look for her in the beginning. On the other hand, if your case has some problems and you're thinking it ought to settle, settle it. Because if you think you have some problems, she'll *know* you have some problems. And she can make you look pretty damn bad in front of a judge and a jury."

At the end of her ninth month in the misdemeanor unit, Barbara Blake asked Jim Tobin to recommend her for a promotion to the felony unit.

"I can't do that," he told her.

"Why not?"

"Because we have an office policy that a new attorney must have a minimum of a year's experience in the misdemeanor unit before he or she can be moved up into the felony unit."

"Why's that?"

"Obviously because an incoming attorney needs at least that much experience trying misdemeanor cases before he's capable of trying felonies."

"I've already had a lot of experience."

"Then there's also the question of office morale. If I ask to have you moved up now, what effect will that have on the other four attorneys here, all of whom have already spent more time here than you? In fact, two of them have already been here twice as long as you."

"Office morale!" She gasped and looked away. "Trial experience! I've already tried more cases to a jury than each and every one of those four have, no matter how long they've been here. And none of them have come close to the number of not guilty verdicts and hung juries I've gotten. So am I to be punished rather than rewarded for the hard work and success I've had because some of my colleagues' feelings might be hurt?"

They stared at each other for several moments. Then Jim Tobin said, "Well, Barbara, a policy's a policy, and it has to be followed for the good of everyone in the office."

Barbara stared some more and then stormed out of Jim Tobin's office.

That exchange bothered Jim Tobin enough that at the end of the following week he spoke to Steve Hastings about it.

"You did the right thing, Jim. We've had that policy in place ever since I've been here."

"I know. But she's not very happy about it. There's no doubt in my mind that she could handle a felony caseload right now. It's just the effect the move would have on the others. Two have been in my unit twice as long as her."

"So why is it still bothering you?"

"I guess I'm afraid of losing her. She could go to any big law firm right now and make five or six times what we're paying her just by flashing the number of jury trials she's had and the number of not guilty verdicts she's gotten."

"So we move her now... What makes you think that she won't stay with us a year or two more and then leave?"

"She loves the trial work here like no one I've ever seen. And as she tries the heavier felonies, the homicides and the death penalties, my guess is she'll find those challenges very much to her liking and not to be found anywhere else. I simply don't want to lose anyone with her talent and work ethic."

A week later just after four o'clock, Barbara Blake was at her workstation packing her things for her move to the felony unit. The five misdemeanor attorneys had workstations in a large room on the ground floor of the municipal court building. A few minutes after she started, she paused, thinking the room was unusually quiet—so quiet, that after a few more minutes she stopped and listened and then walked around the room to see if there was anyone else in it. She was the only person in the room. It was 4:21 and usually most of the attorneys would have returned from court by then. She didn't know what to make of it, but she had to get on with her packing because she wanted to get over to the felony unit before five.

On her way out, she stopped at Jim Tobin's office. "Where's everybody?"

"Everybody?"

"Yeah, the room's empty. Nobody's at their workstations and it's only 4:33."

"Maybe they're still in court?"

"Oh, come on, Jim, you know as well as I do they're usually back by now."

"I really don't know where they are."

"Did you tell them I was moving up to the felony unit?"

"I did."

"When did you tell them?"

"This morning."

"This morning? Why did you wait so long to tell them?"

"Well frankly, Barbara, I thought it would be easier to work and live around here if I waited as long as I could before I told them."

"What?"

"Oh, come on, Barbara, they've all been in this unit longer than you. Some twice as long. I don't think they're particularly happy that we made this move for you, considering you've been here a little short of ten months. There's bound to be some resentment. On top of that, we didn't follow our stated policy."

"I was here when Bob Sutton moved up. They went out and bought a cake and soft drinks for him, just like colleagues and friends are supposed to do."

"Barbara, you've never been a friend or colleague to any of these folks. It seemed to me, and to them, that you always thought they were in your way; they were a nuisance and a bother as you prepared for and tried your cases, which you were always doing. I never once saw you go to lunch with any of them or even sit down here and have a sandwich with them. In the beginning, they invited you to their parties. You didn't go. They stopped inviting you.

You can't tell me you now consider them to be your friends and colleagues."

"I didn't come here to socialize, Jim. I came here to do what I was paid to do, try and win cases. And that's what I did. Just look at my record."

"I know your record, Barbara. It's extraordinary. But when you work with people you just can't run over them and then expect them to be your friends and colleagues."

"I never ran over anyone, Jim. And if you can't see jealousy plain and simple, that's your problem."

Barbara left, hurt and angry.

THE PUBLIC defender's felony unit had its office located on the third floor of the main county building. Each felony attorney had his or own office. So Barbara was surprised and disappointed when the office manager told her that she would be sharing an office with another deputy. "We're full, really. We weren't expecting to add another attorney for quite a while. We're not even considering new applications right now. But Steve came to me this morning and said they were moving you up from the misdemeanor unit. And here we are."

As Barbara Blake followed the office manager down a long hall, she wondered if this space sharing was just a ploy by the office to slow her down, to allow the other deputies to be more comfortable with her success. She had never worked in close proximity with anyone, and it had to be an impairment. Would this person be a man or a woman? Better a woman... No, maybe not. She might turn out to be more competitive, more threatened, and more envious. Yet how could she relate to a strange man in an office meant for one person?

A scraping sound was coming from an open doorway down the hall. When they reached that doorway, the office manager stopped and said, "Greg, this is Barbara Blake, your new office mate."

The man turned from the cabinet he had been moving, looked at Barbara, smiled, and said, "Hi, I'm Greg Olsen. Come on in."

He was a big, burly, blond-haired man with a pleasant manner and a nice smile. "I've heard nothing but great things about you. And I've been trying to move things around in here so that each of us can have a good working space."

She nodded, searching for the right words for her answer and then simply said, "I'm Barbara Blake."

"I'm going to let the two of you get settled," said the office manager and left.

"Why don't you put your things on that desk," Olsen said, pointing. "They just brought that desk in a few minutes ago and it's got your name written all over it."

His smile seemed genuine, but she wondered what else he had been told. Had he been told that her four colleagues had avoided her, giving Jim Tobin's parting words a lot of credibility? Not a word of goodbye or congratulations...

"Let me get this filing cabinet between the two desks," Olsen added. "That should help some. By the way, I moved all my things to the two top drawers. The bottom two are yours. Once I get this cabinet there, if you have a few minutes, maybe we can sit and talk and get to know one another a little better."

Barbara nodded, thinking that it would be very difficult to get anything done in that eight-by-ten room with two desks and two chairs and a filing cabinet. She would have to start working more and more at home. She watched Greg Olsen wrap his big arms around the filing cabinet and lift and drag. In size he reminded her of Bob Johnson, her first husband, but only in size. Already he seemed very different.

Finished with the cabinet, Greg Olsen moved his chair near to where she was sitting. She noticed for the first time that his tie lay rumpled on his desk, and she liked that.

"We better take advantage of these few minutes. The way things move around this place, we'll seldom get a chance like this to talk a bit."

Simple and direct. Good, she thought.

"Where you from?"

"You've already said you've heard things about me, so why don't we start with you. I know nothing about you."

He said he was from Ukiah. He was the oldest of three boys. His father had been a fireman and his mother was a homemaker. He worked his way through college and law school, and in his second year of law school, he married Molly, his high school sweetheart. They had two toddlers, a boy and a girl, who were the light of his life. He had never imagined he could love his kids, or anyone, as much as he loved them. This was his second year with the public defender and he felt lucky to have the job. He didn't plan on being a public defender the rest of his career, but he did think that the trial experience he was getting was invaluable. He had had seven felony jury trials thus far. He lost four, won two, and had one hang, which he would soon have to retry. Wins and losses didn't mean that much to him because he had always thought there were more important things in life than being a lawyer.

She listened and watched him intently. Too often when people spoke of themselves, it had little to do with who they really were. As she watched and listened, it occurred to her that for the immediate future she would probably be closer, in proximity, to this man than to any other human being. She liked most of what he was saying, but how much of it was a reaction to what he had heard about her? Still, he seemed genuine enough. His blue eyes were clear and friendly. His words continued simple and direct. His face had the creases of an outdoor person, a woodsman from Ukiah. His entire appearance bore little resemblance to the slick, smooth faces of the young lawyers she had seen in the big law firms where she had interviewed. Maybe the public defender had hired him to better relate to all the everyday men and women who sat on juries. Clearly she and Greg Olsen seemed to be different people headed in different directions. She could live with that.

When Greg Olsen said, "And you?" she thought it best to be brief, amiable, but guarded.

"I never thought of becoming a lawyer until my parents died in an automobile accident while I was in college." She looked up at him and then away as she spoke softly. "Supporting myself became a big issue then. I had done well in my public speaking classes and decided to go on to law school. Lawyers made more money than teachers. In law school I met a man who joined me in a brief, disastrous marriage. I had done well in moot court and that probably made me think that I would be better suited as a trial attorney rather than a research or associate attorney in a big firm. I, too, was lucky enough to get a job with the public defender. I've been in the misdemeanor unit for almost a year. I worked very hard there and had some success, but I'm fully aware that the cases in the felony unit will be much more difficult. Still, I intend to work just as hard here and hope to become a good trial attorney. I enjoy trying cases and that's pretty much been my life since I started working here."

As they left their little office, Barbara Blake felt at ease with what had happened there.

THEY SHARED that office for thirteen months and became close friends even though they were different people with different goals. Barbara worked all day every Saturday. She worked on Sundays too, and if anyone asked her how long she was going to work on a particular Sunday, she always said, "For a couple of hours." But those hours always extended to most or all of Sunday. Greg, on the other hand, seldom worked Saturdays. If he did, that work was in the office from six to ten in the morning so that he could be with the kids and Molly the rest of the day. He never worked on Sundays. Sunday was church and family.

It wasn't long before Barbara's success rate in the felony unit was the highest, raising resentment and envy by some in the office. Greg, however, saw the other side of that success: the intensity, the inordinate hours of hard work and preparation, and the fear of failure. And he wanted none of it, which Barbara understood.

Greg's success rate with his cases was acceptable, though nowhere near Barbara's. He was liked and respected in the office, which Barbara was well aware of. And Barbara was quick to recognize that she could never work as little as Greg did and attain his success. How did he manage that? She sat in on one of his cases to find out. What she saw was that Greg came across to his jury as a decent, honest, good man, a salt-of-the-earth type who would never deceive or try to deceive anyone. The juries genuinely liked him.

One of the bases for their friendship was their differences—and their recognition and acceptance of those differences. They were each in trial for a major portion of those thirteen months when they shared office space. And at the end of most of those trial days, as they returned to their office tired and worn, worried or dejected or elated, there were always discussions between them about what had happened in court and what was to come. And they brought different points of view and questions that the other hadn't considered—some worthwhile, some not. What mattered most, and what soon became apparent, was that each could trust what the other brought to those talks because the other had no agenda. They could openly discuss anything related to their courtroom experiences and sometimes even personal matters.

Those after-court discussions pretty much came to a halt when during Barbara's thirteenth month in the felony unit, she was given a much bigger office on the other side of the floor. Though the two still sometimes conferred on courtroom matters, the frequency dropped off markedly.

By Barbara Blake's fifth year in the felony unit, she was clearly the best trial lawyer in the office, which spurred her on all the more. She volunteered for the toughest cases and was in trial constantly. Then in mid-December of that year, as she walked back to counsel table after making her closing argument in a double homicide case, she collapsed in the courtroom.

After two days in the hospital undergoing various tests and examinations, her doctor came to her in the evening of the second day and said her illness was owing to extreme exhaustion, and he recommended at least a month's rest from work. Barbara answered that she felt fine and said nothing more. The doctor nodded and said, "You'll be released in the morning. But, we don't want a relapse, do we?" He patted her on the shoulder and left.

Barbara thought the doctor's recommendation of a month's rest was ludicrous. She felt he was ill suited to make that recommendation because he obviously didn't know anything about the work of a trial attorney. Instead she decided she would return to the office in the morning after her release. How to explain her collapse to Steve Hastings she wasn't sure...

As the evening wore on, she became aware of the number of visitors for patients in the rooms near hers. It occurred to her she might not have a single visitor before she left the hospital. Unlike most of the visitors she was seeing, an attorney did not work a nine-to-five job. Everyone in her office was swamped with work. At the end of the day, there was little time for hospital visits.

In the morning Barbara was anxious for her release. The sooner the better to show everyone this was not much of a matter. Twice the nurses assured her that she would be out before noon, which was no relief at all. Then just after 10:30, Steve Hastings and Jim Tobin walked into her room.

"Steve! Jim! What brings you here?" She had seen them approaching and had been surprised and gratified. Now the other patients and nurses would see that she had visitors too—important visitors in suits and ties. But she didn't like the frown on Jim's face. "I was planning to go to the office this morning as soon as they release me and show you I'm fine and ready to get back to work." She thought that should please them. "I was supposed to be released early this morning, but you know how bureaucracies are, slow and slower."

"No," Steve Hastings said, "it's probably better that we came and saw you here."

"Why?" A sinking feeling was setting in.

"Because you are suffering from severe exhaustion. We recommend a month's rest, a month's leave of absence, to prevent a recurrence that could be worse."

"A month's rest!" she said shaking her head and tightening her lips. "I can't do that. What about my cases? The Dorado trial is supposed to start in three weeks."

"Your cases can be reassigned," Steve said calmly and firmly.

"And the Dorado case?" she pleaded.

"I'm sure, given what's happened here, the presiding judge will give whoever's reassigned that case a reasonable continuance to prepare for trial." His look was implacable.

"Steve, you're not being rational."

"I'm being very rational. A quick look at your file told us that you've actually accumulated more than five weeks of unused vacation time." The tone of his words said that he had already decided.

"So?"

"So, I'm going insist that you take a five-week vacation beginning today."

"Why are you doing this to me?" She was crying.

"This isn't meant to punish you, Barbara. In fact, it's a recognition of your remarkable talent as a trial lawyer and of the fierce drive that fuels it. To be carried out of that courtroom on a stretcher after, according to everyone present, another superb effort, tells us that it's time for you to take a break. Stop and assess where you're going, what you want, and at what price... I'll have Lucia send someone over to your house this afternoon to pick up any materials you have there pertaining to the cases assigned to you. And I don't want you in or near the office until your vacation has been completed. Do I make myself clear?"

WHEN SHE got home just after one o'clock the house was cold and empty. She couldn't remember the last time she had been home on a weekday afternoon. She turned on the furnace full blast and kept her coat on. She paced from room to room telling herself that Steve Hastings couldn't do this to her. The two big law firms in town would hire her in a minute at a salary triple what Steve was paying her. That would show him. But those firms were just about money, and trying cases for money had never appealed to her. People were more important. She thought of joining the San

Francisco Public Defender until she remembered that Steve and the public defender there were close friends. The Los Angeles Public Defender had an excellent reputation...but she could never live in Los Angeles.

It occurred to her once again that she had no recollection of collapsing in the courtroom or of being carried out on a stretcher. At the hospital, a nurse had repeated to her what she had been told. As Barbara stood in her kitchen and thought of her blackout, it did concern her but not enough to warrant a five-week leave of absence. She felt fine, ready to try the Dorado case or any case they wished to send her.

THE DOORBELL rang. It was 3:32. She looked out the window. It was Bill Terry, her favorite investigator. No doubt he had come for all her cases. That son of a bitch Hastings wasted no time. At the door Bill said, "I'm sorry Barb. I can't tell you how sorry I was when I heard what happened in court. And now this. I know there's nothing wrong with you and—"

"Stop, Bill, stop... What do you want?" she asked even though she knew exactly what he wanted.

"Well, I was..."

He had an awkward look on his face and she saw that he was staring at the overcoat she was still wearing even as her house blasted hot air against the afternoon cold. Embarrassed all the more, she repeated, "What do you want?"

"I came over to pick up whatever you might have here on the cases assigned to you."

"I, uh, haven't had a chance to put those things together." She wanted him to just go away. "Besides, I don't have any boxes, and it'll take some boxes."

"Oh, I brought boxes. They're in my car. We should be able to put everything you have in them."

We! She didn't want him in the house. But all she could do was nod.

"I'll be right back," he said as he left the porch for his car.

She took off her coat and threw it behind a couch and waited for him. He returned with three boxes.

"Give me those things," she said, opening the screen door and taking the boxes. Then closing the door she said, "I'll be right back," leaving Bill Terry bewildered on the front porch.

Barbara filled the boxes with police reports, court transcripts, and investigation reports. She took the boxes to the front door, which she opened and closed as she passed each box to Bill Terry. As she handed him the third box, she said, "I don't feel good. I've got to get back to bed."

"I'm sorry, Barb. I know how—"

But the front door closed.

She sat on the couch and cried. After all she had given Steve Hastings and his office, how did she deserve this?

SHE MUST have dozed off until it was dark. She wasn't hungry, and instead, she began sipping glasses of wine.

She woke to the early morning sounds of cars on the street. She was still on the couch and it took her a few moments to decide it was Friday. Friday morning and for the first time in six-plus years there was nowhere for her to go and nothing for her to do. Strange indeed. There was no reason for her to get dressed. No reason to rush around the house or worry about being late. No reason to go to Pete's Diner where she had breakfast six days a week.

How serious was the collapse? How bad could it have been when she now felt fine? A week of rest might be needed, but not five. She thought of consulting other doctors and submitting conflicting medical reports to Steve Hastings. Would he listen to reason, relent, and let her go back to work in a week or two? Or would that alienate him all the more, seeing how set he and Jim Tobin were in their conviction? Finally, she got up, showered, dressed in her Sunday jeans and a sweater, dried and brushed her hair, and sat down to coffee and toast.

It was almost noon when she realized her cell phone hadn't rung once. A clip of dejection ran through her. But only the people at the office had her cell phone number, and Steve must have already told them. That phone rang and rang when she was working. Pam Wagner had called her often on that phone, and they had talked of many things other than work. But Pam was married now and spent her free time with her husband. Jill Yeager used to call, but that was a long time ago. Nobody called anymore. Maybe she didn't have many friends. But then, she had never really sought out friends. She had always had her work. That had always taken up most of her time. If she had wanted friends, she was sure she could have made some. But her work had always been her priority.

She thought of the phone calls she had received from her widowed Aunt Claire every Sunday evening for months and months. They were taking up so much time that she finally changed her phone number without telling Aunt Claire. And besides, those calls always turned into depressing laments on loneliness. "It's an animate thing," Aunt Claire would begin. "It's in every part of the house. It's like it wraps its arms around me no matter where I am in the house. And it hurts. It aches. Sometimes I think it lives off the air of my house or that it's part of the air. Because at times when I breathe, I can feel the ache of being alone in the pit of my stomach. So I try to keep busy, not in the house, because no matter how busy I am in the house, the loneliness is always there. I volunteer for things at the hospital and the church and that helps. But I still have to come home to all that emptiness, all that loneliness. At sixty-nine, I can't stay away morning, noon, and night. I can't volunteer twenty-four hours a day, every day. So I'm always faced with the fact that in the end, I have to go home and be alone with that hurt. People die of loneliness. I never thought that was possible. I don't doubt it now.

"I know you're young and alone now and your life is filled with your career. I know you have no time for loneliness now. But your career won't last forever. And when that time comes, be sure you have a mate, a man. I see old couples that are still together and there's no way those two can appreciate how lucky they are to have someone with them. Get yourself a man, a good man, a young man.

The younger the better, because we always outlive men, and sooner or later it seems like we have to deal with this gruesome visitor alone, this visitor who comes to stay."

THAT AFTERNOON Barbara Blake called her grandmother in Kansas. She had some time off, she told her grandmother, and would very much like to go to Kansas and visit with her and meet all her relatives there. Her grandmother was delighted. Barbara said that she would drive so she could see country she had never seen before. She didn't want to fly and show up in Kansas all of a sudden, without much notice. People might wonder, might suspect, that she needed to go.

That evening Barbara Blake returned some overdue books at the law library. She was planning to start her trip the next day or Sunday at the latest. After returning the books, she stopped to read a law review article. It was Friday night and the library was empty. She was almost finished with the article when a man approached and asked if she was a lawyer. When she answered yes, he asked what she knew about the service of process on an out-of-state defendant in a civil lawsuit. She told him that she was a criminal defense attorney and knew nothing about that service except what she had learned in law school. He asked about that and she told him she thought that proof of personal service of the complaint on an out-of-state defendant was required. He told her about an unfair lawsuit being brought against him in Seattle for exorbitant docking fees.

He was a handsome, affable, and seemingly intelligent man her age or a few years older. She listened until the librarian came up to them and said it was closing time. He introduced himself then as Brian Stone and asked if he could buy her a drink.

"Why not," she said and was surprised at her own readiness.

They went to a sports bar across from the law library. Brian struck the right chord when he laughed after she said that she had never wanted to be anything but a lawyer. It took her aback for a moment, but she saw that there was nothing unkind in his laughter. He explained his father had been a partner in a big San Francisco law firm and his two brothers were lawyers. What struck him funny was how hard they worked to have such miserable lives. They knew so little and had lived so little outside the law. They had been chained to the law. His father literally died at his desk at the age of sixty-nine not knowing how to, or being afraid to, break away from the law.

That stung Barbara, so she changed the subject and asked Brian what he did. He answered that he did many things. He traveled; he had lived in different parts of the world; and he wrote poetry, played classical guitar, and painted. He surfed and windsurfed. He sailed, and just last month he had returned from a sailing trip to the Fiji Islands. Only when Barbara asked how he financed all these endeavors did he stumble a bit. His mother, he said haltingly, was a copper-mining heiress who had established a trust fund for him several years before.

One drink led to another, and their laughter grew louder and louder. The more they laughed, the more they laughed at themselves—his blundering on his boat and her botches in the courtroom. Then the bartender came over and said, "Brian, it's almost midnight and I don't know if you're planning to stay here tonight or go over to Port Cato. If you're driving, I think you've had enough. And I know you didn't walk here. So let me put it as nicely as I can...I'm not going to serve you any more."

That settled them. But Barbara didn't want it to stop. It had been a long, long while since she had had such a good time. As they were saying their goodnights, she said, "You know, Brian, except for being in a rowboat with my dad on a little recreational lake when I was a kid, I've never been on a boat."

"Really? Why don't you go over to Port Cato with me tomorrow and I'll show you my boat, and we can get out of the harbor a little ways?"

"I'd like that."

THE HOUSE was as empty and even colder than when she left. But there wasn't a flicker of loneliness anywhere. She had had a remarkably good time with an honest and intelligent man she had met out of the blue. Oh my, how she had laughed at herself, and he too, without a hint of malice. Nor was she in the slightest bit embarrassed by her open plea for more with her obvious line of never having been on real boat before. He had been so quick to extend himself that there was no reason to be embarrassed. He clearly also wanted to continue what they had had that night. And what of her trip to Kansas if she was going to Port Cato tomorrow? It really didn't matter if she left for Kansas on Sunday or Monday, did it?

Barbara drove to Port Cato with Brian late the next morning. Port Cato was a small harbor for sailing and fishing boats along Monterey Bay.

Brian's apartment turned out to be a boxlike, wooden afterthought perched atop one of the pier's stores, a three-room square accessible from an attached, outside staircase. But the kitchen, living room, and bedroom had spectacular views of the ocean and the bay and the beach.

Brian had a twenty-five-foot sailboat, and they went out into the bay that afternoon. The ocean seemed immense to Barbara and its subtle motion made her sit rather than stand on deck. Brian, on the other hand, was in complete control of himself and the boat, standing, pointing, explaining, adjusting the sails, and saying many times, "I love the sea." What impressed Barbara most that afternoon were the smells of the ocean and the freshness of the air.

She spent the night, a wondrous night, in Port Cato. The next morning, as she watched Brian cook breakfast, she wondered how she could have spent her life without a night like they had just had. Worse, how could she spend the rest of her life without a night like that again?

After breakfast, they strolled down the piers hand and hand. Everyone knew Brian. They greeted him and talked to him on the piers, from their stores, and from their docked boats. It was clear they not only knew him, but they also liked and respected him. *How wonderful,* Barbara thought, *to have so many people like you.* Some asked about the boat's condition. Were they still working on it? How much longer? But when someone asked when he would be leaving, Barbara felt a twinge, and then a flush of embarrassment for her reaction. After all she had only known Brian for a few hours. But she couldn't help asking, "Where are you going, Brian? When? Why are you going?"

Brian squeezed her hand and smiled and said, "Why don't you come with me?"

V

They sailed along Mexico's west coast. And he showed her the sea and the sun and the stars as she had never known them before. They docked in small, out-of-the-way fishing villages. Brian was fluent in Spanish and had ease in interacting comfortably with the local Mexicans wherever they were. He read Barbara the poems of Walt Whitman and T.S. Eliot and Wallace Stevens, and he played his guitar for her as they bobbed about on the starlit ocean or sat next to a campfire along the rim of a jungle.

Three weeks into their trip Barbara Blake and Brian Stone were married by a gay expatriate minister, below Puerto Escondido near the southern edge of Mexico, on a long, wonderful stretch of a white sand beach with tall coconut trees swaying behind them and a serene blue sea before them.

Barbara was at her happiest. But as the boat crept up the California coast, she became more and more convinced that she had made a horrendous mistake. Given her workload in the public defender's office, their marriage would never work. When Brian asked what was troubling her, she told him about her position in the office and the demanding time, energy, and skill her assigned cases took. Brian thought about the situation and the next day, reminding her that he knew something about his family's law practices, suggested she open her own practice. There she would be in complete control of the kinds of cases she took and how they would interfere with her private life.

Barbara liked the idea and she told Brian that for some time Greg Olsen had been suggesting that they leave the public defender and open their own law office. The suggestion never went very far because Barbara was well aware of Greg's wife's extreme jealousy. After asking more about Greg and Molly, Brian said not to worry, that he would take care of the matter.

On their first weekend in San Cristobal, Barbara and Brian had a small celebratory dinner at an expensive restaurant. Barbara invited Greg and Molly, and Brian invited two couples. It was a long dinner with several bottles of fine wines and liqueurs served. Brian sat next to Molly the entire evening. Then, as the night was ending, Greg and Barbara announced they were leaving the public defender's office and opening their own law office.

THE FIRST two months of Barbara's private practice were idyllic. A few of the judges, some court staff, and people in the clerk's office assured Barbara and Greg they would be receiving court appointments to get them through the first year of their new practice. Without clients those first two months, Barbara decided to relax and enjoy her time with Brian. Several of their weekends began on mid-Thursday afternoon when they drove to Port Cato, and they typically returned to San Cristobal late Monday morning. Brian cooked early dinners for them Monday through Wednesday, which they enjoyed with a bottle of wine. Their togetherness seemed like it would never end.

But well into their third month of private practice there were still no court appointments and no clients, and the office overhead was getting heavier and heavier. They had hired a secretary who had nothing to do all day except look bright and pretty. There was the monthly rent and office equipment and book and utility payments that had to be made. Those costs and her living expenses without any income were making a significant dent in Barbara's savings. She worried that word had gotten back to the courts that she was only in her office three and a half days a week, making them reluctant to send court appointments. She cut their weekends to Saturdays and Sundays and began spending a full forty-hour week in the office. She felt herself becoming disagreeable with Brian and avoided discussing office finances with him for fear he would think she wanted to ask him for money.

THE MAYOR of San Cristobal had been charged with fourteen counts of bribery. The prosecution's case was based primarily on the allegations of the mayor's chief administrative assistant, who had already pleaded guilty to the same fourteen counts and had agreed to testify against the mayor in exchange for a lenient sentence. The case had dragged on for more than two years and had become something of a laughing stock in the community. The mayor was adamant in his claim of innocence and was refusing to step down unless a jury found him guilty. To some it seemed like the case would never go to trial. One snafu after another resulted in more and more delays. Many thought they were deliberately concocted to keep the mayor in office. The latest problem occurred when the mayor's lawyer of two and a half years withdrew from the case because of a newly discovered conflict of interest. The mayor in turn said he did not have the funds to hire another lawyer, and it would take him at least six months to raise the needed money.

The presiding judge was furious. He knew Barbara's capabilities and that she was available, and he had his clerk arrange a meeting with her early that afternoon. When they met he wanted to know if she was aware of the case, if she felt she could adequately represent the mayor, and if she could be ready for trial in four weeks. "Yes." He then had his clerk place the mayor's case on the following morning's calendar for the appointment of new counsel.

Outside in the parking lot Barbara was delirious with excitement. She danced around her car several times. It was the case of her lifetime. The local media coverage had been overwhelming. There had also been coverage from up and down the state. She was going to be on the biggest stage of her life. And whether she won or lost really didn't matter because she was going to have a chance to show the world what a great trial lawyer she was. Once that was established, there would be no more money problems. At home Brian was happy for her, but he had no idea what her being in trial would be like. She told him again and again that there was going to be a big change in the way he and she lived. But she reassured him that would only be for two months at most. Then, free from overhead worries and with an income, they could once again enjoy the life they had had until recently.

The next morning, she was up before six. There would be a lot of media in court that morning and she had to look her best. She chose her most professional and flattering suit, a light-gray wool that complemented her dark hair. Her pearl necklace and earrings completed the look she wanted. By seven o'clock she was satisfied with her appearance. Brian was still asleep, and she thought it was better not to wake him because he would want to talk and there was no time for talking. While meeting with the presiding judge, she had asked for and received a copy of the court's file, which she felt she needed to review before she stepped into the courthouse that morning. Quietly she left and went to her office with her copy of the court's file.

As SHE expected there was an enormous amount of media at the court that morning. In the hallway the press struggled to get near

her, and she loved it. Never had she received that kind of attention when she was with the public defender. It was only when the
bailiff opened the courtroom doors and shouted for the media to
let the attorneys enter the courtroom that she was able to get near
those doors. This was where she belonged, she thought.

Inside, the mayor said that he was pleased with her appointment. That had not been his initial reaction when he had learned
that he was going to be represented by a young woman. His staff,
however, checked with the public defender's office and relieved
his concern. The presiding judge set a trial date exactly four weeks
away and said emphatically that there would be no further con-
tinuances granted.

It was a brief court session after which the media crowded
around Barbara in the hallway. A good number of their questions
had already been asked and answered before court, but Barbara
didn't mind. She liked the press and they could sense that, which
often ended in a positive slant for her in their stories.

Off to one side in the hallway Bill Terry was waiting. He was
the investigator from the public defender's office that Barbara had
often worked with, and the presiding judge had managed to secure
him for Barbara for this case. Once the media had been handled,
Barbara and Bill had coffee to decide how to proceed. They visited
at the office of the mayor's former lawyer where they found thirty
bankers boxes filled with police reports, witnesses' statements, investigation reports, bank records, and sundry other items waiting for them. A two-and-a-half-hour lunch with that lawyer was
informative. After moving the boxes to Barbara's office, they tried
to arrange them in order of importance. Barbara called Brian and
told him to go ahead with dinner without her and she would just
heat up whatever was left when she got home.

It was after nine when she sat down at the kitchen table. She
was exhausted. As Brian warmed her dinner, he asked about her
day. She hoped he would stop his questions so she could eat in
peace and go to bed as soon as she was finished. On Wednesday
and Thursday nights she came home closer to ten and asked Brian

not to cook for her because she did not want to go bed with a full stomach. Once in bed she was thankful Brian hadn't made any sexual advances.

On Thursday night, Brian suggested they spend the weekend at Port Cato so that Barbara could rest. She agreed. But on Friday night she said she had to work on the case Saturday and maybe Sunday. For the first time Brian was visibly upset. "What about us? When are we going to enjoy anything?"

"This is about us! It is for us! Can't you see that! I went for almost three months without a single client. I had no income and the overhead was eating me alive. I don't know how much longer I could have gone on without a case like this. I really believe if I do well in this case, I won't have to worry about overhead anymore."

On Sunday, Brian went to Port Cato alone. He was already in bed when she came home around nine, and they didn't speak. Nor did they speak on Monday, Tuesday, or Wednesday when she left before seven and came home after ten and Brian was already in bed. On Thursday morning he was up before she left, and he told her he was going to visit his sick mother in Tucson and would stay with her until Barbara's trial began. Barbara was relieved.

THE FIRST day of the trial was strenuous. The local media was definitely outnumbered by media from all over the state, and the court hallway was packed. There was no way Barbara was going to get near the courtroom doors without the bailiff's help. The media's questions repeated themselves: What was her defense? How could she have a defense when the mayor's top assistant had already pleaded guilty to the same charges and was about to testify against him? How could someone so young carry the onerous load of defending a politician who was obviously guilty?

The selection of the jury was made troublesome when three of the prospective jurors said that they could *not* then presume the mayor innocent given the status of his top assistant. That sentiment then seemed to fill the courtroom. When Barbara tried to contest it with more explanatory questions, the judge asked her to move on. At the end of the day the media buzzed with the same question: How could the mayor not have known about and not be involved in his top assistant's misdeeds?

From the courthouse she went to the mayor's office, where a group of his family and friends had questions and suggestions. She dealt with those as best she could as she struggled with the nagging conviction that she had not had a good day in court. Later she and Bill had dinner at Pete's Diner, after which they went to her office and began preparing for the first witnesses.

It was 10:20 when she pulled into her driveway. As she went to her front door, she was still mentally reviewing her questioning of those three prospective jurors and how to avoid making the same mistakes in the morning. She unlocked the door and turned on the light. Brian sprang up from the couch grinning and exclaimed, "I'm back!"

He went to her and hugged her and kissed her inert, open mouth. Then he stood back and looked at her and said, "What's the matter, Barbara? Aren't you glad to see me?"

"Oh no, no, Brian. It's not that. It's just that this has been such a long, tiring day, the first day, and I'm exhausted."

"You look beat."

"Yes, thank you."

"Come on. Let's get you to bed. Tomorrow morning, we can talk about your case. I'm planning on going to your trial every day to watch my talented wife and to give her all the mental and moral support that I can. So let's get you to bed. I know you're probably planning to get up early, and I'm planning on getting up early too."

He took her by the hand and led her gently to their bedroom. She was thinking, *Oh no, I don't want him there tomorrow. I don't need him there tomorrow—or ever. I don't need the added pressure of proving myself to another person, especially him. Not after today.*

In the bedroom Barbara said, "Brian, I don't want you there tomorrow. I don't want you in that courtroom watching me, too."

"What?"

"I don't want you going to court with me tomorrow."

"Well, I'm going. Like it or not."

"Please don't, Brian. I don't think I could bear it."

He looked at her. "You're tired. You need to sleep. We can talk about this in the morning."

BRIAN WAS up before Barbara. He moved about the bedroom and shower as quietly as he could. But when he came out of the shower, she was sitting up in bed crying.

"What is it, Barbara?"

"Brian, I don't want you to come. I don't need another person in that courtroom to prove another single thing to."

He didn't know what to say.

"Try to understand, Brian. This is my first trial on my own. And it's the most publicized trial I've ever had and might ever have. I have to prove myself. I have to shine. I probably won't ever get another chance like this. Not like this. I have to succeed. I have to excel. I don't want to go back to the public defender. I can't afford a poor showing in this case. That will cut off everything I've ever aspired to. The pressure I've put on myself, the pressure I'm feeling now, is immense. I don't need another ounce of pressure."

He didn't know what to say.

"Please, Brian, this won't happen again. One way or another, I'll get over this. There won't be a repeat. And then, you can come to every trial I ever have. I swear to that. But not this one... Answer me, Brian. I can't keep crying. I can't go into court looking like I've been crying all night long."

He looked down and away. He put on his clothes and left the bedroom. She heard him go out the back door. She heard his car start and leave.

When she came home that night, she read his note. "I've gone to Port Cato. I hope things went well for you today. Please let me know when I can come to court and support you. I love you, Brian."

He called on Saturday afternoon. "I haven't heard from you. Are you all right?"

"I'm much better, thank you. I'm sorry I haven't called, but we've been moving at such a fast pace. Most of today and all of tomorrow we'll be preparing for the cross-examination of the mayor's assistant. He's really their whole case and there's so much to prepare for, what with fourteen counts. I really can't talk much longer. We have some witnesses here now that we're about to question. But I'll call you later. Thanks for the call."

On Tuesday evening, Brian received a call.

"Mr. Stone?"

"Yes."

"This is Bethany Rogers. Ms. Blake asked me to call you. I'm working with Ms. Blake on the mayor's case."

"You're Barbara's investigator?"

"No, I'm one of the mayor's staff. Several of us are working with Ms. Blake on the mayor's case. Anyway, Ms. Blake wanted me to call you and let you know that she's fine, working hard, but fine. She cross-examined the mayor's assistant all day today. She did a fantastic job on him. The mayor is very pleased. She's going to continue cross-examining the assistant tomorrow morning, and, if things keep going the way they've been going, it looks pretty good for the mayor."

"Does she want me to come over there?"

"I haven't talked to her about that, sir."

"No, but did she mention anything about my coming over there for the rest of the trial?"

"Not to my knowledge."

"Oh."

"But we'll keep you posted. Have a good rest of the day, sir."

He fought back anger. He remembered her tears and her pleas for no further pressure. And now she had the mayor's staff working with her as well. That added pressure had to be enormous. He waited for Barbara's call the following evening but none came.

On Thursday evening, Bethany Rogers called again. "She said to tell you to hold on, to hold on for a couple more days. I'm not sure I know what that means. But she did an incredibly good job on the assistant. Things look good. The mayor can hardly keep from smiling. I'd better be going now. We'll keep you posted."

"A couple of days, hold on." That wasn't exactly an open invitation to go there. Still, she said it wouldn't be like this ever again. He could wait a couple of more days.

On late Friday, Bethany Rogers called again. "Mr. Stone! Mr. Stone! Now you have to come! You have to come!" The woman was shrieking. "The jury just came back with a not guilty verdict on all fourteen counts! Barbara asked me to call you. Please come. We're going to celebrate at the Fairmont Hotel in downtown San Cristobal. Please come." And she hung up.

Brian stared at the receiver for several moments before he put it down. Fourteen counts of not guilty! That was unbelievable. He was happy for Barbara and happy for himself, too. It was finally over.

At the door to the Fairmont's ballroom a big, strapping fellow was having trouble with Brian's name. "I'm sorry, sir. I have a list here of people the mayor's expecting and you're not on that list... You say you're the mayor's lawyer's husband and your name is Stone...? I'm afraid Stone's not on the list, sir. I have my orders. Only the people on this list are to be admitted. If you ask me, there are too many people in the ballroom already. You'd better calm down, sir. I don't want to have to call security."

Just then Greg and Molly Olsen, who were in the ballroom, saw Brian arguing with the doorman. Greg knew the doorman and went to him and explained, and Brian entered the room red-faced and shaking his head. There were many people in the ballroom already, and Brian could see Barbara and the mayor in the center of a big crowd laughing and talking. Greg and Brian made their way through that crowd. They were deep from Barbara and the mayor when Barbara saw Brian and smiled and blew him a kiss. Brian could see that she was radiant—beautiful and happy.

"She knows you're here, Brian. But she's going to be tied up with all those people for a while. Why don't we go to the bar and have a drink?" Brian nodded and thought, *This thing has to end.*

They drank and talked and munched on salted nuts and cheese and crackers. Time slipped by and when Brian began feeling the effects of the alcohol, he told Greg that it was time for Barbara and him to leave.

"They know I'm Barbara's law partner, so I should be able to approach her. Let me go see where they're at."

He left and returned shortly. "The mayor and Barbara are having a private dinner with his politicos in an anteroom. I think you'd better wait a while."

This case was never going to end and I'd better be careful with the drink, he thought.

After an hour or more, a woman came up to Greg and said something to him in a low voice and left.

"She didn't know you were Barbara's husband. She was in there with all those politicos and she said the drinking was getting pretty heavy. She said I should get Barbara out of there. Come on."

It was Greg who went into the anteroom and came out with Barbara who was smiling but having trouble walking. She kissed Brian, with a "Hi, honey."

BARBARA SLEPT past eleven o'clock the next morning.

"Tired?" Brian said when he saw that she was awake.

She smiled and nodded.

"You should be. Let me go and get us some breakfast. And then we can go over to Cato for a few days, and you can have a much-needed rest."

She smiled and nodded, and as Brian was leaving she said, "I know this will sound vain, dear, but before you start cooking, can you go downtown to the newsstand next to the bank and get all of today's papers? Not just the local ones, but all that he has. I'd like to see what the coverage has been."

Vain indeed. All she could think about, all that was on her mind was the trial. She had dreamt about it, and, from the moment she opened her eyes, she was reliving it—only the highlights, the highlights of good things, except when bad things made the good that followed extra good. The hours she had spent preparing for the assistant's cross-examination had been worth it. Seemingly, by the time the trial began, Barbara knew more about the assistant's participation in the fourteen counts than he did. The pathetic look on the assistant's face became more and more pathetic as she went along in her cross-examination. The way the jury had grown day by day to like her, to admire her, and, finally, to respect her, their verdicts didn't surprise her. She knew what they would be, what they had to be. When she finished her cross-examination of the assistant and went back to the counsel table, the mayor couldn't keep from smiling and saying in a low voice, "Good! Great! Thank you!" In a low voice, yes, but loud enough for the jury to hear, because the judge certainly heard it and turned to Barbara and the mayor and gave them a stern look. When she argued the facts of the case to the jury, from that first minute, she knew that all twelve were hers.

As the days passed, the trial was with Barbara less and less, but then on the following Saturday it was with her throughout the day. It wasn't like she couldn't hear or listen to or answer Brian, she could...but only briefly, because those conversations were superimposed on whatever her mind was replaying from the trial.

As they drove over to Port Cato later that Saturday, Brian suggested that they spend only a day or two in Port Cato and then sail down to San Diego and back for the rest of the week. Barbara agreed. She liked San Diego. Brian knew that and she appreciated the gesture. She decided to take the week off and spend it with Brian in Port Cato.

On Monday morning as they were loading the boat for the trip, a call came for Barbara. Brian answered the phone and knew it was from the presiding judge. He assumed that it had something to do with the mayor's trial and wasn't concerned. But as he listened to Barbara's responses and watched the change in her face, he became worried and then angry. Especially when she said she was in Port Cato and couldn't be in San Cristobal much before two.

"That was the presiding judge in San Cristobal's superior court."

"I know."

"He wants me to meet with him this afternoon."

"What about our trip?"

"I guess we better put it off for a while."

"Why?"

"There's been a rape in the jail and the judge wants to see me about it."

"So? You've talked about rapes in the jail before. Why's this one such a big deal for you now?"

"The victim is a congressman's son who's in jail on a marijuana charge. The case is going to garner a lot of attention. The public defender says it has a conflict of interest and can't represent the accused young man."

"I still don't see how you get involved."

"Well, apparently it's not clear who did what or what happened, and the judge believes that the accused rapist is going to need adequate representation."

"Wait a minute! Wait a minute! Are you trying to tell me that you're getting involved in another hairy case just a week after you finished one?"

Defiantly she said, "I'm not the attorney yet."

"Let's quit playing games. If the judge asks you to take this case, will you?"

"I don't see how I can refuse."

"Fuck you!"

Brian stormed out of the apartment. For several moments, Barbara stood and thought. When she went out on the pier to look for Brian, she couldn't find him. She drove back to San Cristobal and agreed to represent the young man accused of rape. Late that day when she returned to Port Cato, she saw that Brian's boat was gone. One of his neighbors told her that Brian had set sail that afternoon saying that he didn't know when he'd be back.

A MONTH later, Brian's brother called Barbara and said that Brian wanted a divorce. Barbara said that she would not oppose a divorce as long as the matter did not become public.

Barbara never saw Brian again.

BARBARA TOLD no one that Brian had left her. A second marriage to a man she had known for three weeks that ended in three months was more embarrassing than she could publicly endure. It wasn't long before she had to tell Greg. He knew only too well what Molly's reaction would be if she found out. Together they were able to keep the news of Barbara's divorce a secret from Molly for more than three years. When Molly finally learned of the divorce, she went to Barbara's office screaming and throwing things. Barbara moved out of the office the next day.

She opened her own law office and devoted herself to that practice working long hours—days and nights and weekends. She was as good as any criminal defense attorney in San Cristobal. She loved the victories but took the defeats very hard. She had few friends. There was no time for friends, except for Suzie Martin, her secretary, who had left Greg's office with her.

At forty-five, Suzie Martin was five years older than Barbara. A week after high school graduation, Suzie and her high school sweetheart, Glenn, married. Glenn was now a school custodian. Within two years they had two sons, John and George. Suzie liked to tell anyone who would listen that she and Glenn had a "happy, comfortable life." The boys were grown and gone, their house was paid for, and they had a nice cabin up in the mountains. She was an excellent secretary: quick at the computer, good with clients, and skillful at screening and protecting Barbara from unnecessary phone calls and people. Suzie frequently commented on Barbara's life alone. "It can't be easy going home to an empty house after a long day at the office." "I've got to hand it to you, Barb, eating alone every night is not something I'd look forward to." "I don't know how you do it, Barb." At times Suzie was convinced that if Barbara could just find "the right man" all of her troubles and worries would be gone. "Don't worry, Barb, Millie found her husband when she was forty-one, and they're very happy." "You've just had bad luck, Barb. Some people do." Let Barbara even hint about a man and Suzie would be there to listen, scrutinize, advise, guide, and offer her very best opinion. In their two-person law office, she had come to know Barbara Blake very well. There was little Barbara could hide from Suzie Martin. On the other hand, there was little that Barbara wanted to hide from her. Suzie had become her confidante, her only confidante.

VI

THREE DAYS AFTER THE SENtencing hearing, Barbara Blake received three urgent telephone messages from Jacobo Lopez, one of her in-custody clients, saying it was extremely important that she see him immediately. She went to the jail the following morning. Jacobo Lopez had clearly been asleep. He was yawning and scratching himself, his hair was clumped upright in several different directions, and the lower front of his jail-issued T-shirt was scrunched together like an accordion's ribbing. Barbara Blake watched him stretch the last remnants of sleep from his body before he took a seat in the lone, white plastic chair on his side of the visiting cubicle. *Sleep all day and play all night. What else was there for them to do?*

Jacobo Lopez was a confirmed heroin addict. His three prior prison commitments had been for sales of relatively small quantities of heroin. He had been hooked since he was sixteen. Juvenile and adult probation programs hadn't worked. Drug treatment programs and the county's methadone program couldn't keep him off the stuff. Every time he'd been released from custody, he was "into the spoon by noon" as he used to say. He wasn't a violent doper: he didn't believe in muggings or robberies. The only way he knew how to raise funds for his costly habit was to sell retail on the streets. Every cop on the street knew this. But so long as he could provide them with useful information, they let him slide. The more slack they cut him, the more information he gave them. Eventually, the information they wanted was sure to place him in serious physical jeopardy. So Jacobo would return to jail and prison and do whatever he had to do to deal with his demon there. Now he was about to leave on his fourth trip to prison and something very important had come up that needed Barbara Blake's attention. Once seated, Jacobo continued to shake himself, and Barbara wondered how he had managed to get loaded the night before.

"So what's up, Jacobo?" she asked

Jacobo squinted, shifted his head, shifted himself in his seat and squinted some more, and then said, "I got something for you. Real hot. I'm the only one they could trust with it, and I made sure to let them know that I'd take care of business." Then Jacobo looked to all sides, as if some unseen creature might be lurking on his side of the six-by-six-foot visiting cubicle. Seeing no one, he took a small, folded piece of paper out of his underwear. He looked around again, and then he slid the paper through the narrow slit at the base of the visiting window designed for the passing of legal papers and said, "And I'm not gonna lie to you, I didn't open it and I didn't read it. All I know is that it's really important and that it's from this heavyweight dude upstairs in max. It came to me yesterday morning by special delivery."

Barbara Blake opened the folded missile. On a torn, half-page of jail writing paper appeared a cryptic plea. It was written in large, neat, awkward words that said: "MISS BLAKE IT IS URGENTE THAT I SEE YOU IMMEDIATELY ALEJANDRO SOTO." She read it once, then again, and then folded the paper and set it to one side and asked Jacobo, "Who's Alejandro Soto and where'd you get this?"

"Soto's that guy they just brought down from Arroyo Grande on that old murder beef. It came to me special delivery."

"Special delivery? Where's the envelope?"

"I'm talking about a kite. A kite from the third floor. It had to be special delivery because you play hell trying to get anything out of that max up there."

"Who brought it to you?"

"I can't burn my source, Miss Blake. You know better than that. You know *me* better than that."

"How do you know that this came from Mr. Soto?"

"Look, I been knowing the mailman a long time. He's got no reason to be lying to me. And he's been knowing that heavyweight dude up there for a long time, too. Just stop and think. That heavyweight ain't gonna be giving this kite to just anybody. He gives it to a guy he trusts. The same guy I trust. Nobody's got any reason to lie. Besides, have I ever lied to you?"

"Not since you pled guilty."

"That was a cold shot."

"Was this what you were hassling my secretary about all afternoon yesterday?"

"Yeah, I just got the kite yesterday morning and I couldn't get to the phone until the afternoon. But once I did, I kept calling and calling. 'Cause the heavyweight said it was real important."

"Anything else you want to tell me?"

"No. Anything you want to tell me?"

"No."

"That's cold. Not even thank you?"

"Thank you." And Barbara Blake thought no more about that so-called "kite." Alejandro Soto had a lawyer. Greg Olsen could take care of his problems.

Barbara Blake's introduction to Alejandro Soto came from a newspaper account she had read just a few days before his first court appearance. He was being brought down from Arroyo Grande State Prison, where he had been housed for the past eight years in the Security Housing Unit, also known as the SHU, to be tried for the murder of Santos Estrada in San Cristobal County. That killing had taken place almost ten years ago, just a few weeks after the double homicide for which he had been convicted in Dos Palos County and was now serving two life sentences without the possibility of parole. The newspaper article went on to say that because of the Dos Palos convictions, the San Cristobal district attorney had decided at the time not to go forward with the murder charge pending against Soto in San Cristobal. Recently however, a federal court had granted a hearing on the double homicide convictions and there was some speculation that those convictions would be overturned. In light of that, the San Cristobal district attorney had now decided to go forward with the murder prosecution in San Cristobal.

Barbara Blake was familiar with the SHU at Arroyo Grande. The California Department of Corrections had boasted that it was *the* state-of-the-art, maximum security prison in the nation and that it very successfully housed the "worst of the worst." So successful was it that a mammoth lawsuit was brought against it in federal court citing cruel and unusual punishment. Courtroom litigation lasted months. At its conclusion, the trial judge issued a lengthy decision listing a number of grievous violations of the Constitution's proscription against cruel and unusual punishment and ordering radical changes in some of the unit's operations. One such order was leveled at the prison's practice of not removing inmates from a wing after suffering a mental breakdown, to the detriment of other inmates in the same wing, some of who later suffered breakdowns as well.

One of Barbara Blake's former clients had made his way into the SHU and had suffered a nervous breakdown. He was subpoenaed to testify against the prison in the lawsuit, and Barbara had driven to San Francisco to watch him testify. When they brought Henry Gomez into the courtroom, she was aghast. The cocksure, bright, articulate, gangbanger she had represented six years before was now a zombie. He had aged twenty years and lost thirty pounds. He was disoriented and had to be led to the witness stand. Once seated, he turned his head slowly in every direction, dazed, baffled, not sure where he was. To most of the lawyer's questions his answers were, "Huh. Huh." She cried when the judge finally said, "That's enough. I've seen enough," and ordered him out of the courtroom. Henry Gomez had been housed in the SHU for seventeen months and three days.

A few days later, Barbara Blake was in Judge Harold Spencer's courtroom waiting for the Monday morning calendar to be called when several armed sheriff's deputies burst into the courtroom and stationed themselves along the walls and exits. Normally, the in-custody defendants would be brought into the courtroom and seated in the jury box before the judge took the bench. That day the jury box was still empty when Judge Spencer came into the courtroom. "What's going on?" Barbara Blake whispered to the public defender seated next to her. The public defender shrugged her shoulders.

"We'll take one case out of order," announced Judge Spencer. "Case number 96238, People versus Alejandro Soto." Barbara recognized the name and she straightened herself to get a better look at this man who, according to the newspaper, had been in the SHU for eight years.

The door of the holding cell opened just a few feet from the jury box. On the other side of the opened door, chains clanged on the concrete floor announcing the slow, imminent arrival of Alejandro Soto. Barbara Blake's first impression of him was that he was tall for a Mexican, maybe six feet. His red jumpsuit said that his was a crime of violence. The leg irons and the waist chains that kept his hands cuffed to his sides said that he was considered dangerous. The additional armed guards in the courtroom confirmed the above. Then Greg Olsen went to Soto's side and announced he was Soto's court-appointed counsel, which came as a surprise to Barbara.

Now Barbara watched as Greg and the district attorney approached the bench for a sidebar conference with the judge. Then she studied Soto. What she saw was unexpected: unlike Henry Gomez, he appeared to be a physically fit, alert man in full control of his senses. He was standing quietly and calmly in the empty jury box, watching as the sidebar conference turned into a whispered argument. Despite the additional guards in the courtroom, there seemed nothing surly, disrespectful, or threatening about him. Nothing arrogant about the upward tilt of his chin, a sharp, clearly defined chin, as were his nose and cheekbones. Not a typical Mexican face, she thought. His skin was neither brown nor olive but rather a gray-white, probably the product of the sunless, maximum security cells at Arroyo Grande. From what she could see, he had no tattoos. Even his thick, black hair surprised her: it was neatly trimmed and combed. Henry Gomez's hair had been long and straggly.

The more she studied him, the more impressed she became. She had seen thousands of in-custody inmates but few carried themselves as well as Alejandro Soto. He stood straight, not quite at attention, but erect. Though obviously fit, he did not have the bulk of a body builder, and yet everything about him exuded strength. He was paying keen attention to what was going on at the bench. He was neither defiant nor cowering but rather appeared to be very self-confident. And this was the man who had spent almost eight years in the SHU...

The next morning Barbara saw Greg in one of the courthouse halls.

"Why'd you take that case, Greg? Need more grief in your life?"

"Judge Spencer called late afternoon, day before yesterday, and said the DA was bringing down some guy serving two life sentences up in Arroyo Grande and was going to prosecute him on a ten-year-old murder case here. He said it was the damnedest thing he ever heard of, and he needed to appoint somebody. He wanted it to be someone experienced and maybe that would make the case go away sooner rather than later."

"You've turned down Judge Spencer before. So why'd you take it?"

"Actually this guy has a writ of habeas corpus set for hearing in the federal court on the two life sentences. The lawyer handling that writ is Fred Solomon, an old law school friend of mine. I'm sure I've mentioned him to you. He's been working that Dos Palos case for years. Given a bit of his life to it. And he's convinced that the federal court's going to grant his writ and turn Soto loose. He's got me convinced too, and probably the DA as well. That's the only reason they filed on it now. My guess is that this case has big problems. It's ten years old and Randy Davis—it's been assigned to Randy—is already talking to me about seeking the death penalty if Soto won't plead out soon."

"Will they seek the death penalty?"

"I don't know. But the fact that he's already talked to me about letting Soto plead to murder second and having that sentence run concurrent with the two life sentences Soto's already serving, tells me they've got problems with the case. It's awfully early to be talking about concurrent sentences. But let's go down to the end of the hall. It's getting too crowded to be talking about a case of this kind here."

Moving, Barbara asked, "So when does your friend think that the federal court will decide his writ?"

"Who knows? That thing could drag on for another year or it could be decided next month."

"Is your client good for this case?"

"I don't know. He hasn't told me he did it. We haven't got past the "this-is-bullshit" stage. And it may very well be bullshit. But from what I've seen so far, the DA has his share of problems in the case. Not to mention that everything's magnified by an almost ten-year lapse of time since the killing."

"So what kind of a guy is your Mr. Soto?"

"Actually, he's pretty amazing. He's been locked up in the SHU at Arroyo Grande for the past seven-plus years in an eight-by-ten single cell. And just look at him. You saw him yesterday, didn't you? You were in court."

Barbara nodded.

"Just look at the shape he's in. Gets to go out of his cell two hours a week for exercise in an outdoor room the size of a tennis court. That's it, and he's hard as a rock. More than that, he's bright as hell. All self-taught. I don't think he finished grammar school. Reads all the time, anything he can get his hands on. Solomon got him started reading and he hasn't stopped since. Solomon's been sending him books for years."

"What's his rap sheet like?"

"Surprisingly, not a hell of a lot before he decided to go big time. Some small stuff. A couple of petty thefts, a battery, an assault with a deadly weapon that was dismissed, a couple of possessions—one for weed and one for heroin—and then the big time: those two up in Dos Palos County and this one. Still, he's an amazing guy. But don't get me wrong, he's really not somebody I'd like to have over to my house for dinner every Sunday night. And he's already giving me shit, saying I'm not his lawyer of choice and defense attorneys drink out of the same trough as the DAs and the judges. You know the lines. But I'm sticking with this case. My guess is that it just might be winnable. High stakes, and they could get a lot higher, but I don't want to back down now."

"Is he a gangbanger?"

"No, he says he's not and Solomon backs him up completely on that."

"Then what's he doing in the SHU?"

"Solomon says it's because when he went in San Quentin he fought them on everything from his housing to the books he could keep and read. They finally had enough of him, labeled him a gang member and incorrigible, and shipped him off to the SHU."

She thought for a moment and then said, "You know the pressure they put on the guys going into the joint to join one of those gangs is pretty incredible. There aren't many that can withstand it."

"Yeah, but this Soto is not your ordinary guy."

FOUR DAYS later, Barbara Blake saw Alejandro Soto in court again.

She was sitting at counsel table waiting for the sentencing hearing in the child molestation case to begin when they brought Soto out of the holding cell. She had been reviewing Jane Doe's school records and hadn't noticed the extra deputy sheriffs enter the courtroom, nor had she noticed Soto until she heard the clanging of the leg irons on the courtroom floor. When she looked up she saw that Greg was waiting for him near the jury box, and she understood why Greg had taken the case: both the case and the client seemed interesting. Then she returned to her review of the school records.

Once the judge had sentenced her client and the bailiff had whisked him off, she heard the leg irons again and saw that Greg and Soto were leaving the jury box and were making their way to her table. She looked hard at Soto, curious whether what she had seen from a distance a few days earlier was in fact true. He *was* a handsome man who after seven or eight years in the SHU appeared to be in very good physical and mental condition. A remarkable man.

A WEEK later, Jacobo Lopez was on the phone again. "Hey, you better come up here. I got another special delivery from the heavyweight. He's getting on my case. He thinks I ain't delivering his mail. You better do something, lady, before I catch a bum rap."

This note was on a full page of the jail stationery. The big, scrawled, printed letters said: "I CANT BELEVE AFTER OUR TWO MEETINGS OF THE MINDS THAT YOU HAVENT COME UP TO SEE ME. I CAN ONLY THINK THAT THESE FOOLS ARNT DELIVERING MY MAIL. PLEASE COME. IT IS VERY IMPORTANT. ALEJANDRO SOTO."

Meeting of the minds? What meeting of the minds? Did this guy think he was some sort of psychic? It was just as well that he was Greg's client and not hers. Greg was going to have his hands full. She crumpled up the note and threw it in the wastebasket.

Later that afternoon Greg called. "Barb, something's come up. I need to talk to you as soon as possible. It's very important."

"What's it about?"

"I don't want to talk about it over the phone. Trust me, it's important. Can you come over here? Stop on your way home?"

"Yes, but what's it about, Greg?"

"Believe me, it's not something we should be discussing over the phone. How soon can you get here?"

"I'll be there in half an hour...forty-five minutes."

"Great. Thanks."

THE SECRETARIES were gone, and, as Barbara approached his door, she could hear Greg on the phone; his loud voice punctuated by periods of silence and then his loud voice again. She let herself into his office. He was sitting at his desk with the telephone to his ear. When he saw her, he gave her an abbreviated wave with his free hand, followed by an it'll-just-be-a-minute motion and then pointed to the chair across from him. She sat and their eyes met for a moment before he swiveled his chair so that he was no longer facing her. He was arguing with and at the same time trying to calm an anxious client. It occurred to her that she had had enough lawyering for the day. Now as she sat and watched, she saw that the changes fifteen years had brought to Greg Olsen were not pretty. He had gained at least thirty pounds. There were layers of flab under his chin and the top button of his over-starched white shirt refused to stay buttoned so that his loose-fitting tie was holding his collar together as best it could, exposing a layer of grime on the inner collar. His breathing was heavy but shallow and quick, and his big belly was stretching yet another shirt button to its limit. On that shirt were streaks of his luncheon meal. How far had they come—or had they—since their first days in the public defender's office? She had taken much better care of herself, physically at least, but then women always had to be more concerned with their appearance. They had to be "attractive." She despised that word. Attract what? A man? A woman, even? She had neither. Did that mean she was unattractive? *Cut the useless, depressing thoughts,* she told herself. Yet, no matter how much she tried to keep fit, there was nothing she could do about time. Most mornings the crow's-feet at the outer edges of her eyes seemed to be spreading and deepening, and the skin around her upper arms was starting to sag. Even so, she found nothing physically attractive about Greg Olsen.

"Sorry about that, Barb," he said, swiveling his chair back around and putting the phone down. "But you know, you just can't satisfy some of these clients. Threatening to go to another lawyer. Hell, I wish he would. Then he'd get what he really deserves... But, that's not what I called you for. This might take some time. You don't need to be anywhere real soon, do you?"

"No."

"Good."

He leaned forward in his chair, brought his elbows up on his desk, cupped his hands near his mouth, studied her for a moment, and said, "The DA's gonna seek the death penalty in the Soto case."

"What!"

"Yep."

"I thought you said they were offering to let him plead guilty to a murder second because they had a very weak case."

"I did say that and I still think that, but things have changed drastically."

"What happened?"

"Well, the day after I talked to you, Randy Davis came at me again. This time he was much more specific. He said that his office didn't want to spend the time, manpower, or money on this case if it wasn't necessary. What they wanted from Soto was a murder conviction, no more, no less. They didn't care if the time on this new conviction ran concurrent with his life sentences. In fact they would make that part of the plea bargain. But he wanted an answer by Tuesday. Then he would make all the arrangements with the court so that Soto could plead and be sentenced and be back on his way to Arroyo Grande on Wednesday. If Soto wouldn't accept the deal, wouldn't plead, then they would amend the complaint to make it a death penalty case no later than Thursday."

"What'd you say?"

"I told him, of course, that I would have to talk to my client and that I'd get back to him by Tuesday. Frankly, I thought they were still posturing, trying to get us to plead early before we got all the discovery and knew for sure just how weak their case really is. So I went up to see Soto."

"What'd he say?"

"He was outraged. He threw a tantrum, yelling and screaming at me that I was nothing but a fucking dump truck, that I was trying to make him plead guilty to something he didn't do when we hadn't even seen the police reports. Hell, I was just the messenger. If he could have come through that glass partition in the visiting room, he damn well would have. After twenty minutes of ranting and raving, he pretty much lost his voice. Then it was my turn. 'Look, you asshole,' I said, 'I don't give a flying fuck if you plead or don't plead. Let's get that one straight. You want a trial, you'll have a trial. Shit, I've tried more cases than you can probably count to. The only reason I'm sitting here taking all your silly bullshit is because the law says that I have to communicate to you any offer of a plea bargain the DA makes in your case. And that's what I did before you shot your sorry wad off. I never once told you or even hinted that you should plead guilty to something you didn't do. So sit still and shut up and tell me what you want me to tell the DA.' Well, I no sooner said DA when he shot back at me, 'Tell that sorry motherfucker that he can go fuck himself because I ain't pleading to nothing.'"

"So what'd you tell Randy?"

"Well, you know how much I like Randy, the self-righteous little twit. Thinking they had a weak case, I thought I'd have a little fun and make Randy sweat a bit by not giving him an answer until Tuesday at 4:59. So every time he saw me before Tuesday, he'd look at me like a hungry lapdog waiting for a bone and I would just ignore him. A couple of times he came up to me and asked me what we were gonna do and I just told him that Soto was still thinking about it. So Tuesday just before noon, I ran into him at the courthouse and he says to me, 'OK Greg, no more games.

I'm not waiting till five for your answer. What did Soto say?' I couldn't hold back any longer, so I said, 'I'll tell you exactly what he said. He said tell that sorry motherfucker, meaning you, to go fuck himself, because he wasn't pleading to anything.'"

Grinning and nodding, Barbara said, "Whoa! I wish I could have been there."

"The little twit turned beet red. An artery in his neck was thumping against his skin. Had I been six inches shorter and fifty pounds lighter, he'd probably have taken a swing at me. As it was, he just stood there biting his lower lip and glaring at me for what seemed like a full two minutes before he stomped away without a word."

"Wow!"

"I can't say I didn't enjoy that. But there are no free lunches and that little twit didn't wait till Thursday. On Wednesday he amended the complaint making this a death case. Then yesterday afternoon they dragged me and Soto into Spencer's court and arraigned Soto on the death penalty charges."

"How do they get death out of this case?"

"The two Dos Palos murders."

"But the federal court's granted a hearing on them."

"They're still convictions."

"What if they get overturned?"

"They're not worried. They may or may not get overturned. And who knows when, if ever, the federal court will decide. No. In fact Judge Spencer called Randy and me into his chambers after the arraignment and asked if there was any chance of settling the case short of trial. When we said no, he asked me to see him this afternoon to discuss the kinds of resources and funds I was going to need to try the case. I spent most of this morning in the DA's office trying to get a handle on how much discovery there is. There's a lot. I'm going to need another lawyer, a second chair. Judge Spencer agrees. That's where you come in, Barb."

"Me?"

"Oh come on, Barb, you know how much I respect you. There

isn't a better defense attorney around. I trust you. We've worked together. We know each other. We'd make a great team for this case."

All of that was true. But what Greg didn't say, couldn't say, was the other consideration that had weighed so heavily on him throughout the day. This would be their chance, perhaps their last chance, their entrée into that relationship that should have been and now could be. Death penalty cases typically lasted two to five years and could go longer. They would be working long hours, evenings, and weekends together. There could be trips they would need to take together to interview witnesses. The kids would be out of the house in a year and a half. There would be no need to hide. From the beginning, their time together would be legitimate. Once the kids were gone, he would move out of the house and take an apartment for a reasonable length of time until he could move in with her. Then he and Barb would be together, as it should have been long ago. It was a perfect situation.

But Barbara hesitated. "I don't know, Greg."

Fear clutched at him. "What don't you know?"

"The case could go on for years. Most death penalty cases do. You're in a seven-lawyer office. People can cover for you, take cases for you, work on cases you already have. But I'm a sole practitioner and that means there's no lawyer in my office other than myself to take or preserve cases for me. At the end of the case, depending on its length, my law practice could be wiped out. I'd probably be broke or near broke and have to start over from scratch again."

He hadn't counted on this. She was reluctant, or worse? Was she giving him an outright rejection? Fear scraped at him. If she didn't join him he could be tied up with Soto's case for years. As it was now he saw her almost every day at the courthouse or at bar functions. A death penalty case would take him out of the daily courthouse routine. He could go months without seeing her. The kids would be long gone and he would still be going home to drunk and bitter, fat Molly every night. Surely somebody else would step into her life before Soto's death penalty case ended. This was the only real opportunity he would have to get close to her for hours every day, to make himself needed and indispensable, to show her that they were made for each other.

"I'm sorry, Greg," she said as he continued to look past her, "but it really doesn't look like I can help you."

Fear turned to panic. "Wait a minute. Wait a minute. There must be something we can work out here. I appreciate your concern for your law practice but don't turn your back on me now, Barb. Let me think about this. Let me talk to my partners and our office manager about this. There must be a way. Don't say no now. I need you on this case, Barb. There's nobody I'd rather work with. Give me the weekend. Let me figure out how we can make this work. Alright? Let's talk about this again on Monday. Let's meet here Monday evening at six o'clock. OK?"

At 7:18 on Friday evening, Greg Olsen opened the back door and listened for the telltale sounds of who was home. The only sound was the drone of the TV in the family room. *Oh God, Timmy and Jenny are already gone.* He was in no mood to drink, but, without it, it was going to be a long night indeed with Molly. He took measured steps through the laundry room and into the kitchen hoping he could get upstairs to his bedroom and change his clothes before Molly heard him. Then he would decide what to do next.

When he was halfway through the kitchen she heard him. "Is that you, Greg?"

"Yeah. Where are the kids?"

That roused her. She came to the kitchen entryway. "The kids! The kids! Are they the only things you think about in this house? What about me? I live here, too. When the hell are you going to ask how I am? Or even where am I?"

"I can see how you are!" And he regretted that the moment he said it.

"What are you saying? Are you saying I'm drunk? Well, who wouldn't be drunk living with a miserable son of a bitch like you? Tell me, when's the last time you asked me how I was? I'm not even going to ask you when's the last time you kissed me or even touched me. Hell, the word 'kiss' isn't even in your vocabulary anymore. Unless of course you've got some young whore stashed away in some fancy apartment. Look at me, goddamn it! Look at me!"

"I'm looking at you."

"No, look at *me! Me,* the person! When the hell's the last time you looked at me, the person?"

"I am looking at you and I'm seeing that you're drunk again."

"Who wouldn't be drunk living with someone as cold and empty inside as you are?"

They glared at each other. There was hate in their eyes. But those were the truest moments they had spent with each other. Molly lowered her eyes first. "There's takeout on the stove. I never know anymore when the kids are going to be home for dinner on the weekends, and you never call anymore to let me know when you're coming home. Home? Hah! What a laugh! This is a home...? I ordered takeout for myself. There's some left on the stove if you're hungry."

"I'm not hungry. I've got a headache. I'm going up to my room. I'm going to bed."

"Yeah, go on, run upstairs. Hide. Wait till the kids come home so you can sneak downstairs to the refrigerator, and you can feed that swelling gut of yours. I'll be damned if you don't look pregnant."

He moved past her with his eyes downcast. Anything he said or did now would just prolong the agony. Once in his room he closed and locked the door. Then he took off his tie, shirt, shoes, socks, and trousers and lay down on his bed. There had to be some way out of this hell. *Leave,* he told himself for the thousandth time. Timmy was a senior and Jenny was a junior. If he left, he'd see them far less than he was seeing them now, and they were the only warmth and love he had in his life. And how could he leave them with an alcoholic mother and live with himself? But, the truth was he needed them much more than they needed him.

Sometime later, his mind finally relented and shifted to Barbara.

In California, a defendant in a death penalty case can choose to have two trials before a jury. The first trial, known as the guilt phase, deals with whether the defendant has committed the homicide and what degree or how aggravated the homicide was. If the defendant is found guilty of first-degree murder, then a second trial, the penalty phase, takes place. There the jury has to decide whether he should be sentenced to life imprisonment or be executed. Although it was most unusual in death penalty cases, Greg believed Soto's first trial, the guilt phase, was very winnable. He knew most death penalty cases receive substantial publicity. Since Soto was already serving two life sentences and was now being returned from prison to stand trial some ten years after the fact (so that in effect he could be executed), Greg believed the media coverage would be much greater than usual. A not guilty verdict would cement his reputation as one of the leading criminal defense attorneys in San Cristobal County and gain him considerable recognition throughout Northern California. It could mean big money in future attorney's fees.

As lead counsel, his plan had been to try the guilt phase and have Barbara do all the research and motions and try the penalty phase, if there was one. And it had not been lost on him that it was always more palatable and less noticeable to lose a guilt phase trial than it was to lose a penalty phase trial.

But as he lay in his room, the question was how to make the role of the second chair more desirable, more acceptable to Barbara? It took him several hours to reach his decision, although he knew almost from the beginning what he had to do. Nothing was ever easy, nothing was ever without some cost, some price. He reminded himself of that time and again as he veered away from the inevitable. If he didn't pay now, he would pay later. However steep the cost seemed now, it would be infinitely greater in the long run. There was no escaping that reality. Cornered, he conceded, decided, and fell asleep.

Early the next morning, while Molly slept, he called Barbara. "Sorry to wake you, Barb, but it occurs to me that we should talk about this Soto case today, this afternoon if at all possible. I told Judge Spencer that I'd get back to him on this second-chair matter on Tuesday, things like who it would be and what it might cost. If we meet on Monday as planned, and you're still reluctant to come on board, I will literally have no time to find someone else. But not to worry, I think I've worked out something we can both live with."

THEY MET that Saturday afternoon in Greg's office, she in a pair of old jeans and a floppy sweatshirt and he in designer casual clothes aimed in part at concealing his expanding mid-section. She came convinced that she couldn't make the commitment. He came regretting what he had to give up. But when he saw her, despite her sloppy clothes, lack of makeup, and hair pulled straight back and tied with a rubber band, he knew he had no choice. He told her that her role as second chair would not be what it typically would be, that she would try the guilt phase. And, if there was penalty phase, he would try that. He would be responsible for all the research and motions. Her sole responsibility would be to try the issue of Soto's guilt or innocence. It would be, he said, as if she were only trying another run-of-the-mill homicide, no more, no less. Just like those she had tried in the past without jeopardizing her law practice. She was stunned. He was taking on all the grunt work—always the responsibility of the second chair—and reserving little or none of the publicity for himself, while exposing himself to the daunting possibility of losing a man's life.

"Why are you doing this, Greg?"

"Because I need you on this case, Barb...in more ways than you can imagine." He had slipped on the last remark and was quick to try to explain it away. "What I mean is...I'm convinced that a woman would be a much better advocate for Soto in the guilt phase. The jury is going to know that he's already been convicted of killing two people. They're going to be afraid of this guy, probably loathe him, too, going into the trial. As a woman, you can soften those initial impressions in a way that I don't think a man can. You're very good at softening defendants for a jury, Barb. I've watched you. You touch them ever so lightly. When you explain things to them in open court, you get right up next to them, you whisper in their ears. You're completely at ease with them. You smile at them. You smile with them. There doesn't seem to be a trace of fear in you. If a woman as petite and straight looking as yourself has no apparent fear of this guy, then why should the jury? Conceivably he might just seem a little more human than they initially thought."

He watched her. She was pensive, but he had covered his tracks.

"Let's be frank, Greg. No nonsense. We've known each other too long for that. This is a high profile case. You're giving up a lot of profile here, a ton of publicity. In the end, an incredible amount of potentially positive publicity. Why give it up? I know we're friends, and, yes, I'm a woman and that fact could be of some help to your client, but, in return, you're giving up an awful lot. Why?"

"Give me a little credit, will you, Barb. Believe it or not, every once in a while I can hold my ego hostage for the good of the client. You'd be a better advocate for Soto than I would in the guilt phase. Period. End of discussion. We're talking about a man's life here. I can be very objective in that setting. This is a winnable case and you'd have a better chance at it than I would."

"You keep telling me how winnable it is, and I keep wondering what you mean by that."

"The case is ten years old. Much of the physical evidence has been lost or destroyed. Sure, they'll bring in an expert to testify that the gun found at the scene of the Estrada homicide was tested and found to be the same gun that killed Carlos Sanchez and his mother. Other than that, the only other evidence they have is the testimony of Johnny Moncado. Moncado told the cops that Soto shot Estrada as part of a foiled robbery attempt. Soto says Moncado's a liar and that Moncado's the one who shot Estrada. Everything he says makes sense. He says...no, I'd rather he tell you what happened. You know, I'm using Bill Terry as the investigator in the case?"

"Good choice."

"Let's see how well it matches up with what he's told me and Bill. Bill went up to the jail and interviewed Soto and came back with the same story. I sent Bill over to Dos Palos to try to locate and talk to Johnny Moncado. He spent two days over there at all of Moncado's old haunts. Everybody there says that they haven't seen Moncado in four to six weeks. Nobody knows where he went …he just disappeared. My guess is that's about the time the DA's office here contacted him about this case. Bill's cop friends here and in Dos Palos say Moncado's either under a witness-protection plan somewhere or he's split."

"You think the DA's office would push a death penalty case with their principal witness gone?"

"Well, Moncado may be gone now, but I'm sure they think they can get him here for trial. Besides, what have they got to lose? The closer we get to trial, the more the pressure will mount on Soto and the more willing he might be to plead to a murder second to save his life. That way they never have to produce Moncado… So what do you say, Barb? If Judge Spencer called now and wanted you to take another murder case, you know you'd take it. So how does this differ? All you have to do is try the murder case. Me and the people in my office will do the rest."

Barbara Blake thought about it. The opportunity Greg was presenting was a good one. But she had never known Greg or any trial attorney to be so willing to step out of the limelight, especially in a high profile case that was "very winnable." At times, she had thought that Greg had a "thing" for her. But it was a sporadic feeling and a fantasy at best, and certainly nothing she had reciprocated in any way. That could hardly be the driving force here. She looked up at Greg. His blue eyes were as open and honest as they were before juries. She sighed. "I don't know, Greg, let me sleep on it. Any way you look at it, it will still be a big commitment on my part. It's not a run-of-the-mill murder case because if I lose at the guilt phase, it could mean a man's life. Let me sleep on it. I'll call you in the morning."

SHE CALLED Greg the next morning hoping that Molly wouldn't answer. Her contacts with Molly since she and Greg had terminated their partnership had been few, but they were always tense and cold. It was Jenny with her sprightly seventeen-year-old voice that answered the phone. "Hold on Barbara, I'll get my dad." When Greg came to the phone she said, "I'm pretty much committed to doing it, Greg. But I want to talk to him first before I give you a definite yes. Can you get me into the jail to see him this afternoon? I assume you're the only one authorized to see him now?"

"Me and Bill Terry. I'll call over there and talk to whoever's in charge. Can I tell them that you'll be there sometime, let's say, after two?"

"Yes."

VII

Sunday afternoon was unusually quiet on the third deck of the county jail as Barbara Blake got off the elevator. Even better, Joe Rossi was the deputy at the control desk.

"What brings you up here, Ms. Blake, on a beautiful Sunday afternoon?"

"Joe, when are you going to start calling me Barbara?"

"Soon, Ms. Blake. But what can I do for you, ma'am?"

"I came up here to see Alejandro Soto. He's in murder max."

Joe Rossi frowned. "They told me that his lawyer was coming up to see him. I guess I was expecting Greg Olsen. Are you his lawyer too, Ms. Blake?"

"Not yet."

Joe Rossi stopped frowning but the look of concern did not disappear. He turned to his housing chart mumbling, "Alejandro

Soto," although he knew exactly where Alejandro Soto was housed. He needed some time, moments to mask his concern, to choose his words carefully. Six years earlier Barbara Blake had represented Joe Rossi's younger sister, who had shot and killed her husband on the back porch of their home. Joe Rossi was then a twenty-year veteran of the San Cristobal County Sheriff's Department. Conflicted, he helped his sister as much as he could, meeting with Barbara Blake in churches and motel rooms and on county roads, risking his job and his pension and the respect of his fellow officers. Instead of a murder conviction and a life sentence, Gail Goodwin was convicted of manslaughter and received a six-month county jail sentence. The outcome of his sister's case did not change Joe Rossi's opinion of criminal defense attorneys. They were still nothing more than money-hungry whores, cheats, and scum. Except for Barbara Blake. She was different: honest, hardworking, compassionate, and with a heart of gold that made her vulnerable to some of those creeps.

Joe Rossi pulled up several housing cards, although he needed to pull but one, until he came to Alejandro Soto's. "Oh yeah, he's in murder max 8." He pulled out the card, read it, turned it, read the back side, and then looked over at Barbara Blake with a tired, wrinkled look of concern. "He's a pretty bad character, Ms. Blake. Been housed up in the SHU in Arroyo Grande for almost eight years. That's where they keep the worst of the worst, you know. It's none of my business, Ms. Blake, but I really hate to see you get mixed up with this creature. He's already doing two life sentences on two murders. Now I guess they want to gas him for a third murder."

"I'm not his lawyer yet, Joe, and if I do take his case, it'll be on a court appointment. I wouldn't have much respect for myself as a lawyer if I refused to take cases because I didn't like the person or because I didn't like his past record."

"But this is some bad character, Ms. Blake. We can't even pull him out of his cell unless we have three of us there to do it. I've been in the department almost twenty-six years and I haven't never heard of that. Usually you press a button down here at the control desk and the inmate comes out of his cell alone. Sometimes, but not very often, it'll take one of us to pull an inmate out of his cell. A few times, if the inmate's been acting up, it might take two of us. But I've never seen it take three of us. Never. Until this Soto. And they say the word came down from the sheriff himself."

"Joe, I'm sure you know I can take care of myself."

"I do know that, ma'am."

"Where do you want me to wait?"

"Well, today's Sunday and we're light on personnel but heavy on inmate visiting. I'll try to find three bodies to pull him as quick as I can, but it could take a while. You can take your chances and wait or come back after four o'clock when visiting's over. But we'll be feeding then. So I can't guarantee that it will be any quicker later on."

"I'll wait. I know you'll do your best to get him out here as soon as you can."

"Why don't you wait down there in the interview room next to murder max, and I'll see what I can do about rounding up those three bodies."

In the murder max attorney visiting room, attorneys and their clients, separated by a glass partition, talked to each other by the use of wall phones. Barbara hated those phones. How "convenient" they were. That was one of the key words the jail commander had used in their defense: "convenient" for the defense lawyers and inmates. Nonsense. Convenient for the jailers. Convenient for them to eavesdrop and record a conversation between an attorney and a client. Notably, they had been installed only in the one interview room used by murder max inmates and their lawyers. Some of her colleagues had blithely said, "So what. They won't eavesdrop; they won't tape. It's a felony if they do." Right. And who was going to report them to law enforcement? Law enforcement?

She sat and waited, wondering what Soto would be like. It took three deputies to pull him, he had spent almost eight years in the SHU, and he had two murder convictions—two life sentences and now this one. Though it was known as murder max, not all of the inmates housed there were necessarily charged with murder. Barbara Blake had represented a serial rapist, a pedophile, and an arsonist who had also been housed there. But who was this Alejandro Soto?

ALEJANDRO SOTO was committing to memory yet another twenty-five words from *Webster's College Dictionary* when three guards arrived. "OK Soto, strip. You've got a visit."

Sitting on his bunk Alejandro Soto hesitated. A visit? He didn't know anybody in San Cristobal and even if he did, they wouldn't be visiting him. He didn't like it.

"Let's go, Soto. You've got a visit. Strip down."

"Visit? I don't know nobody who would be visiting me here, and I don't want to be talking to no cops."

"It's your lawyer, Soto."

"Oh, OK." And with that he got up from his bunk.

"Strip down and then come over to the door where we can check you out. Then put on your jumpsuit and we'll put the leg irons and waist chains on here."

"Why?"

"Because we're not opening up the door till you're chained up."

"They be 'fraid of you, big fella," came a voice from the next cell.

"Shut the fuck up, nigger," Soto yelled. "I keep tellin' you to keep your black ass outta my business. When I wanna talk to you, when I want something from you, I'll let you know. Meanwhile, stay outta my life."

"I jus tryin' to give you a compliment, homey."

"You ain't no fucking homey of mine, nigger. And I don't need none of your black-ass compliments."

"If both of us didn' know I could kick your ass any time, any day, any place I wanted to, I might could be gettin' pissed. Truth is, I'm feelin' sorry for your li'l brown, Messicun ass."

"Keep your sorriness to yourself, nigger. Mexicans don't need no black-ass sorriness."

Willie Jenkins was a gregarious, likeable giant of a black man whose opinions and humor were always being solicited by the other inmates in the eight-cell maximum security block, except for Alejandro Soto who didn't like or trust him. To Soto, Jenkins was a "plant," someone who, in exchange for leniency for his own case, had been housed next to him with the aim of befriending him and extracting incriminating information from him.

"Jenkins," one of the guards said, "stay the fuck out of this. We got enough problems with Soto without you pissing him off."

With that, Willie Jenkins left the bars of his cell door and went back to his bunk where he could hear Soto mumbling to himself, "Fucking nigger. Fucking nigger. Always trying to stick his black ass in my business."

ONE OF the guards unlocked the cubicle door and turned on a light, temporarily blinding Soto as he stepped into the four-by-five space and shuffled toward the lone object in that space, a white, plastic chair. When he reached the chair he saw her, and the sight of her froze him. She was sitting no more than four feet from him on the other side of the wall and the glass partition. A woman, a beautiful, talented woman. And though he couldn't touch her, this was as close as he had been to a woman in eight years.

"Sit down, Soto," one of the guards said behind him. Soto heard him but couldn't react. "Sit down, Soto," came the order a second time. Again Soto heard the guard, but it might just as well have been the sound of his own breathing. Then the two guards were on either side of him and in one motion they shoved him down onto the plastic chair. They stood there for several moments awaiting a reaction. But Soto was transfixed. He simply stared at the woman four feet from him. He did not see the guards step away, and he did not hear the door close or the lock click behind him.

On the other side of the glass Barbara stared back at his eyes, which, without so much as a blink, were so openly and unwaveringly set on her. "Mr. Soto, Mr. Soto," she said, wanting to break his stare. But he didn't, or couldn't, hear her. Then she saw that the telephone receiver on his side was still hanging on the wall. She pointed several times to the phone but his eyes didn't shift, didn't leave her. She picked up the receiver on her side and with it pointed at his receiver, but his stare was firm. She spoke into her receiver. "Mr. Soto, we have to talk, and the only way we can talk to each other in this interview room is by the phone. So will you please pick up the phone hanging on the wall to your right?" If any of her words were transmitted into his cubicle, he showed no sign of it. The stare continued. She looked away for a minute as if she were not in the least concerned with his staring, but when she looked back, he was still staring.

She was more beautiful than he had imagined. He saw her lips move and he wanted to say something but he couldn't. His tongue was stuck and try as he might to move it, he couldn't. So he stared in wonder of the moment. Not only was she beautiful and talented, but she had come, she had answered his notes, she had come to be his lawyer. And now she was sitting alone with him, almost next to him, so close that but for the glass he could have touched her. She had stared at him the first time he saw her and again the second time. He had doubted. But now she had come because he had asked her to come. She was as attracted to him as he was to her. There was nothing to doubt. He started to shiver. The shiver became a shudder and then hard, spasmodic shakings which he tried to hide, tried to stop, but couldn't.

Holding the receiver up to the glass she mouthed, "Pick up the phone! Pick up the phone!" No response. No eye movement, no nodding, just the stare. Then she saw the trembling, the shaking. Was there something wrong with him? This was not the man she had seen in court. "Pick up the phone! Pick up the phone!" But he only continued to stare. Then she realized there was no way he could reach the phone: both his hands were cuffed to waist chains. The guards had not uncuffed him, and he couldn't reach or use the phone. She stood and leaning as close as she could to the glass mouthed, "I'll be right back. I'll be right back. I'm not leaving. I'm not going anywhere except to get that cuff off your hand." He continued staring, and she saw more trembling. She had to talk to him. She turned and left.

"Joe, I appreciate you doing all you could to pull Soto," she said when she reached the control desk, "but I can't talk to the man. Both his hands are still cuffed to the waist chains and he can't reach the phone, even hold it to his ear."

When she returned to the cubicle, Alejandro Soto was sitting in exactly the same position she had left him in and the stare was still there. Until he had the receiver in hand, there was no point in returning his stare. That would accomplish nothing except to make her nervous. She looked up at the ceiling until that felt awkward. Then she took a copy of the complaint Greg had given her and began reading it slowly, reading isolated words that had no meaning save as an excuse not to look at Soto's staring. A guard entered Soto's side, freed his right hand and arm, took the receiver off the hook, placed it in Soto's hand, and put it to his ear.

"Can you hear me now?"

Her voice was soft and gentle. It had been years since he had heard words with those sounds. He nodded. His face softened, and his eyes fell.

"My name is Barbara Blake. I'm an attorney. Greg Olsen has asked me to help in the defense of your case and I've come to talk to you about that. Can you hear me?"

He nodded. But now his eyes were downcast and she saw him tremble again. He had to stop that, and he had to look at her. "Mr. Soto, I'm going to ask you some questions, background questions that will give me some idea of who you are and what you've done in your life. Then I'll tell you about myself, about my experience as a lawyer. Finally, I'd like to talk a little about your case, not in great detail, just generally for now, so that I can get some idea of your version of the facts. But you'll have to look at me... Mr. Soto, what's your full name and date of birth?"

He tried to answer, he wanted to answer, but his tongue was stuck. He couldn't move it. The more he tried, the more stuck it became. The only sound he could produce was a short, hard, "Uhh! Uhh! Uhh!" until his body shook and he stopped.

"Mr. Soto, Mr. Soto, try to relax. Look at me for a moment."

He couldn't look at her. He wanted to look at her, but he couldn't. He couldn't let her see what a mess he was. How his mouth and throat were trying to force his tongue to move, but it wouldn't move. How he was shaking. She was too beautiful and talented for him. If she saw him now, she would leave and never come back.

"Mr. Soto, please look at me."

The softness and gentleness of that voice paralyzed him all the more.

So they sat in silence, he with his head bent and his eyes downcast, trying to stop the trembling and shaking, and she with her eyes fixed on the top of his head, trying to understand what was happening. The minutes passed. She did not know how to change what was before her, and she did not want to add any more to his obvious discomfort. He was ashamed, and the more ashamed he became, the more he needed her not to leave, but the more certain he was that she would leave. Now there was no reason for her to stay. And once she left, she would never return.

Several more minutes passed. Then she tried again. "Mr. Soto, please look at me." This time he did look up. What he saw was a blur. What she saw were silent tears running down the sides of his face. She looked away. She fought back tears. She had to leave. But she waited, not wanting to tie her leaving to his tears. But she had to leave. Her tears would not be silent. Finally she stood and said, "Mr. Soto, I have to go now but I'll be back in a few days."

When Joe Rossi heard the door to the murder max interview room close, he readied himself. While Barbara Blake had been with Soto, he had called down to the booking unit and had them read him Soto's criminal and prison history. He had taken notes. As much as he liked and respected Ms. Blake, he still saw her as a woman, somewhat naive about the goons she represented. She had a good heart, too good for these animals. When she came to the control desk, he was going to tell her a few things about Mr.

Soto, things he was sure she didn't know. It would be a shame if she got involved with that thug. There were plenty of scum defense attorneys floating around. Let them represent him. They deserved each other.

But instead of coming to the control desk and reporting the close of the interview, Barbara Blake veered off to the elevator and from there, some thirty-five feet away, waved to Joe Rossi and said, "Thanks, Joe. I'm done."

This took Joe Rossi by surprise. With his notes in hand he said, "You got a minute, Ms. Blake? I'd like to run a few things by you."

"Not now, Joe. I'm late. I've got some people waiting for me."

In the elevator the tears came. It was late Sunday afternoon and thankfully the jail lobby was empty, not even the counter deputy was in sight when she signed out. Outside of the jail, as soon as she could stop crying, she called Greg.

"I'm in, Greg. I'll be your second chair."

"Great! You saw him I take it?"

"Yeah."

"How'd it go?"

"OK."

"What'd you think of him?"

"He seemed alright. I wasn't with him very long."

"Did you talk about the case?"

"Not really. I was running late. I'm still running late. I have dinner plans with some friends. I'm going to have to go, Greg. We can talk about this tomorrow or Tuesday. But I'm in. I'd like to have copies of everything you have on the case."

"I've already had copies made. There are quite a few boxes."

"Not surprising. Can you have somebody drop those off at my office tomorrow morning?"

"Sure."

For Alejandro Soto the tears stopped about the time they started for Barbara. *I gotta stop crying,* he thought. *The guards will see, and those fools in the cells will see. Men don't cry. Pussies do.*

But the guards didn't come. Not then or for a long time after. His worry of telltale signs of tears passed, but humiliation set in. *How could I have cried like a baby in front of that woman, a woman who came to be my lawyer and now never will be? I cried like a fucking baby, like a fucking baby. I was shaking like a little punk. If she tells the guards, it'll be all over the jail.*

Two hours and fifteen minutes after Barbara Blake left, the guards came. Joe Rossi had gone off duty without telling the new shift that Soto was in the interview room. The guards didn't seem to know. "Come on, Soto, let's go," the biggest guard said in a typical gruff, brusque manner but nothing more. As he shuffled past the fools on murder max on the way to his cell, he looked. Cell by cell the respect was still there. As he passed those inmates, in the back of his mind was the big nigger: he always knew everything.

"Where you been, homes? Seem like you left us this moanin'. Been gone a mightee long time. No lawyers be comin' up here Sundays. An even if they do, they doan be stayin' no twenty-foh hours. You been huddlin' with the pohleece, tellin' all bout us?"

Alejandro Soto decided to let it go. To answer would just add fuel to the fire. He passed Willie Jenkins without looking at him. But when they reached his cell door, he couldn't help himself. "Shut your fucking black mouth, nigger!"

Once in his cell, Alejandro Soto kicked off his shower clogs, took off his socks, stripped down to his shorts, extended himself on the concrete floor facedown, and began doing push-ups. His goal and standard was to do them as long and as hard as he could. And he did...until his arms ached and his sweat threatened the grip that his fingers and palms had on the concrete. Until he fell flat on his face and he couldn't tell whether the side of his face was lying in his sweat or in his saliva. He lay there only as long as it took him to realize that to stop, to lie there, was another sign of weakness, the very weakness that had dogged him that afternoon. So he rolled over into a sitting position and began sit-ups in the same manner, with the same objective, until his stomach ached and his back felt as if it would break. Then he sat, but only for those moments that it took for the pain to subside and be tolerable. Then he got into a squatting position and burpees began: up, down, squat, kick, up, down, squat for however long it took to feel the hurt so much that he couldn't do one more.

Just then Jenkins interrupted: "Hey homes, whacha doin' in there? You be drivin' the rest of us crazy with all your gruntin' and groanin'!" And he answered without stopping or even slowing his motion, "Fuck you, nigger, another word out of you and I'm gonna twist your head off the next time they pull me out." When he finally collapsed, hours after he began, he fell asleep on the concrete floor in a large puddle of sweat, saliva, and mucous.

As BARBARA drove home, the visit repeated itself and repeated itself. Defendants, especially those who had been to prison, were manipulators, more so with women. Polite, soft-spoken, courteous, thoughtful, ready to tell a woman without the slightest provocation how good she looked. And, inevitably, the pass would come, subtle most times, but there. Usually one or two rebuffs were enough to cut them off. Occasionally she had to be direct: "Look, I'm here to represent you as your lawyer. And, as your lawyer, I'll do the best I know how for you. But I'm not here to be your girlfriend and if you keep trying to make it that, you're going to find yourself with another lawyer. Understood?" But this had been so different. Or had it? Some of these guys were great actors. She thought of the stare...of the trembling. That was not acting, not play-acting. He had tried to speak and couldn't. Instead there were guttural sounds. That was heartrending. And the tears. As real as they could be. He had made no show of crying, no show of the tears. Instead he had kept his head down, trying to hide the tears, looking up at her only after she had insisted. All of this was far from the Alejandro Soto she had expected to meet.

THE NEXT morning when she returned to her office from court, Suzie Martin was waiting for her.

"Have you gone crazy?"

"Crazy?" asked Barbara, closing the outer door to her office.

"Just take a look in your office. There's fifteen boxes in there and more on the way. Barbara, you don't need that case. That man is a beast. The sooner they gas him, the better."

"How do you know more boxes are coming?"

"Because Greg's flunky told me so. Barbara, you're a glutton for punishment. You don't *need* that case. You really don't *want* that case. And I know *I* don't want to work on that case."

"Suzie, I'm in the middle of the Davis case and I have to be back in court at 1:30. I've got a lot of work to do for this afternoon's session, and I have to do it now. We'll talk about the fifteen boxes and Soto's case when I get back from court."

WHEN BARBARA returned from court late that afternoon, Suzie went to her office and said, "You know, Barb, you don't need to be taking these court-appointed cases any more, especially this one. Everybody knows this guy's a creep. The court doesn't pay much and you're doing just fine without them. You've got plenty of paying creeps. You don't need court-appointed ones, especially this one. Remember what you said after the Taylor case? You said you weren't taking anymore court-appointed cases."

There were no free lunches. Suzie was a great secretary. But you always paid in more ways than one for what you got. This was no time to chitchat. She wanted to get to those boxes. "Greg was in a bind," she said. "He needed second counsel and he kept after me."

"Well, Greg doesn't need to be taking these cases either."

Barbara wanted to say: "Go take that up with Greg." But that would only lead to a litany of "what's wrong" and "I'm sorry" and "I didn't mean anything" and she'd never leave her alone. Better to say nothing. She eyed the boxes, all fifteen of them.

VIII

BARBARA BLAKE SORTED
through the boxes. To her relief only two pertained to the Estrada
killing. The rest dealt with the Carlos Sanchez homicide: three
had police reports, lab results, and pre-trial matters; the other
ten boxes contained trial transcripts, appeals, and writ proceedings. Then she went through the boxes again just to be sure. Yes,
only two involved the Estrada killing. From those two she pulled
the police reports. It was after five when she began reading them.
Suzie was gone, and the front door was locked. She wouldn't be
bothered. It had been a long time since she had a "winnable" case
of any kind, let alone a high profile case. She was eager but still
skeptical. There were pages and pages, many of which were redun-
dant and some were just forms. The heart of the prosecution's case
was Johnny Moncado. She carefully read anything and everything

that related to him. When she finished, she sat back and nodded to herself. The prosecution had a weak case.

A WEEK after the Estrada killing, Johnny Moncado was pulled over by a motorcycle cop in Dos Palos for running a red light. When the officer radioed in and learned of Moncado's past, he and a backup officer conducted a search of Moncado's vehicle and found nearly a pound of heroin. Moncado had several burglary convictions and an armed robbery conviction, and under the three-strikes law was facing a life sentence. Moncado never told the police where he got the heroin, repeatedly saying that his life wouldn't be worth a dime if he did. But he did tell them he could help them solve a homicide if they would drop the three-strikes allegation.

Depending on the kind of evidence Moncado was able to produce, the police agreed. Moncado then told them that he and Alejandro Soto had been friends, crime partners and dopers who had shot up together for years. He said that about two weeks after the Sanchez murders, Soto asked him for a ride "to pick up some money from a guy who had been owing him for a long time." While Moncado had been aware of the Sanchez killings, he did not then know that Soto was a killer or even a suspect. He drove Soto to the San Cristobal apartment complex where he later learned Santos Estrada lived, and he waited in the car while Soto went up to collect his money. A few minutes later, he heard gunshots and then Soto came running and yelled, "Let's get the fuck outta here! I just killed that motherfucker!" As they fled, Moncado asked Soto how it felt to kill someone. Soto answered that he would never understand until he had killed someone himself. He quoted Soto as saying, "When you do, you feel like you're God. Because then you know that you've done what only God can do. Only God can take a life. This is my third one, and each time the feeling's bigger, better, and stronger."

Facing a life sentence, Moncado had every reason to lie. That would be made very clear to the jury. Then too, all of his prior felony convictions were crimes against moral turpitude that would paint him as dishonest to the core and not to be trusted. Also, liars have a difficult time remembering what they said a month or even a week before. Try ten years. Johnny Moncado would never be a convincing witness. A weak case? Yes. The only other evidence the prosecution had was the gun, the same gun used by Soto in the Sanchez homicides. But that assumed that the prosecution still *had* the gun, actual physical possession of the gun. After ten years, the gun may well have been destroyed, sold at an auction, or mysteriously disappeared from the crime lab or the police property room. It was definitely a case worth trying.

But something had bothered her when she read the reports, something that was still bothering her. She pulled those pages of the reports again. "You won't understand, Johnny, until you've killed somebody." Where had that come from? She pulled Moncado's rap sheet. Four burglary convictions and an armed robbery. No violence except for the armed robbery. And that could have been anything: a codefendant who had a gun, an unloaded pistol, or maybe even a toy gun. Nothing else in Moncado's four-page rap sheet indicated any violence. Not even an assault. So who would have been more likely to have said that: Moncado? or Soto who had already killed two people? That did not bode well for Soto. "You feel like you're God. ...This is my third one, and each time the feeling's bigger, better, and stronger." The words sent chills through her. She already dreaded having a jury hear those words. That wasn't the man she had seen yesterday. She had dealt with hundreds of defendants. Rare was the one who told *all* of the truth during his first interview. Usually she got little or none of the truth. Yesterday's performance was unlike any she had ever seen. He had said nothing. She was convinced he had tried to speak but couldn't. The guttural sounds were real...the straining around the mouth. The tears and trembling were authentic. Why or how could he have staged all of that? She wasn't even his lawyer then.

None of what she had seen was consistent with a cold-blooded killer who compared himself to God.

Then it struck her how much she wanted Soto to be innocent. Representing a man she knew or thought she knew was guilty was one thing...the usual thing. She did the best she could and gave the best defense possible because the American justice system and her self-respect dictated that. It was quite another thing to defend a person she knew or believed was being falsely accused. There she burned inside. Work was no longer work. It was a cause, a passionate cause. She could work endlessly and tirelessly on the case. She looked forward to the trial. She hungered for the trial. When she finally stood before the judge and jury, she would be cloaked in truth and justice. From what she had just read, from what she had seen yesterday, Soto *had* to be innocent.

IT WAS 8:10 and she hadn't eaten. She wasn't particularly hungry. She wanted to start on the double homicides, the Carlos Sanchez police reports, but she decided she better eat first. She ordered a plate of lasagna at Nick's Diner down the street and was back in her office half an hour later and started on the Sanchez file.

The Sanchez police reports were disappointing and depressing. There was no escaping the fact that the killing had been a cold-blooded, premeditated murder, which had also resulted in the murder of an ostensibly innocent old woman. Those murders would be the vehicle the prosecution would use to ask the jury for the death penalty. Once the jury heard those facts, she and Soto would be in a different world. She thought of the similarities involved in the two killings. Both Sanchez and Estrada were drug dealers and the motives for the killings, as set out in the police reports, were robberies for money and drugs. The Sanchez murders were the prosecution's strongest evidence in the Estrada case. Take those killings out of the case and the prosecution's chances for a conviction were reduced dramatically. It was 11:48 and she had to go home; she had to get some sleep.

SHE HAD lunch with Greg the next day. She could have talked about it with him on the phone, but she wanted to watch his re-actions as they talked. She waited until they had been served be-fore she asked, "What did Soto tell you about the Estrada killing? How did it go down?"

"Didn't he tell you?"

"No, I didn't ask him."

"Why?"

She had decided not to tell Greg about Soto's reaction to her visit. She guessed that nothing similar had happened with Greg during his prior visits with Soto or he would have mentioned it. She wanted to wait to see what Soto was like on her second visit.

"Like I told you on Sunday, I didn't have much time with him. They were having problems finding three guards to pull him, so I waited and waited. When they finally did pull him, I had just a few minutes to let him know who I was and that you wanted me to come into the case as second chair. I had a dinner date with friends that I was already late for, so I had to cut the visit short. I told him that I'd get back to him in a few days."

Greg Olsen looked away and thought for a moment and then said, "I kind of wanted to wait to hear what he told you before I said anything. But I guess it really doesn't matter because he told me and Bill Terry exactly the same thing, and I doubt that he'll vary much with you. He admits that he and Moncado were very tight: crime partners and asshole buddies who shot up together all the time. But he insists, and this appears nowhere in the police reports, he insists that Moncado was with him the afternoon he killed Sanchez and his mother. Moncado didn't go upstairs with him; he was parked around the corner waiting for Soto. Moncado had no idea that Soto was going to kill Sanchez. Soto had only told him that he was going up there to rip off Sanchez. The gun he used was Moncado's.

"Soto says that Estrada was a very big dope dealer and was San-chez's connection. Sanchez had made a lot of money for Estrada and stood to make him a lot more. They were supposedly real tight.

126

Once Estrada learned about Sanchez's murder, he put a $25,000 reward out on the streets for the shooter's head. It wasn't long after, that the word on the street was that Soto was the shooter. Estrada upped it to $30,000 for Soto, dead or alive. Moncado came up with the bright idea of tying up Soto, photographing him bound and gagged, and then taking the photos up to Estrada and asking for half of the money up front before he turned over Soto. Then Moncado and Soto were going to split to Mexico with the $15,000. But Estrada apparently balked, smelled a fish, and went for a gun. That's when Moncado shot him and, in his panic to take everything in sight and get out of there, left his gun behind. The next day, on the word of some snitch, the cops picked up Soto for the Sanchez murders. A couple of weeks later Moncado was stopped by a traffic cop with a pound of heroin on him and you know the rest.

Barbara was relieved. But she needed reassurance. "And you believe him?"

"Yeah...I think so. And so does Bill Terry, and, as you know, Bill has grilled a lot of people. It all fits together pretty well. Soto also told us who Moncado got the gun from. Bill's checking that out. It's been ten years and the chances are pretty slim he'll track the guy down or come up with anything, but if he does, that just puts another hole in the DA's case."

GREG OLSEN visited with Alejandro Soto that afternoon in the jail interview room by phone. "How'd you get along with your new lawyer on Sunday?"

Alejandro was slow to answer. He was still wrestling with his humiliation and wasn't sure what the woman lawyer had told Olsen.

"Ms. Blake came up to see you on Sunday, didn't she?"

"Yeah," he nodded.

"So how did the two of you get along?"

"OK." Still not sure, Soto was waiting for some indication of what she had told him.

"Well, I want you to know that Ms. Blake's an excellent lawyer.

We're real lucky to have her. Death penalty cases usually need two lawyers, and I couldn't ask for a better second chair than her. She's very busy and she didn't want to get involved at first. It took two days of talking to her, of trying to convince her to join us. She finally agreed. She'll be handling the first part of the case, and I'll be handling the second part. She'll be coming up here to see you quite a bit. She's not only an excellent lawyer but she's also a very fine lady, and I'm going to insist that you treat her with all the respect she deserves. Do I make myself clear?

"Good."

Alejandro was more humiliated than ever. She had not wanted to come. Her coming had nothing to do with his kites. The man had to beg her for two days to come. There was nothing about her wanting to be with him, about being attracted to him. And he had made a fool of himself thinking that she had come because of him. He promised himself that there wouldn't be a repetition of Sunday

BARBARA WENT to the jail early Friday afternoon. When she started toward the interview room, the deputy at the control desk said, "Hold on, it's locked. I'll have to let you in."

Locked? It had never been locked before. She followed him to the door and saw that the cubicle was completely dark. Usually there was some light in the cubicle even if it was only the hall-way light reflected in the glass portions of the doors. "There's a light switch on your left," the deputy said as he walked away. She stood for a moment puzzled by the darkness. Then she turned on the light and saw that the cubicle had been completely renovated.

The walls were no longer whitewashed and instead were covered with dark-brown, corklike, acoustic tiles. The plate glass had been replaced by a brown, perforated sheet of steel that had the appearance of a large pegboard. She tried looking through to the cubicle on the other side but could see nothing. The other side was dark in spite of the light on her side. The metal tray extension used for writing was still there, but the white, plastic chair was gone. And the slit for passing legal papers was gone—sealed off. What kind of contraband could someone possibly slip through an eighth-of-an-inch slit? And how was she going to get papers to and from him now? How was he going to sign anything? She examined the acoustic tiles. The whole damn place had to be wired for sound. And cameras...? Wouldn't take much to stuff a camera lens into those black crags in the tiles. What in hell would they want to photograph anyway? Then she saw the phone was gone too. What! That made absolutely no sense at all. Why would they give up their tool for taping and eavesdropping and replace it with this?

"ALRIGHT, SOTO, strip down! Your new lawyer's here."

Each time Alejandro Soto left and entered his cell, he was strip-searched. There were three of them, none of whom he recognized. They were dressed in blue fatigues and were wearing black combat boots. He had been lying on his bunk trying to read but that big nigger had been yapping away with one of the other idiots in the cellblock. When he heard the guards coming, when he was sure that it was more than one guard, he knew they were coming for him. It was early afternoon. His body jerked when he heard "new lawyer." It was her, and there could never be a repeat of Sunday. He was up and out of his bunk seconds after he heard the order. He unzipped his jumpsuit, slipped it off, and stepped out of his shorts. Only then was his cell door unlocked. Two of the guards entered; the third remained stationed at the door.

"OK, arms up." One of the guards ran his hands through the hair in his armpits. "Alright, let's take a look at the mouth. Open wide." The guard rolled his head and his eyes around the outside of his over-stretched mouth. "Christ, you're shivering. It's not that cold in here. What's the matter, afraid we're gonna find something in here?"

Soto looked straight ahead, embarrassed by his trembling. It was her, and he couldn't control it. "OK, let's see the ears. Alright, lift up your balls. OK, turn around, bend over, and spread your cheeks wide open. For Christ's sake, what're you shaking for? You OK?" This time Alejandro nodded, but try as he might, he couldn't stop. "OK, really spread them. I want to get a good look. OK, you can get dressed. Roy, once we get him hooked up and out of here, I want you to give this cell a good searching. The man's real nervous about something."

As soon as Alejandro had zipped up his jumpsuit, he reached for a pocket comb that was lying on the bunk. "Naw, naw, naw," the young guard at the door said, "you don't need to be combing your hair. You're not going on any date, even if your new lawyer is a woman. You're coming right back here after your visit." Alejandro had stopped, bent over in the direction of the comb.

"You want to comb your hair?" the guard next to him said. "Go 'head and comb your hair." Alejandro reached for the comb again, but the moment his hand touched the comb, he began shaking so hard that he left the comb on his bunk. "You don't want to comb your hair? OK, let's go. We got to hook you up."

First the leg irons and then the waist chains and then the cuffs that attached each hand and arm to the waist chains. For the first time ever, Alejandro Soto welcomed the cuffs. They stopped the shaking. Now all he could feel was a quivering, and he didn't think that was noticeable, not under his jumpsuit. He had promised himself that this time there would be no trembling and no tears, that this time he would speak to her like he would to any other person, only more distant and reserved than to any other person. But this visit had taken him by surprise. He had not been expecting her. He had not had time to call up his promises, not until then. As he shuffled toward the young guard at the cell door, the guard said, "Hey, Soto, tell me one thing...how do you rate *two* lawyers? If *I* got picked up on a drunk driving, I probably couldn't afford *one* lawyer."

The young guard was deliberately blocking his path. Soto stopped. The white name tag sewn on his fatigues said Hudson. There was a smirk on his face. "I asked you a question, idiot. How do you rate two lawyers when a working stiff like me couldn't even afford one?" Soto looked at him. It was the bland, blank look he had long since learned to give guards. This one was twenty-four, twenty-five, not much older. Tall, six foot two or three, angular but with a body-builder's girth around his chest and shoulders. He would be a handful. He wore his blond hair in a crew cut but in such a way as to give his head and face the shape of a rectangular block. His blue eyes gleamed with cockiness, and his thin lips were spread and poised for any trouble Soto might want. Soto knew better than to answer. He looked down and away. "Hey spic, I'm talking to you. And when a guard in this jail asks you a question, he wants an answer. We better get that straight right now. Understood?" Each moment of silence brought its own pound of tension.

Jenkins broke it. "Hey Hudson, let the man be. He's chained an' shackled on his way to see his lawyer. He ain't doin' you no harm."

"Fuck you, nigger. Stay out of my business with this greaser if you know what's good for you. Get your ass away from them bars and on your bunk before I come in there and put you on your bunk."

"I jus tryin' to help, man."

"I don't give a good fuck what you were trying to do. You better get your black ass on that bunk like I told you."

"Come on, Huddy, let's go," came a voice just behind and to the right of Soto. Soto turned and saw that it was the older guard, the one he thought was in charge. His name tag said Greene.

"Oh Greenie, so now you're siding with this greaseball and that nigger. Ain't that something. A white, veteran deputy sheriff, who definitely knows better, is siding with brownie and blackie now."

"I ain't siding with nobody, Huddy, and don't even think about trying to guilt trip me, 'cause you can't. Now let's get this show on the road."

Hudson didn't move. Instead he turned to the deputy on Soto's left. "Hey Roy, who's side you on? Mine or the cholo here?"

"Huddy, I ain't on nobody's side. But Greenie's right. Let's get this show on the road."

Then Greene added, "Huddy, Sergeant put me in charge of this detail. If you don't move it, if you don't do as I say, you're not gonna be part of this detail much longer. Now move it. This man's got his lawyer to see and that's all I aim to see happen."

Hudson looked down and took a deep breath and then looked over at Greene defiantly. "OK, Greenie, I hear you. But I just can't believe that it doesn't bother either one of you that we're taking this slimy, good-for-nothing greaseball to meet with his white-woman, court-appointed lawyer. You know who's paying for that, don't you...? We are. Every time we pay our county taxes, we're paying for this shit. And you guys saw her. Not a bad-looking broad. Not that I'd touch her with a ten-foot pole, not that greaser-loving, nigger-loving whore. Bleeding-heart-liberal bitch who gets her rocks off representing these creeps. Probably fucks any one of them on the outside that will let her. That really bothers me...

"Jenkins, I thought I told you to get your big black ass back on your bunk!"

"And I thought I told you to step aside, Huddy!" Greene said. "What you like or don't like, what bothers you or doesn't bother you, I don't give one goddamn bit about. And you, Jenkins, get away from them bars. You're not helping any."

Alejandro saw Hudson's feet shift, and his legs move to one side. They were big feet. Size 13 maybe. He was a big boy but Soto would have relished the chance to go one-on-one with him. It wouldn't be a matter of size. It would be a matter of wills, and he would die before he let Hudson kick his ass. He thought of brushing against Hudson as he shuffled past him. That would set him off, and the other guards would probably pull Hudson off him before he could do much damage. But he thought of her waiting and he didn't want to jeopardize this visit—not be able to make the visit or be so banged up that he would embarrass himself again. So he shuffled slowly past Hudson, staying as far away from him as the cell door would permit. When he reached the corridor and turned, Jenkins's big black face was pressed against and between his cell bars. "Way to go, homey," he said. And for the first time Alejandro Soto let Willie Jenkins mingle in his business.

But not Greene. "Goddamn it, Jenkins, how many times do I

have to tell you to get away from those bars and keep your two cents out of this?" Then he turned and said, "Roy, help me take him down to the interview room. Huddy, stay back and search his cell. The man is too damn nervous about something."

Once Soto passed Jenkins's cell, he felt the shaking again. Shit! How many times had he promised himself that there wouldn't be a repeat? But he was starting to tremble again, even though there was nothing to tremble about. Olsen hadn't lied. And she had said herself that she had come to see him only because Mr. Olsen wanted her to help with the case. She wasn't attracted to him. So why the shaking? What would it take to make him believe that she had not come because he had asked her to come? To ward off the trembling, he began repeating the promise he had made to himself again and again that this time he would not humiliate himself. By the time they reached the interview room, he was calmer. Still, he wished that he had combed his hair.

One of the guards opened the interview room door and turned on the lights. Alejandro was startled by the room's changes. What first caught and held his attention was the chair. The white, plastic chair was gone, and in its place was a dark, heavy, wooden chair with armrests. When he saw the chair a thrust of fear ran through him, and when he looked at the chair's legs and saw that they were bolted to the floor, he panicked. He wasn't going to let them chain him to that chair!

Years before at his first murder trial, the judge had ordered that he be cuffed at his left ankle to a heavy wooden chair bolted down to the courtroom floor. Each morning before the jury was allowed into the courtroom, a cuffed and chained Alejandro, dressed in donated street clothing, was brought out of the holding cell and placed in that brown wooden chair. Then, before the chains and the cuffs were removed, a guard would slip a leg cuff that was attached to the chair onto his ankle under his pant leg. All of this subterfuge was designed to keep the jury from thinking that Alejandro was in custody despite the fact that during the three-week trial the jury never once saw him enter or leave the courtroom.

On the morning when the prosecution's principal witness testified that he had heard gunshots come from his neighbor's apartment and then saw Alejandro run from the Sanchez apartment
with a gun in his hand, Alejandro felt a sudden urge to defecate.
He whispered to his attorney who asked to approach the bench.
In the guarded conversation that followed between the judge and
both counsel, the judge realized that the deputy with the key to
the leg cuff was not in the courtroom. While they attempted to
locate the deputy, Alejandro, still cuffed to his chair, defecated
in the jury's presence. The stench was horrible, and Alejandro's
humiliation was just as bad. Later, one of the jurors said that she
was too ill to continue.

Now at the cubicle's door, Alejandro Soto stiffened. He was
not going to move closer to that chair; he was not going to move
another inch.

"Come on, Soto. Let's not make a production out of this,"
Greene said. "We've heard all about your productions up at the
SHU. You gonna go sit in your chair like a gentleman, or are we
going to have to put you in it like a goon?"

"OK, asshole," the other guard concluded, "we don't mind putting you in your chair." He gave a sharp, shrill whistle and Hudson
came running down the hall.

"No! No! No!" Alejandro protested. But the guards lifted
his squirming body and then dropped and shoved him into the
wooden chair.

"Stop! Stop!" came Barbara Blake's voice from the other side of
the screen. "There's no need for this!"

Alejandro heard her. She was there. She was seeing everything.

"Stay out of this, ma'am! This is no concern of yours!" Greene
said.

"I'm making it my concern!"

"One more word out of you and your visit's going to be terminated!" Hudson shouted. Then they quickly shackled his legs to
the chair's front legs and his chest to the back of the chair and
they were gone.

She could only see an outline of him through the perforated metal but it was enough to see the lifting and slamming down of a body on what had to be a chair. She heard him groan. "Are you alright, Mr. Soto?" She heard the sounds of chains and the closing of a door.

"Mr. Soto, remember me? I was here last Sunday. Barbara Blake's my name. Greg Olsen and I have agreed that the two of us will be working on your case." There was no answer. She dreaded a repeat of last Sunday's silence.

Alejandro heard her words, but he was overcome with anger and shame. They had stripped him of his manhood again. They had done it so many times in the years past that for a long time now he had been telling himself that he didn't care, that it didn't matter. But he always cared, and it always mattered. He would never have wanted anyone to witness it. And now her. He could hear her speaking but the words meant nothing. Then he was aware that she was no longer speaking and there was silence, a painful silence. He knew that he had to speak to her, but he didn't know how to begin or if he could begin.

Then he heard her chair screech and he saw her figure rise and he heard her say, "Well, I best be going."

Words rushed out of him, "Please don't go. Please don't go."

His plea gripped her. She sat down. Now it was she who didn't know where to begin. It would have helped if she could have seen his face, his eyes... Finally, "Mr. Soto, we have to talk."

"I wanna talk."

But so softly that she had to say, "What?"

"I wanna talk." Louder, but just loud enough to be heard.

She cursed the perforated metal screen: she couldn't see him and she couldn't hear him. "Did Mr. Olsen tell you I would be working on your case, too?"

"Yes," he said softly.

"When did you last speak to him?"

"Three days ago."

"You'll have to speak up, Mr. Soto."

He saw her stand. He had begged her to stay. It had been a weak, whiny plea that had squirted out of him. Self-loathing had mired him. Yet, he groveled again, "I wanna talk." He was so shamelessly afraid that she would leave.

"We have to talk."

"Yes, ma'am."

"Mr. Olsen and I worked together for eight years. We're still close friends. We work well together. We talked about your case for several days before I decided to join him, mainly because we're both convinced that the district attorney has a very weak case or no case at all against you."

"Yes, ma'am." All that silly shit about his kites and her being attracted to him burned in him again.

"What?" She couldn't see or hear him. That damn metal screen had to go.

"Yes, ma'am." Louder this time.

"This metal screen's got to go." She was angry now. "I can't see you or hear you. You're chained, aren't you?"

"Yes, ma'am."

"Please, Mr. Soto, my name is Barbara Blake. We're going to be working together for a long time. You can call me Barbara and I'll call you Alejandro, OK?"

"Yes, ma'am"

"What are you chained to?"

"The chair."

"Your body?"

"Yes ma'am and my legs, too."

"That will change. I promise you, Mr. Soto...I mean Alejandro.

"You know that you are now charged with the death penalty?"

"Yes, ma'am."

"What? No, no, don't bother. Just listen to me. I promise you it won't be like this the next time I see you. In a death penalty case, you first have a trial to decide whether you killed this Santos Estrada. I will be your lawyer in that trial. If the jury decides that after thinking and planning to kill Estrada, you killed him, then you will have a second trial in which the jury will decide whether you should be executed in prison. Mr. Soto...Alejandro...did you hear me? Can you hear me?

"Oh, this is ridiculous. I'll be back in a few days. But it won't be under these circumstances."

Glum and angry, Barbara rode down the jail elevator. She thought of complaining to the jail commander about the metal screen and the chains and the lack of a slit to pass legal papers, but Greg was lead counsel and he should at least be present at such a confrontation. She drove to Greg's office.

ANGRY, BLAMING, she said to Greg, "Why didn't you tell me about the changes they'd made in the visiting room?"

"What changes? I don't know about any changes."

She described the changes and concluded with, "And what are you going to do about it, Mr. Lead Counsel?"

Greg Olsen thought for a while and then said, "I don't think there's much either you or I can do about it. He's as big a fish as our county has seen. Double lifer without the possibility of parole facing a death penalty charge here. I can just hear ol' Spencer now: 'Well counsel, under the circumstances, I believe these changes are reasonable and warranted. And as I've said before, I'm not about to start telling the sheriff how to run his jail.' "

"Well then, let's bring a motion. Let's get the media involved. Even they might be opposed to these medieval conditions. At least the legal community will be appalled by them. The federal courts won't tolerate it. Let's go there if we have to."

HAROLD SPENCER and Dave Roberts had been friends for more than twenty years. They met when Spencer was a young deputy district attorney and Roberts was a young deputy sheriff working undercover in the narcotics unit. Roberts had first come to Spencer seeking search warrants in relatively small narcotics cases. As their experience increased, the importance and complexity of the search warrants grew as well. The initial respect and admiration they had for each other continued to grow, and before long their families began seeing each other socially. Parties and social gatherings at the Spencer home always included the Roberts family, and parties and social gatherings at the Roberts home always included the Spencers, breaking an unspoken class line between deputy district attorneys and law enforcement officers. Together they rose in their careers. When Harold Spencer was appointed to the bench, Captain Roberts was the principal speaker at his investiture. When Dave Roberts was elected Sheriff of San Cristobal County, Judge Spencer was the principal speaker at his swearing-in ceremony.

When Judge Spencer walked into Sheriff Roberts's office late that Monday morning, Cathy Wallace, the sheriff's long-time secretary, looked up and beamed, "Good morning, Your Honor. The sheriff's just down the hall. Why don't you have a seat in his office and I'll go down and get him."

"How in the hell are you, Hal?" Dave Roberts smiled from his doorway. It had been months since the two had seen each other. Their handshakes were vigorous, their smiles warm, and Dave Roberts patted Harold Spencer on the shoulder. "I'm alright, Dave, I'm alright. How's it going with you?"

"Oh, I can't complain. Wouldn't do much good if I did, now would it?"

The two men smiled again softly, letting those smiles finish the greeting.

"And what, might I ask, brings Your Honor over to these humble quarters?" Dave Roberts said, seating himself.

"Dave, we got a problem."

"Well, what else is new? But then I'd rather hear your problem than most other folks'. What's the problem, Hal?"

"It's about that guy, Soto. You know the one, the double lifer that the Dos Palos DA convinced our fearless DA he ought to be trying over here on a ten-year-old homicide?"

"Not that guy again. God, will I be happy when you guys can

finally try him and convict him and send him back on his way to Arroyo Grande where he belongs. He's raising hell with my budget. Every time he sets foot out of his cage—not to mention the special visiting room we had to build for him—but every time that man leaves his cell, it seems like I have to deploy twenty of my men to babysit him. Please try him as soon as you can, Hal, and get him out of my hair."

"Believe me, Dave, I do empathize. He's no fun for us either. Every time he steps into my courtroom, the security in there looks like I'm about to start the Nuremberg trials." He paused and then began again. "More to the point, since it's a death penalty case, I've had to appoint two lawyers to represent him. I'm sure you know them both, Greg Olsen and Barbara Blake. Good competent lawyers. Not bleeding-heart liberals or radical defense attorneys. Well, this morning Olsen comes to me and talks to me privately in chambers. He says that Friday, Blake tried to visit with Soto up in the jail but that your men have him so well barricaded in the visiting room that she had a hell of a time communicating with him. Something about a perforated sheet of metal replacing the regular glass panel and the phone being gone. And he's being chained to his chair with no way to pass or receive papers from his lawyers or to write anything. She apparently couldn't see him or hear him, and he couldn't move with all those chains on him. Olsen says he visited three times before the changes in that room were made and had no trouble communicating. He'd like to have it returned to the way it was, which doesn't sound too unreasonable. Olsen doesn't want to have to bring a motion in open court to restore the condition of that visiting room to what it was, but he says he will if the situation doesn't change. If it's as bad as he says it is, I would probably have to grant the motion, which is the last thing I want to do. I'd hate to give that damn media an excuse to start running at the mouth about what a soft-headed liberal I've become and how I'm endangering the safety of the community. Besides, any conviction we get is worthless if an appellate court finds Soto couldn't effectively communicate with his counsel. I'm sure you'll agree that the last thing we want is to have this case sent back to us to be retried."

"So what do you want me to do about it, Hal?"

"Just look into it, Dave, with an eye toward what the law says: that any defendant, no matter how heinous he might be, has the right to effectively communicate with his counsel."

IX

THE ENVELOPE WAS NO MORE than a foot from Alejandro's eyes. It seemed as if he had been looking at it for hours. The edges closest to him were darkened by moisture. The trustee must have tossed it into his cell as he was exercising, and it had to have landed on the edge of the pool of saliva, sweat, and mucous that was still on the floor. He looked at it for a while more, his body and face still prostrate on the concrete. He stared at the envelope. There was nothing to stir for, nothing to move for. It was another one of Solomon's envelopes. Slowly he realized that this was not the kind of envelope he always received. Solomon's envelopes were bigger, whiter, more formal looking. This envelope looked like one of the few envelopes Julia had sent him years ago. He reached for the envelope and turned it faceup. There was handwriting on the envelope. A jolt of hope flashed through him—Julia—and just as quickly disappeared when he saw in the upper left-hand corner that Arcelia Munoz was the sender.

Alejandro Soto was the oldest of five children, and Arcelia Munoz was the youngest. Only seven years separated the three brothers and two sisters. Alejandro had always been Esperanza Soto's favorite child. There had never been any doubt about that. When their father, Domingo Soto, was killed, Alejandro at thirteen became the man of the house. Later, his constant problems with girls, women, drugs, and the law caused Esperanza heartache after heartache. Still, theirs was a very special mother–son relationship and Esperanza always stood steadfastly by her son, to the embitterment of her other children. Yet only Arcelia spoke out against Alejandro. The others were afraid of him. The older the other four became, the less they had to do with him. As time went on they saw Alejandro only occasionally at family gatherings initiated by Esperanza, and then saying little more than hello and goodbye to him and his mocking eyes. Only Arcelia challenged Alejandro's sneering looks, and several times she had to be pulled away from him by the others for fear that he would badly beat her. Alejandro was in jail when Esperanza died and, except for the letter he was holding, none of his siblings had ever had any contact with him there.

With a tired motion Alejandro got up off the cell floor, sat on his bunk with his back against the wall, covered himself with his blanket, and began to read.

Ale: Well, I've got to hand it to you. You finally made the big time. Just like you always wanted. Just like I always knew you would. You were on the front page of yesterday's paper. The headlines said: LOCAL KILLER TO FACE DEATH PENALTY CHARGES. Under the headlines was your big prison picture. You looked awful. But, congratulations anyway. You don't know how happy I am for you. I can't tell you how proud you've made the family. Our big brother finally hit the jackpot.

But before you go to the chair, I just wanted to make one thing clear. So that you can take it to hell with you when you go, so that you can burn in it down there too. You killed Mama! You killed her just like you killed all the others you're going to the chair for. You know it. I know it. Everybody knows it. But no one's ever said it. And since I'm the only one that's not afraid of your phony, bullshit act, I guess it's up to me to say it. You killed Mama! Don't ever forget it. You killed Mama! Don't ever try to run away from it, because you can't. You killed Mama!

She was a good woman. The only fault she ever had was that she loved you. The only sin she ever committed was that she loved you too much. But why am I wasting my time. You've never known what love is and you never will. You're just a cold, ruthless, blood-sucking animal who's taken advantage of too many stupid women all of your life. But Mama wasn't stupid. She *had* to love you. You were her firstborn. Animals like you belong in the gas chamber.

And while you're burning in hell, I hope that the devil and all his little helpers pile on extra logs so that you burn real hot, not just for Mama and the others you've killed, but for all the women you put out on the streets, for all the women you made into whores. Don't think I don't know about that too, because I do. I've known for years. You know Julia and me have become really good friends. She's told me about what you did to her, how you finally put her on the street, too. She's told me how in all those years she was with you, you never once told her you loved her. She's told me she begged you to tell her you loved her, but you never would. But don't worry, Julia's happy now. She's got a *real* man now, not a bullshit macho piece of shit. She's got a *real* man now who works and supports *her* and who has given her two beautiful babies. And who, yes, loves her.

Goodbye, brother dear. Believe it or not, I will be coming up to see you. They tell me that when they execute murderers, family members can go. I plan on making my reservation when they set the date and getting my ticket as soon as they're printed. So I can come up and watch and wave and laugh. So I can come up and watch you die.

Hating you, Arcelia.

Alejandro Soto read the letter again and again, turning from it at times to stare into the past, stunned and angry. Then attempting to refute it line by line. Then simply staring into the past.

ESPERANZA SOTO was a small, delicate, beautiful woman who remained so until the last day he saw her. She had a perfectly proportioned face. A fine nose and full lips. Arched eyebrows that gave her brown eyes almost an arrogance. A smooth high forehead and a delicate chin. There was a softness and gentleness in her face that Alejandro always thought was reserved only for him.

She wore plain, ankle-length cotton dresses year-round, perhaps to hide her deformity, but surely to make it easier to move about on her crippled right leg. She could walk but a few feet without pain. She had stationed chairs and stools throughout the house so she could rest at the end of her brief journeys. In the kitchen there were chairs on either side of the table, a stool at the stove, a stool at the sink, and a stool at a work space between the refrigerator and the stove. She seldom left her house. If she did and went beyond her yard, she would have to be taken by car.

Esperanza told everyone that the crippling resulted from a fall one night off the high, steep, back porch steps. But Alejandro knew better. He couldn't have been more than four years old when it happened. Angela and Enrique were already asleep and Mama was putting him to bed by telling him stories about her childhood in Mexico when Papa came home. He was drunk, and when he was drunk he was mean and scary. *"Vieja!"* he shouted from the front doorway. *"Tengo hambre! Donde esta mi pinche comida!"* Alejandro started to cry, and his mother calmed him and told him she was going to the kitchen to serve his father his dinner and that she would be right back. As she left the room, there were the sounds of shattering glass in the kitchen, the clanging of pans and utensils, and then a loud BAM! And Domingo Soto's ranting began again. *"Aqui yo mando! Aqui yo mando!"* The boy was familiar with his ranting. "Here I rule! Here I rule! All day long I work like an animal on that fucking railroad track. Pick and shovel. Carrying track and ties like a donkey in that blazing sun. Yes, sir. No, sir. Where shall I put this, sir? Is this how you want it, sir? Well, here I'm the boss! Here I'm the sir! This is my house. I pay for everything here. *Aqui yo mando!"* There was a moment of silence. Then he heard his father say, "What did you say?" And then again, much louder, "I said, what did you say?" And the beating began. He knew the sounds. He had heard them too many times before. The splattering of flesh on flesh, the muted and stifled cries of his mother, the thuds of his father's work boots on her body.

The boy ran to the hall just as his mother staggered up from the floor and broke into a run toward the back porch. But his father caught her at the kitchen door, hit her several times, and then threw her against the cement washtrays in the back porch, where she crumpled to the floor. "You wanted to run out of the house, did you?" his father growled. "Well here, let me help you." Domingo Soto picked up the boy's mother off the floor, dragged her to the back porch door, raised her, and then kicked her out and down the back porch steps.

Esperanza Soto was in bed for two weeks after the beating. Fabela, a neighbor woman, took care of her and Alejandro, who was also in bed for several days, with a "fever" they said. When Esperanza Soto got out of bed, she hobbled for the first time, as she would for the rest of her life.

Before that beating Esperanza Soto and Alejandro had been very close. "He's my firstborn," she would explain. After the crippling, they became even closer. Now he was more than her firstborn. Someday, she knew, he would be her redeemer. For the next nine years, consciously or unconsciously, she prepared him for that redemption.

It was when she saw her crooked leg for the first time and felt the pain of walking for the first time that she adopted a stoical look. Now she was a crippled woman with three small children, an illegal alien in a country whose language she did not speak. She was the wife of a miserable, brutal man who tried to blot out his misery with alcohol. "No, Domingo," she would say gently, "let me warm you some more tortillas, Domingo." And she would hobble quietly to the stove.

Not once did Domingo Soto mention that horrific beating or her crippled condition. It was as if she had been hobbling on the first day he met her. But he was well aware of what he had done, an awareness that had a prominence in his stockpile of horrors. He showed that awareness in his subsequent drunken beatings and attempted beatings of his crippled wife, beatings that were about to happen but never did, or beatings that did occur but only briefly. Because Esperanza quickly learned that once Domingo hit her or was about to hit her, she had only to hobble a step or two and a look of terror would appear on Domingo's drunken face and he would stop.

Esperanza Soto bore her husband two more children, Roberto and Arcelia, the products of tear-stained nights when she lay with her legs widespread, but never wide enough to keep her crippled right leg from touching her husband's naked hip. Those births did nothing to displace Alejandro's position in her heart. With the possible exception of Arcelia, none of the other children had Alejandro's strength of character. And he was growing by leaps and bounds. Some day soon, he would be a very big man.

Esperanza's partiality for Alejandro did not escape the other children. Their cries of favoritism started early and plagued Esperanza for the rest of her life.

"How come Alejandro gets more meat than we do?"

"Because he's bigger and he's growing fast and he needs more meat."

"How come Alejandro always gets new school clothes and we don't?"

"Because he's the oldest and there are no hand-me-downs for him."

"But Margarita's the oldest girl and there's no hand-me-downs for her, but you still buy her clothes at the thrift store."

"That's because girls' clothes cost a lot more than boys'."

"How come Alejandro gets to go out and be with his friends after dinner and we don't?"

"Because he's older."

"Margarita's eleven and you don't let her, but you let Alejandro when he was eleven."

"Yes, but she's a girl."

But it was always Arcelia who minced no words. "Mama, how come you like Alejandro more than the rest of us?"

"Oh, sweetheart, that's just not true. Every mother loves all of her children the same."

Even as she spoke them, Esperanza knew that those words were not true. She loved Alejandro more than she loved the others; she loved him as she had never loved anyone. She couldn't explain it. It simply was. He had only to enter the room and she would feel a rush of happiness, and her spirits would rise from wherever they had been. He had always been a good boy, a boy whose few misdeeds always had reasons or explanations. For years he had helped her with everything around the house. She could always depend on him. If he hadn't anticipated a need, she had only to ask and he would be there. At twelve, he was far taller and stronger than she was and even an inch taller than his father. And, there was nothing he couldn't do around the house. It was almost as if she had another man in the house, but one who helped her instead of terrorizing her.

For Alejandro it was always the gentleness and softness of his mother's hand as she stroked his hair while she told him bedtime stories about growing up in Mexico. She told him those stories for years. He begged for the stories, all of which he had heard over and over again. It was not the stories he wanted but rather the closeness, the gentleness, the warmth. It was from those moments that

Alejandro's lifelong love and trust for his mother sprang. As a boy, he told her everything. Later, as he became involved with women and drugs, there were things that he couldn't and didn't tell her, but, even then, he always felt that he could confide in her and trust her regardless of what the situation might be.

The deep respect and admiration Alejandro had for his mother were rooted in the way she kept their family together despite her crippled body; the way she hobbled in the kitchen to cook their meals; the way she washed their clothes and cleaned their house; and the way she acted as mother, father, and arbiter in their disputes and problems. They were rooted, too, in that stoical look of hers that was a reflection of the way she dealt with more than her share of life's adversities and daily coped with a brute husband, yet never whined and complained rather simply endured.

On the other hand, Alejandro Soto hated his father even before the crippling. Even then, he had dreaded the thought of his father coming home while he was still awake. Even then, he had hated his loud voice and his foul words and that sour-sweet smell of cheap wine. After the beating, his hatred increased tenfold, and with the increase came a resolve for revenge. He took to avoiding his father and, when he had to speak to him, it was usually to give an eye-averting, whispery, *"si, Papa"* or *"no, Papa."* In the days following the beating, as Alejandro lay in bed with his "fever," Domingo Soto twice came to his bedside and asked, "How are you, Ale?" Each time the boy kept his eyes down and didn't answer. And each time Fabela, the neighbor lady, said, *"Es la fiebre, Domingo, es la fiebre."* But both the father and his son knew the boy's silence had nothing to do with his "fever."

Often the boy would say to his mother, "I hate him, Mama, I hate him." And always Esperanza Soto would answer, "You mustn't hate your father, *mijo,* you mustn't hate him. He's your father." But the words and the voice were always so weak, so tentative, that the boy heard them to say, "Hate him, my son, hate him."

One day when Alejandro was twelve, the thought occurred to him that Domingo Soto had inserted his penis into his mother's

148

vagina. The thought taunted him. It mortified him. He turned from it. He ran from it. But he had only to look at himself and his siblings for irrefutable, living proof of five such acts. For weeks, it wouldn't go away. He dreamt of it. He couldn't believe it. He wouldn't believe it. There was no way that his mother could have let that pig! Yet he had only to look in the mirror. Worse, after the beating there had been Roberto and Arcelia. He wanted to ask his mother how? Why? How could she have? But he couldn't and didn't and finally concluded, or rather his mind let him conclude, that Domingo Soto had forced his mother each and every time out of fear of more beatings.

After Alejandro had his first sex at thirteen, the torment returned. But now it had to do with the reality of the act, the positioning of the bodies, the awful, complete, physical domination of Domingo Soto over his mother. The need for legs to be opened or spread opened by the hulk of the man unless...she was willing. The horrible, smelly, collapsed body of Domingo Soto atop his mother after he had climaxed. No, his mother never could have acquiesced to that, especially after the beating. Was he still doing it? Of course he was. Would the pig ever stop? Only if someone made him stop.

So Alejandro Soto, who was now four inches taller than his father but much thinner, began lifting weights. The weights belonged to Eddie Ramirez, who had just been released from prison and who now went by the moniker, "Physical Ed," and was now unrecognizable in the barrio because of his immense bulk. Several of the barrio boys had watched Physical Ed go through his afternoon routine in the Ramirez backyard and then they tried their hands at it. After two weeks, Physical Ed solemnly announced that only Ale had what it takes to be a true bodybuilder. Only Ale had the heart, the will, the desire, the discipline to be all that he could be. Thereafter, it was only Physical Ed and Ale who were allowed to touch the weights in the afternoon. Week by week, Alejandro Soto could feel and then see himself getting bigger and stronger.

Soon he wasn't the only one who noticed it. Domingo Soto

noticed it, too. "What are you feeding that boy?" he asked his wife.

"What I always feed him and you and his brothers and sisters. Rice and beans, and meat when you give me enough money." But Esperanza Soto had noticed it, too, and she had asked Ale and he told her about the weights. "That's good, *mijo,* that's good. You should keep it up. You should keep it up." And she began cooking an extra, secret meal each day after Domingo left for work, a special meal of meat and eggs and potatoes that Alejandro ate before the others were up. And then, to avoid suspicion and because he was still hungry, he would sit with the others and have his share of hot cereal and toast and *canela.*

But after a while, Esperanza Soto worried that she might have gone too far with her special meals for Alejandro.

"How come we don't hardly ever have meat anymore? I'm real tired of beans and tortilla tacos," Domingo said.

"Because meat's so expensive these days. Ask Fabela. She takes me. If you give me more money for food, we'll have meat."

The others complained as well. "We have boiled beans, refried beans, beans in chili. Can't we ever have some meat?"

Esperanza Soto paid little attention to their complaints, telling Alejandro privately, "Don't listen to them, *mijo,* they're alright. You have to keep up with your training. It's important, *mijo,* it's important."

Domingo grumbled, "That boy's getting to be as big as this house."

"All my brothers in Mexico are real big men."

"I didn't know that."

"I never told you that."

Now it seemed that Domingo Soto was not as loud and abusive with his mouth when he came home drunk at night, and it had been weeks since he had bullied or laid a hand on his wife.

After four months, Alejandro was ready. He moved his bed as close as he could to the hallway door without raising any suspicion and allowing the best listening position. He didn't know what he would do if his father closed his parents' bedroom door, but he could not remember him ever doing that. His father was usually snoring by the time his mother got into bed, but Alejandro was now convinced that was just a ruse he used until he was certain that all the kids were asleep. The first night Domingo Soto snored deep into the night, or at least until Alejandro could no longer stay awake. The second and third nights were more of the same, and Alejandro was very sleepy by the fourth day, so much so that Domingo remarked, "You've been yawning and yawning. You look real tired. What's the matter, aren't you getting enough sleep?"

After the first week, Alejandro had nothing to show for his vigilance except loss of sleep. Now he was convinced that his father slept for a while and then woke and did it in the middle of the night. He was trying to devise some way of waking himself in the middle of the night without waking anyone else when his mother warned him. "Be careful, *mijo,* you've looked so tired and sleepy lately that I think your father thinks you're sneaking out of the house at night to do some dirty thing. I hope you're not doing that because you know him. He'll stay awake all night trying to catch you."

There had been times when Alejandro had been able to wake himself early by simply reminding himself the night before that he had to get up early. Then one night before he went to sleep, Alejandro repeatedly told himself that he had to wake at two o'clock in the morning, and sometime during the middle of the night he did jolt out of sleep. To his satisfaction, his father was not snoring. He had to be awake. He listened and waited. Then he heard his parents' bedsprings creak. He tensed. The bastard was not going to get away with it this time. But the creaking stopped. He waited, certain that the creaking would begin again. When it did, it was louder and longer, and Alejandro started getting out of bed when it stopped. Then he heard someone coming quietly down the hall. It had to be his father. Quickly but carefully he lay back down on the bed and covered himself. Then the smell and breathing of his father was in the doorway. Alejandro stiffened. Slowly, quietly, Domingo moved toward Alejandro's bed and then gently felt about the bed and along the contours of his body. Satisfied, he left. Then came the creaking of bedsprings again. But then they stopped and within minutes there was snoring.

PHYSICAL ED was annoyed. "What's up with you, youngster? Instead of improving, you're fading. Whadaya got, a night job or some young thing you're hitting on? You better get some rest, boy. I don't need no partner that can't keep his end up."

Alejandro was exhausted and frustrated. He had fallen asleep in class and the teacher had sent a note home saying that he needed more sleep. But the thought of Domingo Soto on top of his mother haunted him, and he was determined to never let it happen again. Still, that night he fell asleep even before his father came home, and the next morning he almost missed his special meal because his mother couldn't wake him.

The next night, after another long, frustrating day, Alejandro was in his room thinking of ways to stop his father when, sometime after eight o'clock, Domingo opened the front door and stumbled into the house as drunk as he could be and mumbling gibberish to himself. The three brothers looked at each other. There were fear and alarm in the eyes of the younger two. Esperanza quickly limped out of her bedroom, hobbled down the hall to the kitchen, and began rewarming her husband's dinner. Domingo Soto fell down hard on the front room floor and for a long while lay there cursing and condemning Esperanza for not having his dinner ready. Then he was up, staggering toward the kitchen, muttering and cursing. Margarita and Arcelia watched, the whites of their eyes exaggerated with fear. Then Domingo was in the living room holding onto the chairs and table as he wobbled toward the kitchen. *"Esperanza! Donde esta mi pinche cena?"* he said, slobbering over and over again. Then he was in the kitchen bumping against Esperanza, backing her into a corner, and she had her head down trying to avoid the spit and mucous that his sputtering words were carrying. When Esperanza's back was against the wall, Domingo grabbed at her neck and she cried, "No, no!"

From behind, with both his hands on Domingo's shoulders,

Alejandro tore Domingo from his mother and flung him against the sink. Domingo slammed into the sink with a loud thud and then sank to the floor. Alejandro jumped on top of his father and punched the drunken man's face again and again shouting, "You motherfucker! Don't you ever touch my mother again! Hear me, motherfucker? Don't you ever touch my mother again!" The splatter of flesh striking flesh rang out in the kitchen. Soon there was blood, and his brothers and sisters were crying, "Stop, Alejandro! Stop!" while Esparanza looked on in shock.

Winded and momentarily out of breath, Alejandro got up off his bleeding, motionless father and for a moment stood staring down at the unconscious man. Then a new wave of rage came, and Alejandro started kicking his fallen father, screaming, "Get up, you motherfucker! Get up!" And when the beaten lump of a man wouldn't move, Alejandro took him by the legs and dragged him to the back porch and there picked up the crumpled man as he shouted, "I said get up, you motherfucker! Get up!" And when he had all but Domingo's feet off the ground he threw his inert body against the cement washtrays and for the first time a groan came from Domingo as he crashed and crumpled once again to the floor. But Alejandro wasn't finished. "Get up, motherfucker! Get up!" And when that human lump refused to move once again, Alejandro dragged him to the back porch door, picked up the bleeding pulp of a man, and threw him out and down the high back porch stairs. From the back porch door, Alejandro yelled at the motionless mass, "Motherfucker, don't you ever set foot in this house again! If you do, I'll kill you!"

That night and for the five succeeding nights, Alejandro Soto slept on the floor next to his mother's bed waiting, hoping, daring his father to enter their house again.

IN FACT, Domingo Soto never set foot in that house again. Five days later he was crushed by a speeding locomotive while he was riding on a tiny, track handcart. It was never clear how the speeding train and the slow-moving handcart got on the same track.

Some of Domingo Soto's fellow workers thought he might have been drinking. But there was never any satisfactory explanation for the collision, and the railroad company brought the matter to a quick conclusion by awarding Esperanza Soto a lifetime pension.

WHEN ALEJANDRO Soto stopped reading Arcelia's letter, when he stopped looking into the past, he thought to himself: *I never did tell Julia that I loved her, I never did.*

X

"**I**'M NOT GOING UP THERE AGAIN
until they change that goddamn torture chamber so that I can effectively communicate with my client!"

It was late Friday afternoon of the following week. Barbara had gone to the jail to visit Alejandro Soto under the assumption that the murder max visiting room had been returned to its original state. Greg had said as much. But when she and the deck officer reached the door to the attorney's side of the cubicle, her breath caught. It was pitch black in the cubicle, just as it had been on the previous Friday. As soon as the deputy unlocked the door, she reached in and turned on the light switch and her lungs filled with anger. The room was exactly as she had left it the week before. She turned and walked hurriedly to the elevator.

"Hey, where you going, counselor? They're gonna pull your client!" the deck officer shouted.

Without stopping, without turning, she said, "You and they can do whatever you want! I'm out of here!" Then she drove to Greg's office.

"CALM DOWN, Barb," Greg said when he saw her.

"Calm down, my butt! I thought you told me this thing was taken care of!"

"What I told you was that Judge Spencer said he'd take care of it."

"Well he hasn't, and another week's gone by and I still haven't been able to talk to my client!"

"*Our* client."

"Well start acting like it then!" She saw the sting in his flinch but didn't care. "When's the last time you saw him?" She still didn't care. "So when did you last go up to the jail, Greg, to see *our* client?" Taunting and knowing she was taunting.

"For your information I was up there last Saturday. I saw those ridiculous changes. I talked to Judge Spencer first thing Monday morning. Told him we'd have to file a motion if changes weren't made, and he said he'd take care of it."

"Well he hasn't!"

"Apparently not."

"So let's file the motion."

"Calm down, Barb."

"What are you afraid of, Greg?"

His face reddened. "Afraid?"

"Yes, afraid. There's absolutely no reason why we shouldn't file that motion. No court other than this one would deny it. I'll file it under my name. I'll argue it. I'll take whatever flack or fallout comes from it."

Greg Olsen took a deep breath and looked away. There was nothing to be gained by working himself up to her pitch. She hadn't looked away. She was challenging him. He didn't like it.

"Look Barb," he began calmly, "you're missing the big picture here. This is a big case. It could go on for years. We're going to

156

appear before Judge Spencer on a lot of matters before we get to trial. His decisions on those matters could really affect the outcome of this case. Now he pretty clearly indicated to me on Monday he'd rather we not go public on this and that he would take care of it. Why ruffle his feathers so early on with a relatively unimportant issue?"

"Relatively unimportant! Wake up, Mr. Olsen! This is a death penalty case and I can't communicate with my client! How much more important can anything else be? Get real, Greg!" She could see him flushing even more, but it didn't matter. "Any appellate court would say that this is a violation of Soto's right to counsel. Even Spencer knows that. I for one am not going to wait around for weeks to talk to my client—our client—until Spencer gets to the task, if ever. I'll tell you what, Mr. Olsen, over the weekend, I'm going to draft *my* motion to effectuate *my* client's right to counsel under *my* name and signature, and if that cubicle hasn't been changed by Monday, I'm filing *my* motion on Tuesday. And if you and your patron Judge Spencer don't like it, you can get rid of me. Not being able to see, hear, or talk to my client in a death penalty case is just plain bullshit!" Then she turned and left.

GREG OLSEN caught up with Judge Spencer as he was leaving the courthouse for the weekend. "Judge, can I have a few words with you please?"

"What is it, Greg?"

"Judge, on the Soto matter... We were up to see our client in the jail this afternoon and nothing's changed. We weren't able to communicate with him. We're into our second week now of not being able to communicate with our client. I know what your feeling is on the matter, Your Honor, but if something isn't done soon, we're going to have to file a—"

"There've been no changes in the visiting room?"

"No, sir."

"You're sure of that?"

"Yes, sir."

"Well, there will be very shortly."

By mid-afternoon on Monday, county workers were busily re-vamping the conditions in the murder max visiting cubicles.

MEANWHILE, ALEJANDRO Soto had returned to his motto: Do the time; don't let the time do you. He had lived by that maxim for years. It was only when Barbara Blake had entered the picture, or he thought she had entered *his* picture, that he lost sight of that. And he had paid dearly for it, suffered humiliations that could have been the end of him had they continued. Thankfully, that had been for a span of only two and a half weeks. Now he was back to his old routine. Five o'clock breakfast. Stretching for half an hour. Then a two-hour workout followed by a "bird bath" using the tiny sink in his cell. Next came a cleaning of his cell, particularly the toilet and the sweat-stained floor, using his single towel or T-shirt as a mop which, along with his underwear, he then scrubbed with a sliver of soap in the little sink, rinsed them, wrung them out, and hung them to dry on his cell bars. Then he read until lunch from the new supply of books that Fred Solomon sent him: a novel, a history, and a biography. After lunch he walked for thirty minutes in that eight-by-ten cell, six paces in one direction, return six paces, back six paces, counting as he went to gauge the full thirty minutes. Next came *Webster's College Dictionary* and twenty-five new words that he was committing to memory. Then he took a nap that ran anywhere from half an hour to an hour, followed by more stretching and more reading until dinner. There was a single television set mounted high on the opposing corridor wall in the center of the cellblock. The set was on whenever the block's lights were on, and no one ever challenged Soto's "right" to watch an hour of national and local evening news and an hour more of whatever program he chose, if he chose, after that. Then, there was some brisk, brief stretching and some limbering exercises. Reading until the lights went out at nine o'clock concluded his day.

That regimen had kept him sane and healthy for more than

eight years, and it would continue to do so until he was either physically unable or he died. For two and a half weeks, he had lived with the pain and despair of a single intrusion. He had been a pathetic idiot to even think that someone as beautiful and intelligent and talented as one of his lawyers was physically and romantically interested in him. She had no such interest in him, that was now crystal clear. So now there was no need for all those frantic promises never to humiliate himself again when she visited— because it would not happen again. Whether she came alone or with Olsen, it would not happen again. Of this he was certain.

Willie Jenkins still nibbled at being an intrusion with his questions and comments, but less so as day by day Soto simply ignored him. Not even Deputy Hudson could cause Soto more than a passing sneer. Since Barbara Blake's last visit with him, Hudson had taken it upon himself to appear at Soto's cell in his fatigues and combat boots at different times of the day or night, though not every day, and would simply stand there for a moment or two, sometimes saying, "Just checking on you, Soto," but most times saying nothing at all. And when he was certain that Soto had seen him, he would turn and leave. But Soto had dealt with Sanders for years and next to him, Hudson was nothing but a punk kid.

Ten days after Barbara Blake's visit, he heard the banging and the drilling and the thumping begin down at the other end of the cellblock. Maybe the lawyers would be coming soon or, then again, maybe not.

The banging stopped on Wednesday. Late Thursday afternoon, he heard three guards at the cellblock door. Maybe it *was* the lawyers. Almost as he thought it, an inmate near the door shouted, "Hey, Soto, your lawyer's here!"

Jenkins chimed in, "Damn, you sure popular, homey, three visits in less than two weeks, an I ain't even seen my lawyer once in three." Alejandro Soto sat up in his bunk, shifted to its edge, stared at the opposite wall, and began readying himself. He didn't know which one it was. That didn't matter.

The guards no sooner passed Jenkins when Deputy Hudson

announced loudly, "Hey Soto, your white whore lawyer's here. Get ready, greaser."

Jenkins didn't like it. "Hey Hudson, that ain't no way be talkin' bout a man's lawyer."

"Yeah," two inmates down the line agreed.

"That's rank, Hudson."

"Cold shot, Hudson. Uncool."

Deputy Greene bellowed out, "Alright, everybody knock it off! And that includes you, Hudson! You start up like that again, and you're off this detail!" Hudson smirked and looked away. "OK, let's get on with it!" Greene ended.

Soto was already standing naked with his back to the bars. All of their chatter had meant nothing to him. He was welcoming a chance to meet with her a third time. When the strip search was completed and the chains were in place, he turned and saw Hudson standing tall and wide in the cell doorway. Soto shuffled toward him and then stopped. Hudson looked him up and down, let out a "huh!" and then stepped aside. As Alejandro Soto shuffled down the corridor, he recalled his trembling of two weeks past and thought, "How stupid."

It HAD been nearly two weeks since Barbara had agreed to represent Alejandro Soto and she had yet to have a conversation with him. When she went to the jail to visit him on Thursday afternoon, she didn't know what to expect, and she was surprised by what she saw.

From the moment the door opened and one of the guards stepped aside, he was in complete control of himself. He looked at her from a distance of five feet before he began his shuffle to the white chair. He nodded slightly, a look of recognition, of acknowledgment.

There was nothing diffident or awestruck in that look. He was the tall, physically fit Mexican she had first seen in Judge Spencer's court some three or four weeks before. But at this closer range...much better-looking. He stood erect and moved with confidence and purpose. He sat down and one of the guards handed him the receiver from the wall phone. The guards left and for a moment there was an odd silence before Barbara said, "How are you Alejandro?"

"I'm fine."

His words were clear and his eye contact direct, which again surprised and impressed her. After some small talk and background information Barbara went to the heart of the matter. "Alejandro, I'd like to talk about your relationship with Santos Estrada. Before his death, how long had you known him?"

"I didn't know him. Never met the man in my life."

"You were never with him?"

"No."

"Never talked to him? Over the phone even?"

"No."

His eye contact was unswerving, not a flinch, remarkably open. He seemed convincing. "Then tell me what you know about the Santos Estrada killing."

He first flatly admitted killing Carlos Sanchez and his mother without making any attempt to excuse or explain those acts. Then he told of his relationship with Johnny Moncado. He went into considerable detail regarding the reward that Estrada had put on his head and the problems it caused him on the streets. He told in specifics how Moncado had conceived and put into operation his scheme to collect half the reward money without killing or turning Soto over to Estrada. He reiterated clearly and concisely what Moncado had told him about the shooting of Estrada. She took notes where she thought she might find inconsistencies or where she thought anyone creating a set of facts would have difficulty in recalling and retelling it in a like manner a second time around. When Alejandro finished, she questioned him, in fact cross-examined him, about the afternoon with Moncada at Estrada's home. Alejandro held up well and was every bit as good in his second recounting as he was in the first. He certainly seemed to be telling the truth, and the more she weighed everything he said, the more convinced she became that he *was* telling the truth. Equally impressive was how he told the story. He had a quiet, matter-of-fact style about him. He was firm without being forceful, convincing without appearing to advocate. Above all, he exuded strength —strength in the way he held himself, in the way he looked at her, in the way he listened and watched. Women jurors would find him appealing...if they could get past the Sanchez murders.

Before she left, she told him she would visit him once or twice a week at a minimum. She did this with all her serious cases. Even if it seemed there was nothing to discuss, the fact that the client knew he would be seeing his lawyer that week was always a good thing. But given the gravity of this case, she doubted there would ever be a week when they wouldn't have something to say to each other. She also said it seemed highly likely he would be testifying in his defense, and his testimony stood to be the most important piece of evidence in the case for the defense. Not only would she prepare him to testify, but they would also get to know each other well enough so that a nod or a pause or even a shifting of her eyes meant something to him while he was on the stand. What she did not say was that the more often she saw him, the greater the probability his trust and confidence in her would grow to the point that he would readily accept her advice on all the important decisions to be made in preparing for and trying the case.

When Barbara left the jail, she was uplifted. She was certain he was telling the truth. He was very strong, both in appearance and character. He would make a great witness.

SHE SAW Alejandro once or twice a week during the month that followed. As much time was spent getting to know him as the case itself. He was open and truthful, she thought. Although when it came to family matters, he tended to be terse. There was an obvious reluctance to discuss them. He hadn't gotten along with his father. He hadn't known him very well. He was a drunk. He was run over by a train, probably when he was drunk. He loved his mother, a wonderful woman who worked hard to keep the family together. She was beautiful but crippled after falling down some steps when she was a young mother. He and his mother were close. His brothers and sisters were younger and did not see, or at least appreciate, the effort she had made to keep the family together. He never had much in common with his brothers and sisters. Now it was worse. He never really liked school. It was boring. A lot of his friends didn't go to school. So when he was sitting in a classroom, he was always wondering what was going on...what he was missing out there in the streets.

After the first month she began to feel as if she had known Alejandro for a long time rather than for just a few weeks. They were at ease with each other, comfortable. Their greetings were warm and casual; if not quite friends, they were at least like neighbors or classmates. Now they spoke of things other than the case: of news and sporting events, of history and religion, and even of evolution. His eyes were always open and attentive, relaxed—except when the matter of his family came up. In those moments he would tense up, and his answers became curt.

There was a change too when she questioned him about one particular prior arrest, an assault with a deadly weapon charged as a felony that had been dismissed. He flatly refused to discuss it, saying it was not a prior conviction and couldn't be used against him, so why bother. She waited a while and then reintroduced the matter of prior arrests. Once again, with the exception of the assault with a deadly weapon charge, he explained the circumstances and final outcome of each arrest candidly and in great detail. The two petty thefts involved walking into stores during their busy hours and being caught on one occasion with a bag full of cigarettes and on the other occasion with a case of whiskey. Both times he was heavily addicted to heroin. The arrests for marijuana and cocaine preceded the heroin addiction and were small quantities in his possession for recreational use. The battery was his second arrest and involved a street fight with some "south siders" who had come into his barrio looking for trouble. He gave one of them what he was looking for: a sound beating.

Barbara saved the assault charge for last and when she raised it she was met with reluctance and annoyance. "What's that got to do with anything?" he asked. "Those charges were dropped. They're not prior convictions. The DA can't use them against me."

"I'm not so sure about that, Alejandro. The DA can definitely use it in the penalty phase of the trial, and, depending upon the state of the evidence in the guilt phase, he might well try to introduce it there. How can I raise an objection if I don't even know what it's about? At any rate, I should at least have some idea of what was involved. There are no police reports on it and nothing that I'm aware of that deals with that charge."

Now he was surly. The frown on his face was emphasized by the way he slowly turned from side to side and looked away as if he were thoroughly disgusted with her, which made her think that she had hit on something. For the first time he appeared evasive. Now she had to know.

"Alejandro, I'm your lawyer. Whatever it is, whatever happened, you have to tell me. I need to know it all so that I can prepare your defense. For me there's no worse court scenario than to hear something that is detrimental to my client's case for the first time during the trial. Tell me, Alejandro, I need to know."

Alejandro Soto continued turning slowly from side to side and staring. Finally, he nodded to himself, turned, and said, "OK, I'll tell you. It was my uncle Mario...Mario Soto, my dad's brother. He was over at the house drunk, raising hell with my mother and my brothers and sisters. I came home and told him to leave, to get out. But he wouldn't leave. So I made him leave."

"Did you hit him?"

"Yeah."

"With what?"

"My fists."

"How much did you hit him? How badly?"

"Bad enough so that he was flat out on the sidewalk unconscious and bleeding, and someone called the cops."

"That was your first arrest?"

"Yeah."

"How old were you?"

"Eighteen."

"And the charges were dropped?"

"Yeah."

"Why?"

"Because he wouldn't show up to court. He wouldn't testify. He knew what he did was in the wrong. So he wouldn't press charges."

Then he was silent. His eyes were focused on the writing shelf just below his side of the glass. He had said all that he wanted to say. To press further, she thought, was probably a mistake.

WHEN BARBARA returned to her office, she searched through Bill Terry's interviews of Alejandro's siblings. His two brothers and one of his sisters had little to say of any importance, and what they did say was all pretty much the same. They had had very limited contact with Alejandro over the past seventeen years. They knew nothing about the killings or his lifestyle. When their father died, he more or less became the head of the family. He was strict, but he wasn't a bad brother.

Arcelia Munoz was an entirely different matter. Her first words to the investigator had been, "You don't want to call me as a witness. He's a rotten son of a bitch. Always has been and always will be. I hope he gets the chair because that's what he deserves." She told the investigator that after their father died, Alejandro appointed himself the head of the family. He was always bigger than everyone and terrorized all of them. He had two standards, one for himself that allowed him to do anything and everything he wanted and another for them, which was that they had to do everything he said, when he said it, and how he said it. He beat his siblings and intimidated his mother. Everybody was afraid of him. They lived on their father's pension, and when Alejandro was old enough to cash checks, he put himself in charge of the money too, making their mother turn over the pension check to him as soon as it came. Whenever Alejandro wanted something, he bought it, no questions asked. Whenever anybody else wanted or needed anything, they were questioned again and again about their need and then made to wait until he said he had enough money to pay for it. He always thought he was better than the rest of them and was always telling them so. He called them less than "mediocre." Where he got that word from, Arcelia never knew. As they got older, he ridiculed their schoolwork, their jobs, their boyfriends and girlfriends, and, in the case of Manuel, he ridiculed Manuel's young wife and two children. Yet he became nothing more than a drug addict who never worked and who "put his women out on the street to work for his drug money." The investigator's closing assessment was: "Arcelia Munoz is the bright, articulate, outspoken, youngest sister of our client. She thoroughly hates her brother and does not hesitate to detail her reasons for hating him. She would make a very poor witness for the defense, and, in fact, we had better hope the DA doesn't contact her and call her as a witness."

But there was no mention of Uncle Mario anywhere. From what little Alejandro had said, the entire family might have been present and the beating had been charged as a felony, which in all likelihood meant that it had been a severe beating. A severe beating of one family member by another that left the beaten party bleeding and unconscious in the street had to be memorable. Yet, not a word.

Barbara called Arcelia Munoz that afternoon. Arcelia was hostile from the beginning. "Who are you...? Well, I feel sorry for you because he won't appreciate anything you do for him and he's going to the chair anyway... Why should I talk to you? I've already talked to your investigator for over an hour and that's an hour more than anyone should give that creep... No, I'm not afraid to talk to you. When it comes to my big brother, I can only tell the truth and that's what I'll do."

The drive to Dos Palos was just under ninety minutes. Arcelia Munoz's home surprised her. The investigative report said only that Arcelia Munoz lived in Dos Palos with her husband and two young daughters, and it gave an address. She had assumed Arcelia and her family lived in the old, run-down east side of town. What she found instead was a spanking-new, middle-class home, in a tract so new that none of the homes had lawns or shrubs. Sheets were hung over most of the windows. As she walked up to the front door she chided herself for her stereotyping.

Still another surprise was Arcelia herself. Pleasant, pretty, petite, and very self-assured, she greeted Barbara with unexpected composure and led her through several bare rooms of hardwood floors and stark-white walls to a family room, just off the kitchen, that had a couch and two armchairs. "It's going to take us a while," Arcelia said, "but we'll have this place looking like a home. Can I get you a cup of coffee or tea?" She was half Alejandro's size and except for her hair and eyes, there was little resemblance. While Arcelia was in the kitchen, two dark-eyed girls of three or four came to the doorway of the family room and stared. Then a dark-skinned man came up behind them and said, "Hi, I'm Paul and this is Cindy and Lisa. Say hello, girls." But the girls were content to stare. Then Paul turned toward the kitchen and said, "Honey, I'm taking the girls over to Joe's house with me," and they left.

When Arcelia rejoined her, Barbara asked about the house and Arcelia's family, hoping to get a better sense of her than she had from the investigative report and their telephone conversation. Open and cordial, Arcelia clearly enjoyed talking about her new home almost as much as she did talking about her daughters. But once the subject changed to Alejandro, a different person appeared. Her mouth tightened, her brow furled, and her eyes hardened. She sat up in her chair and raised her feet so that the weight of her legs was resting on the balls of her tiny feet. Then she began. It was almost as if she had scripted what she had told the investigator: Alejandro's self-appointment as the head of the family; his autocratic rule; his bullying, intimidations, and beatings; his diversion of the family pension to himself; and his arrogance and ridicule of the things the others loved or enjoyed. She went on for at least twenty minutes, providing example after example, needing no prompting or questions from Barbara, rather fueling and refueling her memory with the recall that her anger provoked.

When she stopped, Barbara asked, "Was there ever a time that you loved your brother?"

Now Arcelia looked at Barbara oddly. "Of course we did," she answered, seemingly surprised that Barbara had to ask. "We all did."

"When was that?"

"Before my father died."

"What was there to love about him?"

"He was the oldest and he was nice to us then. My father was always drunk and he was a mean drunk. Ale was always trying to protect us from him then."

"And your mother, too?"

"Yes. Ale really loved our mother then. And she loved him a lot, too. He did everything he could to protect Mama. Finally, when Ale was thirteen and bigger and stronger than Papa, Papa came home drunk one night and started in on Mama again. He hit her, but he hit her for the last time because Ale beat the holy hell out of him and threw him out into the street and told him never to come back. And he didn't... Five days later he was run over by a train and died."

"I'm sorry."

"That happened so long ago and I've thought about it so many times—talked about it, mentioned it so many times—that now it's just like saying that the sun came up this morning."

"Was it better at home after that?"

"Oh, much better."

"When you loved Alejandro, were there any other reasons you loved him besides the fact that he protected the family from your father?"

"Yes. He was big and strong and good-looking and really charming when he wanted to be. None of the other kids on the street messed with us because they all knew that Ale was our big brother. He was so smart. One time not just his teacher but the principal, too, came to our house to talk to Mama. They told Mama that Ale was so smart that he could do anything he wanted to, become anything he wanted to be, if he would just go to school. They kept saying it was such a sad thing for them to see Ale wasting his mind. But nobody could make Ale go to school. If he went, it would be for just a few days and then he would be out on the streets again. He always used to hang around with older guys who never went to school. He would say that when he was in school, he couldn't sit still because he was always thinking about what he was missing on the streets with his friends in the barrio."

Arcelia had softened again, and in the process she looked somewhat confused. Her self-assuredness had deserted her. She was twisting one hand around the other and now she looked tentatively at Barbara, almost as if she were afraid of Barbara's next question.

"So when did it change? Right after your father left?"

"No, not then. For a while we were OK. Ale was doing everything he could to keep us together. Then...it did change."

"When? What caused it to change?"

Arcelia Munoz was out of words. She fiddled with her hands some more. She shifted in her chair. She looked at and away from Barbara several times. She set her mouth to speak and then relaxed it again.

"Arcelia, I have to know. Whatever you might think of your brother, I have to know."

She set her mouth twice more before she began. "Ale really loved Mama. I'll give him that. And she really loved him, too. She was crippled, you know, and, after Papa left, Ale was always doing everything he could to lighten her load. Once Papa was gone, we ate every night at six. No matter where Ale was or what he had been doing, Ale always made sure that he was home at least one hour before and one hour after dinner. That way he could help Mama with dinner and cleanup and make sure that we helped, too. I can remember coming home from school and a lot of times seeing just the two of them sitting at the kitchen table laughing and talking. She was always telling him about Mexico and what it was like growing up there as a girl. She told him everything: about her *bodas* and fiestas and even about her *novios.* They'd just be sitting there laughing and talking, a lot of times about stories that all of us already knew by heart.

"When Ale was sixteen, somebody gave him an old car that didn't run anymore and he fixed it up on his own so that it did work. It was an old heap and he only used it to take Mama to the store and to *mandados* and sometimes for a little ride out in the country because she could barely walk and she loved it when he took her out there. They were so close that, of course, the rest of us kids were kind of jealous. Roberto used to call them 'the old married couple,' but not to their faces...at least not to Ale's face."

Arcelia paused and looked up at Barbara, tapping the back of her thumb against her closed mouth, as if she was trying to decide whether she should go on and tell that woman more. Then she nodded and said, "OK. Everything was going along fine until one day, about five years after Papa died, his brother, Uncle Mario, showed up from Mexico. None of us kids knew him, but Mama did. Right off the bat, Ale didn't like him. Maybe it was because he looked just like Papa. Whatever it was, Ale didn't want him around. But Uncle Mario didn't have no place to go. He had no money and no job, and Mama convinced Ale to let him stay until he got on his feet. Ale did that alright. He waited until Uncle Mario got his second paycheck and then Ale told him to leave. Uncle Mario stayed away for a few months, and then he started coming around, not every day, but maybe once a week. When he came he always brought something: a chicken, a dozen tamales, sometimes even a sack of beans or flour. Then he started giving Mama money, not a lot, just a few dollars here and there to help us get by a little better. Ale didn't like the money part. He wanted Mama to give it back. But Mama was always reminding Ale that Uncle Mario was blood, that he was only trying to help, and that we had to treat him like family. Winter came and the rains put Uncle Mario, who was working construction on the highways, out of work for a while. We didn't know that, but now he had a lot of time on his hands. Then one afternoon, Ale came home and found Uncle Mario in bed with Mama and all hell broke loose. I wasn't there when it happened, but my sister Margarita came home right after it had started and Ale was beating the hell out of Uncle Mario—so much that she called the police. She thought Ale was going to kill him.

"That's when Ale changed. That's when he got mean, started pushing us around, hitting us. That's when he took over the money. That's when he started watching Mama. He started coming and going at weird hours, like you could never tell when he was going to be there or not be there. Sometimes, he would leave in the morning and say he'd be back in the afternoon and then he'd double back twenty minutes later, leave again, and come back in forty minutes. If he said he was going to be gone all day, you knew he wasn't; he'd stop by two or three times during the day, not say anything, just sit, look around, be there for anyone's guess how long, and then leave again. At night when he was with his friends, he'd still manage to come home two or three times during the night and then leave again. We all knew he was watching Mama.

"Then he started staying home a lot, especially during the day. At first we thought it was because of Mama, but we were wrong. What we didn't understand then was that all of his friends were gone. A few had jobs, but most of them were locked up in jail or prison or the Youth Authority. He tried to get a job but he had dropped out of school in the ninth grade, and all there was for him was work in construction, work with a pick and shovel, and he was too proud to do the work Papa and Uncle Mario had done. That's when he started ridiculing us. He made fun of our homework and our classes, our friends and dances, our boyfriends and girlfriends. Manuel went out for track and was a pretty good runner, but Ale made him quit. He found more and more things for us to do around the house and in the yard, and he did less and less. He never hit Mama, but she was afraid of him. He made her feel like a sinner and she walked around like Mary Magdalene or something. A sinner only he could forgive. But Ale didn't know how to forgive anybody.

"We all left the house as soon as we could. Manuel got married when he was sixteen and moved out. I lived at my girlfriend's parents' house for the last half of my senior year. Then it was just the two of them in that house. At first Mama would invite us over for Sunday dinner, then just for the holidays, then just for our birthdays, and then not at all. Because Ale was miserable and he made us all miserable. His smart mouth was always cutting and humiliating us.

"None of us knew what went on in the house between them once we left, but it must have been hell because Mama cut her wrists. It wasn't one of those attention-getting things. She almost died. She was in the hospital for two weeks. The weird thing was they really loved each other. When he found her bleeding, he picked her up and carried her out into the middle of the street where he forced the first passing car to stop and rush her to the hospital. The nurses told us that Ale was hysterical when they got there. He never left her side for two weeks. He slept in a chair next to her or on the floor. He ate whatever we brought in. He wouldn't leave. After a few days, we had to bring him clean clothes because he stank. And he cried and cried. Ol' Mr. Macho Man cried like a baby. He didn't care who saw him or what anybody said or thought, he just cried. The day they released Mama from the hospital, Ale took her home. Then he moved out. He didn't say anything to anyone; he just moved out and never went back. He got a job at the Chrysler plant and for a while he was sending Mama money every week. Then we heard that he had quit his job and was hooked on heroin. It doesn't take long for the word to get around in that town, especially in the Mexican community and especially if it's bad. At one time or another all of us, except Mama, saw him on the street and he looked terrible: skinny, dirty, a lost look in his eyes, and a gray color to him. I've always thought he never went back to visit Mama because he didn't want her to see the way he looked then."

She stopped again and looked all around the room at nothing and then said, "You know it hurt Mama real bad when we told her he was hooked on that stuff. But for a while we kept telling her and telling her—kind of like we were trying to show her we were the ones, the good ones, she should have loved, not Ale. It broke her heart when he got charged with those two murders. And it destroyed her when he got convicted and was given those two life sentences. She died two weeks later."

Now, Arcelia Munoz was clearly uncomfortable. She fidgeted with her hands again, she shifted her feet, and then she alternated looking at Barbara and at her hands. It was as if she had said too much, revealed too much. The early autumn sun was beginning its afternoon slide creating shadows within the new home and adding somberness to the family room.

"What's the matter, Arcelia?"

"Nothing," she said, convincing neither of them. "You must think we have a pretty weird family."

"Not really. More often than not I find this kind of hate among family members isn't really unusual. And I always ask myself, if family members can't get along, how in the world can we ever expect nations to get along? No, your family's not weird."

Then Barbara tried to present enough facts about Alejandro's case so Arcelia might at least entertain the notion that her brother might be innocent of the Estrada killing. But Arcelia's reaction to any mention of the homicide was to turn stone cold.

As Arcelia was walking her to the door, Barbara said, "You know, Arcelia, when our investigator interviewed your brothers and sisters, their answers to what Alejandro had been like when they lived with him were quite a bit different than yours."

"Oh, what did they say?"

"They said that when your father died, Alejandro became the head of the family, that he was strict but that he wasn't a bad brother."

"They said that?"

"Yes." Then Barbara stopped short of the door and turned to Arcelia and asked, "Why do you think your answers were so different than theirs?"

Arcelia Munoz thought for a moment, but only for a moment, and then she said, "Probably because I loved him a lot more than they ever did."

ON THE drive home Barbara was offended. Alejandro had lied to her, if not outright lies, then lies of concealment. The relationship with his mother had been twisted, perverse, sick. And yet all he had said to her was that they had been "close." He had beaten two men over her—his own father and his uncle. He had battered his uncle until he was unconscious and bleeding. He should have been grateful the police had come. He had beaten the "holy hell" out of his father and thrown him out into the street. Five days later his father was run over by a train. "Probably drunk." Was there a causal connection between the beating and the train? Who knew? He had punished his mother, as only he could, until she cut her wrists. Then, in hysterics he had carried her out to the street. For two weeks he didn't leave the critically injured woman's side. But he had lied to Barbara. His calm, open, sincere looks had all been a ruse. Still, why was she so offended? What made him any different than the hundreds of other defendants who had lied to her? This was a death penalty case, for one. His life was on the line. It seemed certain that they were going to trial. How could she effectively represent him if he lied to her?

Thinking of the sick mother/son relationship, Barbara Blake wondered what the husband/wife relationship must have been like. Julia Cruz had been listed in the prison records as Alejandro's wife. Oddly, other than those records, there had been no mention of Julia Cruz in any of the discovery the DA had given them. God only knew what happened between those two. Better to interview her before the DA did. She and Bill Terry should go out and talk to her.

Greg Olsen disagreed. "Really, Barb, what does Soto's ex-wife have to do with the defense of the Estrada murder?"

Barbara left it there. But in her mind, just as Arcelia had shed so much light on Alejandro, Julia Cruz stood to explain at least as much and probably more. For the rest of the day and into the night, the thought returned. She woke to it in the morning and decided to do it. She didn't need Bill Terry...she'd go alone. Greg wouldn't like it, but then he didn't need to know about it unless she turned up something important and then all would be forgiven. She called Arcelia.

"Yes," Arcelia answered, "I know where she lives. But I know she's not gonna want to get involved. She has a different life now, a better life. She's married. She has a good man now and two little kids that she loves a lot. She's not gonna like it if I give you her phone number or tell you where she lives."

"She doesn't have to get involved, Arcelia. I don't see any way she can be called as a witness. But just like you did yesterday, she can tell me things that will give me a better understanding of your brother. Things to emphasize or stay away from in the trial. I didn't say this outright yesterday, Arcelia, but I think you can tell from our conversation, I think Alejandro's completely innocent of these murder charges. I'm not talking about the Dos Palos murders, I'm talking about this case. He's innocent. He didn't do it."

"I'm glad you think so, 'cause I don't."

"Arcelia, remember yesterday when I was leaving and I asked you why your statements to my investigator about your brother were so different than those of your brothers and sister?"

"Yes."

"You knew I was asking why yours were so bitter compared to theirs, didn't you?"

"Yes."

"Remember what you said...'Probably because I loved him a lot more than they ever did.'"

"Yes."

"Love like that never dies, Arcelia. I need Julia's phone number. I need her address. Your brother needs them."

She decided to return to Dos Palos that afternoon. She wanted to talk to Julia Cruz before she saw Alejandro again. If she didn't go then, there would be no time during the week. She decided not to call and instead to arrive unannounced, unexpected. She was taking the chance even though Julia might be out on a Sunday family outing. But the chances were probably greater that a phone call would end any possibility of ever meeting and talking with Julia Cruz.

THE NEIGHBORHOOD had to be the bleakest part of Dos Palos. Wood-frame houses built quickly and cheaply fifty years before to accommodate a passing housing boom were none the better for the wear due to a combination of shoddy beginnings and then neglect and abusive disregard. Front yards no longer had lawns. Instead they had row after row of deep rain ruts and had become the current and previous owners' private parking lots with four or five cars, some running and some wrecked, parked just a few feet from front doors. Broken windows abounded. Many were boarded over with plywood, some were patched with an array of materials from the inside, and others were simply ignored, leaving gaping holes where the wind and an occasional curtain passed through. Large gaps of siding were missing, having been put to better use by the houses' occupants. Most of the houses were dirt-streaked and badly in need of paint. Screens were mostly gone or torn. As Barbara pulled up to a faded green house with the remnants of four old cars parked in the front yard, Arcelia's words rang in her mind: "She has such a different life now. A better life." *What must her life have been like with Alejandro Soto?*

She was glad she had come before dark. She knocked on the front door. The hinges that had once carried a screen door were now rusted, twisted, and abandoned. No answer. She knocked again, harder, louder. There was some movement behind the large window to her right, which was covered with a dark-blue blanket. The edge of the blanket closest to the door was slightly pushed aside, and she saw a pair of eyes peek out at her and then disappear behind the blanket again. She knocked a third time. There were sounds and then vibrations behind the door. It opened, but only partially.

"Hi, I'm Barbara Blake." Now she could see her, see the puzzled look on her face. "I'm Barbara Blake," she repeated with her friendliest smile, and the door opened more. She had a very dark complexion, darker than most Mexicans, and she was taller than most Mexican women as she looked to be five foot six or seven. *So his taste runs to dark, tall women.* A loose, long, worn-cotton dress almost hid the two round-eyed, young kids who had their arms wound around each leg. Barbara smiled at the children and said animatedly, "Hi, there!" This seemed to puzzle their mother all the more. She had sad, dark eyes but a pretty face and a quiet dignity about her.

"What is it?" she said softly. Her jet-black hair was pulled straight back in the custom of Mexican Indian women.

She must have been very beautiful in her day, thought Barbara Blake. "Ms. Cruz, I—"

"No, my name is Jimenez."

"That's your married name, correct?"

"Yes."

"But your name was Julia Cruz before that?"

"Yes."

"Mrs. Jimenez, I represent Alejandro Soto and I'd like to talk to you about—"

The woman pulled back. "Oh, no..." And she started to close the door.

"Please, Mrs. Jimenez, I need to talk to you."

"Oh no, I don't want to talk about that. I don't want to go back there. Please go."

"Mrs. Jimenez—"

"No, please go. My husband just went to the store. He'll be back any minute. He knows nothing about Ale. He doesn't need to know. He deserves not to know. He's a good, hard-working man. We don't need this in our lives. Please go before he comes. You'll cause so much hurt if you stay and he comes home."

"Maybe I could talk to you alone sometime when he's not nearby?"

"No, please. That life was hell. I don't want to go back there.

177

I try not to think about it. I have nightmares about it. Please go before he comes." She closed the door leaving Barbara stung and embarrassed. She shouldn't have come. But then, she had to know. She had to see for herself.

SHE DID not see Alejandro until the following Thursday. She had thought of seeing him on Tuesday, but Greg had gone instead. She asked Greg not to mention Uncle Mario in his visit. The lies or at least the half truths Alejandro had told her continued to bother her, and she wanted to be the first to confront Alejandro about both beatings. But she was conflicted about how best to approach him. An outright confrontation might be the worst approach. It might damage the attorney–client relationship she had worked so hard to develop with him. But what kind of relationship did they have given his lies to her? How best to signal to him that she knew the full stories behind both beatings and allow him to divulge them without losing the confidence she had gained with him? As she rode up the jail elevator she decided to let the matter rest for now and to send Bill Terry out again later to talk to family members. Then she could attribute her new information to the second set of interviews rather than reveal that she had gone directly to Arcelia.

But once the guards left and he gave her that open, attentive, relaxed look, she said, "Why have you lied to me?"

"Lied to you?"

"Yes, lied to me."

"About what?"

"About the beating you gave your uncle Mario."

"I didn't lie to you."

"You did and you're lying to me again right now by saying that you didn't lie to me."

"How did I lie to you?"

"You said your uncle came over and was drunk and wouldn't leave so you ended up beating him."

"I did."

"Why do you continue to lie? You found him in bed with your mother. You flew into a rage, then beat him, and threw him out."

"How do you know that?"

"Arcelia told me."

"You talked to Arcelia?"

"Yes."

"When?"

"Saturday."

He looked away and lowered his head. The seconds passed. A minute. Almost another.

"Why did you lie to me, Alejandro?"

He looked back at her and said, "Do you think I wanted to tell you that I came home and found my mother and uncle in bed having sex? I loved my mother. I love her still. She's dead now. Why would I want to dese...desecrate?...her now? How could what they were doing in bed twenty years ago have anything to do with who killed Santos Estrada?"

His words made perfect sense, which enraged her all the more. But he had lied to her and now he was talking his way out of it. "And what about your father? What about your father?"

"What about him?"

"You told me that your father was a drunk who got run over by a train probably when he was drunk. Why didn't you mention that five days before he got run over by that train you beat the hell out of him and threw him out of the house for good? When that train hit him, maybe he was drunk because of what you had done to him. But you said nothing about that."

"That was almost twenty-five years ago. What's that got to do with Santos Estrada? Why should I have told you about that?"

"Because it shows a pattern of violence. That's why. Because murder is a violent crime and that kind of behavior could be construed as showing you might be more prone to commit murder than if that were not in your background. That's why. That's..."

But she wasn't making much sense now. She was stumbling and staggering. Her accusations seemed silly now.

Offended and angry, Alejandro answered forcefully, "Did Arcelia tell you, too, that I started hitting my father only after he started beating on a cripple just like he had done time and time again before that? Did Arcelia tell you about the beating I watched one night when I was four? When he knocked my mother around the kitchen until she fell and then he kicked her and kicked her and then dragged her into the back porch, picked her up, and threw her against the cement washtrays? Did she tell you that? And when she bounced off those washtrays, he picked her up again and threw her down the back porch steps. She wasn't crippled before that night. I was the only kid who could remember how pretty she was and how fine she walked before that night. Did Arcelia tell you that, too? Hell no! She wasn't even born then. Did she tell you how many nights I've dreamed about that night? How during the day or night, any time that I'm awake, I can close my eyes, or I don't even have to close my eyes, and I can still see him beating on her, kicking her while she was down, picking her up and throwing her against those washtrays, and then tossing her down those back stairs like some dirty dog. Did Arcelia tell you about that too? Come on, answer me! Did Arcelia tell you about that, too?"

Now it was she who had her head downcast. Thoughts of cut wrists and the life he must have given Julia Cruz raced across her mind. But even in that state of mind, she understood how disconnected those things were from Santos Estrada. Shame and confusion burned hot. She stood and said, "This is going nowhere. I'll see you next week."

XI

It was at least an hour before they came for him. Later he would think that had been a good thing. He would not have been able to hide his anger and hurt had they come for him as soon as she left. He had learned long ago never to show a guard his anger, hurt, or frustration. Most guards would take that show of emotion as a sign of weakness, something to be laughed at or ridiculed. With a guard like Hudson you were just opening yourself up to abuse—mental for sure and maybe even physical.

He was boiling when she left. She had called him a liar several times. He had not lied to her or anyone for at least ten years now. Once he quit heroin, he stopped lying. It was as if he had made a commitment to himself never to lie again, because while he was addicted to heroin, his entire life had been a lie. He lied about everything. To the other junkies, he lied about how much of a stash he had, afraid that they might ask him for a taste or even rip him off. To his connection, he lied that he had some guy who owed him "big time" and was gonna pay him that night, but that he needed just a little taste to get by 'til then. To his fence, he lied that nobody had seen him take the cigarettes or followed him out of the store to the fence's house, and, that in any event, he had stopped by a friend's place before coming to the fence's place. To Julia, he lied that he would never ask her to turn a trick for them again because next week he was gonna start moving some stuff for his connection and they wouldn't be short no more. To himself, he lied that the ever-increasing amount of heroin he was needing just to get normal, not high, just normal, not sick, was not all that much. Once he left the heroin, there was no need to lie. Life is what it is. Don't twist it, don't stretch it, and don't try to make it the panacea it's not. Tell it like it is. Stop all that self-deception, all that bullshit.

For almost ten years now, he had told it the way it was. He had lied to no one. He had not lied to her. When he yanked his naked uncle out of his mother's bed, he could smell the booze on his breath. He told him to get out but his uncle wouldn't leave. He kept saying, "It's not what you think, Ale! It's not what you think! Your mother and me are in love!" He kept repeating it even as he kept telling him to get the hell out of there, to get his clothes on, and to get the hell out of there. But he wouldn't go, even as he started hitting him, even as he fumbled with his clothes, he wouldn't go. Until there was blood splattering from his mouth, until he knocked him out the front door. But what did the fact that his mother had been in bed with Uncle Mario have to do with Santos Estrada? What jury needed to hear that? Why did he have to tell her that? She had never answered him. Yes, his father was probably drunk when the train ran over him. No, they were never close. He never lied to her. He just hadn't told her about the beatings. But what did the one savage beating he gave his father for the twenty or thirty savage beatings his father had given his mother have to do with who killed Santos Estrada? She had never answered him about that either.

There was the hurt, too. For several weeks she had treated him and spoken to him, if not as a friend, then at least as a near equal, raising him in his own mind several levels. Then, on the say-so of Arcelia, after one conversation with Arcelia, she had treated him probably the way she felt she should have been treating him all along: as a liar, a murderer, a criminal, and someone far beneath her.

Yes, it was a good thing they had not come for him sooner. By the time they did come, the rage had passed. He was still angry, but the rage had passed. It was a good thing because his right hand and arm were unchained and free, and Hudson had been the first in the cubicle and hadn't hesitated to mock him. "My, my your white whore girlfriend has finally come to her senses. Gone almost as soon as she came. I wouldn't want to hang around with you people for very long either. Damn you greasers sure do stink! Don't you know what soap is for?"

Greene had exploded. "Goddamn you, Hudson! Shut your big fucking mouth and get your butt away from him and come out here in the hall! I'm getting fed up with that mouth of yours!"

"Greenie, I'm sorry," Hudson said in an insincere tone, "but it just pisses the hell out of me that this two-time murderer gets two lawyers to represent him on a cold case that he should have pled guilty to weeks ago. Worse than that, you know damn good and well who's paying for them lawyers, who's paying to house and feed him here while he lays in his bunk all goddamn day and reads and watches TV...we are."

"I don't give a good goddamn what pisses you off, Hudson!" Greene shouted. "Go tell the Sergeant that, and, while you're there, ask him to get you off this detail 'cause I'm sure as shit tired of all your bitching and raising hell with Soto. Roy, let's you and I get Soto back to his cell. Hudson, lock up down here."

The shuffle back to Soto's cell was solemn and silent until they reached Jenkins's cell. Jenkins took one look at Soto and said, "Oh, oh. We in for a whole lot of gruntin' and groanin' now." And they were.

AFTER SHE left the jail, Barbara's anger passed through several phases. Outrage came first. Because he had continued to lie to her. Because he wouldn't admit that his half truths were lies. Because he wouldn't deal with truth, the ultimate issue, and in a case of this magnitude it was absolutely necessary that he be completely forthright with her. At her office, the moment she walked through the door she had to contend first with Suzie and her interminable questioning and prodding and then with an elderly couple whose son had just been arrested on suspicion of murder. She struggled to keep a calm, controlled demeanor and listen as attentively as she could while the anger burned within. At 6:40 when she was finally alone, she found that her ire had simmered and now she was feeling some embarrassment. She had lost control of the situation at the jail. After all, she was the attorney and it was her responsibility to maintain control of the interview no matter how volatile the circumstances. She had called him a liar and raised her voice, and he in turn had yelled at her and berated her. No client had ever spoken to her like that. There was still anger in her. He had shown her a complete lack of respect.

Just before going to bed that night, she admitted for the first time that the fact his mother and uncle had been in bed together twenty years ago, as well as the beating that Alejandro had inflicted on his father or the beatings that his father had given his mother years earlier, probably had no relevance in the Estrada case. Still, he should not have spoken to her as he had, and he should have had the courtesy to hear her out on the potential relevancy of the beatings.

She woke at five o'clock the following morning completely embarrassed. Any first-year law student would have known that the lies she had accused Alejandro of would never be admissible in a court of law. And she had even gone to Dos Palos to interview Julia Cruz. There was little information Julia could have given her that would have been admissible, and, as it turned out, she wouldn't speak to her anyway. She hoped her attempt to interview Julia would never come to light. What had gotten into her? Maybe the case was getting the better of her... Maybe it would be good to get away from the case for a few days... Take a long weekend.

SHE WENT to see Alejandro late Thursday afternoon. For the first ten minutes they were deferential and almost shy, tripping over themselves to be considerate, one of the other. Not once did they mention their meeting. It was as if it had never happened. She started the visit by discussing the court's desire to set a trial date and what were his thoughts on a date. It was a subject they could meander around, get them talking, settle them down, let the awkwardness pass. He paused, thought, and then said, "You know, it makes no never mind to me. I'm not going anywhere soon, and in a lot of ways this jail's a lot easier to do my time in than up at the SHU. I guess the later the better. But you know a lot more about these things than I do. So whatever you think is best, is OK with me."

She told him of Bill Terry's efforts, without any luck, to track down Johnny Moncado. Without Moncado, the prosecution had no case. She said that Bill Terry thought Moncado might be on the run, that the DA really didn't know where he was. He listened and watched and thought too, listening just enough so that he could comment or answer if asked to do so, but mainly watching— watching her high, smooth, forehead; her soft, clear hazel eyes; and the small, moist mouth that moved with such ease. He was watching and thinking, *Who is she, who is this woman, and what's she all about?*

She said she wanted Alejandro to meet Bill Terry again. Soon she would bring Bill with her for one of the visits. She said that a meeting like that always seemed to make a difference, a big positive difference, with an investigator's attitude toward the case—

because then the investigator actually knew the person he was working for, as opposed to just knowing a name on an assignment sheet.

He wondered, *Is she married?* He knew nothing of her personal life even though the prison files told her everything there was to know about him.

She said that she had worked with Bill Terry for years, first in the public defender's office and now in private practice. She trusted him implicitly with every phase of the case's investigation. He had been a major factor in winning one of her much publicized cases.

She never said she wasn't married and she wore no ring on her left hand. But that meant little. Still, she never mentioned a husband. She could be living with a man. And those long, fine legs in the courtroom...not many men would let those legs be. She had to be involved with someone.

Barbara paused and saw him watching her intently and thought: *Such a shame. Such a vigorous, bright, handsome man. Such a waste. The probabilities are that he will die in Arroyo Grande's SHU.* She went on about Bill Terry's total commitment to that case.

She never mentioned kids, which doesn't mean that she doesn't have any. But people who have kids were always ready to talk about them. He knew so little about her, and yet he was afraid to ask, afraid she'd say something like: What does this have to do with the case?

He was still attentively watching and listening to her when she realized how much she liked but was also disturbed by the attention he was giving her. She went on, "No one expected the verdict of not guilty in that case, and much of it was due to Bill Terry's work and effort."

She takes her job so seriously that there probably isn't much room for anything else in her life. What does she want? What is she after? What makes her tick?

Then she said that she wanted to know everything Alejandro knew about Johnny Moncado. Here his mind couldn't wander. She noted once again the quickness and nimbleness of his mind despite all those years in isolation. She asked question after question about Moncado, until it seemed that she knew everything there was to know about him.

He felt twinges of shame over his earlier fantasies and sorry beliefs that she was attracted to him. She was all business. She had no time for such foolishness. Certainly not with him and maybe with no one, or at least not with a man.

Next she moved on to the trial. "I want to make sure that you understand the process of a death penalty trial from beginning to end. This trial will certainly be one of the most important events in your life. And the more you know about the process, the better able you will be to help Greg and me with your defense." It was a long-winded explanation that began with the applicable statutes, wound into the case law, then moved into selecting the jury, and finally included the trial itself. There was much that Alejandro was hearing for the first time. He paid strict attention, and yet he continued to be baffled by her. Not the legal concepts. But by her, the person. He had never been around a woman like Barbara Blake before. Her life seemed to be totally involved with the law. She was a pretty, attractive woman, and yet none of that, or all the things that went with it, seemed to matter to her. He became so perplexed by her, that at one point, while she was explaining a recent U.S. Supreme Court case, he blurted out, "What do your kids think about all this?"

"My kids? Think about what?"

"About your life with the law?"

"Alejandro, what my kids, and that assumes that I have kids, may think about my life with the law is completely irrelevant to this discussion. Now, I'd like to continue, if I may."

He winced, but he should have expected that answer. She seemed a bit irritated but quickly resumed her cool, detached lecture. And still he knew nothing about her.

As she was leaving, at the door to the cubicle, she turned and picked up the phone again and said, "Alejandro, I want to apologize for my conduct at our last visit. I was completely out of line."

"No, it was all my fault. I got all shook up, and I shouldn't have."

"No, really, I—"

"No. No. It was all my fault."

"I guess we'll have to leave it that way then. Goodbye."

She continued her practice of visiting him two or three times a week. He looked forward to those visits. They were the highlights of his day...of his week. Not only did it mean that he would leave his cell for an hour, sometimes even two, but it also meant that he would have a conversation with a beautiful, intelligent woman, something he had never experienced before. And he came to understand that if he bided his time, if he picked the right moment in their visit, he could move Barbara away from the case and onto almost any topic that wasn't personal. They talked about local, statewide, and national politics and events. They talked about religion. They talked about books—about his favorite book, *Crime and Punishment.*

"Do you think Raskolnikov was justified in killing the old woman?"

"What do you mean by justified? Do you mean blameless?"

"No, not blameless because he committed the act. What I mean is, can you understand why he killed her? As a woman, as a lawyer, can you understand that?"

"I understood it. But it was intentional. It was still wrong. It was still a crime."

"Is there ever an intentional killing that may not be wrong, not be a crime?"

"Self-defense."

"Aside from self-defense?"

"I don't know. Maybe. Possibly."

After many of these conversations he returned to his cell exhilarated. Because he, Alejandro Soto, an uneducated man, a nothing, had been able to hold his own in any and all of those conversations with a brilliant, accomplished woman.

SHE ALSO enjoyed those exchanges and was fascinated by the questions he asked and the positions he took. Sometimes they were childlike, while at other times they bore the cynicism of a world-weary, old man. He seemed to be interested in, or could become interested in, everything, and his ignorance never made him self-conscious. Often when she left the jail, she was saddened by the fact that it had taken two murders to develop such a fertile mind.

THERE WAS another change that had taken place after Deputy Greene's last warning to Hudson. Now, whenever the three deputies pulled Alejandro for a visit, Hudson said nothing. Sometimes he glared and even grunted at Alejandro, but that was all and that only occurred when the deputies were pulling him for a visit with Barbara Blake, never when the visit was with Greg Olsen. Hudson's silence had a ripple effect. Because now Jenkins came to his cell bars and merely watched as the guards pulled Soto for or returned him from a visit. If he said anything, it was only to bemoan his own fate. "Hey homey, look to me like you gonna beat your case with all them lawyers comin' to visit you every week, an me sittin' here not seein' my lawyer for months."

XII

Greg saw Barbara appro-
aching in the court hallway and stopped her.

"Think you'd better handle the Soto matter tomorrow morning?"

"You're not going?"

"No. Soto doesn't need two lawyers in court to pick a trial date. Not to mention how much it would piss off Spencer to have to pay two lawyers for picking a trial date."

"But you're the lead lawyer, Greg."

"So? You're the one who's going to be trying the guilt phase that begins the trial, and the date selected tomorrow should fit in more with your schedule than mine. Once the trial starts, we'll both be in there. Until then, there's no reason for two of us to be there just to pick a trial date. As I've already said, Spencer wouldn't like it."

"I don't have any problems with that. I can do it."

"Good. Call my office with the date once you get it."

"OK."

He watched as she walked away, watched her swaying hips and her fine legs. His day would come. In a few months they would be together day and night and even on weekends. He would make the most of that opportunity. He knew he would. But then he looked down and caught a glimpse of his huge belly. His belt was nowhere in sight. The shirt button at the peak of that mound seemed ready to pop. He had to start watching his weight. He had to start exercising. If he didn't, he might blow everything.

For the rest of the day and into the following morning, there was a certain excitement she felt whenever she thought of the hearing. She had had many such hearings but had never felt excitement like this. And yet there really was nothing to be excited about. The judge would take the bench and ask both lawyers what dates they proposed for the trial. Usually there was some disagreement and then the judge would question both sides and set a date. Those hearings seldom took more than five minutes, and the courtroom was always empty. *So why the excitement?* she asked herself. Maybe because it was the highest profile case on the court's calendar, and there would be a reporter or two in the courtroom. Then too, she would be making her first appearance in a death penalty case, something that most criminal defense attorneys never attain, and on behalf of a client who some perceived to be the worst of the worst.

She was ten minutes early and the courtroom was dark and empty. The bailiff let her in and went back to his desk outside the judge's chambers. She sat alone at one of the two polished, eight-foot-long tables set two feet apart facing the judge's dais. Her table, the defense table, was to the left of the prosecutor's table, which in turn was always a few feet from the jury box. Six feet behind the counsel tables was a railing that separated the judge and the lawyers from the spectators. The judge's dais stood four feet above the courtroom floor so that the judge could look down at everyone and everything from a seated position. To the immediate right of the dais, some two feet lower, was the witness stand, and to the right of that was the jury box. On the back wall between the witness stand and the jury box was a large steel door. Behind the door was the tunnel that brought inmates from the jail to the courtroom. The tunnel was 150 feet long and could be shut down at the foot of the jail stairs that led down into it or at the other end of the tunnel at the foot of the stairs that led up to the courtroom. There were holding cells along the tunnel walls, where inmates could await the call of their cases or simply be segregated. At the top of the steps leading up to the courtroom was a landing with three-foot benches on either side next to the courtroom door. The steel door was situated close to the jury box so that whenever court was in session and a jury was not sitting in attendance, twelve to fourteen inmates could be brought into the courtroom, instead of one at a time, and seated in the jury box while waiting for their cases to be called.

She was wondering what it would take to prove to the district attorney that Alejandro was innocent, short of a trial, when there was a long, loud, hard rapping on the locked courtroom door. Only a prosecutor would dare rap that hard on a courtroom door. It had to be Randy Davis. Randy Davis, small and slight, joked past the bailiff at the door and bounced confidently into the courtroom. Randy Davis was a deeply religious man who every year took his entire family to Bible camp for their summer vacation. As a prosecutor, he was on the side of God, doing the work of God by bringing to justice evil men and women who had violated the law. He worked hard. His conviction rate was high, and the few cases he lost had to be the work of the devil through some "slime-ball" defense attorney. Defense attorneys were no better than their clients and, in some cases, worse—because they at least had an education and should have known better. They had no business standing in the way of justice, obstructing it in any way they could. Money and greed. There was no other way to explain a defense attorney unless it was that he or she was possessed by the devil, which on a few occasions he thought was actually the case. When the chief asked him if he would be willing to prosecute Soto's case, he jumped at the opportunity. "Are you kidding! I'd love to have that case. That man is evil. He needs to be put to death. He's been a scourge on this earth and its people for too long now."

He was very formal with defense attorneys in and out of court and usually addressed them as Mr. or Ms., even though he had known some for more than ten years. He had a hard time being civil with defense attorneys, and Barbara was no exception. There was a time when he wondered about Barbara. She appeared to be honest, hard-working, and not altogether greedy, but then he learned that she had been twice married and divorced and had no children and that was enough for him.

"Good morning, Ms. Blake," he said as he reached his counsel table.

"Good morning, Randy."

But by then he was already busy putting his papers in order. If he heard her, it didn't matter.

Six armed deputies came into the courtroom and stationed themselves at strategic positions. Other than the bailiff, the court clerk, and the court reporter, there was no one else in the courtroom.

"Is he chained, Chris?" one of the deputies asked the bailiff.

"Oh yeah, he's always chained."

"What kind of chains?"

"Leg irons and waist chains with cuffs."

"Good."

Then Judge Spencer entered from the door to the left of the dais, quickly climbing up the steps onto the dais, motioning as he did to the bailiff that no one need stand for his entry. "Remain seated!" the bailiff said loudly.

Judge Spencer took his seat, arranged some things on his desk, turned on his microphone, looked around the courtroom, and said, "Alright, Mr. Bailiff, bring out Mr. Soto."

Two of the guards followed the bailiff to the iron door. There he took a huge key from a leather holder on his belt, and the lock clicked loudly. When Barbara heard the first clinking of the chains, she stood at counsel table as if to greet him. He entered like so many animals she had seen in movies and on television, stopping and looking in every direction, trying to get a sense of where he was. When he saw her, he stopped looking. Then the guards nudged him forward. She had seen him in court twice before, but now he seemed bigger.

"Do you want Mr. Soto in the jury box, Ms. Blake, or at counsel table with you?"

She hadn't considered that, but didn't need to think twice. "At counsel table, Your Honor."

"Very well," he said nodding to the guards and the bailiff to move him.

As Alejandro Soto shuffled across the courtroom floor between two burly guards with the bailiff trailing behind and the chains clinking, he seemed at once pathetic and yet somehow strong and menacing. She was still standing as the guards led him around the table, and she pointed needlessly to the empty chair beside her. Then the waist chains and leg irons rubbed hard against the chair's wooden back and legs. As he sat down, they emitted a dull screeching sound.

"Counsel, I assume that Mr. Soto is right-handed. Are you going to want his right hand free? Will there be any need for him to take notes?"

She didn't think so, but she decided it best to ask Alejandro. "May I have a moment, Your Honor?"

"You may."

She leaned over and bent down an inch from his ear, "Are you... are you..." And she smelled him, a strong, rich, male smell, and for several moments she was aware only of his smell.

He turned and whispered something to her, something she didn't hear because now she felt his warm breath touching, caressing, and spreading all along her face. Maybe she said something because the whispering stopped but the smell returned, and then he whispered again and his warm, soft breath against her face sent a tingling sensation throughout her body. But the judge was waiting...the judge was waiting. She saw Alejandro shake his head no, and she had enough composure to say, "No, Your Honor."

"Very well, then. This case has been on the court's docket for quite some time now and we have yet to set a trial date. I fully understand the gravity of the charges and I certainly want to give counsel on both sides sufficient time to prepare for trial. On the other hand, we need to set a date, a reasonable trial date, and if as that date approaches, counsel can show good cause for a continuance, this court would certainly be inclined to grant that request. But for now, let's set a trial date. Mr. Davis, what date would you suggest?"

"If we set the date in December, which is three months away, we're going to run into vacation plans and the holidays. My suggestion would be mid-January to the first week in February. Both sides ought to be ready by then."

"Ms. Blake, how does that sound to you?"

She had heard little of what either had said except that they were going to set a trial date. Perhaps it was the blank look on her face that led Judge Spencer to say, "Would you like to confer with your client?"

"Yes, yes," she nodded. She leaned over, wanting more of what had happened just seconds before. It was there again: his smell, rich and strong; his breath, all the same, mesmerizing her; and her desire to remain in that mesmerized state. But they were all watching, so she whispered something, what she did not know, and he whispered once, then again. She heard the second whisper: "Makes no never mind to me. I ain't going no place."

That was enough to elicit, "We agree, Your Honor."

Then he was gone. Then they were all gone and she remained slowly, deliberately, giddily putting her things in her briefcase, smiling and smiling to herself and thinking, *I have never, but never, felt like this before.* She took the back stairs down to the foyer rather than the elevator for fear that someone would see the silly smile she knew she was wearing. Outside, the sky was a brilliant blue, the sun perfectly warm, and birds were singing and hopping from branch to branch. It was a wonderful, glorious day.

As she walked to her car still smiling, she realized she couldn't go to her office. Suzie would ask about the hearing. "How did it go?" "Were there reporters there?" "What was he like close up?" How could she answer that last question without Suzie sensing something? She could hide nothing from Suzie.

What was the trial date? Trial date? Trial date? In all that confusion, or whatever it was, she had not noted, heard, or taken down what the trial date was. She had gone to court for a trial date. Judge Spencer had presumably set a trial date, but she had no idea what it was. She had no recall of what Judge Spencer had said. Panic penetrated. *Not only would Suzie be asking, but also Greg had probably already called the office to find out the trial date.* With those thoughts, the smile and the mood deserted her. No one should ever know what had happened in court that morning. She felt empty and vacant inside. She turned in every direction not knowing where to go or how to get there.

Passersby were starting to notice her. She couldn't continue to stand on the sidewalk aimlessly. It was 10:55. She was in no condition to be seen by anyone she knew. She went to her car and decided that she had enough time to drive out to Santa Silvia, an old refuge of hers. Santa Silvia had once been a thriving fishing village at the foot of the bay but now was a collection of deserted, weather-beaten shacks abandoned by a bay that had permanently receded several hundred yards out to sea. A thin film of polluted water lapped against the rotting pier poles at high tides. She walked along the pier to a useless jetty. She walked out to the jetty's point and then sat and stared out toward the water's edge.

What she had felt in the courtroom was not only gone, but it frightened her. How could she continue to represent Alejandro Soto when just being near him had so rattled her that she was completely unaware of a trial date? And this was a death penalty case. If she withdrew from the case, she would probably never have contact with Alejandro again. There was nothing in the lawyer's code of ethics that she knew of that would require her to withdraw from the case because of the feelings she had experienced.

Still, she knew she couldn't competently represent Alejandro if she continued to have that feeling in the courtroom. She told herself that it was a passing thing, something she could overcome or even learn to ignore now that she was aware of what could happen. And, nothing could ever come of that feeling. Alejandro was a twice-convicted murderer who was serving two life sentences and with whom she probably had very little in common. If she already felt compelled to hide what had happened in the courtroom that morning, how much more difficult would it be to live in the open with anything going beyond that feeling? There was no reason to withdraw from the case so long as she could control and ignore that feeling if it were ever to rise again. Life was an endless stream of worrisome problems. She had been able to handle most of them, and most of them came to nothing anyway.

She looked over at the deserted shacks and thought of the old fishermen who had first settled there. What had their hopes and dreams and fears been like? Eighty years later, nothing that had mattered so much to them was important to anyone now. A calm came over her, and she sat at the jetty's point for a while longer and then walked back to her car.

IT WAS 12:50 when Barbara Blake got back to San Cristobal. She drove to her office. What had happened in court that morning would not happen again. And she was ready for Suzie. She had her entire script laid out: Court had run a little longer than expected. She had met an old college friend at the courthouse and had taken an early lunch with her. She had turned her cell phone off when she went into court and had forgotten to turn it back on until just a few minutes ago. That's why she hadn't gotten any of her calls. She had jotted the trial date down in the file, which was still in her briefcase in her car. She couldn't remember it offhand now, but she'd give it to her when she got back from court later that afternoon. She didn't have time to talk then because a client's family was waiting for her at the courthouse. She had just rushed back to the office to get a couple of files she needed for afternoon court.

But it turned out that Suzie was not in the office; she had gone to lunch, leaving a note saying that Greg had called wanting to know the trial date. Not a problem. The court's file should be in the clerk's office by then and she would look at it for the trial date long before Greg got to the courthouse for the afternoon calendar.

In court that afternoon, while she sat with other lawyers waiting for her case to be called, she resolved many times there would never be a repeat of that morning and she was staying on the case. Becoming involved with Alejandro could mean the loss of her license to practice law and the loss of her respect and reputation in the legal community, and, perhaps, it could even force her to move to Southern California or another state. Now, rather than joy, the morning incident was causing her embarrassment.

When she returned to her office, it was Suzie who was ready. "Where were you?"

"I was in court."

"I'm talking about this morning."

"I was in court."

"Court didn't take all morning. It was 12:15 when I left for lunch and I still hadn't heard from you."

"When I got out of court, I met an old college friend of mine. We talked for a while and then decided to have an early lunch."

"Why didn't you answer your cell phone? I called several times."

"I forgot to turn it back on when I got out of court."

"Greg's been calling wanting to know the trial date, and I didn't know where you were."

"I saw Greg in court this afternoon and gave him the date." That stopped Suzie. Barbara was satisfied with her aplomb: she had made good eye contact and her voice had been calm and deliberate. She had left no hint of anything out of the ordinary. She moved past the reception area, down the hall to her office, thinking that it had been a lot easier than she had anticipated. But Suzie followed her, something she didn't realize until she was seated behind her desk and looked up to see her standing at the door.

"What's he like?"

She hated Suzie at times like this. Why the hell couldn't Suzie leave her alone? "What's who like?" she said, knowing only too well who Suzie meant but needing time to gather herself.

"Your client."

"Which client?" Still gathering herself.

"The one you were in court with."

"I was with three this afternoon and three this morning." She had recovered enough now, she thought, to talk about him matter-of-factly.

"Come on, Barbara, don't play games with me. I'm talking about that Soto guy."

"I was in court with Alejandro Soto this morning for less than five minutes total. That's the first time I've been to court with him. And he didn't seem any different than he is when I visit with him in the jail." From the look on Suzie's face she knew she had marched past whatever suspicions, if any, Suzie might have had.

"I saw a picture of him in today's paper. He's not bad looking."

"Oh." The less said the better.

"I had lunch with Merrilee and she saw him once in court with Greg, and she thought he was real good-looking, a hunk."

"Oh...well, that might be. I guess he's just not my type."

"Are you trying to tell me that you haven't noticed?"

"Suzie, I've represented men far better-looking than Alejandro Soto. I'd be in big trouble if I started appreciating all of their good looks. That's just not part of the package for me, Suzie. It can't be."

BACK AT his cell, Alejandro thought about the Moncado case and what it meant for him. *So they really want to execute me. And they've decided that the only way they can do that is through a trial. Today in court was their beginning. It's a reality now,* he thought as he sat alone on one of the benches next to the big door, waiting for the guards to come and take him down the tunnel to the jail. *They're really gonna put me through a bogus trial for something I didn't do so they can kill me. They'll get me for sure that way, won't they? It doesn't matter what Johnny Moncado says or doesn't say at their trial. That white jury will never get past the Sanchez murders. They'll think I should've gone to death row for them. They'll think I am wasting their fucking time again. Death row here I come. But with all the appeals everyone says they won't get to me for twenty years. Twenty years. I'll be almost sixty then. That's not too bad, any way you look at it.*

Then he heard them coming. When they were about a third of the way up the tunnel, he saw them. Greene, Hudson, and Roy. "Come on down those steps and meet us at the gate, Soto," Greene said in a loud voice.

Alejandro rose and, slowly maneuvering his leg irons, approached the bottom of the stairs just as they reached the gate that was a replica of the cell doors in the jail: six long bars and three crossbars. As Greene was unlocking the gate, Hudson said, "Hey spic, you and your girlfriend have a good time?"

Greene wheeled around. "Goddamnit Hudson, I've warned you for the last fucking time."

"Greenie, what're you getting so riled up about? I was just asking the greaser how it went in court."

"That's not what I heard."

"Greenie, when you're talking to a spic, you talk like a spic. And that's how they talk. You've heard them. They don't talk like civilized people. They don't talk like you and me."

"Hudson, I don't want you saying nothing more to Soto. Nothing. Is that clear?"

"Greenie, I was just asking him in his lingo how it went in court."

"Nothing, goddamnit. Nothing."

"Alright, alright. Don't have a fucking stroke."

The walk across the tunnel was slow, silent, and grim. When they reached the door that opened up onto the stairs that lead into the jail, Greene moved to the forefront to unlock it. Hudson was on Soto's right, a foot to the side of him and a foot behind him. Roy was on Soto's left. As Greene was unlocking the door, Hudson punched Soto hard in the kidney. Soto gasped and buckled. Greene turned and saw Soto bent over. "What's the matter?" he said. Soto looked at Greene for a moment, straightened himself, and shook his head, nothing.

Jenkins was at the cell bars as they passed him. He said nothing until the guards were gone. "How'd it go, homes?"

A bolt of anger ran through Soto. "I ain't your fucking homes, you black bastard! How many times do I have to tell you! I ain't your fucking homes! Look at me! Look at my arm! Do I look like a fucking nigger? Fuck no! And I ain't no fucking nigger! Can't you see that!"

"I don' know why you be gettin' all crazy, homes. I jus askin' about your case."

"Fuck my case! Fuck your case! For all I know you're probably one of those snitch plants they put next to me so they can fry me when I go to court. Do I ever ask you about your case? Fuck no! And I don't give a good goddamn about your case. So why should you give a good goddamn about mine?"

"Homes, my case ain't shit. Jus a little stealin' from a junkyard. But yours be the main act, homes. Be life or death. Don' get no bigger than that, homes."

Sitting on his bunk, Alejandro gritted his teeth and then yelled, "Well then, what the fuck are you doing locked up next to me with your chickenshit beef unless you're a rat?"

"Don' know why they put me here. 'Cept maybe they be tired of me comin' and goin' an they wanna scare me. Snitchin' out dudes ain't never been my style, homes. Never was, never is, never will be. You don' get it, homes. I like you, I respect you, I see through all your tough-ass talk an I jus' wanna be your fren'."

"Mexicans don't need no fucking friends."

"Everbody needs a fren', homes. 'Specially in here."

XIII

Barbara spent an inordi-
nate amount of time preparing for her Thursday afternoon jail
visit with Alejandro. The visits usually ran an hour or a little more
and she had long since reached the point where she made only
mental notes about what she wanted to cover with Alejandro on
any given afternoon. But this Thursday was different. She had obtained copies of Johnny Moncado's testimony in one of his previous trials and had carefully read the transcripts, outlined parts
of them, and prepared a three-page list of questions for Alejandro that would easily take an hour to ask and get answers to. She
knew why she had gone to those lengths. If this was what it took
to remain on the case, then so be it.

She was guarded when he maneuvered into his side of the cubicle. She quickly started in on the Moncado transcripts. When she
looked up at him to ask her questions, her looks were direct and

brief before she returned to the transcript and her notes and questions. Several times she said, without looking up from her materials, "We've got a lot to cover, Alejandro, and now that we have a trial date, we have no time to spare or waste." He was baffled by her schoolteacher-like approach. Gone was her easy, relaxed manner and her soft smiles. It was probably the court date that was making her uptight.

But the questions went faster than she had thought. She had only five questions left and a good part of the hour remaining. She laid her left arm flat on the writing shelf, turned it a bit so that she could check her watch without appearing to be looking and then looked. Seventeen minutes left. Her mind went into a flurry. What would she do with that remaining time? She couldn't just leave. He would suspect something. His mood was already stunted. She looked up at him, almost as if to ask him, and their eyes met and for the first time that afternoon she didn't immediately look back to her papers. She felt herself turning red, warm, then hot and knew she should look away, not let him see. But she also wanted more than anything on earth to keep looking, blinking, and blushing into his eyes. When she finally dropped her eyes after one, two, three minutes—she didn't know how long—she was embarrassed and ashamed, knowing full well that she should never have let happen what had in fact just happened. She stared down at her papers aware that she should leave, get out of there, but not knowing how without adding to her shameful mess. Finally she simply stuffed all of her papers into her briefcase, stood and said, without looking at him, "I've got to go," and left.

WHEN SOTO was returned to his cell, Jenkins said, "Whas up homes?"

"Fuck you, nigger!"

"Look to me like your lawyer dumped some heavy shit on you."

Nobody could piss him off more, get to him more, than that filthy nigger. "Fuck you, nigger, and shut the fuck up! If I want to talk to you, I'll let you know."

He needed to think now while it was still clear in his mind, while what he had just seen, no doubt about it, was still fresh in his mind. She was stuck on him. He turned her on. There was no doubt about it. But what to do about it? There was nothing he could do about it, not there in his cell...not anywhere. If he could be free for an hour, just one hour, then he'd do something about it, then she'd see. One minute he was proud, flattered that he could turn her on. The next minute he was miserable because now he wanted something, now he needed something that he could never have. How much easier life was when you wanted nothing, when you were content with what you had or at least accepted what you had. She was a lawyer, yes. She was his lawyer, yes. She was a woman, yes. And she had just given him every reason to believe she could be his woman...yes, yes, yes. But how in his locked-up situation could he make happen what he now so desperately wanted to make happen? There was no way out. Until this trial was over, she would always be so completely within reach and yet so completely unreachable. Unless of course he fired her, told the judge he wouldn't go to court if she continued as his lawyer. The thought of her no longer being there left him empty, while at the same time the thought of her being there tortured him. There was no solution. For two or three hours a week he could think she was his and bask in the way she reacted to him. Then for the rest of the week he would wonder what she was doing, who she was doing it with, and, worse, who she was fucking. He slept badly. She was there, and she wasn't there. He was having her...someone else was having her. Every morning for the next days when he woke, he regretted having seen what he so unmistakenly had seen that past Thursday.

As Barbara left the jail, she knew she had to withdraw from the case. If what had just occurred were ever to happen in open court, not only would Judge Spencer remove her from the case on the spot, but she'd be laughed out of town by all the other lawyers—and the State Bar might even take action. She drove home. Suzie had probably left the office by then, but why tempt the gods. Once home, her first impulse was to call Greg and tell him she was withdrawing from the case. But she had to have a reason. She couldn't tell Greg she was withdrawing because she couldn't look at their client without turning beet red and getting flustered and mesmerized. Unless she had a good reason, Greg would never agree, especially now that they had a trial date. Where would he find a suitable replacement? But down deep, she didn't want to withdraw from the case. It was winnable, one that could bring her the kind of media exposure and praise that she hadn't had in a long while. And withdrawing would also mean she would not see him again...or have any more contact with him. She was thirty-nine and had never felt like this about a man before and probably never would again. She went to bed knowing she had to tell Greg in the morning.

But by noon of the next day she could not claim any of the principle reasons lawyers use for withdrawing from a case: a conflict of interest based on her prior representation of another individual involved in this case who had an adverse interest against Alejandro, a deep-seated conflict with the client himself, a conflicting calendar schedule, or a medical excuse. The first three she had already discussed with Greg and had assured him that they were nonexistent. The last would require a letter or declaration from a physician stating that continued participation in this case would be detrimental to her health. Such a letter might ruin her chances for future court appointments to serious cases.

The weekend went by and she did not call Greg. And with each passing day, she was becoming more and more convinced she could and should stay on the case. Over the years, there had to have been millions of women in different settings who had worked for or with men who they found themselves attracted to with little or no hope of seeing something come of it and who still continued working under those conditions. What had happened in court had been a complete surprise. Thursday's visit was a clumsy attempt at denial. Now that she was fully aware of the attraction, she had to learn to live with it. Rather than restrict the interactions with Alejandro, it made more sense to have increased contact with him...more visits with him. The more she saw of him, the sooner the electricity would fizzle. You could only be around someone or something so long before that person or thing became commonplace. The more often she saw him, the sooner Thursday's sensation would wear away. And there was every reason to see him more often now that a trial date had been set. But would her attraction hinder his defense? The answer seemed clear enough. She valued him as she had never valued another client. Despite his history, there was so much potential there, so much potential good. If anything, the attraction would spur her on and drive her. This would not be laborious work.

So the dance began. For the next two weeks, she saw him two or three times a week. There was always some aspect of the case that needed discussion. More often than not they got sidetracked on national and world politics, history and books, the weather—things that casual acquaintances or even friends might talk about. She did reach a point where she could look at him without blushing or becoming transfixed. But they both knew and knew that the other knew, too.

They had been talking about the Vietnam War when he could hold back no longer. "Are you married?"

It took her by surprise. She was flattered and pleased and yet her answer was, "Alejandro, what does that have to do with your case?"

"Nothing. But are you married?"

She flushed a bit and shook her head in supposed exasperation even though she was more impressed by his persistence. "No, I'm not married. But really, Alejandro, we should get back to the case."

"Are you living with a man?"

"Alejandro!"

"I want to know. I need to know. It's very important for me to know."

How did he always seem to know exactly what button to push? "No, I live alone." Far more than he had asked for. But she wanted him to know.

"Do you have a boyfriend?"

Now she was both pleased and disturbed. "Alejandro, please... No, I don't have a boyfriend. But we have to get back to discussing the case. We can't keep talking like this. This little, makeshift visiting room could easily be bugged."

"Bugged?"

"Yes, bugged."

"But isn't it some kind of felony for cops to do that?"

"Yes, it is. But what makes you think that would stop them? Talking like we just were could get me thrown off the case."

"No."

"Yes."

THAT MARKED the beginning of the end of Alejandro Soto's hostility toward Willie Jenkins. "Hey, Jenkins." Now it was Alejandro Soto who was standing at his cell bars and Willie Jenkins who was lying in his bunk some ten feet away.

"Whas up, homes?"

"Why don't you come up here next to me so we don't have any of these other fools listening in on what don't pertain to them."

"OK, man, but whas up?"

Then Jenkins was standing at his bars on the other side of the wall that separated the two cells, and Alejandro asked in a low voice, "How long you been jailing in this here jail?

"Oh, 'bout tweny, twenty-five years."

"Is it twenty or twenty-five, man? It's important."

"Let's see... Twenty-three years...an six months. Why, homes?"

"You think they're bugging the attorneys' visiting rooms?"

"Wouldn' put it past them, homes."

"No, I'm not asking what you wouldn't put past them. I'm asking if you've ever known or heard of the goons bugging the attorneys' visiting rooms?"

"I know for sure they been buggin' families an frens' visitin' rooms cause they done did it to me once an twice to my road-dog crime parner."

"But what about the attorneys' visiting rooms?"

"Well, lots a folks talk about it, and a few swear they do cause there's no otha way they could be gettin' the evidence they're gettin'. One of my lawyers swore up an down they did it. Othawise it had to be him who snitched me off cause there's no otha way they got what they got unless my own lawyer snitched me off."

"But ain't it a felony if they do that?"

"So what cop is gonna be turnin' in another cop to the cops? An they only need one or two of them to plant that bug an no other cops need to know about it... So what happen? Whas the problem?"

"Well, I got a woman out there."

"You got a woman out there! I be dog. Here I thought you was the Lone Ranger an you got a woman out there. You never said nothing about no woman. An nobody but your lawyers come see you. Everybody knows you done eight years in the SHU. So how can you still have a woman?"

"It's my old lady from years past. We've been off and on for years. Anyway, she wants to be on now. She lives down south by San Diego, so she can't come up to visit me. She's barely making it. No car. Three kids. On welfare. But now she's calling my lawyer and telling her things to tell me. Problem is, she's been talking about things that could hurt my case. So my lawyers been asking me about them and I don't even want to talk about them if that visiting room is bugged. See where I'm coming from?"

"I do an I wouldn' trust that room for nothin'."

FOR WEEKS Alejandro refrained from using any words that could be construed as personal. Instead he had to rely on her looks and smiles and the softness of her voice, none of which were nearly enough to assure and reassure him that he was the man in her life, the only man in her life.

What made it doubly difficult was that she could ask and did ask, had every right and reason to ask, for everything there was to know about him. Nor could he sway in any of his responses, because she had all the exhaustive prison files on him as well as his old probation reports. Then without any warning, she settled in on the Carlos Sanchez homicides.

"We haven't ever really talked about those killings. How they came about. Why they came about. What actually happened. I've read all the police reports, but those are their words and their deductions. You didn't give the police a statement and you didn't testify in court. No one has ever heard from you what happened, how it really happened, and why it happened. And, believe me, I need to know."

She did need to know, more for herself than for the case. Because she had reached a point again where she thought she had to withdraw from the case, suffer whatever consequences came to her as a lawyer but to preserve her well-being and sanity. Yes, she had overcome the blushing and the feeling of being entranced by him, but she had been drawn deeper and deeper into him. She thought of him constantly. She dreamed about him. She was seeing him three times a week, sometimes four, and some visits for more than an hour. Afterward, she would relive each meeting for hours. She started counting the time until she would see him again. But more and more, she was haunted by the two murders. She hated the secrecy—or was it that she was living a lie? She dared not tell anyone, breathe a word to anyone, of what was now becoming, or rather already was, the most important thing in her life. She couldn't continue to live with this shame, this fear, that someone would discover them. How, everyone she knew would say, could she have possibly developed feelings for a twice-convicted murderer? They would laugh. They would be disgusted. They would trust her with nothing. She would have to leave town...go some place where no one knew of her or him, perhaps even another state. And yet, oddly enough, she still knew only what the police had said about the two murders. Because he, the only living person who had been present, had said nothing. After fifteen years of practicing criminal law, she knew police reports were not always accurate.

So she began by suggestion: it would probably be helpful if she heard from him what had happened on that fateful day. Then it became a legal necessity: if he testified, and she felt he had to, he could be badly damaged on cross-examination if his lawyer didn't know what had actually happened that day. Finally it became mandatory: even if he chose not to testify, the prosecution could still raise the two killings as similar acts and his lawyer would be powerless to defend against what would probably be the most devastating evidence in the case. One way or another, Alejandro Soto had avoided discussing the prior murders. Barbara persisted until it became the focal point of their visits. Still he resisted.

He knew from her first suggestion that he could not tell her. As the visits passed and her requests increased in number and intensity, he used every ploy, every means he could, to run out the visit without telling her. To tell her would mean that he would lose her, and he had never known a feeling like this. His mother had loved him, unconditionally loved him, but that had been all. He didn't know what this woman wanted or how she stood to gain anything from him. But at times, her eyes, her words, her smiles, and her laughter clearly told him she wanted to be with him and she enjoyed being next to him—even if separated by glass—and she desired him. She had fostered in him previously unknown feelings of warmth, worth, hope, pleasure, and satisfaction. At times, he was convinced he had someone who cared for and about him. At times, he was bold enough to think she was his woman—this beautiful, talented, intelligent woman. And though her feelings for him were a mystery to him, he accepted them more often than he denied them, enjoyed them at least as much as he had suffered with them.

The fear and dread of losing her...that was why he couldn't tell her. To tell her was to reveal himself, and if she saw him for what he was and who he was—and he could imagine the look of horror on her face—she would leave him. But then the day finally arrived. She began by saying, "Alejandro, I'm not going to say another thing and I will sit here in silence for the next hour until you tell me about the Sanchez killings."

So they sat for an hour, occasionally, doggedly, looking at each other, their eyes pleading for understanding but neither speaking. As she left she said, "The next time I come, Alejandro, the first thing I'm going to do is ask you is if you're prepared to tell me. And if you don't tell me, I'll leave then and there, maybe for good. I can't take this any longer."

HE INDEED came prepared for her next visit. As soon as the guards were gone, he took out a sheet of paper he had concealed among his other papers and on which he had written several lines, and, he pressed it flat against the glass for her to read. It said: "I will tell you what you want to know. But first I want you to tell me what your feelings are for me. You don't have to say it over the phone. You can write it on a sheet of paper and put it up to the glass like I'm doing and then slip it under the glass. Then I'll tell you." This device was commonly used by inmates when they were visiting with family or friends if they believed the visiting room was bugged, since there was no legal proscription against eavesdropping on non-attorney visits. So certain was he that once she heard about the Sanchez murders, once she saw him for what he was, she would leave him that he wanted a piece of paper, something physical, to always remember what he once had.

She read and reread the words pressed against the glass. Then she thought some and read the message again. It would be stupid to put her feelings in writing and then pass that paper to him. Inmate cells were always being searched by guards. If something like that were ever found, the repercussions would be grave. She thought some more. Then she said, "Alejandro, I'm here, like it or not, first as your lawyer. If you won't tell me openly and freely, without any conditions being placed on it, about the most damaging piece of evidence that the district attorney has against you, one that could lead to a death sentence, then I'm going to have to ask the court to allow me to withdraw from your case."

He studied her. There was no blinking and no blushing then. She meant it. She wasn't playing games. But the tone of her words and her look were still warm and caring. Would she really withdraw if he didn't tell her? She said she would. What was the greater risk? Not tell her—and he didn't think she was bluffing—and she'd withdraw? Or, tell and maybe she would or wouldn't withdraw?

"I'll tell you. Where do you want me to start?"

"From the beginning."

"What's the beginning? How I met Carlos Sanchez? Why I met him?"

"All of it."

XIV

HE LOOKED DOWN. HE
caught and held his breath. She would never understand. It would
end everything. But he had no choice. "I guess you could say that
it started at the Chrysler plant," he said softly.

"I can barely hear you."

Louder, "I was twenty-three, and it was the first job I ever had
for more than a week. I had finally left my mother's house, and I
had to work. My brothers and sisters were making my life and my
mother's life miserable because I was still freeloading there. So I
left. A friend of mine was working out at Chrysler putting bolts
into cars for eight bucks an hour, which was pretty good money
at that time. I figured if he could do it, I could do it. They put me
on the assembly line right away. The cars never stopped coming.
My job was to put eight bolts, four in the front door and four in
the back door, on each car before it passed me. Can you imagine

what it's like standing at an assembly line putting four bolts in the front door and four bolts in the back door for eight hours a day, five and sometimes six days a week? I used to look at the old-timers, the guys who had been doing it for ten, fifteen, sometimes twenty years and just wondered how in the hell they did it. I used to tell myself I'd never be doing it for twenty years because I'd put a gun to my head long before that. I used to ask myself is this all there is to life? I wasn't married and I didn't have no kids to support like the rest of those poor saps. I didn't *want* to get married and have any kids. That just meant slavery to me. Then I would *have* to work like they did, for as long as they did. That's probably one of the big reasons I was never with a broad very long. I just wanted to party and they wanted a...a...'commitment' was the word some of them used. They just wanted to get married and have kids and settle down.

"So I'd ask myself, standing there with a wrench in one hand and bolts in the other, is this all there is to life? Lots of times the answer came back to me in the singsongy way we memorized it in after-school catechism classes: 'God made me to know, love, and serve Him in this life and to be happy with Him in the next.'

"There was no God in my life then, still isn't. I just could never get over the idea of this Great, Good God and all the suffering in the world. So I used to stand there thinking and waiting for my next car: I don't have no God, no wife, no kids, maybe that's why I'm so miserable now. But I sure as hell don't believe there's a next life. One's enough." He shook his head.

"Anyway, I'm getting way off track. It took me more than two months to figure out that more than half the guys on the line were either loaded or drunk. Most of the guys that were loaded were loaded on weed. It wasn't long before I was loaded on weed too, with a wrench in one hand and bolts in the other. It helped a lot. That old assembly line didn't really matter that much after all, and the future would be whatever it wanted to be. But I had to be careful how much weed I used because after too many joints nothing mattered. My eyes got real bloodshot after my first joint, so I started wearing shades indoors, outdoors, everywhere. Then I knew why at least a third of the guys on the line wore shades.

"One day an old friend of mine, Willy Granados, was giving me a ride home from work when he said to me, 'Hey, Ale, I just scored real big. Wanna go to my pad and catch a little taste?' 'Taste of what?' 'Smack, man, real good stuff.' I had never tried heroin. I had always used weed and I had tried coke and speed, but never heroin. For one thing, it was always too expensive for me. For another, I had seen too many guys get really strung out on it, and I didn't like what I saw. But it had been an ugly, ugly day on the line and I figured one time's not gonna string me out and it wouldn't hurt none to see what it was like. 'Sure,' I said."

She was watching him carefully, watching for any change in his demeanor, any hesitation, any confusion, or excessive repetition, anything that would indicate that he was lying or not being completely truthful. She had seen none yet.

"Well, old Willy tied me down and shot me up and I swear he shot me straight up into paradise. I was in heaven, better than heaven. Everything was great...wonderful. I didn't have a care or a worry. I was never happier and haven't been since. It was better than sex, way better. I just floated and floated in happiness. Everywhere I turned there was just more and more happiness. When I came down, when I came out of it, I knew I had to do it again. I knew I had to have it again. Getting strung out didn't even cross my mind. There was no way I was about to let that thought in. You know how you have to eat to live? Well I knew I wanted smack to live.

"For two months I had the ride of my life. But within the first two weeks I had been needing a little more and a little more to reach my high and after two months I was out of money. And then I had my first taste of being sick. Every joint in my body ached. My head felt like someone had split it open with an axe and was still pounding. I had a fever but I was freezing. I was sweating and running cold chills at the same time. I wrapped myself in every blanket I could find but was still freezing. My stomach felt like it was tied in one big knot. I was convulsing, and every convulsion felt like it was one big jerk that was going to tear me apart. When you're like that, nobody wants to be around you. People would stop by and then take off as soon as they saw me. Finally a couple of dope fiends felt sorry enough for me to let me have some of theirs. They gave me just enough to stop me from being sick. At times I wonder if they had really done me a favor after all. Maybe if they had left me alone, I would have kicked once and for all right then and there. But that's bullshit. It was going to take more than one sickness to make me kick. Still once I was 'normal,' I found this fear way down deep inside me, a fear like I had never known, a fear that if I didn't have the stuff I would get horribly sick again. So I jumped on the junkie bandwagon. I became a criminal.

"From then on I did anything and everything I had to do to get my next fix. I wasn't working anymore. I had hung up my job after two weeks of happiness. But that didn't matter because I could never have earned enough money at any job to keep me supplied with smack. So it was steal, steal, steal. I didn't turn armed robber. That wasn't me—at least that's what I thought at first.

"There were three fences in town. Dirty motherfuckers! They were the real criminals, greedy bastards, taking advantage of strung-out hypes. They'd buy anything we stole. But we'd be lucky if we got a third of the market price on the new items. And one, to boot, had a compadre who was a sergeant in the police department. Anyway, if they saw that we were really strung out, sick, or about to get sick, then their offers would go lower and lower.

"I started with cigarettes. In those days the stores stacked their cartons of cigarettes in open shelves just like they did everything else. Well, I'd walk into a store with a couple of big shopping bags under my arms, walk over to where the cigarettes were, fill my two bags with cartons, and walk out of the store just like any other paying customer. A few times I had to run for it. But as soon as I was far enough away from the store, I stopped and told whoever was chasing me, 'You take another step toward me and it could be the last one you take.' That worked.

"Then there were the beer runs. Whenever anyone could get their hands on a pickup truck, two or three of us would jump in and then look for and follow a beer truck making its deliveries. We'd wait till the driver pulled up to a big store—one where he would have to wheel in a big load and take it deep into the store. Once the driver was past the store's door, we'd pull up alongside the truck on the street side so that nobody in the store could see us, and then we'd start loading cases of beer into the pickup as fast as we could. We pulled those beer runs quite a few times and we only got caught twice. Actually I never got caught because as soon as the cops were on our trail, we'd jump out of the truck and run in different directions. Both times the other guys got caught but I didn't."

Now it was he who looked at her, looking for any sign of disgust or scorn. But he saw none.

"I became a damn good thief. One of the few things I've done well in my life. The secret was be as natural as you can be and fit in with what's going on all around you, and you can be as bold as you want to be. A lot of dope fiends couldn't believe what me and Johnny Moncado were pulling off for a while. Refrigerators and TVs and, a couple of times, stoves. We would dress up in white coveralls and blue baseball caps and walk into Sears or one of the big stores with our hand trucks on a Friday night or Saturday when they were real busy. We would walk right into the appliance department, load up a couple of refrigerators or TVs, and head right out the front door, like we were on our way to deliveries. Then we just walked right around the corner to Johnny's pickup truck. It worked real well for a few months until one Friday night Johnny tripped and a refrigerator fell on him. He must have been a hell of a lot more loaded than I thought. But then, I was pretty loaded myself.

"When Johnny went to jail for his refrigerator, Julia and I hooked up. It was the first time I really liked nodding out with somebody. We were dope-fiend soul mates. I don't think we had sex more than five times in the eleven months we were together.

It was more than enough just to sit in a room, any room, side by side or across from each other and get loaded. Two of us on the same high at the same time was great, and we dug it. Between my stealing and her working as a streetwalker, we were able to keep at it for quite awhile. But then it came down to the same old thing: our habits had become too big for the money we didn't have."

For the first time he thought he saw her flinch at the name Julia. Then he was sure he saw her flinch at the mention of sex with another woman.

"Our connection for a long time was Carlos Sanchez. Carlos was a strange man. He didn't use dope, never had to. He lived alone in a ratty old flat that he owned. He never married, had no girl-friend or boyfriend. He sold a lot of dope and because he never used, he never kept the dope on him or close to him and was very careful who he sold to and how he sold. He made himself and San-tos Estrada a lot of money. Although you could never tell that by the way he lived."

She saw absolutely no change in his demeanor at the first men-tion of Carlos Sanchez.

"Carlos had a dog, a giant Doberman pinscher, the meanest-looking dog you'd ever want to see. Saint, Carlos called him, and in a way Saint was really a saint to Carlos. Except for one hour a day, Carlos always had Saint at his side. All Carlos had to do was snap his fingers and point to whoever was annoying him and Saint would growl and get up on all four and bare his teeth at the poor sap. Every afternoon between three and four, Carlos would close shop for an hour and take a nap. Then one of the three Mexican boys Carlos kept at his mother's house about four blocks away would come and take Saint for his daily exercise. Carlos made it clear to all his customers that anyone who came looking for dope between three and four during the day would be put on his shit list, and he wouldn't sell to him for a month. If it happened a sec-ond time, then he wouldn't sell to him again period. One thing you have to understand is that Carlos always had good shit and you never had to worry you'd OD on his stuff.

"The three Mexican boys, they were really Indians, came from a village deep in Mexico. How they ever got here, no one knew. And Carlos rotated them. Every six months to the day, the three that had been there were gone and three new ones were there to take their place. They looked to be in their late teens or early twenties. But it's hard to tell with Indians, and every one of them was a dead-on Indian. Being from Mexico they must have spoken Spanish, but I never heard them. They always spoke their Indian language and, sure as hell, Carlos spoke to them in that language too. Where he learned it was anybody's guess. They lived with Carlos's mother. The old woman had a rickety, old house on a huge, overgrown lot. All the dope fiends were always betting their asses that's where the dope was. But the old lady had three Dobermans as big and mean-looking as Saint, and everybody said the Mexicans carried small machetes, but I never saw one. Anyway, with the three Dobermans and the way the Mexicans handled themselves, there wasn't a single dope fiend that was about to start snooping around the old lady's property."

Now Alejandro was very much matter-of-fact, telling of people and things that had been the core of his life.

"The way Carlos ran his operation was you could go to his flat pretty much anytime—except from three to four in the afternoon—ring his bell downstairs, talk into the squawk box, and, if he let you in, go upstairs. The flat had two apartments: one upstairs and one downstairs. The one downstairs was always empty. When you got upstairs, he'd ask you what you wanted. You could never say dope because he was always afraid you might be wired for sound. If you said dope, you were outta there. Instead you had to say you wanted to put some money on the horses and he'd ask how much and want to see the money. Once he counted it, he'd say that he'd see what he could do and he'd push a buzzer on the wall. Within a minute or two, one of those Mexican boys was in the room. They got there so fast that some of us thought they lived or at least were stationed downstairs. Later I found out for sure that they came running from where Carlos said they lived: at his mother's house.

Carlos would talk just a few words, never more than that, in that weird-sounding Indian tongue to the Mexican that came, and then you would follow the Mexican out into the street in whatever direction he chose until he pointed for you to stop and wait. In a few minutes, he'd be back with the dope.

"Everybody was sure Carlos had a big stash of cash in his house. Where else could it be? No one ever saw him out in the street, and banks would be real suspicious of a bunch of big, steady, cash deposits coming in from a guy who didn't seem to have a job or a business anywhere. But Carlos always had the Mexicans and Saint and a gun close by, and he was always telling you that he and Mr. Big were in the racing business together and that if anything ever happened to him or his money, Mr. Big would take care of anyone and everyone who was behind it.

"Carlos usually wanted only one customer at a time up at his pad. But I was up there a few times when other junkies were up there, too. Now I think he let me be there just so he could have the pleasure of watching me watch them. Those few times were when the other poor saps were really hurting, when they were already starting to shake and they had no money or not enough to score. Carlos loved to toy with them. 'Now why do you want to be coming up here when you know that you're not in any position to put anything on the horses?' he'd say. He loved to see them grovel, beg for it, promise him anything, do anything for just enough so that they wouldn't get sick. He had one guy lick Saint until Saint came. Watching him, I know that Carlos enjoyed it more than the dog did. He had two straight dudes try to fuck each other, and he laughed like hell the whole time as those poor chumps took turns trying like hell to do each other with their limp things."

Here he had expected some sort of reaction—shock from Barbara—but there had been none. Instead there was an absolute stone-cold look on her face.

"I should have known my day would come. And it did, but with Julia. It was toward the end, before I killed the son of a bitch. Me and Julia were hurting real bad. The first time he had Julia go down on him while I tried to sodomize her. It went on and on until, in between all his laughing, he came. The second time an old junkie named Cookie was up there begging too. He had the two girls licking each other and me licking the girl's butt that was on top. He said he wasn't going to give us anything until one of the girls came. We must have tried for half an hour with no luck. He laughed so hard that I think he finally cut us a break because his gut was hurting so bad from laughing, and he buzzed for one of the Indians. When you're strung out that bad, hating yourself isn't even a consideration. You have to have the stuff, not to get high, because at that point you'd have to be one of them rich musicians to have enough money for your next high. All you want, all every bit of you wants, is not to be sick. And when you get enough not to be sick, to ward it off one more time, to be 'normal,' as some of the idiots say, then it's just a few minutes, an hour at the most, before you start thinking that in the very near future you're gonna need another fix, and there's no time or room in your mind to be hating yourself or the situation you've put yourself in."

Barbara knew that he was waiting for her reaction to the perversity, but she was too intent on evaluating him to react as he expected and perhaps wanted.

"The third time it was just the four of us: me, Julia, Carlos, and Saint. He had Saint fuck her. I know Julia had done her share of streetwalking but nobody deserved that. He didn't make me do anything except watch, and he watched me watch as much as he watched them. Something snapped that night, something snapped then and there. When the dog came and fell off Julia, I knew what I wanted to do. I knew what I had to do. As we were following the Indian, Julia was crying silent tears and all I could do or say was 'I'm sorry, Julia.' I'll never forget what she said: 'You gotta do what you gotta do.' Nothing more, nothing less, no production, no drama. I gave her my share of the dope that night. I probably felt some guilt, but I gave her my share of the dope mainly because I knew then what I had to do and I knew I had to start then. I told Julia I was going to kick cold turkey and she said, 'You crazy?' and I said, 'I never been saner.'

"I took all the blankets we had and I went to see old Freddie Garcia, an ex-con and an ex-junkie who had kicked cold turkey and who still lived in the barrio and was always preaching kicking. 'I wanna kick, Freddie,' I said. And he said, 'You sure?' And I said, 'I never been surer.' He locked me in his basement with some crackers and water. I've never been through a rougher week. The only thing that kept me going was Carlos. By the ninth day Freddie would open the door when I asked him to open it, but not before then. Until then, it only opened when he wanted to open it. I came out of the basement at the end of the second week. I didn't go back to Julia. Not then...I couldn't. Freddie let me stay with him. I had a lot to think about, a lot to plan."

Now he saw that her focus on him had become even keener. Her eyes had narrowed almost as if she were expecting him to lie.

"For the next two weeks, I watched Carlos's flat and the Indians as best I could without being seen. The first thing I noticed was that while everybody, including the Indians, rang the downstairs buzzer to go upstairs, whenever one of the Indians took Saint for his walk, he came out the back door downstairs. Nobody knew that you could get upstairs from the downstairs back door. After watching the Indians and Saint leave for a few days, I ran up to the door once they were gone and saw that the only lock the Indians were probably using when they left was a press-point lock on the inside knob. Hell, I must have busted open fifty of those with a credit card when I was burglarizing houses. The next day I had a credit card with me and after waiting for ten minutes I ran up to the door and...click. Sure enough.

"The next thing I learned was that the Indians always went to the mother's house for the dope. No big surprise, but then we never knew for sure. The dope wasn't in the house itself but somewhere in that huge yard, because once they got past the fence, they went around the house someplace and never went inside even when the old lady was standing on the front porch. And the fence must've had an electrical current running through it because the Indians always stopped a foot or two in front of it and made this weird sound and usually waited for grandma to come out on the porch and croak something back before they touched the gate. It made me wonder if the money wasn't somewhere in the yard, too."

The planning sent chills through her. But he was too calm, too matter-of-fact to be lying. Everything made sense...and fell into place.

"But that's not what I told Johnny Moncado. He was a greedy bastard who I always suspected had his own private little stash hidden somewhere that he would never share with anyone no matter how sick they got. I told him only that I definitely knew where Carlos had his money hidden up in the flat. I told him about the back door and that I would be wearing a mask and a cap and gloves and long sleeves so that Carlos would never know it was me if he woke up. I told him I was taking a gun with me just in case Carlos woke and made an issue of it with his gun. I told him to be parked around the corner so that we could get out of there fast. The split would be 60–40, and he was more than satisfied with that.

"Once I saw the Indian leave with Saint, I waited ten minutes before I ran to the back door. Inside I didn't bother with the mask or the gloves or the cap; I kept them stuffed in my pocket. All I needed was my gun. I took that out of my waistband and for the fourth or fifth time that day made sure it was fully loaded. The stairs were to my right and a lot of them were warped with age. I found the spots on each step that had been nailed down and walked only on those spots hoping not to creak. Halfway up the stairs there was a small creak that stopped when I stopped and I shifted my shoes. When I got up on the landing I started shaking, and I cursed myself over and over again and stood still for a minute or two until the shakes calmed down. I had come too far, suffered too much, to blow it now. But when I turned on the landing I saw there was another door that led into Carlos's apartment that seemed to be closed too snuggly not to be locked, and my body sank. If it was locked, if I had to force it, he'd probably get me before I could get him. I had no idea what was behind the door and I was just glad that I had seen Saint leave earlier.

Step after careful step I made my way to the door. I looked at the old black doorknob and wondered how much it would squeak only to have the door be locked from the inside. Carlos had probably locked it as the Indian and Saint went out. I cocked my gun. If we had a shoot-out and I got hit, it didn't matter so long as I got him. I turned the knob and it turned easily and completely without a squeak. Then I carefully put my weight to the door. It gave and swung open. I was in the kitchen, and I could hear Carlos snoring down the hall in the front room where everybody paid their 'horse money' or did his bidding. I took off my shoes and socks. My bare feet would give me a better sense of the old floor. I moved toward the hall and felt the floor give a few times and stopped and replaced my lead foot. I could hear Carlos snoring clearer and clearer.

I went down the hall to the front-room door. There he was sprawled out on his back on his favorite red couch—a couch that had witnessed so many of his pleasures. His gun was on a lamp table less than a foot from his right hand. I could have shot him from the doorway. I thought about it and thought about it. No, I wanted to be sure that I snuffed the filthy pig once and for all. So I took step by slow step toward him. I started trembling but not shaking. With each step my extended right arm was bringing my gun closer and closer to his fat head. Then I was next to him and I brought the gun to within an inch of his temple. But I didn't pull the trigger. I wanted to enjoy the moment and squeeze as much pleasure out of having him at my ultimate mercy the way he had had so many others at his. I held the gun there, what, a minute or five minutes, I don't know. But then I started to shake again. Finally, as the shakes were getting too strong, I gritted my teeth and screamed, 'You rotten cocksucker!' and shot him twice in the head with his skull and flesh and blood splattering all over me. I was still shaking as I watched the blood pour out of his head.

And then I heard a scream behind me and I turned and shot, emptied my gun into the doorway, and watched her fall. It was only as she lay quivering and bleeding that I saw that it was his mother. And I ran."

As Alejandro told of the step-by-step stalking, she was crying. When he recounted standing over Sanchez, gun in hand, gun an inch from his temple, and waited, wrenching every modicum of pleasure from this final act, she nodded. When the shots killed first Sanchez and then his mother, she felt that not only Alejandro, but she as well, had been vindicated. And he had not lied.

XV

Barbara couldn't stop the tears. She wanted to say something...something like, she knew, she understood, it was OK, and it didn't change anything. Say something foolish...anything. She didn't care if the cubicles were bugged. She had to let him know she understood. She had to say something... But when she looked up, her tears flowed all the more and they embarrassed her—left her speechless and feeling foolish. She was his lawyer first and foremost, and now this. She shoved her notepad and pen into her briefcase, stood, and left without a word, too ashamed to let him see her like that for another moment...to hear her like that.

She started for the elevator and then stopped. She could hear guards talking at the control desk, and she was still crying. It would be her luck that one of them would ride down in the elevator with her. She had to stop crying. But even if she did, her eyes would still be puffy and red and her face streaked with eye make-up. They all knew who she was, that she was Alejandro's lawyer, and she was coming from an interview with him and she was crying. The word would spread. It would get back to Judge Spencer and even Greg. She could hear Greg say, "What the hell were you doing crying in the jail after seeing Soto? What'd he do to you? What'd he say to you? What's going on between you two?" Then she was conscious once again that she was standing in the jail hall-way and that a guard could come by at any time.

She reached into her briefcase and put on her dark glasses, and for several moments the third floor of the jail went completely dark. Then she could make out the dim light over the elevator door. There was no one standing there. She moved as quickly and quietly as she could toward it. When she reached it, the desk guard interrupted his conversation some twenty-five feet away and asked loudly, "Finished, counselor?" She had already pushed the elevator button and she managed a yes without turning. The elevator light flashed "3" and she heard the elevator settle to a stop. The door begin to open without anyone approaching from the control desk.

She breathed a sigh of relief and stepped into the elevator and pressed "G" before she saw him. He was tall, young, and angular with a blond, burr haircut. He was standing in the back corner of the elevator staring at her. Her first inclination was to keep her head down so that he wouldn't see the awful shape her face had to be in. But that would be a giveaway. She raised her head and stared straight ahead at the panel opposite her. He said nothing. But out of the corner of her sunglass-covered right eye, she could see that he was staring at her. As the elevator slowed for the first floor, he moved next to her so that his left shoulder was inches from her. He was wearing blue fatigues and a name tag that said "A. Hudson." When the elevator door opened, A. Hudson went to his left and she to her right into the jail lobby and then out the front door.

Once in her car, there was another outpouring of tears. She started for home. She was in no condition to go to her office. Halfway home, she turned and headed toward Brown Town, a collection of run-down buildings in east San Cristobal that was at once a skid row and a commercial center of sorts for brown and black people. When she was a public defender, nearly 75 percent of her clients had come from Brown Town. "Hope" was a forgotten word in Brown Town. Those who could and did work were primarily day laborers who boarded rickety trucks and buses in the morning darkness to be driven to farms and ranches. Drunks frequented Brown Town's one, dried-up park more than anyone else did. Pimps were readily noticeable in their flashy clothes and cars. Small-time drug dealers supporting a habit were on the constant lookout for old and new customers. Old, white-haired, brown-skinned, bow-legged, apron-clad, Mexican women went about their endless errands as if blind, seeing nothing, disturbed by nothing, and yet unmolested and unnoticed themselves as they filled their indestructible, plastic shopping bags with meager buys. Throughout the day, different bands of young gangbangers came strutting through Brown Town with their defiant swaggers and unmistakable clothes, displaced sons of illegal aliens, rejected by the mainstream culture just as they rejected their own, ultimately heading nowhere except to juvenile hall and then jail and finally prison. Broken windows, tarnished buildings, filthy streets, and splattered sidewalks...Brown Town.

When Barbara reached Brown Town, she made sure that her doors were locked and her windows were up before she joined the slow procession of cars down the main street. As she crept along, she watched the parade of people and, as always, wondered how they survived. Alejandro had come out of a Brown Town and, but for the two killings, might well have survived and even excelled. The irony was that after his description of the two killings she now understood his earlier question, heard those earlier words over and over again, "Is there ever an intentional killing that may not be wrong...not a crime?" Brown Towns had to be better places without people like Carlos Sanchez and his mother. Meanwhile somewhere in Bali or Monte Carlo, Brian Stone was sipping a daiquiri on a balcony overlooking a beautiful expanse of water, and somewhere in California, Bob Johnson was closing another loan for corporate America.

When she got home, she called Fred Solomon. It was well past six and she fully expected to leave a voice-mail message. But Solomon answered his phone. She introduced herself and said that in preparing for trial, she had become convinced that the prosecution would use the Sanchez killings as similar acts and wanted to know what, if any, flaws or weaknesses in the prosecution's case Solomon had found in his review of the record on appeal. She listened patiently while Solomon pontificated. Finally, she was able to put to him the only question she had really called to ask, "What are Alejandro's chances?"

"Chances for what?"

"For a reversal."

"As you well know, the federal courts don't grant an evidentiary hearing everyday. It's one in hundreds, even thousands."

"But what are *his* chances?"

"I'd say seven out of ten."

Fred Solomon had made her day. Barbara Blake slept well that night. But she did not see Alejandro for the next ten days. She had much to consider and she needed the time and the space away from him. Nor did she ask Greg about his visits with Alejandro in the interim.

SOMETHING WAS wrong and Willie Jenkins knew it. "Hey homes, whas goin' on witch you, man?" He moved to the cell bars. "You OK in there man?"

"Mind your own fucking business, Jenkins"

"You are my business, homes. Since we been next-door neighbors, I ain't never seen you like this. Nothin' worse than to die all alone in a jail cell."

"Mind your own fucking business, jigaboo, if you know what's good for you."

"Homes, if you was one of them silly-ass li'l gangbangers with all your compadrays backin' your play, I might could take notice. But you ain't. And even tho you be workin' out all the time, that don' mean you're in any condition to take on ol' Jenkins. Hate to tell you, homes, don' matter how good condition you're in or how tough you think you is, I'm twice your size and you wouldn' last ten seconds with me."

Willie Jenkins was right. At six foot five and 250 pounds he was a giant of a man. It made little sense for Alejandro Soto to be threatening him. Besides, sooner rather than later Jenkins would tire of talking to himself.

"Homes, we suppose to be nachural enemies. In the joint they keep us segregated, but here we're almost cellies. I like you, homes. Ain't too many dudes like you, black, brown, or white in this place. If you was just a regular ol' taco, I wouldn' give a shit. You could just up an croak in your cell if you wanted to. Wouldn' be no never mind to me. What's up with you, homes? You ain't been workin' out, don sound like you been readin'. I ain't heard you yellin' at all them fools to shut the fuck up. You ain't been eatin'. I seen your trays go back with everythin' on them. That's goin' on almost a week now, homes. Somethin's wrong. You OK? I guess I just hate to see a good man go down."

She hadn't come in a week, and, lying on his bunk, Alejandro Soto knew it was over. He should never have told her. He should have trusted his instincts. He knew this would happen. His world could never be her world. It was too big a change, too much for her to swallow. But she had insisted. She had threatened to leave the case if he didn't tell her. He should have called her bluff. But at the time he didn't think she was bluffing. No, Carlos Sanchez and his mother had been too much on her mind for too long a time. Even if she had backed down then, she would have come back to it. There had been no way out. None of that mattered. All that mattered, all he could think of, feel, be tormented by was the thought that he had to see her, that he needed and wanted more than anything to see her again, be with her again, even if it were only on the other side of a piece of glass.

He couldn't eat, sleep, read, or exercise. All of that seemed trivial and beside the point. When his mother had died and word of her death had reached him in prison, he had felt a sense of loss but nothing like this. This seemed completely hopeless, ongoing, and eternal. He tried to console himself with the thought that sooner or later it would have ended anyway. Life being what it was, he would lose his appeal in San Francisco, a jury would convict him in San Cristobal, and he would end up on death row where there would be no reason for her to see him. But that didn't diminish the pain now. Seeing her and being with her until all those things came to pass would be infinitely better than what he was going through now. He had always been contemptuous of the word "love." He despised the word. It was a woman's word. They coated everything with it. It was silly and stupid. The only time a man could legitimately use it was when he was referring to his mother. Otherwise men used it only out of weakness, lust, or manipulation. But if as he lay on his bunk for days tormented by the need to see her and be with her, if this was what the word meant, then he loved her.

Sunday came, nine days since he had seen her. He thought once again of writing to her. But he was certain the guards would read whatever he wrote, so what could he say that he really wanted to say without getting her thrown off the case? "I need to see you! Alejandro." "Need" was too strong. It would make them suspicious. Then for sure they would bug the cubicles.

"It's very important that I see you." What could be "very important"? That was worse than "need." "Please come and see me." "Please" wasn't him. They would suspect that this was something more that an attorney–client relationship.

Just then he heard two or three guards unlock the block gate and start down the corridor and everything within him leaped and then strained to listen. *It was Sunday and only she came on Sunday.* When they were a few cells in, he was certain that it was only two guards. Twice they had used only two guards to pull him and seldom did they use two guards to pull other inmates. *No, sometimes they used two guards to pull other inmates.* He sagged. But the two guards kept coming and they never used two guards to pull Jenkins. In a second they would be at and past Jenkins's cell. He felt a huge burst of excitement. But they stopped at Jenkins's cell.

"OK, Jenkins, get your jumpsuit on, your old lady's here to visit you. Bud, he's gonna give your cell a nice clean search while you're gone. That shouldn't worry you, should it? You got nothing to hide, do you?"

"Why you guys be fuckin' with me. You know I got nothin' stashed in my house."

"Come on, Jenkins. Move it. We ain't got all day."

Then Jenkins and one of the guards were gone. *It wasn't her.* The letdown after any hope, no matter how small, was getting worse. He lay on his bunk wondering where she was and what she was doing.

TWICE DURING those ten days, Greg Olsen visited Alejandro. As much as Alejandro was hoping that Barbara's name would come up during those visits, it didn't. Hudson's demeanor whenever Greg came to visit Alejandro was markedly different than when Barbara came to visit him. Not that he was pleasant or even civil, but he simply didn't go out of his way to denigrate Alejandro. During Olsen's first visit, Greene was still in charge of the three guards. During his second visit, Hudson was in charge.

"OK, Soto, get your ass up. You got an attorney visit." It was Hudson. "For your information, there's a new sheriff in town. Me. Your celebrity trip is over, starting now. So get your ass up."

Two young deputies he had never seen before accompanied Hudson, and he immediately reemphasized who was in charge. "Tim, you take the door. Once Jack and me are in, lock it till we're ready to come out. Old Greenie had me keep the door open the whole time. I think that's just asking for trouble. Jack, you come on in there with me and help me check out this idiot and chain him. Alright, Soto, get the shorts and T-shirt off. We're coming in."

When he was naked and standing at attention with his back

to the cell door, they entered. "OK, bend over and spread those cheeks. And I mean spread them wide. From now on we're gonna be damn sure that you're not trying to sneak anything outta here to try to pass it to one of them poor excuses you have for lawyers... Goddamn you got a shit-caked, smelly asshole. Fucking greasers always stink. When's the last time you've gone out to the shower, three weeks? Jack, take a look. I just had breakfast and I'm liable to puke all over this sumbuck. Now don't tell me he's clean 'cause he's not. But has he stuffed anything up there?

"OK, now turn around and face me. Alright, open that mouth. Wide. Wider. Tongue up. Tongue down. OK, arms up. Jack, check his armpit on your side. Thanks. Now run your fingers through his hair."

"Through his hair?"

"Yeah, through his hair. Remember that fucker George Jackson smuggled a gun into his cell by hiding it in his Afro?"

"Yeah, but this guy doesn't have an Afro."

"Goddamn it, just do as I say. We're dealing with a three-time murderer here who's facing the death penalty. He's got a lot of hair up there and he's got nothing to lose by trying to smuggle some-thing outta here. OK, get your jumpsuit on, Soto, and let's chain him up, Jack. Mr. Big's special treatment days are over."

XVI

On Sunday morning as the bright, autumn sun illuminated the closed blinds of her bedroom windows, Barbara, in the warmth of her bed, embraced with finality the fact that she was madly, hopelessly in love with Alejandro Soto and the feeling was wonderful. Let everything be damned. She loved him, she loved him, she loved him. And she was going to enjoy and revel in the moment forever. For nine days she had wrestled with the fears and the doubts and the absurdity of the situation, but the fact that she loved him won out. She could live with the two killings.

All of her life she had wanted to fall in love. Twice she had married and had hoped and thought she was in love, only to be rapidly disappointed. But even in the beginning of those marriages, it had been nothing like this. She loved everything about him: his strengths, his weaknesses, his intelligence, his flaws, his biases, everything. She loved it all. Recently she had gone to a wedding. She had been standing next to a group of girls no more than ten or eleven years old when the bride and groom exited the church to a shower of rice and cheers. They stopped and kissed and the girls jumped and screeched, "Another one! Another one! Another kiss!" And when the bride and groom kissed again, the girls' screeches grew louder. Their faces stretched with excitement and joy as they leaped and leaped, screaming for still more kisses. *Someday,* she thought, *each and every one of them will be that bride.* Later at the reception, when the bride tossed a bouquet into a crowd of enthusiastic and expectant young women, the excitement, the cries, and the jumping was much the same. *Someday it will be them too.* As Barbara lay in bed on that bright, autumn Sunday morning, she knew, without a doubt, her day had come.

For nine days her mind had badgered her with fear after fear. Her options had been two: withdraw from the case by whatever means or fight the good fight. However perilous the second option seemed, it made the most sense. If she withdrew from the case now, there was a good chance she would never see Alejandro again. If she were not his attorney of record, she would have no basis for contact with him. On the other hand, the Estrada case was very weak. Johnny Moncado had every reason to lie, and given the number of felony convictions he had for moral turpitude, his credibility as a witness left much to be desired. Then too, Bill Terry thought there was a good chance Moncado had fled the area. Without him, the district attorney had no case. Either way, the Estrada case should be resolved by the end of February—most probably in Alejandro's favor. Then there were Fred Solomon's statistics. One defendant in hundreds was awarded a hearing in the Federal Court of Appeals as Alejandro had been granted. Of those, seven out of ten had been granted relief. In six months, Alejandro could be a free man—free to be together with her for the rest of their lives. With that eventuality in mind, Barbara was certain that she could maintain the control and decorum to proceed as his attorney undetected.

So many of her fears had been variations of what would people think: judges, lawyers, friends, secretaries, neighbors, and even the State Bar. Not only what would they think, but also how would they react? When he was out of custody, if he was successful in his court battles, and people learned about their love, they would be ostracized. He would always be considered a twice-convicted murderer. They would have to move to another part of the state or perhaps another state...somewhere where they were not known. Her parents were dead and she had no siblings, but her grandmother was still alive—the same sweet old woman who had answered her questions about how would she know when she was in love by saying, "When the time comes, when he comes, you will know." But how would Grandma react when she took her love, a twice-convicted murderer, to meet her? And how would they support themselves? She could support him...but for how long? Who would hire him? Then too, how long would she want him idle? And what would they do in their spare time when the physical newness wore off? They came from such different backgrounds. In a different city or state could they, or would they, need to hide his identity? At times, it seemed insurmountable—doomed before it even started. But in the end she loved him and that was all that really mattered. It was now or never, and she wanted the now. She couldn't pass up the now. It probably would never come again. Of that she was certain. So she turned and turned and smiled again and again in the warmth of her bed and her love.

She was still in bed when just past noon, Greg phoned to tell her that Bill Terry was certain, based on conversations with a cop friend, that the district attorney still had in its possession some videotapes of Johnny Moncado and his friends that had not been turned over to them. Greg was in trial and he asked that she set a discovery compliance hearing before Judge Spencer as soon as possible, preferably no later than Tuesday.

She saw Alejandro the next day. The visit was brief. There was so little time. The compliance hearing was set for the next morning and she had to prepare for it. Then too, she had made an appointment with her hairstylist and she needed to do some shopping. She hadn't been paying much attention to her appearance lately and a look in the full-length mirror on Sunday afternoon had been very disappointing. But her visit with Alejandro was warm and wonderful, however brief.

HE HAD given up hope of ever seeing her again when the guards came to pull him on Monday midday. He watched Hudson carefully both before and after he announced, "Get ready, Soto, you've got an attorney visit." It had to be Greg Olsen again, coming to tell him that she was no longer on the case. Hudson's quiet, bland, disinterested look said as much. Hudson's silence and lack of brusqueness as they made their way to the cubicle furthered Alejandro's worst fear. But then he saw her and closed his eyes, perhaps in relief or perhaps to make certain that when he opened them again he wasn't dreaming. As they seated him, he studied her for any negative look, but there was none.

She said she had come to tell him about the hearing the next day. She repeated what Greg had told her about Bill Terry's conversation with his friend. When she paused he said, "I missed you." The words and his voice were soft and warm and left no room for misinterpretation. She nodded and looked down, looked away, looked back at him, still nodding and then quickly wrote on a yellow legal pad that she held up to the glass, "Believe me, I missed you too."

The visit could have and should have ended there because for a long while they simply stared at each other with caring eyes. But gradually fear crept into her mind—they could be listening, they could be watching—and she broke away. She seized on Johnny Moncado, but the gibberish she spoke made no sense whatsoever. Finally, she stood and said, "I have to go." But they had said with a few words and looks all that needed to be said. At least for then.

LATE MONDAY afternoon when Barbara walked into High Fashion

Hair Style, Renee Walker looked up from a sink where she was washing combs and raised her hands and eyes as if to say, "Hallelujah!" but instead she said, "Oh Barbara, I'm so happy for you!"

"Happy for what?"

"Oh sweetheart, I've been styling women's hair for more than thirty years. They come in here for all kinds of reasons. But when they come in here like you just did, with their eyes glowing and their faces beaming and their bodies swaying, they can never fool me. They're in love. Congratulations!"

JUST BEFORE eight that evening, Barbara went shopping. She bought a new suit, one with a pencil skirt that hugged her hips and thighs and a fitted jacket that accentuated her curves. Though she had never worn perfume to court, she bought a bottle of Chanel No5. Lastly, she bought a pair of spiked high heels to allow her hips to sway as they had never swayed in a courtroom before.

THE NEXT morning at 10:30, the courtroom was empty save for Barbara, Randy Davis, the court clerk, and the bailiff. At 10:34, six armed deputy sheriffs entered the courtroom, locked the hallway door behind them, and, without a word to anyone, stationed themselves around the courtroom. Seconds later Judge Spencer took the bench. "Bring out, Mr. Soto," he said. The bailiff, followed by two guards, went to the courtroom's holding cell and unlocked the steel door, and Barbara heard the first clanging of the leg irons. She watched the opening intently and her heart sank when she saw him. He looked so small and helpless chained between those two burly deputies as they led him to the jury box. "Your Honor, I ask that Mr. Soto be seated next to me at counsel table and that his right hand be freed so that he can take notes." Her voice had quivered, and she hoped no one had noticed it. Judge Spencer nodded. "Yes, that will be the order." The deputies changed their direction and for a moment her eyes met his and if the anguish she had felt seconds before were any kind of doubt, it was swept away. She was certain.

He, on the other hand, felt chagrined to have her see him like this in the ornate setting of that courtroom, chained and shuffling clumsily and loudly across the polished hardwood floor, dressed in a faded, soiled, red jumpsuit—in every way the least and lowest of all the creatures present. He called up and clung to an image of himself on his cell floor stretching every muscle and gritting every tooth for those last push-ups so he could accept what was and not go beyond. He lowered his eyes and carefully, slowly, made his way to the counsel table.

At the table, next to what was to be his seat, one of the deputies said, "Hold it, Soto." He stood perfectly still as the deputy fumbled with the waist-chain lock. Out of the corner of his eye he saw her, seated less than three feet away from him, without any glass or metal between them, saw her looking up at him and watching him. And everything within him leaped and turned and raced and collided. Gone was any semblance of the exercises, any meaning of the exercises. All that was present and all he was conscious of was the tumult she was causing in him. "Have a seat, Soto." He was only too glad to have a seat and let the chair rather than his shaky legs support him. Now seated, he could smell her, and the hair on his left arm, the arm closest to her, stood up and for a moment he thought that hair had somehow touched her arm and he shuddered. Then she leaned toward him and touched his bare forearm gently with her fingertips, and he jerked, tensed, and stiffened. She whispered in his ear, "The notepad and pencil in front of you are so that you can take notes or jot down anything that you might want to call to my attention." He heard none of it. He felt only the softness and warmth of her breath in his ear, and he knew that her lips had to be less than an inch from him. He felt hot and light-headed.

She felt him jerk and sensed the tension and stiffness that followed, and she loved it. As she whispered to him she saw his eyelids droop and heard his breath get heavier, louder, deeper. She loved it.

Judge Spencer called the case and noted for the record that the district attorney and defense counsel were present, as well as the defendant. Then he said, "Let the record show that I have read and considered the briefs that have been submitted on this discovery issue and unless there is something further that either side wishes to present, I am prepared to rule. Counsel?"

Randy Davis answered, "May I have a moment, Your Honor?"

"You may. Ms. Blake?"

"May I have a moment to confer with my client, Your Honor?

"You may."

Once again her hand went to his arm, but this time it was the flats of her fingers that settled gently on it as she leaned toward him and whispered, "Everybody in the courtroom is or will be watching me whisper to you. I am going to whisper several things to you and after each sentence I am going to ask you if you understand. If you do, nod... Alejandro, I love you. Do you understand?" He blinked several times, knotted his brow, and thought for several moments before he nodded. "No matter what happens, I will always love you. Do you understand?" He paused again, digested it, and then nodded many small, rhythmic nods. "Someday we will be together. Do you understand?" Now he turned his head and looked at her with a bland, calm stare and nodded twice slowly. Then she rose. "Your Honor, after speaking to my client, the defense is prepared to submit the matter on the briefs. However, if the district attorney chooses not to do so, then I request that the court permit me to respond in kind."

"Of course. Mr. Davis, what is the People's position?"

Randy Davis began, but Alejandro Soto heard none of it. What he heard were the sounds of someone speaking, but that was all. He felt hot, feverish, though he knew he had no fever. At the same time joy, despair, belief, doubt, trust, distrust, satisfaction, and fear were colliding within him. He reveled in her words and then feared them. There was bliss in those words but dread, too, that someday she would come out of her delusion.

Randy Davis went on about the defense attorney's misinterpretation of the case law for a full ten minutes, repeating himself over and over. Only once during that diatribe did Barbara dare turn and look at her client. When she did, it was what she had done thousands of times with other clients, to see if they understood what was being said and to see if they had any concerns with what was being said. But what she saw this time was the man she loved—strong, handsome, stoic—listening quietly and patiently and with enormous dignity. Near the end of Davis's soliloquy, she saw that Judge Spencer was becoming irritated, shifting in his chair, and beginning to tap a forefinger on the bench, which was never a good sign for the presenter. "Anything else, counsel?" he said three times before Davis answered, "No, Your Honor."

"Counsel?" he said turning to Barbara Blake.

"I think not, Your Honor. But may I have a moment to confer with my client?"

"Certainly."

This time she gently folded her fingers around the curvature of his arm so that the palm of her hand, so that her whole hand, was warm against his forearm. This time her lips brushed against his ear ever so slightly before she began whispering. He shuddered. She felt his shudder and loved it. "Everyone is watching, so nod if you understand. Do you know that I love you?" He nodded but now without a pause. "Do you believe that I love you?" He looked up at the judge and then cautiously nodded. "Do you know that I will do everything I can to ensure that someday we'll be together?" Now he nodded self-consciously, afraid that they were arousing suspicions. "Do you love me?" He blinked several times and then, for a moment, sat wide-eyed before he nodded yes, yes, yes in short, quick nods. She stood again. "Your Honor, after conferring further with my client, the defense will submit the matter."

Judge Spencer did not mince his words. "Mr. Davis, by no later than four o'clock this afternoon I want you to obtain copies of any and all statements the police may have obtained from Johnny Moncado and any and all persons who have indicated that Johnny Moncado has incriminated himself in the shooting of Santos Estrada. Furthermore, by five o'clock this afternoon I want all of those statements turned over to the defense. Have I made myself clear? This case is scheduled for trial and I intend to begin trial on the date set. I am continuing this matter to Friday's calendar at 10:30 to deal with any and all matters regarding the order that I have made here today."

Elated, Barbara turned to whisper something more to Alejandro but in doing so saw that he was erect, enormously erect. Now it was she who shuddered and she managed to whisper only, "I'll see you on Friday morning, Alejandro." Then she stared and watched as he rose from his chair and she gasped at the size of his hard-on. Once standing she saw him stoop as if to conceal his hunger. Soon there were two deputies standing beside him, one of whom said, "Straighten up, Soto," and she watched the erection disappear.

She took her time gathering her things wanting to savor what had happened, where it had happened. Finally the bailiff said, "Barbara, you're the last one out. The doors are locked. Make sure they catch as you leave."

She sat for several moments more thinking and reliving those moments—especially those last moments when he tried to hide himself. Each time she remembered those final moments it pleased her, made her happy, and, yes, excited her. True it was only a part of whatever they had, but it was an important part. It was only when she stood to leave that she realized she was wet.

She went home from the courthouse, bathed, changed her clothes, and had lunch. Only then did she go to the office. She wasn't there very long. Twice Suzie had caught her staring out her office window. "What's the matter, Barb?"

"Nothing's the matter."

"You sure?"

"Of course I'm sure. Nothing's the matter. Now can we leave it at that? Nothing is the matter." She reached for the nearest set of papers and brought them to a reading distance.

"I'm sorry. I...uh..." Then she was gone.

Less than an hour later, Suzie was standing in her doorway again. This time Barbara had no idea how long she had been standing there or how long she had been staring out the window. "What's the matter, Barb?"

Barbara Blake thought for a moment and then looked back at Suzie and said, "Why should there be something the matter? I happen to be looking out the window and from that you deduce that something's wrong. For all you know, I could have been watching the birds." There was irritation in her voice.

"Come on, Barb, we've been together too long for that. Something's eating you. Why can't you tell me?"

"Suzie, there is nothing eating me. When there is, you'll be the first to know."

"It's this Soto case, isn't it?"

"Damn it, Suzie!" She slammed her hand on her desk. "I've got a lot to do this afternoon and I don't need you in here questioning me. Now leave me alone."

A few minutes later, Barbara stuffed her briefcase with the afternoon work she had set for herself and she left the office. As she reached the door, Suzie said, "Oh, by the way Barb, I've been meaning to tell you, but haven't had a chance to, I really like your hair."

"Thank you," she said without turning or even pausing. *Does Suzie suspect? Has she tied the new hairdo and her preoccupation with the case to Alejandro? How could she suspect? Well, let her suspect. She can suspect all she wants. She could never prove or know anything.*

She was home no more than five minutes when the phone rang.

"How'd it go today, Barb?" Greg asked.

"Good. Fine. Judge Spencer ordered them to turn over everything they or the cops have that incriminates Moncado."

"By five tonight, right?"

"How did you know?"

"Spencer's clerk told me."

"How did you know I was here?"

"I called your office and Suzie said she thought you'd gone home. She said you hadn't told her anything about a packet coming from the DA's office."

"Damn that Suzie."

"No, no. She's a good secretary. I hope you don't mind but I asked her to stay at least until 5:15, unless the packet came before then. I told her that if the packet didn't come by then to call either me or you."

She did mind. Who gave Greg and Suzie the authority to run her office? But it was true, she hadn't mentioned the all-important discovery packet to Suzie. She had completely forgotten about it. Her mind was elsewhere.

"Are you OK, Barb?" He could hear the irritation in her voice, and he hated hearing it. Hated himself for being so needy when it came to Barbara. There was no one he wanted to offend less. No one he wanted to like him more. He wanted to say, "Stop. Hold it, Barbara. You know I would never do or say anything to hurt or offend you." But he couldn't, not then. Someday, perhaps.

"I'm fine. Why?"

He could hear the added irritation in her voice. He'd succeeded only in upsetting her more and in perhaps making her think that somehow he was dissatisfied with her, which couldn't be further from the truth. He shifted everything to Suzie. "Well, Suzie thinks this case might be getting to you. She said you looked very tired and preoccupied when you got back to the office today and you were a bit on edge."

If Suzie had been there, she would have fired her on the spot. "Damn it, Greg, Suzie's way out of line. She'd better start being a secretary and stop being the junior partner she thinks she is or she's going to be looking for another job."

"Calm down, Barb, calm down. We...she means well and she's very devoted to you." He had almost slipped.

"Well, for your information, the Soto case is not getting to me. And if I was preoccupied, it would probably be because Randy fought so hard to prevent us from getting what the cops have that I've been wondering what's in their files to provoke that kind of opposition."

"I was just thinking...I know you've got a busy schedule on Fri-

244

day...I could probably handle the Soto motion then if I could get Judge—"

The thrust she felt was quick and sharp. So was her response. "Greg, I argued the motion in court this morning and I'm going to finish it, OK?" No one was going to take Alejandro from her, not even Greg.

"OK, OK. I was just trying to help." And he was just trying to help. But everything he said seemed to turn out wrong. How demeaning it was to try so hard to please and fail so miserably.

"Thank you, anyway."

When she hung up the phone, the torment began. Greg had to know or suspect something. How often did one lawyer finish litigating a court matter that another lawyer had begun and almost completed? Never, unless the first lawyer had become seriously incapacitated. Suzie had told him that the case was "getting" to her. Then he discovered that she had left the office early, without mentioning the delivery of the important discovery packet. Would he go to Judge Spencer and tell him in confidence that he was uncomfortable with her handling of the case and ask the judge to relieve her as second counsel? Then she would never see Alejandro again. But suspecting was a far cry from knowing, and what could Greg know? Nothing. Unless, of course, Alejandro had said something to Greg, told him about her whisperings in court... But when? Greg was in trial. No, Alejandro would never mention those whisperings to Greg. Or would he? But why had she whispered those things to him in open court in the first place? How stupid of her! How insane!

Now the whisperings that had recently given her so much joy lashed out at her. Greg suspected something. Why else would he have wanted to relieve her midway through the motion? Even if Alejandro hadn't told him, she was now embarrassed by the way she had forced nods out of him. What real value did any one of those nods have? What else could he have done there in court but nod? And if the court ever found out that she was telling her client that she loved him and demanding to know whether he loved her during the litigation of an important motion in a death penalty case, she might very well be suspended or even disbarred. How could she have been so reckless and callous?

She found no relief in sleep. Throughout the night, her dreams were filled with scenes of suspension proceedings before the State Bar. The proceedings took place in a huge outdoor amphitheater. The stage was long and large. Plain, thick concrete, like the jail's, made up the floor, the pillars, and the overhang. There were only two people on the huge stage: she and Judge Spencer. He was in his black robe, sitting behind an elevated wooden desk and she was standing to his left some thirty feet away in her new suit and shoes and smelling of perfume. The audience was packed with the entire county bar. The public defenders and defense counsel were seated closest to the stage, the district attorneys behind them, and then the civil bar with the women seated behind the district attorneys and the men behind them. There was a great deal of murmuring from the audience about her and her romantic interlude during an important court hearing in a death penalty case. She could clearly hear it as different segments of the audience looked up at her in disbelief, disgust, and shock.

For a long time she stood waiting for the proceedings to begin. Her new, spiked high heels were hurting and her skimpy new underwear was cutting into her upper thighs. Judge Spencer sat silently looking out at the audience, not once looking at her. He sat in the only chair on that enormous stage and after a while it seemed as if she had been standing for hours. She had dreaded the proceedings, but now she longed for them to begin. But they wouldn't begin and try as she might, she couldn't stand there and ignore the titters and stares and disgust of the patrons. *Was that part of the punishment?* she asked herself. No, after a while she was convinced that it *was* the punishment. Because the disbarment was a given and had in effect already happened. Now she must stand before her peers and be exposed for what she was: a fraud, a liar, a cheat, and worse, much worse. A woman so needy that she had stooped to the ultimate low, the disgrace of all disgraces in their profession: to take advantage of a pathetic, chained defendant whose death was being sought by the state and, in effect, force him to acknowledge his love for her in open court. No, even worse. Force him to make love to her there in open court, under the counsel table while the court conducted one of the most important motions in the case, popping up from under him to answer the court's questions or refute the prosecution's allegations and then returning to her filthy interlude under counsel table only to be discovered when she let out one long, loud primal scream.

But the proceedings wouldn't begin. And her sweat became grime, so thick that it made a paste out of her eye shadow, which in turn glued her eyelashes together so that she couldn't see, only hear and feel her greedy accusers. But then she did not need to see because the sneers and smirks and disgust had been indelibly imprinted in her mind forever. She was about to scream out, "Stop! Stop! I'm guilty! Take me! Do what you want with me!" when she heard the chains and without thinking, without needing to think, she exerted more force than she had ever exerted or would ever exert in her life and burst the grimy seal on her eyelashes and saw him. Only it wasn't him... Wait, yes, it was him, coming slowly up the steps to that great, gray stage, shackled and bent, the chains so large and heavy he could barely lift his legs, so large and heavy he had wasted away to nothing...was a skeleton of himself—weak, dirty, unshaven, and unkempt, so changed she hardly recognized him. But then, maybe that was how he always really looked, maybe that was what she never wanted him to look like before.

Then he was on the stage, on the other end of the stage, and for the first time Judge Spencer turned and spoke not to her but to him. "Is this your woman?"

"Yes, Your Honor," came the cracked, broken voice.

"Now, before I sentence you to death, you understand that I have the discretion to overturn the jury's finding of death, and I can sentence you instead to life in prison without the possibility of parole?"

"Yes, Your Honor." In hardly more than a whisper.

"Is that the woman who seduced you and forced you to copulate with her in open court under the counsel table while we were hearing the defense's motion to compel discovery?"

"No doubt about it, Your Honor."

"What was that?"

"Yes, Your Honor, that's her."

"And did she say that if you did not copulate with her in open court, she would make your defense a shambles, ensure that the jury would invoke the death penalty?"

"Yes, Your Honor."

From across the stage she screamed, "He lies! He lies! He forced me under counsel table! You don't understand! My tight new suit and new underwear had nothing to do with it! It's not fair! I didn't blow in his ear! Not intentionally, anyway! I merely whispered!"

Then the audience broke out in unison, "Whore! Whore! She lies! She made him do it!"

Then Judge Spencer said, "Having considered all the evidence in this case, the court finds that—"

And Barbara woke, sweating and shaking.

"So WHAT's up with you, Ale? You mighty quiet over there. Ain't said a word since you came back from court. How'd it go in there, man?"

Alejandro welcomed Willie Jenkins's words. He had wanted to talk to Jenkins from the moment the guards locked his cell door behind him. But he didn't know what to say or how to begin. He was afraid that if he wasn't careful, he would reveal Barbara Blake as his woman. Then too, he had never spoken to anyone about his feelings, and these feelings were so different that he didn't know where or how to begin.

"It went good, man."

"Good how?"

"Good because my lawyer kicked the DA's ass. The judge told him he had to give us everything the cops had on their rat by five o'clock today."

"Tha's good, man."

"But that's only half of it. My woman from San Diego showed up."

"She did?"

"Yeah."

"Was she lookin' good, man?"

"Oh yeah, real good."

"Tha's a good sign, Ale. Once they stop lookin' good when they come to court or visit you, you probably on your way out. She gonna come by and visit you, man?"

"Naw."

"You mean she come all this way from San Diego and she's not gonna visit you?"

"Her mother's real sick down in San Diego and she had to get right back."

"Tha's a long way be comin' from jus for court and head right back. You say she's on welfare. So she musta come up on the bus then. Thas a long way to be travelin' on a bus. That woman must *luuvvv* you."

"I think she does, man."

"You think! Man, tha's a long way for any woman to be comin' for an hour or two and then turn 'roun and head back! I wouldn' be *thinkin'*, I'd be *knowin'* that that woman *luuved* me if she did that for me. Not even Sandy did that, and I *know* she luuvs me. So you didn't even talk to her then, huh?"

"Well...kinda. I mean she talked to my lawyer before court and told her a lot of things to tell me."

"Like that she luuved you?"

"Yeah, she said that."

"Tha's good. They luuv to be recitin' that when they luvv you. Start worryin' when they don'... Did your lawyer tell her that you luuved her back? Tha's important."

"Oh yeah."

"Tha's good. They got to be hearin' that. Those words are soul food for them. Say 'em right and everythin's gonna be fine. Sometimes it's better to say 'em wrong than not say 'em at all."

"Jenkins?"

"Yeah, man."

"Mind if I ask you a personal question?"

"Go ahead on, Ale. I ain't got nothin' to hide. 'Cept if it be too personal, I'll tell you."

"How in the hell have you been with the same woman for seventeen years? I don't know anybody these days that does that. The old-timers used to do it. But they never had any choice. Money was always a problem. Besides, they were always getting some on the side. But I don't hear you saying that. You know what I mean? I don't hear you saying you're getting some on the side."

"Lemme tell you like it is, Ale. When I was a youngster in Chicago playin' music, I had all the women I could handle. I mean *all* the women. You sing and play them love songs and that's the key to their hearts and pussies. When I come out to Frisco an' San Cristobal I had my share of women, too. But lemme tell you this, gettin' that pussy is just the beginnin'. Cause then you got to be with 'em an there ain't no free lunches anywheres. You can quote me on that. We all got problems, we all got hang-ups, mens and women. But it takes a certain kinda person, a certain kinda woman that can look past herself and luuuvv you for who you are. Sandy's not much to look at, not anymore, but I do know she luuuvvs Willie Jenkins, just plain ol' simple Willie Jenkins for who he is. And I been round long enough to know that that pasture ain't greener on the other side. Fuckin' with some other broad means I might could lose Sandy. Maybe she wouldn' leave me. I ain't talkin' 'bout that. I mean I could lose the feelin' she has for me and I don' wanna risk that. She's the bes' thing I ever had with anybody. I plan to be with that woman till the day I die."

ALL WEEK long the minutes ticked by slowly. She was everywhere and yet so far away. She was with him when he did his push-ups and sit-ups and burpees. Trying to keep his count was impossible. Most times he couldn't get to ten before she was there. A look of hers, something she had said, her touch, the warmth and softness of her breath on his ear, and then he could only remember that he had not gotten to ten and now had no idea how many burpees he had done or how long he had been doing them. She was with him when he read. He never seemed to get past the second sentence in anything he was reading. His eyes would continue to work down the page and maybe even as far as the next two pages before he would stop and acknowledge that he didn't remember a word he had read, and he had been swept away by her again: a lock of her hair brushing against his cheek, the way she stood when she spoke to the judge, her voice and, yes, the whispered, "I love you." She was with him when he ate, when he stood over or sat on the toilet bowl, when he spoke to Jenkins. It was as if he were starving and could smell and even taste food but not eat it, as if he were thirsty and could feel and taste water but not swallow it. Every hour and even before an hour passed, he subtracted another number of minutes from the enormous amount that he had calculated on Tuesday afternoon that would have to pass before he could see her again on Friday. He wanted nothing more...would be fully satisfied with just seeing her on Friday morning. But Friday morning refused to come.

It was Deputy Hudson who finally announced the arrival of Friday at 5:05 that morning as he rattled Alejandro's cell bars. "Get your ass up, Soto. Sergeant wants us to move your ass now. Doesn't want to shut the jail down for your silly-ass, ten thirty court date." It was then that Hudson struck his first blow. "Come on, come on. Don't want to keep your girlfriend waiting. She'll be here in five and a half hours." He struck again later as he locked Soto in one of the special holding cells at the beginning of the tunnel. "Damn Soto, you stank! You should have showered this week. Your girlfriend's not gonna appreciate your smell."

He thought of Hudson's words several times as he sat in that special holding cell. He didn't smell. He had showered the night before. *What did Hudson know? What could he know? He had not been in court with them on Tuesday, and he had never seen them interact. Or had he? Were their visits being videotaped. No, she had assured him that they wouldn't dare. No, Hudson was just an asshole.*

SHE WAS sitting at the counsel table when he shuffled into the courtroom. Her eyes met his and their fondness caused him to look away lest the deputies see. He met her eyes again as he approached the counsel table but their gleam and boldness made him look away again. As soon as he was seated, she leaned toward him and touched his forearm with her fingertips sending a current through him that stiffened him. Then her mouth was next to his ear and the warmth of her breath sent a chill through him. She whispered, "I missed you terribly since Tuesday. If you missed me nod, but please don't nod if it isn't true." He nodded not once but several times and then looked up to see two guards staring intently at them, so much so that he turned and whispered back, "They're watching us."

"So let them watch. What can they see? Nothing. I'm your lawyer and I've whispered to my clients thousands of times."

When Judge Spencer took the bench, he wasted no time. He turned to Randy Davis and said, "Mr. Davis, have you turned over to the defense all the materials in your or law enforcement's possession as ordered by this court on Tuesday?"

"Yes, Your Honor."

"Did you receive the ordered materials, Ms. Blake?"

She rose and Alejandro Soto noticed she was wearing a brown, full skirt instead of the blue, tight-fitting skirt he had greatly admired on Tuesday. "Yes, Your Honor."

"Very well then. Is there anything further to be heard in this matter, counsel?"

"No, Your Honor."

"No, Your Honor."

"Very well then. The trial date remains as originally set. This court will be in recess."

As Judge Spencer rose, Barbara Blake said what she had thought of saying many times since Tuesday, but now she said it in as calm and nonchalant a manner as she had never imagined she could. "Your Honor, may I be allowed to confer with my client in the holding cell for a few moments?"

Without the slightest hesitation Judge Spencer said, "Why yes, of course," and left the courtroom.

Then the guards surrounded Alejandro and one of them said quietly, "Alright Soto, let's go." She watched as he rose, watched as they cuffed his right hand to the waist chain, watched with an unanticipated calm. She gathered her things as they led him around counsel table and said quite matter-of-factly, "Thank you for the discovery, Mr. Davis." Then she fell in on the heels of the two guards who were right behind Alejandro and moved slowly toward the holding cell door with the confidence of someone expecting to rightfully prevail. For the first time, the dragging of the chains on the courtroom floor didn't bother her. In fact, in a strange way she welcomed the sounds, perhaps because she knew that she was about to overcome them. She felt her skirt softly rustling against her thighs and freshly shaven, bare legs as she marched in that solemn courtroom procession. As they turned toward the holding cell, she was almost certain the holding cell itself, as well as the stairwell behind it and the tunnel below, would by then be clear of all other inmates, and the jail guards would not come for him until the deputies in the courtroom called for them. Alejandro and the two deputies climbed the three steps to the cell door and she waited patiently, calmly, below as the deputies unlocked that great iron door. It was only after she heard the door opening and looked up to see the space behind it becoming larger by the moment that excitement surged within her and she told herself, *Stop it!* Alejandro moved past the door and into the cell, and the guards took a step toward the door and turned to her and waited for her to step up, which she did with the same calm she had possessed as she had followed them. "How long do you think you'll be, counselor?" She caught a glimpse of Alejandro standing just inside the door and shunned that glimpse knowing she needed to maintain her demeanor to answer. "Oh, five or ten minutes. Shouldn't be any longer than that." Calmly, evenly.

She moved inside the door and motioned for him to sit on one of the side benches. He looked in the direction of the bench but before he could move the great door slammed shut behind them and the lock clicked and echoed loudly. She had planned to look down the stairwell and as far back into the tunnel as she could, but once the door shut they were standing face-to-face, less than a foot apart. They stared into each other's eyes, he with a self-conscious, half grin and she with a shaking of the head in disbelief and satisfaction. Then without a word, without a warning, she leaped up onto him wrapping her legs and thighs around his waist just above the chains, hooking her feet behind his back and crossing her arms tightly around his neck. She pushed him backward, staggering him and almost causing him to fall. She kissed him hard on the lips and then thrust her tongue into his mouth. He stood stunned, trying more than anything to keep his balance as her tongue roamed. Then she pulled her head back, but only a few inches, only to that point where she could look into his eyes and whisper, "I love you! I love you! Alejandro, I love you!" Her legs began slipping down his sides and she said, "Hold me, darling, hold me. Don't let me fall. Let me stay as close as I can to you, at least for these few minutes."

He opened his hands and extended his fingers and pulled on the waist chains as hard as he could and cupped parts of her thighs and buttocks and lifted her above the waist chains again and became a participant. He reached for her mouth with his and then thrust his tongue hard and wet into her mouth. His fingers dug into the softness of her flesh, and then he strained to have the tip of his iron-hard dick touch her thighs or her buttocks or any part of her through his red jumpsuit, but to no avail.

Their mouths parted again and she gasped, "Oh my darling, I love you so much! More than anything else in the world, I love you! Do you love me? Tell me! Tell me!"

"Yes! Yes! Yes!"

"No, say it! Say it! I want to hear it! I need to hear it! Tell me! Tell me!"

"I love you! I love you!"

"Oh, my darling, I love you so much! Tell me again, again!"

"I love you! I love you! I do love you!"

"Oh!"

They kissed again, another full, open kiss, their tongues doing what they could not otherwise do. This time when she drew her head back, he said, "Press yourself against me! Hard, as hard as you can!"

"Like this?"

"Yes, harder!"

"Like this?"

"Yes! Now rub!"

"Like this?"

"Yes!"

"Ohhh!"

There was a sound somewhere below them. They stopped, tensed, and listened, their eyes as round and alert as their ears. She looked over his shoulder but saw nothing. There was a second sound from down somewhere in the tunnel. She slipped down off him and quickly straightened her clothes and hair and motioned for him to sit on one of the benches. She wiped the wetness from her face and dabbed her eyes hoping the mascara and eye shadow had not spread. Her heart pounding, she fumbled with and finally opened her briefcase. She retrieved the first batch of papers she touched and began sputtering sentences in a legal jargon that he did not understand.

From the other side of the tunnel someone said, "Jones, what the hell are you doing in this tunnel?" There was no response. "I'm not gonna ask you again, Jones. What the hell are you doing in this tunnel?"

Then a second voice said softly, too softly, "This be where they left me, suh."

"How come you're not in one of them holding cells?"

Again softly, the voice said, "You gonna have to take that up wid Mistah Hudson, suh. I ain't got nuttin' to do wid that."

There were sounds of keys, a lock, and an iron door opening and closing and finally, "You better get your ass up to the second deck, pronto."

At the other end of the tunnel and up twenty stairs, Barbara Blake and Alejandro Soto sat frozen side-by-side on one of the benches on the landing staring at the grimy concrete wall across from them. Sweat had formed on her forehead and her clothes were sticking to her body. He sat as much confused as he was concerned and with an abiding conviction that something bad would come of it.

"Who was it?" she asked.

"I don't know." He had heard the name "Jones"...but he knew no Jones in the jail. The inmate sounded black but he wasn't sure, and the only black he knew in the jail was Jenkins.

For several minutes after she heard the voices at the other end of the tunnel, Barbara sensed that the world as she knew it was crumbling around her. She was sitting just inches from Alejandro but for all intents and purposes she was sitting alone. He was not a part of the crumbling chaos. Then she heard a key in the door and she picked up the sheaf of papers she had taken from her brief-case, shifted away from Alejandro, turned her back to the door, and brought the papers within reading distance. The door opened.

"Any idea how much longer you'll be counselor?"

She turned her head halfway to the door and without facing it said, "We'll be through in a minute or two."

The door closed. Now more than ever she had to compose herself. In a few seconds she would be coming face-to-face with several deputies who would probably look at her closely. She rummaged through her briefcase for a mirror. Her mascara had run a little under her right eye and her hair in front was a mess. She dabbed beneath the eye with Kleenex. Alejandro Soto quietly watched but she was not aware of him. She brushed her hair briskly until it was in place. Then for the first time she saw that he was watching her. All she could say was, "This never happened. No matter what anyone says or does, this never happened. It's our word against some snitch who's trying to shorten his sentence. In the long run, his word will never be good enough. Do you understand? It never, ever happened. It would destroy me and your case. I've got to go now. The deputies are waiting. I don't want to make them any more suspicious than they already are. Remember, it never happened."

She rapped on the door with her keys. The door opened. She smiled at the deputy. "I'm finished." She stepped quickly past him and the other two deputies in the courtroom without looking at them.

ONCE THE guards were gone, Jenkins said, "Wha's the matter, Ale? You didn' look too good passin' my house."

"Nothing," he said, because he wasn't sure what or how much he could tell Jenkins. All he knew for certain was that he had to find out who Jones was, and it was likely Jenkins might know Jones. But he needed time to sort out what had happened from what he could tell Jenkins. "I need to talk to you, man. But I need to take a dump first. I almost crapped in my pants waiting for them to come and get me."

"OK, Ale, just don't stink up the place too much. You know I got to be breathin' here, too."

A few minutes later Alejandro Soto was at the far front-right corner of his cell clutching the bars and saying quietly, "Hey Jenkins, something's come up and I don't need these other fools hearing anything about it. So step on over here, man, where I can get at you."

"Wha's up, homes?" He was a breath away.

"Keep it down, big fella, there's rats all over this place."

"OK. So wha's up?"

"You know a guy in here by the name of Jones? I think he's a black dude."

"Jones...Jones. I don't know, Ale. Been a lotta dudes come in here since I been up here in max, and, like you, I ain't been down to the main line.... Black dude? I only know two black dudes name Jones who do time 'round here. Wha's he look like?"

"I don't know. I didn't see him."

"Well, you gotta be tellin' me more bout him than that. Where you run into this dude?"

"I was up in the holding cell for court three. You know, up there at the top of the stairs sitting on one of them benches talking to my lawyer, real confidential-like. We were talking about some real heavy stuff that I can't get into, but it's probably gonna win my case for me. You know they always clear the tunnel and every-thing for me wherever I go in this place. So me and my lawyer were talking in regular voices, and all of a sudden we hear this dude coughing way down there in the tunnel where we can't see him. After a while one of the guards on this side of the tunnel sees him and asks him what he's doing there and why he's not in one of those special cells down there in the tunnel. But the rat won't talk. So the guard pulls him. He was listening to us real quiet and sneaky like. He's gotta be a plant or a rat on his own."

"Why you thinkin' he's black?"

"Cause he talked like you when he finally answered."

"How you know his name is Jones?"

"That's what the guard called him."

Jenkins was silent for several moments before he said, "I don' like it."

"What don't you like?"

"From what you been tellin' me this dude be in protective cus-tody and the only black Jones I know who does time in protective custody is Bobby Jones, and he is one big muthafuckin' rat. I mean big time. Plants hisself all over the jail and then goes runnin' to the guards with everythin' he hears to lower his beefs. He's no good."

"You sure it couldn't be the other Jones?"

"Naw. That Jones is always on the main line."

Alejandro Soto was silent. A tinge of heat ran through him. It increased when he remembered that Jones had mentioned Hudson's name. Anything that rat knew, Hudson would know. Hudson had probably planted him there. After all, Hudson had been calling Barbara his "girlfriend." He had to get word out to her. But how... without being detected?

XVII

Outside the courthouse
the apocalypse continued. The sun was shining in a brilliant blue
sky but Barbara saw none of it. She was enveloped in fear, chaos,
and self-destruction. She didn't know where to go or what to do.
It was 11:15 and she dared not go to her office. Suzie would see.
She had to be back in court at 1:30 and needed to pick up a file in
her office before that. That gave her two hours to try to get a hold
of herself. She went home. She dropped her briefcase next to the
kitchen door and went to the front room and sat on the edge of
her couch and stared off into the destruction that enveloped her.
Everything she had worked so hard to attain was gone, and there
was no way to undo what was done. Almost two hours later, nothing had changed, not even the position she had been sitting in.
She needed to get to court, but she needed to pick up the file first.

"WHERE HAVE you been? I've been trying to reach you for the past hour," Suzie said—always one to escalate any crisis, no matter how big or small, two or three notches.

"Oh, I must have forgotten to turn on my cell phone after I left court," she answered blandly as she walked past Suzie toward her office without a look.

But Suzie followed her. "Greg's been trying to get hold of you. He says it's important."

An increment of fear pricked at her and she was thankful that she had her back to Suzie as she searched for the court file. "I'm going to court right now and I'll probably see him there," she said, still bent over. "Anything else?"

"No," said Suzie, deflated.

"OK, I've got to run now. I'm going to be late. Be back by 3:30 or 4:00. See you then." She was past Suzie and out the door, and Suzie was none the wiser. Greg had apparently not mentioned the holding cell. Suzie would never have held back on something like that. But what did Greg want? What did he know? Better to find out now over the phone rather than face-to-face in the courthouse.

Once in the car she called him. "Greg, Barbara," she said, more nonchalantly than she ever could have in person. "Suzie said you called...that you needed to get hold of me. What's up?" She waited, at the ready. She would know in a moment.

"No big deal," he said, but he was thinking, *just another chance to talk to you.* Her shoulders loosened and sank some more. "I was just curious how much of a chance you've had to look at the discovery Randy gave us on Tuesday."

Complete relief for a moment followed by a pinch of incompetence revealed. "I glanced at it and listened to a bit of it, but not much more than that. I've really been busy, but I'll get at it tonight, for sure"

"I'd appreciate it if you would and then get back to me. I saw Randy in court this morning after your hearing, and apparently there are some videotapes, including one in particular of Moncado, that Randy says the cops claim were misplaced and therefore never turned over to him. Talk about bullshit. Probably some pretty heavy stuff on those tapes. Call me tonight at home if you get a chance to look at them." He did want to hear her reaction to the tapes, but he knew he was needy as well.

On her way to department six, Barbara ran into Randy Davis. He motioned her over and in an apologetic manner began telling her about the misplaced tapes. She listened, just enough to know it matched what Greg had already told her. She was more concerned with Randy's eyes and his manner of speaking. She watched. There was nothing accusatory there, nothing to indicate that he had heard or knew anything about the holding cell. She could be, she wanted to be, magnanimous. "Nothing to worry about, Randy. We all make mistakes. I haven't had a chance to look at those tapes yet, but I plan to do so later today. But, I don't see a problem. We have the tapes now. We're still a couple of months away from trial. We have plenty of time to review them and do whatever we have to do once we've seen them."

As soon as she reached department six, it was apparent that her case that afternoon was going to be reassigned to another department because there were three preliminary examinations ahead of her. She was reassigned to Judge Spencer and her immediate reaction was, *Oh no, not there. If any judge knew about the holding cell, it would be him.* She took the court file and rather than wait for the elevator, hurried down the back stairwell. The sooner she reached department three the more of an opportunity she would have to talk to his clerk and bailiff before Judge Spencer came out on the bench. If Judge Spencer had heard anything, chances were they had heard something too. Talking to them beforehand would give her a chance to improve on the blanket denial she was prepared to give everyone.

But Judge Spencer was already on the bench when she arrived, and he was angry. "Counsel, this case was assigned here twenty minutes ago. Where is the district attorney?"

"He's on his way, Your Honor. We were just told to report here a few minutes ago, Your Honor."

He looked away as if he didn't believe her, didn't trust her, as if he knew. She tried to recall her denial but couldn't remember it. She groped for a new denial, any denial, but words wouldn't come. Judge Spencer asked his clerk to call department six to find out where the district attorney was. Then he turned back to Barbara and said, "Will counsel approach the bench on an unrelated matter." Fear numbed her. She made her way slowly to the bench. She couldn't look at him and didn't know what she would say. *Act shocked, act surprised,* was the best she could think of. When she reached the bench she said meekly, without looking up at him, "Yes, Your Honor." He turned off the microphone on his desk and moved it to one side. Then he leaned forward and said quietly, "Counsel, I simply want to commend you on your compliance motion in the Soto case. It was timely. Sometimes we forget to do the little things that can have significant consequences." Without looking at him she said, "Thank you, Your Honor" and wanted to cry. Just then the clerk announced that the district attorney was on his way.

Once the case was called, the district attorney asked for a continuance. As Barbara left the room, she told herself again and again that no one knew, no one had seen, and there was nothing to worry about. But out in the hallway it occurred to her that even if Judge Spencer had not heard, his bailiff might have. Word spread quickly among deputy sheriffs. If the bailiff had not heard by now, then no one had heard, no one had seen. She went back to the courtroom. It was empty except for the clerk and the bailiff.

"Hey Joe, I saw in the paper that Amy's pitching fall ball for a traveling team." One sure way of getting parents to open up, to talk freely, was to ask them about their kids, especially if the kids were doing well.

"Yeah, I'm so proud of her. Everybody's been asking me about her. She's really throwing great. College coaches are coming to her games now. Who would have ever thought..." He was beaming. He hadn't heard anything. No one had seen them.

Once home, Barbara skipped dinner and began watching the

three videotapes. What Greg had suspected proved correct. The Moncado tape was of the original police interview with Johnny Moncado some ten years before. It differed significantly in important areas from his most recent statements about the Estrada killing. The other tapes were interviews with two people that Moncado had spoken to shortly after the homicide. They provided still further versions of the events of that day as told to them by Moncado, just days after the killing. Barbara was elated. The day was turning out to be a very good one after all. Johnny Moncado's testimony would never hold up in court. Someday Alejandro would be a free man. And no one had seen them. But they had to be more careful from here on in. Still, she was glad to have taken the chance to show Alejandro how much she loved him.

She called Greg and told him about the tapes. It was exactly what he had suspected. Then he said, "We've got to show those tapes to Soto as soon as possible. He can probably give us more insight and background before we turn them over to Terry to do some follow-up. I'm still in trial for at least another week. You're going to have to show Soto those tapes in the next couple of days. Set it up with the jail and then sit down with him and..." There was little she heard after that. The image of her sitting alone next to Alejandro for two or three hours in the interview room was all her mind would hold.

"How soon can you get in to see the tapes with him? Barb...? How soon can..."

She heard him the third time. "Sorry, Greg, I was just trying to figure out my calendar. I don't have it with me. If you could set it up with the jail, I could probably see him."

"Me set it up? Why would I set it up? I'm in trial, remember."

"I'm sorry. I just thought that since you're the lead attorney you might want to."

"Come on, Barb. When can you get in to see the tapes with him? The sooner the better."

"I can set it up on Monday and then see him on Wednesday at the latest."

"Good." It would have been better if he and Barb could have watched the tapes together with Soto, but Bill Terry should start corroborating those tapes as soon as possible.

That night Barbara lay in bed thinking, while elated, she had not counted on being alone with Alejandro again so soon. She had assumed there would be more time—time to let things settle a bit more, to rethink what had happened, to see him first in the visiting cubicle to gauge his reaction to that morning, and more time to be certain no one had seen them. But Greg rightfully wanted the viewing as soon as possible. She would have to visit with Alejandro on Monday to tell him of the viewing and, more importantly, to see how he was reacting to their morning.

THAT SAME night, Alejandro lay in his bunk pondering how best to contact Barbara with word about Jones and Hudson. The more he thought about it, the more he concluded his only option was to call her office collect with a message that he needed to see her as soon as possible. To do that he would have to ask for the portable phone and once it was rolled down to his cell, the guard would ask for and dial her office number. If Jones had seen them, and he was by then certain that Hudson had planted Jones in the tunnel to spy on him and his "girlfriend," Hudson would be told immediately about the phone call and probably its contents, which would make Hudson more vigilant than ever at their next visit. She had warned him the guards might be bugging their visits. Why else would Hudson have planted Jones down there? Where did this girlfriend business come from unless they were taping their visits? He was thinking of Hudson, thinking that he would put nothing past him, when suddenly Hudson was standing at his cell door with two of his goons.

"OK, Soto, up and at 'em. Back to us and down with your shorts. Don't touch or pick up anything."

So this is the beginning, he thought. Strange how he had no fear. Subconsciously he must have been expecting this visit. *Even sooner,* he thought. *Remember,* he heard her repeating, *it never happened.*

It was the rat's word against theirs. Against *his* word the rat wins, against *her* word they probably win. *Unless Hudson has photos...* something he hadn't counted out.

"Alright, spread them nice and wide, Soto."

Then Hudson's hand was on his back as he bent over and spread. But it wasn't the usual rough, gruff hand.

"What's up, Hudson?"

"Soto, the sooner you understand that I'm running the show, I'm calling the shots, and you do as I say when I say, the easier this whole process is gonna be on all of us. OK, we're gonna put the chains on you just like this, buck naked. But don't get your balls in an uproar; everybody's getting the same treatment. Put 'em on him, Tommy. Some of the other guys are already set."

He didn't know what was going on, but Hudson's manner and voice, his tone, didn't seem like he was busting him for anything. Then he heard deputies in Jenkins's cell and voices and commotions in other cells and knew it was a surprise search of the entire block.

When they chained him four showers down from the shackled Jenkins, Jenkins said, "They're lookin' for dope. Some of those other fools be axin' real crazy lately. Hope you ain't got no dope in your house, Ale."

"Aw, shit no. Don't use the stuff anymore. Wouldn't use it even if I had it. You hear anything about that Jones rat?"

"Naw, ain't heard nuthin'."

"You'd think if he had snitched me out about anything this morning they would have rolled me up by now."

"Ol' Hudson woulda had your ass in solitary by now if he heard somethin'. But what could that rat snitch you out about, Ale?"

"Nothing. I just don't trust rats. Never have, never will."

There had been something different about Hudson, something different in the way he had handled him this time, and something different too in the way Hudson had handled himself. Just as blind people develop their other senses so they can hear, smell, and feel things that those with sight can't, so, too, Alejandro was convinced after so many years in prison that he had developed a sixth sense about people—about who they were and how they were dealing with him, who could be trusted and not trusted. It was that sense that told him to watch Hudson closely when he and his goons came for him in the showers.

"OK, Soto, let's go. Your cell's clean."

There was a change. The gruffness was gone. It was almost as if Hudson were talking to him as one man to another. Hudson had given him an explanation of sorts. Short, true, but Hudson had never bothered explaining anything before. On the way back to the cell there wasn't the slightest shove or push from Hudson, the way there usually was, the way a dog or any beast is prodded. At the cell he had said, "OK, that's it. Let's go guys." No smart cracks, digs, or other demeaning remarks. For whatever reason there had been a change in Hudson. Maybe only for the day, but a change for the better. In any case, this would not have been Hudson's reaction if Jones had seen anything or even if Hudson had planted Jones in the tunnel. There would have been far more serious repercussions by now. No guard would have let anything like the holding cell incident slide, least of all Hudson. They were safe. There was no need to call her.

ON MONDAY morning in department seven, the bailiff and his neighbor bailiff were visiting when she walked into the courtroom.

"Hey Barb, how's it going?"

"Good morning, Ms. Blake."

No, they hadn't been seen. Bill Mowatt, a detective sergeant, stopped as he came into the courtroom and said, "That's a helluva case you've got now, counselor." Theirs had been a relationship of long-standing respect. "I keep wondering how long it's gonna be before you stop working for the bad guys and come on over to our side. The good guys could use your talent." They smiled. All her worry, her fear, had been for naught. But she couldn't afford to do anything like that again. It had been a badly needed wake-up call.

After court, she went over to the jail commander's office to make arrangements for viewing the tapes. Lieutenant Barkley was on duty, a by-the-book man. He was always very formal, and that day was no exception.

"How long's it going to take you, counselor?"

"Well, I've got three videos, one that's close to two hours. The other two aren't nearly as long. I'd say three hours, more or less."

"Alright, I'll slot you in for Wednesday morning, nine to twelve thirty. Is that OK?"

"I think so. Thank you, Lieutenant."

"You're welcome, counselor."

Nothing there. Eye contact as solid as ever, she thought as she left. Her only concern now was Alejandro and what his reaction had been to Friday morning. There could never be a repeat. But then, only she was to blame. He had been and would always be chained. No matter what he might want, she was the only one who could execute anything.

Barbara went to the jail that afternoon. The deputy on duty at the sign-in counter was more than cordial, friendly even. The desk guard on the third floor was a new, pleasant man. As she made her way to the visiting cubicle, she couldn't help but think that there were times when she was all but certain she would never see Alejandro in that cubicle again.

When the door closed behind him on his side of the cubicle, Alejandro's smile was immediate, warm, and wide, and she loved it. He picked up his phone and looked at her. She had yet to pick up her phone, but she mouthed, "I love you." He blinked and blushed. So she mouthed it again, "I love you," and he turned away with a boyish grin and she loved him all the more. Then she picked up the phone and in her best, lawyer-like voice said, "Alejandro, I have here three videotapes that were supplied to us by the district attorney pursuant to the court's order." She leaned over and with one hand rattled the videos about in her briefcase while with her other hand she held up a legal tablet to the glass which read, "Darling, there is absolutely nothing to worry about. Nothing. Believe me, nothing. But we must be careful in the future. I love you. Nod if you understand." He nodded.

Then she went into a long, detailed explanation of the contents of the tapes. Only after that did she tell him that they would be viewing the tapes together on Wednesday morning in a jail interview room. When he became visibly excited, she felt a warm satisfaction. As she was about to leave, she mouthed, "I love you" and then held up the tablet that now read, "If you love me, I need to see your lips say it, not so that they can hear but so that I can see and know. Please say it. " And he mouthed, "I love you, I love you, I love you."

Her unspoken words were still ringing, singing, in his mind as Hudson and his goons led him back to his cell. He seemed to be floating. The chains seemed lighter, weightless even; he couldn't hear them and he wasn't dragging them. Or if he was, it didn't matter. The goons weren't taunting him and, even if they had, it wouldn't have mattered. Hudson said something to him but not gruffly, and he nodded and Hudson let it be. "I love you," she had mouthed. He still wasn't sure what that word meant, but it didn't matter. It was the feeling. The closest things he had experienced to that feeling had been his first and second highs on heroin. But the heroin had only acted on *him*. Here, the feeling acted on him, but he had acted as well: he loved her. A word had been needed to express that feeling and someone had chosen "love." Let it be. Somehow she loved him too. It was clear. She couldn't hide it. He saw it in her eyes...the gleam in her eyes. They glowed. He saw it in her smiles, in her grins. He saw it in the softness of her face when she looked at him, when she tilted her head and nodded yes.

Jenkins said, as he passed his cell, "You back already, homes?" and Alejandro nodded. As they took the chains off him, as Hudson and one of his goons took those wasteful things off him while the third goon guarded the cell door, as if there were anywhere he could possibly go, he felt the "I love you" again and again and it didn't matter what they guarded or what they said or how they took off the chains. Even Hudson must have sensed it, because once again his voice seemed human as he left. Then Jenkins said, "Wanna talk, Ale?" and the softness in that black voice, the music in that black voice, said, "I love you."

"In a while, homes, in a while," and he lay down in his bunk to feel her "I love you."

THE INTERVIEW room in the jail's basement was eight by ten, painted white, and bare except for a television and VCR set on a metal stand in one corner and a metal table with four chairs. The room was windowless, but the top half of the door was made of a thick glass that could be covered over by a shade that rolled up and down. It was used primarily for inmate interviews by court-appointed psychiatrists and psychologists. It was also used for viewing videos by inmates and their lawyers. One of the chairs was bolted to the floor, and an inmate could be chained to it at the request of any of the interviewers. The reason given for the glass and shade was that sometimes the doctors felt more comfortable with the shade up, depending upon whom they might be interviewing.

That Wednesday morning as Barbara waited to be taken to the interview room, she expected to find the shade up and Alejandro chained to the bolted chair. She was determined to ask that the shade be drawn and that he not be chained to the chair, and, if her request was not granted, she would go to the jail commander or even to the court if need be. To her surprise the shade was drawn and Alejandro was not chained to the chair, although he was wearing the waist chains and leg irons. As soon as she entered, she signaled to him not to say a word as she carefully looked around the room and at the shade for any kind of surveillance. Satisfied, she turned and smiled and said, "I'm sorry, Alejandro, but I just wanted to be sure." He too smiled and said, "I know." She felt the urge to go to him and at least take hold of his hands, if not kiss him, but restrained herself. There could not be a repeat, especially with that shade on the door and God only knew who was stationed outside. She placed her briefcase on the table and pulled out the chair opposite him. She took out the three videos, looked up at him, and smiled, happy and satisfied to be in a room with him. She selected the Moncado tape and then walked around the table toward the television set. As she did, her hip slid ever so slightly against the side of his shoulder electrifying her.

WHEN SHE entered the room his breath caught and his chest reached for more and more air until it was full, until discomfort forced a release. But she said nothing, nor did she smile, and his heart dropped. Although it was only momentary, because she signaled and then he saw what she was doing and he appreciated her all the more. Finished, she turned and smiled and it was as clear as anything he had ever known that she loved him. She took a seat across from him, close enough so that their legs could touch unseen under the table. She looked in her briefcase. She was no more than three feet from him then and there was nothing between them. He watched her, waiting and wanting her to look at him. When she did, she smiled and the glow on her face said it again. She took one of the tapes and walked around the table so that she was inches from him. Her hip brushed finely against the side of his shoulder. He wanted to touch her, grab her, but he was chained. Or so he thought, until she was past him, until it was too late and he remembered that the deputies had released his right hand and arm before they left. But she would pass again and this time he would be ready. When she returned he reached for her and his right hand fell against her left thigh and he pressed his fingers hard into the softness of that thigh. And for a moment she paused and let him, but only for a moment, before she continued around the table with her eyes pressed firmly closed.

WHEN SHE felt his hand on her thigh, she stopped. There was nothing more she could have wanted then than to have his hand pressed hard against her thigh, pressed hard against any part of her. But she knew this room, more than any, could be bugged, and there was a guard standing just outside that porous door. She bit her lip and squeezed her eyes shut and moved again to the other side of the table and quickly sat and scribbled a note that read, "Darling, there is nothing more I could ask for than for you to touch me, anywhere, everywhere. But we can't. They could be watching and listening. This room could so easily be bugged. I love you. Some day soon we will be together. Try to be patient."

Then she announced that this was the Johnny Moncado tape and what she wanted him to focus on, look for, and make note of. But she was distracted...because her mind kept reminding her of the pressure of his right hand pressed hard against her left thigh and that he was free, free at last to do whatever he wanted to her with that hand. She pressed the "play" button and the tape began. Johnny Moncado in living color in an interview room with two cops. She watched the tape intently for five and then ten and then something less than fifteen minutes before she dared look at him. When she did he was looking at her with his back to the screen, with his back to Johnny Moncado and the two cops, and with the forefinger of his right hand he was signaling for her to go there, to go to him. She shook her head no, but he wouldn't be denied. He mouthed, "One kiss, just one kiss," holding his forefinger upright and still indicating one. Again she shook her head no, but he continued. Until it occurred to her that if they were watching, if they were videotaping them, they would have been in the room by then. And if they were audiotaping it, they had said nothing to give themselves away and the sounds of Moncado and the cops would obliterate any sounds they made. She raised one finger and mouthed, "Just one," and he nodded. She went to him and he kissed her and held her and groped for her as Johnny Mocando lied in living color behind them. He groped for and found and caressed her breast and then her stomach. He found her pubic hair and more. He fingered her until she was ready and then he brought her head down toward him and together they struggled with the jumpsuit's zipper, struggled past the waist chain, until he was exposed and enormous and she kissed, licked, and sucked. Until the door imploded and there was a room full of shouting guards, and she was dragged out of the room with her blouse unbuttoned and her brassiere half on and her pantyhose hanging well below her knees.

XVIII

Iᴛ ᴡᴀs 10:46 ᴀɴᴅ ᴛʜᴇ ᴊᴜʀʏ ʜᴀᴅ just returned from its morning recess when Judge Marlene Tate took the bench. After the bailiff's pronouncements, Judge Tate asked the deputy district attorney to call her next witness. As the deputy district attorney went out to the hallway, the phone rang and the bailiff, after mumbling, "Yes, sir," motioned for the court clerk to take the call. The court clerk took the call, listened for a few seconds, and then turned and whispered something to Judge Tate who rose and said to the jury, "Ladies and gentlemen, please remain in your seats. I have an important call I have to take. I'll be just a few minutes," and then went into her chambers. When she returned to the courtroom, she said to the lawyers, "Will counsel please approach the bench."

At the bench she looked to Greg Olsen and said quietly, "Mr.

Olsen, the presiding judge has asked that you go to his chambers immediately."

"What about the jury, Your Honor?"

"I'll take care of that. But please try to return as soon as you can."

When Greg Olsen got down to the second floor, he saw Judge Spencer's bailiff standing in the hallway holding the courtroom door open. He quickened his pace wondering what had happened... what in the hell had gone wrong? At the door to the empty courtroom the bailiff said, "Go on back, Greg. He wants to see you right away."

Judge Harold Spencer was seated at his desk staring out a window when Greg Olsen entered. He turned, and his face was furrowed and red. "Greg, we've got a huge mess over at the jail. Apparently the sheriff deputies have arrested Barbara Blake and are holding her in custody, and my guess is they are questioning her as we speak. I have a call into the sheriff but haven't been able to get hold of him. I want you to go over there as her lawyer and stop this nonsense or at least intervene until we can get some cooler, saner heads involved."

"What?" Greg Olsen couldn't believe what he had just heard. "What!"

"I don't know what's going on over there. I've heard everything from escape plans to sex with and the smuggling of weapons and narcotics to that Soto fellow. From what I can make out, it's absolute chaos over there."

"Barbara..."

"I want you to get over there as her attorney and stay with her until you think it's safe to leave her. That should calm things down a little. I'm hoping to hear from the sheriff soon, but until I do, she best be represented." He shook his head in disbelief. "She's always been such a fine, honest lawyer in my court. I have nothing but respect for her. I can't believe any of this. Go on, you'd better get over there. When you're able to leave her, I want you to report back to me."

Greg Olsen was startled, confused, and apprehensive. "Yes, sir." He wanted to stay, talk, find out what the judge knew or had heard. But if Barbara was really under arrest, he had to get over to the jail right away.

He hurried out of the courthouse toward the jail entrance a block away. On the courthouse steps his cell phone rang.

"Greg, have you heard about Barbara?" It was Bill Terry. His voice was tight and quick.

"Yeah. I'm on my way over to the jail now. What have you heard?"

"I've got it from a very good source that Barbara was giving our client Soto a blow job in the psych interview room while she was showing him the videotapes."

Greg's stomach dropped. "He must have been forcing her."

"No, no, no. It was all voluntary. They've got it on film. Apparently this young, hot-dog deputy who's been escorting Soto in and out of his cell for the last couple of weeks has been videotaping and audiotaping them. He even planted a snitch on them."

Greg Olsen stopped walking. The thought of Barbara blowing Soto was more than he could fathom. He fought off the image, but it kept returning even as he tried to answer Bill Terry. "You're kidding me!" was the best he could do. He was overcome with rage toward Soto. "They can't do that," he went on feebly. "Any cop knows that."

"Apparently they're claiming the attorney–client privilege goes out the window once the lawyer and his client are planning a crime. I think they've arrested her. They're holding her in custody down there in the jail's basement."

"What crime?" He was only half involved, his other half was battling the image.

"I don't know."

"How good is your source?" *This could all be bullshit. Barbara would never stoop to...*

"Very good."

"Who is he?" Too many of those cops were liars.

"Don't put me on that cross, Greg. You know I can't go there."

"I've got to get over to the jail." He had heard enough. Or at least all that Bill Terry could tell him.

"Keep me posted."

"No, you keep *me* posted."

Barbara... He stood for a moment trying to make some sense of it. There was hurt now as he wrestled with the image, straining to keep it out of his consciousness. How many times, when they were young lawyers, had he thought of leaving Molly for her? Except for the kids, he would have. Without a doubt. *Barbara...* The bittersweet feeling he had when he learned that she had married that playboy, worthless sailor. Bitter, because he had lost her, lost what might have been one day. Sweet, because she deserved more than the solitary, lonely life she led. *Barbara...* And yet, as he had grown fatter and fatter, and Molly joined him in his race toward obesity and complained and whined more and more each day about everything, and the kids were for all practical purposes grown and gone, as all these things came to pass, Barbara became more attractive still. And now this. She deserved so much more than this. *Barbara. Under arrest and being grilled.* He broke into a run but five steps into it he wrenched his knee and let out a loud groan and several curses.

At the front desk Greg Olsen flashed his bar card and said, "I need to go down to the basement to see my client, Barbara Blake."

"I'm sorry, sir, but the jail is on lockdown. No one is being permitted in or out of the jail for at least another three or fours hours," said a diffident desk deputy.

"What! Are you telling me I can't see my client?"

"I'm telling you that the jail is on lockdown, sir."

"I want to speak to the jail commander."

"Lieutenant Barkley's not here, sir."

"Where is he?"

"He's down in the basement, sir."

"Well, you call him and tell him that attorney Greg Olsen has a court order from Judge Spencer to see his client Barbara Blake, and if I'm not permitted to see her I will be seeking a contempt order against him and the sheriff."

"I'll see what I can do, sir."

The deputy left the front desk, and Greg Olsen could hear him on the telephone in the adjoining room. When he returned he said, "There'll be a deputy here shortly to take you down to the basement, sir."

Lieutenant Barkley was waiting for him at the end of the west hallway next to the room where Barbara was being held. "Good morning, Mr. Olsen." He was a tall, thin, well-groomed man who never seemed to lose his composure. He was no different now.

"Good morning, Lieutenant."

"The front desk said that you wanted to speak to me?"

"Yes sir. I represent Barbara Blake. It's my understanding that you've arrested her and are holding her here in custody."

"I wouldn't go that far, Mr. Olsen."

"Is she free to leave then, Lieutenant? Can I take her with me now?"

"I wouldn't go that far either, Mr. Olsen."

Well Lieutenant, if she's not free to leave, then under the Miranda case she's in custody. Correct?"

"We haven't decided yet whether she is or isn't in custody, Mr. Olsen"

"Well, until you make that decision, can I take her to my office, and once you've made that decision I will surrender her if need be?"

"No."

"Alright then, let me inform you once again that I represent Barbara Blake, and, as her attorney, I do not want anyone from law enforcement questioning her without my permission. Furthermore, I'd like to see her now, please."

Lieutenant Barkley looked at Greg Olsen with cool detachment for several moments before he said, "Alright, we can make that arrangement."

"Where is she?"

"She's in there," he said, pointing to the room on his right. Then he turned to a deputy behind him and said, "Please ask the detectives to step out here."

It was a few minutes before two disgruntled detectives left the room with sour looks for Greg Olsen. "You can go in now, Mr. Olsen," the lieutenant said.

She was sitting at a metal table with her head resting on her forearms and her face down. She did not look up when he entered or when the door closed behind him. Her hair was tousled covering most of her arms and all of her face. He couldn't tell if she was crying. He watched her. He didn't know how to begin. Then he said, "Barbara." She looked up and saw him and said, "Oh, Greg." She had been crying, and she started crying again. She rose, took a halting step, and then went to him. "Oh, Greg!" She threw her arms around him and he held her as her head jerked with sobs. He had never held her before and now he was self-conscious, mostly because of his girth. There had been so many times that he wanted to hold her when he was fit and firm.

He thought of Alejandro Soto's fit, muscular, fat-free body and at the same time fended off the image of Barbara and him. The thought of Barbara's mouth on Soto made him nauseous. He hated Soto. Was it a pure, physical, animal attraction? He hadn't known her first husband, but the few things she had said about him, a banker now, gave him the impression that he was softer, flabbier than himself. The irresponsible sailor husband had been a scrawny thing. Maybe it was just a fascination with a brute, muscular, male body, something she had never experienced before. Her uncontrollable sobbing brought him back. She wanted and needed to be held by him regardless of the flab.

He held her for a long time without a word being spoken. The loud, jerking sobs turned to quiet sobs and then to soft, silent crying and then to nothing but the need to be held. He thought of all the times as a criminal defense attorney he had told himself that nothing about human behavior could surprise him anymore. He had been wrong again. When she was breathing softly against his chest he said, "Barbara, what happened? I have to know. You have to tell me."

"Nothing happened." She pulled away from him.

"Barbara, they're holding you here. I'm sure they tried to question you before I got here. They want to charge you with a felony or felonies. This is no laughing matter. I need to know what happened so I can deal with them."

"I love him." Defiant. "That's what happened. I love him."

This took him by surprise. It stung. It hurt. It was real. These were the words of a twice-married, almost-forty-year-old lawyer. Gone forever were his theories of force and an animal-like attraction, and in their place were the realization and pain that Barbara might very well be in love with Alejandro Soto. He put that thought aside. He reminded himself that he wasn't there to deal with matters of love but rather to represent her. He was there then to find out from his client what had happened. He would deal with his own pain later.

"Were you making any plans to help Soto escape?"

"God, no! We're going to win this case, Greg, and as soon as the writ is granted, Alejandro will be free. Why would I want to help Alejandro escape?"

He wasn't as certain as she was about the case and the writ. What he was certain of was his disdain for the familiarity with which she used Soto's name—Alejandro. "Were you sneaking any drugs or weapons into the jail?"

"Oh Greg, you know me better than that. No, no!"

He had thought he knew her better than that. "Was there any sex involved?"

"I made love to him. That's not a crime."

He didn't want to ask the next question, didn't want to hear the answer from her lips. But there was no way around it. "What kind of love?"

"I orally copulated him. That's not a crime. I love the man. And that's not a crime."

Greg Olsen felt more pain. His first impulse was to answer, "It should be." But instead he said, "No, that's not a crime," and shook his head in disbelief as he attempted to rid himself of that image. Then he added, "You know, they videotaped you and him."

"Videotaped...? Videotaped?"

For the first time, he thought the act was bringing her a sense of fear and shame.

"They have a tape of Alejandro and me?"

He nodded. Now there was a sense of satisfaction: the act was causing her some remorse, some shame.

"You mean they'll circulate that thing as some sort of evidence?"

"My guess is that it's already being circulated among the deputies. Cheap thrills, you know."

"They can't do that! What Alejandro and I did is not a crime. You've got to stop them, Greg. I know half of the department."

"I'll do what I can. But my guess is that most of the department has at least heard about it by now even if they haven't seen the tape. You know how word gets around."

"Oh, my God! Oh, my God!"

She began crying again, quietly, and he watched her torn with empathy and resentment.

WHEN GREG Olsen stepped into the hallway again, Randy Davis was standing there with Lieutenant Barkley. He never thought he would see the day when he would be happy to see Randy Davis, but dealing with him would be easier than dealing with the stiff, indecisive lieutenant. He could expect some answers from Davis.

"What brings you here, Randy?"

"Same thing that brought you here, Greg."

"Well, is she under arrest? Is she in custody? Are you going to charge her with anything? If not, I'd like to take her home. How's that for getting to the point?"

"Not bad."

"Which one or none of the above?"

"I'm still working through it here with Lieutenant Barkley."

"Come on, Randy, you don't have a crime here, and you know it."

"I wouldn't be so sure, Greg."

"I've heard the rumors. Escape plans? No. Smuggling contraband into the jail? No. Consensual sex with an inmate? Probably. But that's not a crime. What penal code section makes it a crime? Now I understand that you'll have to talk all of this over with your boss before anything's decided, but in the interim, why not release her to my custody? If you decide to charge her with something, I'll surrender her. You know I've always kept my word in the past. But if you won't agree to that, I'm going to walk over to Judge Spencer's department and ask that he release her on her promise to appear. And I'll bet you your next paycheck that he'll do it."

"I can't release her to your custody, Greg. At least not until I've talked to Jim about it."

"Well, I guess I'll go over and talk to Judge Spencer then. But please, I don't want anybody from law enforcement talking to her while I'm gone." As he was leaving, Greg Olsen paused and said, "By the way, Randy, don't you really think you've got the wrong person in custody here?"

"What do you mean?"

"Well what about the deputy who's been filming and audiotaping their visits for the last couple of weeks? Deputy...Deputy...," he said turning to the lieutenant.

"Deputy Hudson."

"Yeah, Deputy Hudson. Isn't it still a felony for a peace officer to tape conversations of an attorney and his client when the client is in custody?"

"It depends."

"Depends on what, Randy? What are you going to be able to show that justified Deputy Hudson's filming of my clients two weeks ago, ten days ago, or last week? Not much, I bet."

WHEN GREG Olsen stepped into an empty department three in the courthouse, the bailiff said, "Go on back, Greg, he's waiting for you." He did not expect to find Sheriff Roberts also sitting in Judge Spencer's chambers.

"Well, what's going on over there, Greg?"

"As near as I can make out, Your Honor, they've had her locked up in a basement interview room for over two hours now and neither Lieutenant Barkley nor Randy Davis can decide if she's been arrested or if she's in custody or whether any charges will be filed against her. They're also refusing to release her to my custody even with the understanding that I will surrender her if they do file charges. One curious note is that a Deputy Hudson has been taping her visits with Soto for some time now, and, as far as I'm concerned, he's the one who ought to be in custody on felony charges. Believe me, when I leave here I'm going over to the DA's office and demand that they file charges against him."

"Now, now, calm down, Greg," Judge Spencer said. "We don't need to start airing this thing out in public. The last thing we want is to get the media involved. The less that is said about this, the easier I think it will be to resolve it for everyone concerned. Now it may be that Ms. Blake has not committed a crime, nevertheless, I'm dutybound to report this matter to the state, and I will do that. What action the State Bar decides to take against Ms. Blake is out of my jurisdiction. Now the sheriff and I have been talking, and it may well be that Deputy Hudson has overstepped here, but this is the first time, to my knowledge, that anything like this has happened in all the years I've been in the criminal justice system. To air something like this out in public and have our criminal justice system pilloried up and down the state, to have every defense bar in the state pointing to us as the perfect example of underhanded law enforcement methods isn't called for. And, my guess is that whatever action the State Bar takes against Ms. Blake won't bar her from the practice of law for the rest of her life. She's a good lawyer, a dedicated lawyer, and I'm sure that some day she'll want to return to the practice of law whether it's in this county or somewhere else. It's also in the deputy's best interest, if he's charged with anything or disciplined in any way, to settle the matter as quietly and expeditiously as he can. What I'm asking is that we work through this calmly and quietly. Do you understand, Greg?"

"Yes, sir."

"Do you agree?"

"Yes, sir."

"Good. It looks like we're all in agreement. Sheriff Roberts wants to make a call. We were just waiting for you to return and brief us before he did so. Dave, why don't you just use my phone."

Sheriff Roberts's call was brief and to the point. "Lieutenant, Mr. Olsen is coming back over to the jail in a few minutes. I want you to release Ms. Blake into his custody as soon as he arrives. Thank you."

WHEN GREG Olsen returned, Randy Davis and Lieutenant Barkley were sitting in the hallway next to the room where Barbara was.

"Did you talk to the sheriff, Lieutenant?"

"Yes, sir."

"Is it alright for me to leave and take Ms. Blake with me?"

"Yes, sir."

"Any problems with that, Randy?"

"None except that if we decide to file charges you agree you will surrender Ms. Blake within an hour of our notifying you by phone?"

"Agreed."

Barbara had returned to the chair and the metal table once again with her face buried between her forearms on the table. She didn't look up until he said, "Barbara, get your things and let's go."

"Go where?"

"Out of here. Home."

She looked at him doubtfully. "You mean they're not going to do anything to me?"

"Not now. Maybe later. We'll have to play that one when and if it comes. Come on, get your things. Let's get out of here."

She started to cry and went to him again and threw her arms over his shoulders and around his neck. "Oh, Greg, thank you."

God, how he cared for her. Too much so, too much to put his arms around her then. Somewhere in his consciousness he made a resolution to stop eating and drinking so much and to start working out at the gym.

"Come on, let's go."

She cried some more and pressed against him for a while longer. Then she stopped, stepped away, dried her eyes, and went to the table to gather her briefcase. He waited for her at the door but she was slow in coming. Her face and eyes were downcast and her body was bent. It was the shame. This proud, capable woman was about to step out into a hallway and jail filled with deputies from whom she had always commanded respect. She edged closer and closer to him until their bodies were side by side. There had to be a better way. "Why don't you wait here, Barb," he said, "while I go out and talk to the lieutenant about letting us go out the back way. There's no telling what might be waiting for us in these hallways and in the lobby." She seemed not to have heard him and so he asked, "Don't you think that's a better way to leave?"

She nodded.

He slipped out of the room in such a way that no one in the hallway could see her. The lieutenant was still there but he had not expected Randy Davis to still be there. *Probably wants to gloat as she leaves,* he thought. The lieutenant agreed that it would be better if she left through the booking area.

When he reentered, she slid behind the door as he opened it. He closed the door and said, "We're going to go now, but out through booking. A lot less people there." She reached for and took his hand tightly. They stepped out into the hallway, he first and she closely behind him still clutching onto his hand. There were five or six deputies in the hallway plus the lieutenant and Randy Davis. There was a heavy silence and stillness as Greg Olsen walked and Barbara Blake slunk past them. She saw none of them and spoke to no one, using his hand rather than her eyes to guide her out of the jail.

Once outside, he said awkwardly, "Where to?"

"My car. It's across the street in the parking lot."

"Going home?"

"No, I don't want anybody to find me."

"Well, I may need to be in touch with you. If they decide to file charges, I'll have to turn you in. But I'm sure Spencer will order you released on your own recognizance."

"I know. But for now, I'm going to rent a motel room. As soon as I do, I'll call your cell and let you know where I am. If I go anywhere, I'll call and tell you."

"How long are you going to rent a motel room?"

"I don't know, Greg. Probably until I can face people. I can't do that now."

THERE WERE four deputies standing in a loose circle around Alejandro Soto who was now seated in a chair with his right wrist attached to the waist chains when Deputy Hudson returned from across the hall where detectives were beginning to question Barbara. His first words were, "Chain that son of a bitch to that chair. One wrong move by that Mexican shit-eater, and I'm liable to kill him." Then, as two of the deputies were chaining Alejandro Soto to the chair, Hudson said to Alejandro, "Fucking spic. Thought you and your white whore could put one over on us, didn't you? Well you're fucked. I got your asses down on film. We know all about your shit. I've got all that stupid cunt's messages against the glass on film."

Alejandro sat looking down at the rectangle on the floor between his leg irons. He was worried about Barbara. There was nothing they could add to his two life sentences, but what would this do to her? For sure they would take her off the case, and he would probably never see her again. But what would they do to her? She had given him so much, more than anyone had ever given him. She had taught him love. She had made him feel worthwhile, if only for a few weeks. And for that she was about to pay dearly. He should have known; Hudson had been making it too easy.

He hadn't been listening to Hudson, but now Hudson bent down and put his face next to his and said, "Goddamn greaser gets a white whore posing as a lawyer. She must have fucked everybody in sight to get that bar card she loves to flash around. You get her to suck on your dick and you really think your human. I'm so tired of you cholos filling our jails and welfare rolls. Why don't the whole goddamn bunch of you go back to that sorry-ass country of yours where you belong?"

"This is our country," Alejandro answered quietly without lifting his head. "It was ours long before any of your grandfathers ever came here."

"What'd you say, spic? You're telling me this is your country?"

"In 1848 the U.S. invaded Mexico and took over Mexico City. Mexico had to give up Utah and Colorado and Arizona and Nevada and California. This was our land. You took it from us."

"Bullshit! Got yourself a white whore posing as a lawyer and now you're going around thinking you're educated."

"I'm not educated, but I read. You should try it sometime."

"You rotten motherfucker!" Hudson grunted, swinging his closed fists and hitting Alejanadro Soto in the face several times. He kicked at Alejandro's legs and then at his chest knocking Alejandro and the chair over. He moved quickly to where Alejandro had fallen and began kicking him repeatedly in the face and head.

One of the other deputies grabbed at Hudson, yelling, "That's enough! That's enough! You're gonna fuck him up him real bad!"

"Fuck you, Byrnes! Stay out of my business!" Hudson shouted, pushing Deputy Byrnes aside and turning back to Alejandro.

This time Byrnes jumped on Hudson and wrestled him to the floor. "That's enough, Huddy," Byrnes repeated, "you're blowing it for all of us!" And he held the struggling Hudson on the floor.

"Stop, Huddy! It looks like he's hurt real bad," said another deputy.

"Yeah, Hud, you got to stop, man. There's gonna have to be some explaining to do," added a third.

Hudson finally heard them. "OK, OK," and he stopped struggling.

Minutes later they carried the unconscious Soto to a solitary confinement cell and left him there, at least for the night.

XIX

HE WALKED BARBARA TO
her car. They were two people with so much to say, saying nothing. At her car, she opened the door and turned and looked at him
for the first time since the interview room in the jail, she on one
side of the door and he on the other. It was a long, open, resigned
look. Still they said nothing. She wanted to tell him that she was
sorry...but sorry for what? That she had fallen in love with Alejandro? That was nothing to be sorry about. Sorry about the case?
He knew that. Sorry that she had fallen in love with someone other
than him? He knew that, too, just as she had always known his
attraction for her. In the interview room she had seen him gulp
and swallow when she said, "I love him, I love him." And again,
when she said, "I made love to him...I orally copulated him." All of
that was better left unsaid. The only thing left to say was a repetition of "thank-you, Greg." And she said it again, quietly, earnestly,

"Thank you, Greg." But that was all. There was so much Greg Olsen felt he wanted to say. But he could only nod and look away.

He watched as she drove erratically out of the parking lot, watched until the car was gone from sight. He stood for a few moments more toying with what might have been, not wanting to return to what was now. Then he saw people lining up on the courthouse steps for the afternoon session, and he remembered that he had a jury and client waiting for him in Judge Tate's courtroom. He glanced at his watch: 1:17. He hurried to the courthouse. He had to tell Judge Tate before the jury was seated that he was in no frame of mind to continue that afternoon. At the courtroom door the bailiff said, "The case has gone over till Monday morning. The presiding judge called and said that you'd be tied up with that death penalty case at least until then. I called your office and left word. I'm surprised you haven't heard."

He considered going to the jail to visit Soto but thought better of it. He'd have to see him soon, tomorrow for sure. But for the moment, it was probably better to let things settle. There was no telling what he might say to Soto now. Then too, it had already occurred to him he might want to ask the court to allow him to withdraw as his attorney. He had a lot to consider. Tomorrow would be soon enough to see Soto. He looked at his watch again: 1:27. Suddenly he was very hungry. A steak sandwich, some fries, and a cold bottle of beer at Jake's BBQ sounded awfully good. Faintly his mind reminded him of his resolve to stop eating and drinking so much. But he needed to calm down. The day so far had been hell, and he was starving. There was so much to think about, so much to decide. One bottle of beer would calm him. One bottle of beer wasn't going to hurt him. Tomorrow he'd start in earnest and cut back on his eating and drinking.

In the fifteen years that Greg Olsen had been a criminal defense attorney, he had prided himself in never having refused to represent a defendant because of the nature of the charges or who the defendant was. There were criminal defense attorneys who routinely refused to take rape cases or child molest cases or death

penalty cases and attorneys who refused to represent sexual preda-
tors or previously convicted child molesters or defendants charged
with three strikes. Greg Olsen believed that if a lawyer held himself out to be a criminal defense attorney, he had a moral obligation to represent to the best of his ability any individual who
could afford his services or any court-appointed defendant. It was
not a question of winning or losing because, contrary to television and movies, criminal defendants seldom won. Rather, it was
simply a question of providing the best defense possible under
the law. No more, no less. No games, no tricks, no lies. Any fear
or distaste one might have for the case or the defendant had to
be set aside. But now he represented Alejandro Soto, a man who,
as he raised his first taste of beer to his lips, he despised. What to
do about Soto? Clearly Barbara was off the case. But should he,
or could he, continue to represent Soto?

The second swallow of that cold beer went down easier, tastier,
than the first, sweeter than the sweetest ice-chilled Sierra Mountain water. It calmed him and soothed him far more than the first.
What to do about Soto? The question jiggled in his mind. The
question was ever-present and yet he couldn't or wouldn't stop
the jiggling, wouldn't face it squarely. He was awfully hungry.
Maybe that was it. The steak sandwich arrived with a mountain
of french fries. Two huge bites of the sandwich washed down by
two big gulps of beer and a handful of fries, and he was ready to
seriously consider the question. But first he ordered another beer.

He waited for the beer and as soon as it came, he took a long
swig of it and then he was ready. He despised the son of a bitch.
If Soto got the death penalty, he, as his attorney, would probably
be entitled to a seat at the execution. He'd arrive early, take a seat
in the front row, and watch his client's face twist and grimace as
he died. Nothing could please him more. He picked up what was
left of the sandwich, examined it, and thought, *Damn good sandwich, best steak sandwich in town.* No, he couldn't represent Soto
any longer. Not hating him as he did. He added a little more salt
to the fries and then rubbed the grease and salt off his thumb and

forefinger before he picked up another one. He picked up two instead, bit off the ends, and shoved the rest in his mouth. He loved french fries. On the other hand, with the new Moncado tapes, he was more convinced than ever that the case was winnable. Judge Spencer would assign him a new second counsel. He would let the new attorney finish preparing the penalty phase of the case and try the guilt phase himself. If there was a penalty phase trial, and he seriously doubted it, he already knew enough about the case to try that as well. Soto's was a high profile case. The San Cristobal and Dos Palos media would be saturated with it. A not guilty verdict would probably make the wire services. A win in this case would put him among the top two or three criminal defense attorneys in the county. His income would triple even as his caseload shrank. There was absolutely no reason why he couldn't try and win Soto's case and still hate him.

That seemed to settle it. He took two more swigs from his second bottle of beer and ordered a third. He was almost finished with his sandwich and fries but he was still hungry. He waited for his third beer to wash down the remains of the sandwich and fries. *Hell, why not order another steak sandwich and fries and just kick back and relax... The noon crowd is long gone and the restaurant is quiet and deserted. Why not?*

He had nothing on his office calendar for the rest of the afternoon. But he thought of Barb and the promises he had made to himself in that awful interview room. She would get over this border brother soon enough. Both of his kids had one foot out the door and certainly didn't need him like they did before. The thought of another year with Molly seemed as bad as a life sentence. Barb wasn't a lost cause yet. As soon as she got over this infatuation, he'd put his cards on the table and do what he should have done years ago.

Barbara... He hadn't heard from her yet. She had to be settled in her room by now. He needed to know where she was in case he had to surrender her. She knew that. Why hadn't she called? Probably too ashamed. And with good reason. That video of her and that animal had to be making the rounds in the sheriff's department. The judges surely knew by now and the DA's office too—maybe even the public defender's office. He should call her. She definitely needed moral support. He had the afternoon free. He called.

"Yes." Her voice was quiet, cold, and abrupt.

"Barb?"

"Yes."

His spirit sagged. There was nothing welcoming about her voice. It was terse and the tone said, "What do you want?"

"Barb, it's me, Greg."

"Yes, I know."

The two additional words added nothing except more indifference and coldness. Now he did not know where to begin. The silence that followed was even more chilling. He had to say something. The waitress gestured for his plate. He shook his head no but the gesture gave him his next words. "Barb, I was just sitting down here at Jake's about to order my lunch when I thought that you were probably pretty hungry by now. Can I order us each a steak sandwich and bring them over to the motel. Maybe we could eat and talk and—"

"I'm not hungry." Curt...even brusque.

"Well then," he said flailing, not willing to face the obvious, "maybe I could come over and bring my sandwich and talk. I'm sure there's a lot on your mind and as your lawyer I should be absolutely clear on what your position is on a good number of things."

"Isn't talking premature at this point? Don't we have to wait and see what they do first?"

That angered him. "Barbara, I don't even know where in the hell you're at. I'm your lawyer. I'm supposed to surrender you on an hour's notice if they file charges. Where are you?"

"I'm in a motel."

"What motel?"

"Greg, you have my cell phone number. You can contact me at any moment you choose. I'm minutes from the jail. There's really no need to tell you where I am. Short of having to surrender myself, I really don't want to talk to anyone right now."

"Fine." He was hurt, crushed. He wasn't just *anyone.* "Goodbye." He sat staring off into space until the waitress approached again. He ordered another steak sandwich and fries and when those came, another beer.

It was 4:34 when he got home. Molly and the kids were out. Good. The last thing he wanted was to deal with Molly's fat-ass whining. He took two beers with him into the family room and turned on the television. The evening news had begun. Same old shit. Another catastrophe the media had dug up somewhere in the Middle East. What would the media do without catastrophes? He switched channels at the first hint of a commercial, but the next channel had a commercial on as well. He switched again. Same result. It was neither the top nor middle of the hour. The bastards were in a conspiracy to force him to watch a commercial. He hit the mute button. Now who had the last laugh? At two minutes to five he carried out his plan to relieve his bladder and grab two more bottles of beer out of the refrigerator, thereby avoiding an inundation of commercials and also fortifying himself with enough beer so that he wouldn't have to deal with Molly no matter when she arrived or what she said when she did.

HE WOKE to cold and darkness. It took him a while to orient himself. He was still in the family room and the television was off. The house was silent, and the door to the family room had been closed. The bitch had shut him out of the family that night. He expected that from her, but the kids could have at least come in and said good night. He was thirsty and wobbly. He made his way to the kitchen. Dirty dishes everywhere. Lazy bitch couldn't even load the dishwasher. An empty bottle of Merlot said it all: she had been drunk on her ass. He went upstairs. He passed Molly's open door as he staggered toward his room. She was snoring loud and hard. It was gross and disgusting.

He woke to an overcast sky, a slight headache, and the gnaw-
ing question of what he would do with the Soto case. He was still
vacillating, but it was clear he had to see Soto that morning and
Judge Spencer before the end of the day. The kids had already
left for school. Molly was still in bed. She wasn't snoring. He felt
sure she was feigning sleep so she wouldn't have to talk to him.
Fine by him...made it that much easier. He showered, shaved, and
dressed. The sight and odor of the dirty dishes in the kitchen was
even more repulsive than it had been the night before. *Dirty, lazy
bitch,* he thought as he went out the kitchen door.

No sooner was Greg Olsen out of his driveway than Alejandro Soto appeared center stage in his mind. Now it seemed as
if he could think of nothing else. He had to see him today, and
the sooner the better. He probably should have seen him yesterday, but he couldn't have contained his rage then. He would have
regretted anything he would have said to him yesterday. He hated
the bastard.

*How could she have fallen for his bullshit? Over the years she must
have had hundreds of guys come on to her in the jail, only to fall for a
three-time murderer. How could she?*

There was no way he could continue representing Soto. *Why go
visit Soto at all? Just go directly to Judge Spencer and ask to be relieved.*
There was no way he could sit next to Soto in a courtroom for
a month and not try to strangle him. No, he had to see him; he
had to hear him out at least. Wasn't he the one who was always
pleading with the prosecutors and the judges to hear his clients
out? Nor could he forget that this case was very winnable. Why
let some other lawyer reap the rewards of all his hard work? This
case could make him. *No more small potatoes for Greg Olsen.* He decided to stop at the Koffee Kup for some coffee and something to
eat, something to soothe his head and stomach. He drank three
cups of coffee and slowly tried to swallow down a bowl of hot
cereal. After half a bowl he was certain he would vomit if he took
another spoonful. Like it or not, he had to see Soto and he had
to see him now.

HE WENT to the jail and up to the third floor cubicle where he always saw Soto. In the cubicle he felt the cheap, white, plastic chair buckling under his weight. He had to stop eating and drinking so much. *But why? What did it matter now?* He was still undecided about Soto. He would make his determination once he saw him. Hopefully then he would at least have a better sense of what had actually happened and how it had happened. Bill Terry's sources weren't necessarily infallible—probably second or third-hand hearsay. Hear Soto out. It was a very winnable case. He snapped out of his uncertainty long enough to realize that he had been waiting for twenty-five minutes. He went to the guard's station, but the guard wasn't there. He waited another ten minutes and then went out to the station again.

"I'm sorry, sir, but he's in the infirmary. They'll bring him up, but it will be a while. I didn't know he was in the infirmary."

In the cubicle he scoffed. *He didn't know he was in the infirmary, ha!* Those bastards will do everything they can to inconvenience defense attorneys. Or was Soto feigning an illness so he wouldn't have to face him? Another twenty minutes passed. Now he was fuming.

"Look, Deputy, I've been waiting almost an hour now. Where in the hell is my client?"

The guard was wide-eyed. "I just now got a call from the infirmary. They say they can't move him until a doctor has seen him, and the doctor won't be in until 11:30. They suggested that you come back at one o'clock and report to the infirmary first because the visit may have to take place there."

Now he was certain Soto's sudden illness was a sham, a ploy, to avoid seeing him. Soto knew he and Barbara were close and had worked together for years. In Soto's world that would have meant sex, intimacy, and a parting of ways once Greg's wife discovered the affair. Barbara still being the good-looking woman that she was, Soto would have guessed that Greg was still attracted to her and wanted to resurrect their liaison. And Soto would have concluded that Greg would be deeply offended by what had happened.

Greg Olsen reported to the infirmary at one o'clock, having decided that if Soto wouldn't see him, he would march over to Judge Spencer's court and ask to be relieved. The on-duty guard was quick to dispel his resoluteness. "Yes, sir, we've been expecting you. We were told that you'd be returning at one. The visiting rooms are just down the hall on your left. Why don't you take the first visiting room, and we'll bring him out for you as soon as we can."

It was only a matter of minutes before he heard the leg irons. The eight-by-eight visiting room was bare except for a small metal table and two chairs. This would be their first contact visit. The dragging sounds were coming from a hallway on his right but at a distance. He watched that hallway wondering whether he would be able to maintain eye contact and hide his outrage from Soto.

Gradually the chains grew louder. When he finally saw Soto he was startled. Soto's face was a swollen mass of red, blue, green, and yellow. His right eye was swollen shut, and there were black stitches that ran down and through his left eyebrow. The left side of his upper lip was swollen and stitched—so swollen that it appeared to be touching the bottom of his nostril. His arms had random welts of red and blue, and he was limping badly and shuffling in small broken steps.

Oh my God, he thought, *they've beaten the holy shit out of him.* Two guards, one on each side of him, seemed ludicrous: a man shackled by waist chains and leg irons who could barely move and probably could barely see. Slowly, very slowly, he made his way into the room, and Greg Olsen moved around the table so that he could sit in the chair closest to the door. With great effort he sat down, the guards at the ready to catch him if he fell on either side. Seated, his head hung over the table. He said nothing to Greg Olsen nor did he acknowledge him in any way. As the guards left, one pointed and said, "There's a buzzer behind you. Buzz if you need us or when you're ready to leave." The door closed. He heard the key in the door and the lock turn.

They sat in silence for a long while, one man staring at the stitches, the swelling, and the discoloration of the other, and the other sitting hunched over the table as if dazed or unconscious. One man sat conflicted and tried to call up the rage and hatred that had dogged him for the past twenty-four hours but found himself flooded by empathy instead. The other man sat there perhaps not knowing or perhaps not caring that he was there. Finally, the conflicted man said, "What happened, Soto?" But the other man did not hear him or did not want to hear him. After a while Greg Olsen asked again, louder and now with some irritation, "What happened, Soto?" Still no response. Now the irritated man rose and leaned over the small table and shook the other man's shoulder, "I said, what happened, Soto?"

The shaking roused the other man because he grunted, "Huh? Huh?"

"I asked you what happened."

Now the other man answered drowsily as if coming out of a slumber, "She was sucking on my dick."

"What!"

"She was sucking on my dick."

"I don't want to hear that! Do you understand? I don't want to hear that!" He shouted angrily, pressing his fingers into the other man's shoulder and shaking him very hard. "I want to hear what happened!"

"She was sucking on my dick and—"

Then there was the ugly, unmistakable splatter of flesh on flesh, and for a moment the blow lifted the dazed man off his chair and then sent both the man and the chair crashing to the floor where the dazed man lay groaning.

Greg Olsen turned and pressed the buzzer and immediately recoiled because of the pain in his right hand. The hand was reddening, and he stuffed it into his pants pocket and leaned on the buzzer with his left hand. A guard came running. He looked for Soto and when he saw him on the floor said, "What happened?"

"I don't know. He just passed out and keeled over."

He left the infirmary with his right hand in his pants pocket.

In the lobby, the on-duty deputy was standing near the sign-out sheet. He thought of using his left hand to sign out but felt that it might draw more attention than it was worth. His right hand was red and hot and seemed to be swelling. He was sure he had broken it. When he gripped the pen, the pain was excruciating. He scrawled something as lightly and hurriedly as he could and left the jail.

The pain was shooting up through his entire right arm. It was 1:27, and he needed to see Judge Spencer before he took the bench for his afternoon calendar. He had to see a doctor, and there was no way he could wait around until Judge Spencer finished his calendar. If he went to the doctor now he would probably return with a heavily bandaged right hand that surely would provoke questions and suspicions. He half ran, half walked to the courthouse. Judge Spencer's courtroom was filled with attorneys, inmates, and spectators. The bailiff, telephone in hand, was about to summon the judge to the bench when Greg Olsen arrived and said, "I need to see the judge now! It's about the Soto case, and it's urgent!"

The bailiff altered his message and then said, "Go on, back, Greg. He'll see you now."

Harold Spencer was standing at his desk clad in his black robe. "What's the problem, Greg?"

"Judge, I've got to withdraw from the Soto case."

Harold Spencer rubbed his hand back and forth across his mouth and studied Greg Olsen.

"I'm sorry, Judge, I know you have your afternoon calendar and a courtroom full of people out there, but I felt that I had an obligation, in light of what happened yesterday, to inform the court of my decision immediately."

Harold Spencer now held three fingers across his mouth and studied Greg Olsen for a few moments more before he said, "Calm down and sit down. Let's talk about this. And you needn't worry about my calendar. This is far more important. Now tell me, what's the problem?"

"I just saw Soto a few minutes ago, Judge, and because of what happened yesterday I find I have such an overwhelming hatred for the man... She's like a sister to me, Your Honor. No, she's...," his voice cracked and his eyes watered, "she's actually closer to me than my own sister. As you know, we started out in the PD's office together. We were law partners. We're still very close. I've always confided in her about problems in my cases, and sometimes even my own personal problems. It's as if he did this to a member of my family. I...I..." He stopped. His throat had tightened and he was afraid he'd cry if he continued. His right hand was hurting even more.

Harold Spencer hadn't taken his eyes off Greg Olsen. There was no doubt that his emotions and feelings were real. But now he was thinking of Dave Roberts and how he would howl when he told him that he was going to have to appoint two new attorneys to the Soto case, that the trial date in the case was going to be continued, and that instead of having Soto in his jail for another three months, he probably would have him there at least another year. With the added escapades of Deputy Hudson and all the motions that would bring, it could be a year and a half...maybe more. It seemed like everyone was pressing him to get the Soto case to trial and get Soto back to Arroyo Grande, but no one more than Roberts. The heightened courtroom security with as many as nine additional deputies needed every time Soto came to court, the special guards needed to pull him from and escort him back to his cell, the complete jail lockdowns every time he came out of his cell, the overtime it was costing Roberts, and then yesterday's fiasco... Roberts wanted Soto out of his jail and he wanted him out now. But as he watched an emotionally choked-up Greg Olsen, Judge Spencer had no alternative. The last thing anyone needed was to have Greg Olsen file a formal motion to withdraw, which he would have to grant, and have the entire matter aired in public before the media.

"Alright Greg, have my clerk put the matter on Monday afternoon's calendar. I was going to relieve Barbara Blake from the case then anyway. You won't have to say much on the record. In fact, I'd appreciate it if you didn't. Just say a conflict of interest has arisen and you're asking for the two of you to be relieved. Don't forget to alert Randy Davis. He will need to be here."

"Will Barbara need to be here?"

"No, that won't be necessary. My guess is that the State Bar will have placed her on interim suspension by then. So why draw any unneeded attention to that? Have any suggestions on who I can appoint to replace the two of you?"

"No, not really. But then you shouldn't trust me with anything that might help Soto right now."

Harold Spencer needn't have worried. The next morning, the Federal District Court denied Alejandro Soto's petition for a writ of habeas corpus. That same afternoon, the San Cristobal District Attorney dismissed the murder charges against Alejandro Soto, and that evening, he was transported back to the Arroyo Grande State Prison.

Two DEPUTY sheriffs rolled a heavily medicated Alejandro Soto out of the San Cristobal County Jail's infirmary on a gurney. Four other deputies accompanied them. All seven boarded a helicopter in the jail parking lot. Two hours later at Arroyo Grande State Prison, a guard at the receiving unit said, "Whoa! What happened to this guy?"

One of the sheriff deputies answered, "Well, Mr. Soto's not as tough or as smart as he thinks he is, especially around those young gangbangers we've got down there in the jail. Even if he's a Mexican, too."

XX

Barbara Blake learned in the local paper that the Estrada murder case had been dismissed and Alejandro's writ of habeas corpus in the Sanchez case had been denied. Randy Davis had given the federal court's denial of the writ as the reason for their dismissal of the Estrada case, saying that his office now felt it was senseless to waste taxpayers funds trying a man who now, with all certainty, would serve two life sentences in prison without the possibility of parole. There had been no mention of her in the article.

She had called Greg's cell phone twice that day and left messages for him to call her but he did not return her calls. She was too embarrassed to call his office. His secretaries had to have heard by then. She thought of calling him at home, but Molly certainly knew and even if Molly did not answer the phone she might be in the room and eavesdrop on their conversation. And that was more than Barbara could bear. She went to bed convinced that Greg was avoiding her calls. But what was she to do? Lie to him? Lead him on? Give him false hope? She was not in the least bit interested in Greg Olsen, now less than ever.

She called Greg again the following morning, reminding herself that this was not about Greg or her, it was about Alejandro. There was no answer. She left another message. Greg returned the call late that afternoon. His voice was cool and distant.

"You called?"

"Yes. I wanted to confirm what I read in this morning's paper. Have the murder charges been dismissed?"

"Yes."

"The writ was denied in federal court?"

"Yes."

"There's no doubt about that?"

"None."

"I see." She did see, all too clearly. Greg's words struck her harder than the newspaper article. There was a finality to them, a certainty that was too often missing in the media's reporting of legal proceedings. And his voice, his tone, his choice of words signaled a finality to a friendship of many years. There was nothing more she could think to say, nothing more she wanted to say. She waited for him to say something—not end it like this.

Finally, he did say something, in that same dry, solemn, precise tone he had just adopted.

"You should know that last week, Judge Spencer notified the State Bar of your episode in the jail with Mr. Soto. This morning he received notification from the State Bar that you have been placed on immediate interim suspension pending their investigation. You will not be permitted to appear in any court or act in any capacity as an attorney until you are otherwise notified by the State Bar. Judge Spencer will be reassigning your court-appointed cases, and you should do the same with your privately retained cases as soon as possible. He also said the State Bar sent a letter to your office informing you of the interim suspension. In light of that, the district attorney's office has decided not to press any criminal charges against you."

It was she who said good-bye and he who hung up the phone without another word.

She had thought as early as high school that she might want to be a lawyer. Hard work and perseverance helped her become one and later gained her the respect and admiration of judges and peers. But when she hung up her cell phone, it was gone. The identity she had worn for so many years had been taken away from her in seconds. She was no longer a lawyer. She didn't know what she would do or where she would go. And where would Alejandro go? Was he still at the jail? It didn't matter if he was because she had probably been banned from the jail as well. Had they shipped him off to Arroyo Grande, or would he go elsewhere? She called the jail. The woman's voice was curt and businesslike. "We have no one by that name in custody here." Now she felt completely alone.

It was another long, disjointed night in the motel bed—sleeping some, lying awake some, dreaming, and thinking. Too often not knowing or remembering whether she had been awake or asleep, whether she had thought or dreamt of things. And all those thoughts and all those dreams dealt in one way or another with a sense of total loss.

She woke with the realization that she had to call Suzie. The week before, she had called her office at night and left Suzie a voice-mail message. "Suzie, a family emergency's come up and I have to leave the state. I don't know how long I'll be gone but it shouldn't be much more than a week. Call Greg's office and have them appear for me on all my cases and continue them at least a week. Reschedule my office appointments for at least a week, too. Thanks. Sorry I haven't gotten to you sooner, but I've had my hands full. I'll be checking in with you." She had been thinking and hoping that perhaps nothing more would come of the Wednesday incident other than her removal from Alejandro's case. Hudson's tapes and eavesdropping were clearly felonies and would draw every local lawyer's wrath and fuel their long-standing distrust of law enforcement. The sheriff's office and the district attorney's office might very well want to keep the matter quiet and therefore be satisfied with her removal from the case. But now Greg had said the State Bar had sent notification to her office...and Suzie opened her mail every morning. She had to call Suzie. As she was dialing, she wasn't sure what she would tell her.

"Good morning, Ms. Blake's office."

"Suzie."

"Where in the hell are you?"

"What do you mean where in the hell am I?" Barbara's voice rose.

Suzie's voice became even stronger, more emphatic. "I mean exactly what I said. Where in the hell are you!"

"That's none of your business."

"That's bs! It's all of my business! You've left me here for more than a week now to deal with all your angry clients and all the angry lawyers demanding to know where you are—taking their frustration out on me, calling me names, swearing at me. I've never been called a liar so much in all my life, when in fact you're the liar, the biggest damn liar that's ever lived. You've being suspended by the State Bar. I've got the letter right here in my hand. Did you happen to notice how I answered the phone, my dear? 'Ms. Blake's office.' Because I nearly got my head chewed off by a very angry lawyer yesterday who said you were no goddamn lawyer anymore, and I better stop answering the phone with 'law office' or he was going to report you to the State Bar again. Now, one more time, where in the hell are you? Because I'm sick and tired of taking all your crap...all the crap the you should be taking."

Barbara Blake stiffened and fell silent. Suzie had never spoken to her like that before, but there was much truth in what she said.

"I asked you, where are you?"

"I'm in town," she said quietly, subdued. She never wanted to speak another lie as long as she lived.

"Where in town?"

"At a motel."

"A motel! You don't belong in any motel. You belong here, answering for all the lies and crap you've heaped on yourself. You and your three-time-murderer boyfriend. If it's true what they said you did—and they've got videos of it so it must be true, so don't bother denying it—then I don't want to be associated with you. So you better get over here so I can leave, before I leave the way you did...by deserting everyone and everything."

"You can't talk to me like that," she said, but with little conviction.

"I can talk to you any way I want, Ms. Tramp, Ms. Ex-Lawyer, Ms. Nothing."

Again Barbara Blake was silent.

"Are you coming or aren't you?"

"I can't get there until five thirty."

"Five thirty! You gotta be kidding! What are you afraid of? To be seen by everybody in the building? They all know. They've all been asking. They all think I'm crazy for being here. That's what you're afraid of, isn't it? That they'll see you and they know... What's the matter, aren't you proud of what you did with that beaner? Well, I won't be here at five thirty. And I won't be here at two thirty or eleven thirty or forty-five minutes from now. If you're not here in half an hour, I'm gone. Half an hour. And you can deal with your mess yourself. Do you hear me?"

"Yes, I hear you."

"Do you understand...half an hour?"

"Yes, I understand," she said softly.

"Good." The click of the receiver followed.

Barbara Blake sat beaten, staring vacantly at a wastebasket, hearing a phrase she had heard years before in a history class. "The worst tyrant is the ex-slave." The phrase repeated itself again and again. *But Suzie wasn't a slave,* she protested, *I always treated her well.* But the phrase played on. "The worst tyrant is the ex-slave."

On Sunday night, Barbara Blake purchased a navy-blue sweat

suit from Long's Drugs. She also bought changes of underwear, white cotton socks, a head scarf, and a pair of shower thongs. When she returned to the motel that night, she changed her clothes and threw them into a dumpster. Thereafter, whenever she went out, she wore the sweat suit, the thongs, the scarf, and a trench coat and dark glasses that she had in her car.

She got ready by disguising herself—hopefully beyond recognition. The scarf covered her hair completely and was drawn and tied tightly over her cheeks and jaw. The dark glasses reached above her eyebrows and covered a portion of her cheeks that the scarf left exposed. She buttoned the trench coat to the top and pulled up the collar, completely concealing her neck. It was only when she opened the door and saw the beautiful sunny day that she understood how ridiculous she looked and how much attention her outfit would draw. She started to cry but forced herself to stop—her eyes were already red enough. She had to leave. She was out of time and options.

She drove to her office. She thought of circling the block a few times to see which cars she recognized in the parking lot to give her some idea of who was in their offices and who might be leaving. But there was no time for that. She parked and hurried to her office without anyone seeing her.

The office was empty except for Suzie who looked up from her desk and said, "My, my, my, look who's here. And in disguise no less. Barbara, who are you trying to hide from? Who are you trying to fool? Yourself? That silly outfit you've got on wouldn't fool my dog. Tell me, just who are you trying to fool? Everyone knows what you've done. Everyone knows you've been suspended. You're not a lawyer anymore. You're nothing."

"Suzie, please, I came to—"

"No, no, no. You listen to me for a change, missy. I've had to listen to you for years. I've had to put up with your condescension for years. I've had to put up with you looking down your nose at me and everything I have, everything I am, for years. And now Miss High and Mighty, you're nothing. Because you got caught with your mouth on your boyfriend's dick—and he's a three-time murderer. You lied to me. You lied to the court. You lied to the guards. You lied to Greg. You lied to the taxpayers. You took their money so you could go into that jail and suck on that animal's dick. I'm sorry, but that's the only way my stomach will let me describe it. What you did and what you are repulse me and everyone else that knows about this."

Shattered, she said, "Suzie, please, I didn't come here to—"

"No, you're gonna listen to me, Miss Accomplished Lawyer. You've always held yourself out to be my superior. Better educated, better qualified, better connected, at least two and three social classes above me and mine. Well, Miss Grande Dame, how many other dicks have you sucked on in the jail? I'm sure you've sucked the big dicks of some of those hunks you defended and were always talking about. And how about the guards? I'm sure you tried theirs, too. You were always bragging about how much the guards did for you. But you never mentioned what you had to be giving them. No wonder you always had those mouth infections. What did you tell the doctors, or did you just offer them some too? Did you—"

"Stop! Stop! Get out! Get out! This is still my office! I pay the rent here! Get out!"

"Get out? I'm not leaving till you pay me what you owe me! And you owe me plenty! Two weeks pay, severance, vacation pay, and—"

"I'm going back to my office. Write down what I owe you and I'll pay you."

A few minutes later Suzie knocked on her door. Barbara Blake took the sheet from her and shut the door. Once she had written out the check, she went out to the desk where Suzie was sitting in the reception area, handed her the check, and returned to her office. Moments later she heard the front door close, and she went out and locked it. She spent the rest of the day and early evening closing files and writing letters and refund checks to clients, explaining that she was no longer practicing law and referring them

307

to Greg Olsen's office for continued representation. Then she called Beth Cohen, an old friend and colleague at the San Cristobal Public Defender's Office. Beth Cohen had gone on to become the head of the Alternate Public Defender's Office in San Diego. She told Beth of her suspension and the reason for it. She said that she wanted to leave San Cristobal and was hoping Beth knew of a law firm in San Diego that might need a paralegal for criminal defense work. Beth hired her on the spot.

It was dark when she left her office and drove to her home for the first time since that Wednesday. As she pulled into the driveway, she had the feeling she was about to enter a house where she had lived long ago. She took all the clothes and personal effects that she could fit into her car and left.

BARBARA BLAKE checked out of the motel early Monday morning. Instead of heading south however, she headed north for the two-hour drive to San Francisco. Fred Solomon was not in his office when she arrived but his secretary said that she was expecting him shortly. She was staring blankly at an opened issue of *Newsweek* when he walked into the office. He glanced at her, said good morning to his secretary, and continued on into his office. He was not what she expected, not at all. He was a small, round man—perhaps a few years older than herself—balding and wearing small, round, wire-rimmed glasses. Everything about him seemed soft, cherubic even, from the roundness of his stomach that began just above his thighs and ended just below his shoulders to his round, pleasant face and eyes, they were all soft. And yet, Greg Olsen held him in great respect and Alejandro seemed to as well.

The secretary rose and followed him into his office and closed the door behind them.

"Who is that out there? Is she waiting to see me or Larry?" he asked.

"She's waiting to see you."

"I didn't think I had any appointments this morning."

"You don't, and she doesn't. She just walked in this morning and said she had to see you about a case you were handling. She said it was important. I told her you were going to be tied up for most of the day, and she said that she didn't care that she'd wait all day if she had to. She said it was important."

"Did she say what case it was?"

"No, and I didn't ask her."

"Did she give you her name?"

"Yes. Barbara...Barbara...Barbara Blake."

The name registered but Fred Solomon couldn't place it, not immediately. *Barbara Blake...Barbara Blake. Oh yes.* "What time am I supposed to be in court?"

"At ten."

"And with the Commonwealth luncheon and court after that, I probably won't be back in the office much before five. I'd better see her now. Send her in."

He watched as she entered with a sort of diffidence. Forlorn and unadorned, she was still a pretty woman. Forty give or take. He gestured with his hand to one of the two chairs across from him and watched as she arranged herself in it. She wore a black trench coat, but he guessed that she was still physically attractive. Once settled, she looked at him for several moments before she spoke. It was an open look with an abundance of dignity and poise. And, he felt...a touch of sadness. How could this woman have been attracted to Alejandro Soto? What could there possibly have been in it for her?

"Mr. Solomon, my name's Barbara Blake."

"Yes, my secretary told me. I know who you are. We spoke on the phone a few weeks back."

"Have you talked to Greg Olsen recently?"

"Yes, I have."

"So you know about my situation?"

"Yes, I do."

She looked away, looked at the windows and the open sky ten feet away. Then she looked back at him and said, "All of it?"

"All of it." His sadness deepened. How could she have fallen for Soto? What could she possibly want or get from him?

But more to the point, what did she want now from him? He had done all he had known to do in Soto's case, everything there was to do and the court had still denied their petition.

She told him that she wanted him to file a certificate of appealability in the federal district court and, if that failed, to file in the federal circuit court and, if that failed, to take it to the United States Supreme Court.

As Fred Solomon sat and listened to her long-winded request, he found himself becoming piqued by what was sounding more and more like a demand and then an implied accusation of incompetence on his part for having lost the writ.

Quick to sense that budding resentment, she said, "This by no means is intended as a criticism of your work. I thought you did an excellent job, brilliant in fact. Sadly, too many lawyers would rather play golf on Friday afternoons than be bothered with work. I don't mean to be getting all worked up about this, but the Miranda issue is a very viable one, one the Supreme Court could take an interest in. Don't you agree?"

"I raised it. We filed sworn declarations in support of our request for an evidentiary hearing. I expected that the court would want to take oral testimony, but instead it decided the matter on those declarations."

"I didn't know that."

Then he said, "Do you have any idea how long one of these cases can take, Ms. Blake?"

"Years. And please, call me Barbara."

"OK, Barbara, how many years?"

"I don't know. Ten, fifteen..."

"For your information, I was just reading a case last week in which a writ was finally granted twenty years after the defendant was convicted. For twenty years, the man sat in prison before his conviction was overturned. Twenty years his lawyers worked on his case. I have the case citation right here someplace."

"No, no, that's not necessary, Mr. Solomon."

"Please, call me, Fred."

"Yes, Fred."

"I may not be living twenty years from now. Besides, I can barely keep up with my practice now as it is. Where am I going to get all the time required to take this case up again? And who's going to pay me?"

"The court will pay you."

"Yes, very little and very slowly."

"I'll do all the work."

"You can't practice law."

"That's true, but I can work as a paralegal. I'll do all the research. I'll draft all the pleadings. All you'll have to do is sign the pleadings as the attorney of record and appear in court occasionally."

"And who's going to pay you? I don't believe that ethically I can turn over court funds to you, and I'm not in any position to pay you out of my own pocket."

"I'm not asking that you or anybody pay me. This would be a labor of love, believe me."

The labor of love phrase irritated him. "How will you support yourself?"

"Fortunately, money isn't a problem for me."

"Trust-fund baby, eh?"

"No. My monetary needs are not great. I live frugally and I have savings and a house I can sell if need be."

They sat in silence. Then she said, "Fred, we have a viable issue here. And you know Alejandro's worthwhile or you wouldn't have sent him all those books month after month. How many other clients have you done that for? He's worth saving. It's our obligation. Isn't that why we're defense attorneys?"

"Please don't try to guilt-trip me. That's not needed here. I'm not a child. Nor am I a new, just-out-of-law-school, wet-behind-the-ears lawyer. That's more offensive than it's useful." Now he was very irritated. But he also knew that he was very trapped. He knew he couldn't turn his back on Alejandro Soto, not when she was offering to do all the work. And he wondered why a woman like Barbara had never entered *his* life.

They agreed that Fred would have a copy made of his entire file—more than ten banker boxes—and have it shipped to San Diego. Once Barbara had studied it, she would call him and they would begin to decide how best to proceed with Alejandro Soto's appeal.

XXI

HEN ALEJANDRO WOKE, HE
said, "Barbara. Barbara." He remembered calling for her in his
sleep, but she hadn't come. He called for her again, louder, "Barbara! Barbara!" She didn't come. No one came, not even a guard.
He didn't know what part of the jail's infirmary he was in, but it
was a cell—not unlike the single cells in the SHU's pod...with a
commode and a cot and a solid door. The only differences were
that a light hung down from a canopy on the ceiling and there
was a wooden chair at the foot of the cot.

He started to get up from the cot, but a sharp pain on his right
side laid him down again. There was pain in his neck every time
he turned it. They had beaten the hell out of him, not just Hudson,
but Olsen, too. That bastard Olsen. Somehow he had to be made
to pay. "Barbara!" She had to see what they had done to him—sue
them...get Olsen disbarred.

Why hadn't she come? She was still his lawyer. The sex they were having in that basement room was consensual. In his earlier years of jailing, he had seen guards catch inmates in acts of consensual sex. Nothing ever happened to them. Because it wasn't a crime. Sometimes they were put in separate cells, but only sometimes. Barbara was his lawyer, and there was no way they could separate them or have some judge try to make him give her up as his lawyer.

He turned himself on his left side. There was some pain, but nothing like the pain on his right side. He must have slept because the slipping of a food tray into the cell woke him. He was hungry and needed to use the commode. Gently, carefully, he pushed himself up off the cot. But as soon as he put weight on his right foot an excruciating pain made him sit again. Beads of sweat gathered on his forehead. Later he hopped on one foot to get to the commode and then the food tray.

The pain was less the next day, and when Barbara didn't come to visit, he remembered how the guards had grumbled about having to take him out of the patient section of the infirmary for the interview with Greg Olsen. That was not the normal procedure, they kept saying. He thought he'd be out of the infirmary soon and then Barbara could visit him as often as they wanted.

The following day Alejandro was examined by a cranky old doctor who sat in the wooden chair as much as the examination permitted. His answer to Alejandro's question about visitation in the infirmary was, "Young man, I'm here to medically examine you and not answer every random question you may have." The old doctor did say, "I don't find any broken bones, but you must have been in one helluva altercation." He gave Alejandro some pain pills and concluded by saying, "I'll see you again in a couple of days, and we should be able to get you out of the infirmary and back to your pod soon after that."

"My pod?" Alejandro repeated several times to himself during the day. "Since when do they have pods in San Cristobal? That old fool is really out of it!"

On the fourth day, it was the lieutenant who came in first, followed by two guards. "How you doing, Alejandro?"

"What are you doing here? You don't know a goddamn thing about this case. Why did they bring you down here?"

"Where do you think you are, Alejandro?"

"You know damn well where I'm at, Lieutenant, and it's got nothing to do with you."

"Alejandro, you're in the SHU. They brought you back three days ago."

"Bullshit! I got a murder case pending here in San Cristobal County. There's no fucking way I could be in that shit hole of yours. I've got to be in court."

"Alejandro, that murder case down there was dismissed. They dismissed it because the court of appeals denied your writ of habeas corpus. You're back here at the SHU doing your two-consecutive life sentences without the possibility of parole."

"You're fucking lying!"

"We'll see. You were heavily medicated and pretty banged up when they flew you in. So much so, that it was thought better to put you here in the infirmary until the doctor had a chance to take a good look at you. He has examined you and he thinks you'll be ready to go back to your old cell in a few days. Nobody's occupied it since you've been gone."

"Bullshit!"

"You can 'bullshit' me all you want, but you'll see soon enough that you're here again." The lieutenant shook his head. "Probably for the rest of your life."

"Bullshit!"

"Well, I just thought that once you were awake, we should at least tell you where you are and why. That's all I've got to say." They started to leave but the lieutenant stopped and turned and said, "By the way, the captain's ordered that there's to be absolutely no communication between you and that female lawyer that was representing you in San Cristobal. That means no letter writing, no mail, no visits, and no phone calls. Nothing. I thought you should know that. I'll see you again once you're in your old house."

Alejandro told himself that this had to be a bad dream. A day later, he knew it wasn't.

The doctor came and examined Alejandro again and then said to the guard with him that he'd probably let them take Alejandro back to the pods the next day.

During his first eight years and three months in the SHU, Alejandro had lived by the prison motto, "Do the time. Don't let the time do you." How well he knew that there could be no survival in the SHU if he let the time do him. So he had fought the time. He had stuck to his rigid schedule of exercises and reading and learning, and he watched himself growing. He had been doing the time. He was beating the time.

But he had not counted on Barbara coming...or on her loving him and he loving her.

IN THE courtroom, she leaned next to him and said softly, "I'm going to be whispering several things to you, nod if you understand... Alejandro I love you, do you understand? No matter what happens, I will always love you, do you understand? Someday we'll be together, do you understand?

"Everybody is watching, so nod if you understand. Do you know that I love you? Do you believe that I love you? Do you know I will do everything I can so that someday we'll be together? Do you love me?" He nodded and nodded.

IN THE holding cell she had gasped, "Oh my darling, I love you so much! More than anything else in the world, I love you! Do you love me? Tell me! Tell me!"

"Yes! Yes! Yes!"

"No, say it! Say it! I want to hear it! I need to hear it! Tell me! Tell me!"

"I love you! I love you!"

IN THE interview room she had held a yellow legal tablet up to the glass, which said, "If you love me, I need to see your lips say it. Not so they can hear, but so that I can see and know. Please say it." And he had mouthed, "I love you, I love you, I love you."

From the time he woke in the infirmary, he repeatedly heard and saw her and himself in the courtroom, in the holding cell, and in the interview room. When he knew that he wasn't dreaming, that he was going to spend the rest of his life in the SHU without her, those moments increased in repetition and intensity. They were torture infinitely worse than the physical pain.

After the doctor left the second time, Alejandro decided that he wasn't returning to the pod. He thought of his beautiful, gentle, kind mother. He had known her before she was a cripple. He had witnessed the permanent pain his brutal, drunken father had inflicted on her. Yet, the longer he lived, the older he got, the more he understood his father's brutality: how he came home at night drunk and yelling, *"Aqui yo mando!"* "Here I rule." What had his life become laying railroad track, like a coolie, in the blistering heat and the freezing cold? He remembered, too, how he and his mother had planned and then took their revenge until they drove his father to his suicidal death. *What could they have done differently?* he asked himself.

He remembered the Chrysler plant and the soul-busting, mind-crushing monotony of the assembly line. How car after car, hour after hour, day after day, and, for many workers, year after year, they took to wearing sunglasses on that line to hide their blood-shot marijuana eyes. How different were those sorry saps from his father? *Not much,* he thought.

When he met heroin, he remembered how he had thought he had escaped the doom of that assembly line. For a few weeks he had a blissful existence: happy—happy as he would or could ever be. And then came heroin's inevitable, costly sickness and the criminality to ward off that unbearable sickness. He took Julia down that road with him. Julia must have loved him. But what did he know about love then? Nothing. Arcelia was right: he never told Julia that he loved her. Together he and Julia fell in with Carlos Sanchez, a truly evil man, and Carlos's facilitator mother. Time after time they witnessed Carlos's distorted perverseness on needy junkies, until Julia became his subject. All of which led Alejandro to Freddie Garcia's basement for two weeks to kick the habit cold turkey, so that he could kill Carlos. He murdered Carlos and his mother in cold blood in retribution for their evil and to make his world a better place. He could never understand why society had punished, rather than rewarded, him for eliminating that evil. Instead he was sentenced to serve two life sentences in prison without the possibility of parole.

Sent to the SHU, he developed a system of exercise and learning to ward off insanity and suicide. For eight years he lived successfully under that system and developed himself physically and mentally. Then he met Barbara. She gave him and taught him love. Being with her for an hour or minutes showed him how wonderful life could be. She gave him a reason to live. She promised that some day they would have a life together. Without her, he didn't have the will or desire to return to living a life simply to avoid insanity and suicide. Living like that until death seemed too bleak. He was not returning to the pod.

What had also increased was his interest in the light canopy in the ceiling. During the doctor's first visit, Alejandro noticed that the light canopy was loose. In between the doctor's two visits, he was able to pry the canopy open enough to feel two iron rods above the ceiling. After the doctor's second visit, he tested the rods' strength and found that each could carry his full weight. For several hours after that visit, he carefully ripped his bedsheets into long strips. By standing on the wooden chair he was able to tie and knot two of the bedsheet strips around one of the rods. He made a noose from the two strips. He couldn't live, didn't want to live, without Barbara.

120 DAYS

Ronald L. Ruiz is the author of a memoir, *A Lawyer* (2012), and five previous novels—*Happy Birthday Jesús* (1994), *Giuseppe Rocco* (1998), *The Big Bear* (2003), *Jesusita* (2015), and *Life Long* (2017). Born and raised in Fresno, California, Ron was educated at St. Mary's College, California, University of California, Berkeley, and University of San Francisco. He practiced law from 1966 to 2003 as a Deputy District Attorney, a criminal defense attorney, and a Deputy Public Defender. He was appointed to the California Agriculture Labor Relations Board by Governor Jerry Brown in 1974 and later served as the District Attorney of Santa Cruz County, California.

www.ingramcontent.com/pod-product-compliance
Lightning Source LLC
Chambersburg PA
CBHW070542260626
47161CB00002B/483